FREE TO RUN

TRACEY JERALD

FREE TO RUN

Free to Run

Copyright © 2018 by Tracey Jerald. All rights reserved.

ISBN: 978-1-7324461-2-0 (eBook)

ISBN: 978-1-7324461-3-7 (Paperback)

Editor: One Love Editing (http://oneloveediting.com)

Editor: Trifecta Editing Services (https://www.trifectaedit.com/)

Cover Design: Amy Queau – QDesign (https://www.qcoverdesign.com)

To my parents for ensuring I grew up knowing I could do anything, be anything, believe in anything. Who taught me about the importance of strength, truth, and trust. Who worked hard and loved harder – you've always been the standard I held my life.
This book is for you.

THE LEGEND OF AMARYLLIS

There are variations regarding the legend of how amaryllis flowers came to be. Generally, the tale is told like this:

Amaryllis, a shy nymph, fell deeply in love with Alteo, a shepherd with great strength and beauty, but her love was not returned. He was too obsessed with his gardens to pay much attention to her.

Amaryllis hoped to win Alteo over by giving him the one thing he wanted most, a flower so unique it had never existed in the world before. She sought advice from the oracle Delphi and carefully followed his instructions. She dressed in white, and for thirty nights, appeared on Alteo's doorstep, piercing her heart with a golden arrow.

When Alteo finally opened his eyes to what was before him, he saw only a striking crimson flower that sprung from the blood of Amaryllis's heart.

It's not surprising the amaryllis has come to be the symbol of pride, determination, and radiant beauty. What's also not surprising is somehow, someway, we all bleed a little bit while we're falling in love.

PROLOGUE - ALISON

TWO YEARS EARLIER FROM PRESENT DAY

"More," I moan, pushing back against the body behind me. His deep laugh is his only response as he taunts me with what I want so desperately—him.

"More of what, Alison? This?" He tightens his hand on my hip and pushes his cock deeper inside of me. He swivels his hips, causing me to gasp from the pleasure. "Or do you mean this?" He slaps his other hand against my pussy, landing directly against my distended clit. I moan long and loud. My heart is pounding so hard it might jump out of my chest. I can hardly breathe, only seconds away from my third orgasm of the night.

The arrogant bastard laughs before leaning over my shoulder, forcing himself deeper. My head arches back against him, leaving my neck vulnerable.

He immediately takes advantage.

Soon, my already slick channel is dripping down my thighs as he simultaneously pounds into me, while lightly slapping my sensitive clit. Every bite he takes of my neck is sending more jolts of pleasure down to that particular nerve center. I'm primed to explode.

"Let go, Alison. I want to feel you squeeze my cock like a vise. Give it to me." His voice is ragged in my ear, right before he bites down on it.

And I sail over the edge, moaning his name.

"Keene..."

His hand slides through my drenched sex, then up my body to capture my nipple. He squeezes it, prolonging my orgasm as he pounds into me. "Give me another one, baby. Come on," he urges.

And like a helpless doll, I comply.

My body is his slave and his to command. It's been this way since the first time. I have no idea why or how, but I have to explore this connection, and I've never wanted to do that before.

Never before tonight.

Not before meeting Keene.

Even as I feel him shudder through his orgasm, I'm already thinking about the next time. How will he take me? The chair? The shower? We've already been against the wall and twice on the bed— one of those times, his emerald-green eyes were locked onto mine as I rode him—and now this.

Jesus, I'm addicted to him already.

Eventually, my breathing slows. I'm almost asleep when I hear him whisper, "Baby, you need to clean up. You can't go to sleep like this."

Nodding, I move to stand. He's by the side of the bed, his gaze raking over me. Pulling me to my feet, he pushes my hair back from my face and drops a soft kiss on my lips. "Start the shower."

"Okay." I reach up and pull his dark head down to nuzzle the scruff on his cheeks. The same scruff that scraped the skin between my thighs earlier. But I don't care. "I'll see you in a minute."

In the dark of the hotel room, he kisses my lips. "Go." Patting me on my ass, he pushes me toward the en suite bathroom.

Starting the shower, I collect myself before walking back into the bedroom, wanting him to join me.

One foot crosses the threshold of the bedroom, and I gasp at what I see.

"What the hell?" The words are out of my mouth before I can stop them. My afterglow has vanished to never-never land.

"Shit." Keene quietly closes the door before he can finish sneaking out. He turns with his head lowered and leans his back against the door.

"Seriously? I know you didn't exactly slap a ring on it, but for fuck's sake, Keene. I thought you had at least a healthy amount of respect for me before you stuck your dick in me tonight!" I yell.

"Lower your voice, Alison. There's someone else in the suite," he warns me.

"It's my sister. Who the hell cares?"

"I do." He hisses.

I take a deep breath to hide my hurt. "Of course. After all, we barely know anything about each other. I have no idea of whether our fucking a few minutes ago impacts your day-to-day life. You merely suggested I get into the shower. Walking in to find you almost completely dressed, carrying your pants and shoes to sneak out of my room gives me zero reason to draw any conclusions. Why don't I help you out a bit?" Stomping past him completely naked, I reach for my suite door and swing it open. "Get out."

His lips part in surprise, but he doesn't argue. "Alison..." But I don't let him finish. His chance was lost the minute I walked back into the room.

"Don't let the door hit you on the way out. Thanks for a hell of a night," I smirk.

Keene searches my face before muttering under his breath, "Fuck," and skulks barefoot to the main door.

After I let my emotions out in the shower, I belatedly wonder about the woman's name tattooed on his thigh.

And then I throw up.

1

ALISON

PRESENT DAY

The edge of pain. I push through it. I know how far I can go before I'm in danger.

With my playlist driving me, I'm determined to conquer the last part of the mountain trail in front of me. My stride is sure over the uneven terrain in the early Connecticut summer warmth. Reaching for my running belt, I snag my GU Energy Gel and take a quick slurp, knowing I need the extra push of energy to make it to the summit.

As I climb higher and higher, the early-morning heat of the summer sun burns my skin. Beads of sweat fall faster between my breasts and are captured in my running top. My blue running shorts brush against my skin, reminding me with barely a wisp of movement that they're there. Thin tree branches occasionally lash out at my bared stomach, but I ignore them as I thunder past.

I lean my body forward a little as the incline increases. I'm almost to the top. The trees are starting to thin out, so I know I'm close.

Jumping from side to side in a half run, half lunge, I maneuver the final yards to the top of the stone steps that level out at the end of the trail to the sweeping view of the Berkshire Mountains, overlooking my hometown of Collyer, Connecticut. I hold my arms over my head in victory, while taking in deep breaths as OneRepublic pours into my ears.

Another personal battle conquered.

I've been working my way up the difficulty of this trail for a long time. Sure, I'd hiked it almost as soon as I'd heard about it at Tabor's Sporting Goods, but it's not the same as running it. Not to me.

Once my breathing is back in its normal range, I unsnap my running belt and sit on a smooth, rocky ledge to enjoy the view.

I can't say much about the natural wonder around me, other than recognizing poison sumac enough to avoid it, but I see beauty in the hummingbirds darting around in the early Saturday-morning light. Hoping to get a decent picture my sister Holly, a photographer, will appreciate, I pull up my phone app and quickly snap a few. After a few photos, I attach them to a message in our family chat, saying, "Finally conquered this bitch running. I am so getting extra mocha today." Knowing this will only piss off my brother, Phillip, who constantly bemoans the need for exercise but loves extra-rich lattes, I hit Send with a smile.

It's difficult to explain how I lose myself while running. I'm in my head, but I'm out of my own thoughts. I'm hyperaware of my surroundings, and often I can forget my day-to-day frustrations.

Today, my thoughts have been wandering to things I so rarely think of while I'm out running.

Sex.

Great sex.

Phenomenal sex.

And my thoughts, of course, jump to sex with Keene Marshall.

He's my newest brother. At least according to my adopted sister Cassidy. Phillip, Emily, Cassidy, Corinna, Holly and I aren't what you would call a conventional family. We adopted one another as we found each other, gradually becoming a cohesive unit. You'd never know it started as a result of the kind of abuse people only read about in the newspapers. Well, we lived it.

Cassidy never knew her blood brother Keene existed until she fell in love with her now husband, Caleb Lockwood. Through her courtship, Cassidy met Caleb's best friend, Keene. I roll my eyes at the memory. Did they recognize each other? No. Have an immediate kinship? Hell no. It was more like a Roman fight to the death, with Cassidy delivering the final blow when she realized Keene was the man I hooked up with the night of our brother Phil's wedding.

It took a while for them to tolerate each other, and then Keene began to realize little things about Cassidy that should have been obvious to someone searching for their long-lost sister for the last seventeen years. My childhood crush, Sir Arthur Conan Doyle, would have had apoplexy at how long the two of them took to figure out they were related. The clues were right there.

Now we're all adjusting to our new normal. Our family has grown so much from the six of us who had originally moved here.

We all get on our knees every day and thank God that Phil married our brother-in-law Jason. Divine intervention was definitely involved, with Phil literally falling into Jason's life. Cassidy's recent intimate wedding ceremony to Caleb a few months ago didn't leave a dry eye. Not even mine. Quickly, I do a sanity check. Jesus, I wonder if my other sisters are dating?

Letting out a breath, I realize I'm safe from the family expanding, other than Cassidy's upcoming baby. The men Em, Holly, and Corinna typically date aren't the kind you'd bring around the family dinner table. And no one should expect me to bring anyone permanent into our circle.

I'm at a loss on how to handle the situation with Keene. I shake my head, thinking about how much has changed in such a short period of time. Keene is a member of our family now, meaning I have to stop thinking about the incredible sex we had at the Plaza Hotel in New York the night of Phil and Jason's wedding. And at my house the night of Cassidy and Caleb's wedding.

Groaning, I roll into a sitting position and bring my forehead to my knees. I know I'm not solely to blame for what happened; Keene was an active participant. God, was he ever.

It can't happen again. Despite my openness to meeting someone, I haven't gotten laid since. It's not like I'm saturated with chances to meet a ton of men. Most of my time is spent working as the lawyer for our wedding- and event-planning business.

Time to stop daydreaming about what Keene did with his sexy mouth and get on board with our new reality. I stand and walk toward the edge of the rugged terrain, making myself a promise that somehow, I will get past this lingering desire I have for him so I can help Cassidy settle into her new family dynamic. There has to be someone alive in this world for me to have a relationship with, where it won't be so complicated. Where they'll accept that I just want companionship.

And smoking hot sex.

Heading down the running trail on the opposite side of the way I came up, my legs eat up the miles at a much-faster pace on my way back to Collyer.

Toward my well-deserved and anticipated mocha.

THE TOWN of Collyer is more alive as I make my way back toward its center. Every quarter of a mile or so, I hear the toot of a horn or see a random arm shoot out to wave. When I see Ava and Matt, the owners of The Coffee Shop, roll up next to me riding Matt's Harley, I laugh and try for a quick sprint to outrun their Hog. Matt guns it and salutes me before taking off. Knowing they're on their way to open the place my highly anticipated mocha is located encourages me to increase my stride.

I turn down Pine Lane and run the last quarter mile at a sprint.

As my foot touches our property, my arm immediately raises for me to see the stats on my tracker. About six miles in a little over an hour and fifteen minutes, including my break on the mountain summit. I smile and slow to a walk on the lush green grass surrounding the farm.

Walking down the lane to my house, I inhale the cool morning air and admire everything we've worked for. About ten years ago, after we all became emancipated and decided we'd had enough of life in the South for a while, we moved to Collyer. Not long after, we went in together and bought a piece of land about a mile and a half off Main Street. It was a choice piece of real estate that ate up a good portion of our savings. Fortunately, Phil, Emily, Corinna, and Holly, the more artistic members of our family, saw the vision of what it could be.

I still cringe, remembering the look on my siblings' faces when I told them it would take years to realize our dream. Even now, as the chief financial officer and chief counsel of Amaryllis Events, our family wedding and event planning business, I'm always the buzzkill.

Luckily for us, we got the land for a fraction of what it would have cost had it been fully developed. Over time, we've taken the worst-looking property in Collyer and turned it into a showplace. Our dream is a reality—one we talked about in the darkest hours before dawn when we'd hang out gorging out on junk food in our trailer in South Carolina. We dreamed of a place where we could grow old together and no one knew who we were or where we came from. Where the only thing we could see was beauty outside our window, instead of trash from the nearby trailer. And we did it. The six of us who never should have succeeded.

Leafy green Connecticut oaks towering over the drive provide shade for me to cool down as I walk back to my cottage on our property. When we renovated, we each chose our individual home site, based on the seven foundations already located on the property. My home is situated on the farthest original foundation, which backs up to an extensive tree line. When I first saw it, I imagined how gorgeous the winters would be with the view of the pines tipped with snow. I dreamed I would build my house with my bed facing the trees, so I could snuggle under the covers and enjoy the beauty on cold winter days. Also, it was the farthest back from the main farm gate. I wanted the distance when I went out to run. The location of my cottage gave me an extra half mile to warm up and cool down. Even though it was the last property left—since I encouraged my siblings to choose first —it's the one that suited me best. I ended up with everything I wanted.

We each pooled an equal amount of money to convert the main

barn, which overlooks the lake, into a communal space. It's the center of our little village, with a restaurant-grade gourmet kitchen, gym, game room, and a living room that easily holds thirty or more, with an original stone fireplace dominating the space. The one good thing about the way we live is that we all have our own space to avoid death by sibling. At the same time, when we want to be together, we're no more than a mile apart with plenty of space to be with each other.

As I look up at each of my family's homes on my way in, I know they're likely empty. It's Saturday, and there's a small wedding going on. Holly, my youngest sister, who's my age at twenty-seven but younger by six months, is likely at the wedding site taking stunning photos. Phillip, our florist, and Corinna, our baker, are already at the local country club with their deliveries. Knowing my siblings as I do, I suspect Cassidy, our CEO, and Emily, our designer, will be at our offices in the event there are any last-minute catastrophes they need to handle. While I know I have the luxury of time, it's likely minor chaos will erupt down at the office, so I decide to forego the bath and hit the shower instead.

I rarely feel like I contribute enough to this family as it is. If there's anything I can do, I want to be around to help out.

2

ALISON

I find myself speeding into town, narrowly avoiding an accident when I turn into the parking lot of Amaryllis Events. Waving my hand in the air where my convertible top is open, I hear a couple of beeps. Must be someone used to my crazy driving, I surmise. Glancing around the parking lot, I find Phil's BMW, Em's Rover, and Caleb's Porsche. Figures the newlyweds wouldn't be too far apart on a weekend. Grinning, I make my way up to the porch.

While Phil was the first to fall in love with Jason when they met at Candlewood Lake, the private betting pool we have within the family has Corinna going down next, due to the volume of men she dates. I mean, the odds are decent on at least one being a winner. Holly, our dreamer, always has her face glued to her camera lens, but she's a knockout. She also hasn't let the issues of our pasts touch her too much. I have pretty high odds as well, though I scoff at the idea of it.

Em is a more prominent possibility than Cassidy, despite her refusal to date any man seriously. She's the quintessential ice princess. Sadly, each guy wants to break the frost around her heart.

None of us, especially Cassidy, ever thought she would be able to let go of her past to date, let alone fall in love. I consider it a miracle that about nine months after they first met, Cass and Caleb were married and expecting their first baby.

I decide to run inside to see if anyone needs anything before I walk to The Coffee Shop. Cass, Phil, and Em are most likely hanging around inside the mansion we converted into our offices to make sure nothing needs their personal touch for the reception scheduled at eleven this morning. I know Corinna will head back to her bed the minute she's done delivering the wedding cake she spent most of the night decorating.

Swinging open the stained-glass door, I hear Phil and Em bickering from the direction of her design space.

Em's area is flooded with natural sunlight streaming in through her bay window. Filled with jewel tones and littered with pillows made of every color and texture imaginable, beautiful stained-glass dream catchers capture the sunlight, throwing bright colors around the room as you walk in. Antique art deco posters decorate the walls. This room is Em's soul in living color, the part of her that no one but family gets to see.

It's here I find Phil and Jason lounging against the pillows on the floor. Cassidy—probably ordered by her husband, Caleb—is lying on Em's chaise, with him on the floor by her feet. Mugsy, Em's elderly rescue dog, woofs a welcome.

Em looks up from where she's passing out cups from The Coffee Shop when I walk in. Her dark blue eyes widen in surprise when she sees me. "What are you doing here?"

I saunter over to her. "Nice greeting, Em. Did you get me one?" I wonder if they saw my text and guessed I'd want to celebrate with chocolate. "How did you know I'd come by?"

Uncomfortably, Em ducks her head. "Actually, I didn't. I'm sorry, Ali. We figured you'd be enjoying your day off." She tips her head at Cassidy, who's sipping her standard cappuccino—now decaf due to the baby—with an expression of pure bliss. "Cass bet that there was no way you'd come in since you weren't scheduled."

I pause in the act of dropping kisses on varying heads or cheeks around the room. "Wow. I always feel guilty you guys work harder than I do on days we have events. Way to make me feel worse." I decide to claim a seat by the wall, sliding down it to sit.

"Yeah, but you get us paid," Phil pipes up, trying to lessen the blow. "And since we all like money, we let it slide." Laughter fills the room. All but mine.

I pull out my phone and look through the pictures I took this morning, trying not to let my hurt feelings show.

Cassidy's still laughing as she rubs a hand over her already protruding baby belly. She looks further along than the four months the doctors swear she's at. It must be because she's so petite. "Don't worry, Ali. You'll have plenty of extra work soon enough. You'll wish for days when you didn't have to be here. And no, you don't get to pay yourself more for having to deal with Whirlpool."

They all laugh again at the narrow look Phil sends Cassidy. I can't help but smile too. Cassidy's nickname for our older brother is inspired by a washing machine—living with him is like being on the spin cycle. "Be careful, little girl. Just because you're going to be a mama soon doesn't mean I won't exact revenge."

"Oh yeah? How?" she sasses him. Since falling in love, her personality shines, lighting up everyone around her. I only wish she could forgive me for being cautious with Caleb and not accepting him right off the bat.

"Maybe by telling your husband about the night we taught you how to give a blow job," Phil taunts. He looks at Caleb, whose grin says Cassidy already neutralized his threat. Phil sputters indignantly. "Damn you, Cass. That was a family dinner. You're not supposed to share what happens at those!"

"Caleb is family, remember? There was an event a few months ago? I wore a white dress? Veil? Announced I was pregnant?" Cassidy recounted, raising her eyebrow.

I sit back and cross my legs at the ankles. I wish I had my mocha. That's all I wanted to celebrate my personal accomplishment. I don't need to post pictures of my trail run all over the internet. I only need the personal satisfaction of a job well done and a celebration with double chocolate.

"Ha!" Phil says, still in a snit. "We'll have to see what comes up at dinner tonight since the whole family will be there." He emphasizes the word "whole." My head snaps in his direction so fast, I swallow the ends of my hair in my mouth. As I pick them out, I think fast. What family dinner tonight?

Suddenly, the spot where I'm sitting feels like it's covered in a bed of poison sumac. I shift uncomfortably, as if my skin is trying to peel off my bones. My teeth clench. Even my breathing alters.

I'm trying not to let my discomfort show before I look over at my oldest sister. Maybe Phil didn't mean the whole family, as in the inclusion of a recently added brother who I can't get out of my brain, short of an exorcism with our local priest. My hope is lost when Cassidy, who's resting her hand on Caleb's shoulder, beams at me, saying, "Yeah. Keene's back from DC. Since everyone's in town tonight, Caleb and I wanted to share some news. So...the farm at six?"

"Sure, she can make it," Phil interjects. "It's not like she has other plans."

Actually, I do. I'm supposed to go on a blind date with a guy I met on a social media app not too long ago. That being said, I'm more than a little affronted that my family is so cavalier about my social life.

Hiding my face to avoid anyone catching the expression plastered there, I nod.

Standing abruptly, I decide to leave, overwhelmed with being perpetually punished for a misconstrued statement in the heat of the moment. "Then I guess I'll see you all tonight."

"Thanks, Ali. We appreciate it," Caleb murmurs, scrutinizing me.

I make my way to the door as I say to everyone, "Have a lovely afternoon together."

I close the door carefully behind me.

As I start to walk down the hall, I hear Em ask, "What's up her butt?"

"I don't know. Maybe she sat in some poison sumac. You know she's allergic to it," Phil quips.

Laughter floats through the closed door at my expense.

Coming in was a mistake. It feels like that more and more lately. Then again, ever since my last fight with Cassidy nothing seems right anymore.

∾

CASSIDY, if you just sign the prenup, you'll be protecting yourself on top of the company. After all, Caleb is the first man you've ever really been with. By doing this, you'll be protecting him, us, and yourself...

My words come back to haunt me as I race out the front door of Amaryllis Events. Even though I felt, and still feel, the advice was sound—to my sister who fell in love with the first man she ever dated, it was a declaration of war. I must hate Caleb. I must resent her because of Keene. Taking a pragmatic approach to our business caused such a fight I was surprised to be included in the wedding. In fact, two months later, I'm still being punished for it.

Escape. All I need to do is escape. Maybe if I can get away fast enough, the pain in my chest will ease up.

The summer breeze dances around me, rustling the ends of my hair. Jumping in my convertible, I just drive, taking a turn to head out of town and onto the twisty roads that lead to the peaks of Collyer. My little car wants me to let it go, so I drop it into third and punch the gas. I feel the response through the purring of the engine beneath my feet. With no real destination in mind, I fast forward through my playlist until I find a song that matches my mood.

Our past emotional wounds had barely scabbed over when Corinna, Holly, and I first met Phil, Cassidy, and Em. Wounds inflicted by being pawned out by our respective blood relatives to pay for their drug issues. My daddy's little nasty habit was cocaine; something he picked up after my mother died.

I did everything I could to Phil, Cassidy and Em, trying to force what it was they really wanted from us. We had nothing left to give at that point. God, looking back, I can't believe with the shit I spewed, but they didn't walk away. One thing I was adamant about was refusing for Corinna, Holly and I to be separated. We held each other's hands in the terrifying dark my father and his partner trapped us in and then through those equally frightening first moments out of captivity.

Even though we never knew each other before our time trapped in that horrific shipping container, I felt a bond snap between us. Then when we became six, our lost souls found a new home. All we lost we found. Together.

Once we changed our names, I chose Alison since it was my mother's middle name. Louise Sibley ceased to exist except in the darkest recess of my mind. I wanted nothing to associate me with my father.

If I have to applaud Max Sibley for anything, at least he tried to sell me in a state with some of the strictest human trafficking laws in the nation. He got 144 years on top of his drug charges. He won't be out in his lifetime.

My sisters always claim I'm the life of the party, the person who lights up a room with a smile, yet I hardly know who I am. It's why I started writing some of my thoughts out, to get rid of these emotions no one would ever associate with me. I feel like I'm going mad with no one to talk to. So many people think I have it together, and I do for the most part, except for love or anyone getting too close to my heart.

Love, that feckless, backstabbing bitch. That turncoat traitor. The hand that will disappear to let you fall into the bottomless well.

Men are such liars, such assholes. I'd learned the hard way to be wary of them. Look at what happened when I needed things like food and shelter. The price for that landed me on an auction block to benefit Dad.

I also need to remember what happens when I ask a man to rescue me from a silly dare, and the connection I felt that enticed me to blow off my brother's wedding reception to sneak up to my suite. How could I forget his emerald-green eyes that looked into the depths of my soul every time his body connected with mine? I only need to remember him sneaking out without his pants on, eager to run away.

Bastard.

I should have just ruined the shoes instead of ruining my... No. I refuse to call it my heart.

Blinking rapidly behind my sunglasses, I downshift into a tight turn. After everything that happened when I was a teenager, I have zero tolerance for lies. I wholeheartedly believe in telling the truth, especially to myself.

I have no problem with people choosing to live their lives how they please, but don't lie to me. Don't pretend to be something or someone you're not.

And I'm done lying to myself about Keene Marshall.

I was nothing more than a one-night stand to him. Correction, a two-night stand. Not that anyone knows that. It's unpleasant having to accept I've been nothing more than a warm place for him to stick his cock in when he needed a release.

Pressing my lips together, I get my bearings before turning back toward town.

Sighing, I realize I have to find the protective shield I wear for anyone who's not allowed inside my heart. That means they get the dazzle, the charm, and the smile, but they'll never see behind it to the real me.

How does that saying go? Burn me once, shame on you. Burn me twice, I'll take a torch to you...or some shit like that.

Turning my car down the next street, I make my way back to the farm for a family dinner I don't particularly want to attend, knowing I'll have to force a little more dazzle into my smile because of one particular family member.

The only thing keeping me from bailing out of this fiasco of a night is my curiosity over Cassidy and Caleb's announcement.

3

KEENE

"I repeat, is that understood?" I coldly address the room full of analysts sitting in front of me.

I'm holding my iPad that contains the files Caleb forwarded to me earlier. Their colossal mistake caught by our more seasoned analysts in New York managed to delay my leaving the Reston, Virginia, office of Hudson Investigations by several hours.

"Mistakes like this will not be tolerated. Consider this a written warning for everyone in this room. On this assignment you work as a team; therefore, you take your punishment as a team." I pause for brevity. "You will also lose your jobs as a team if there's not more attention paid to details."

The silence that settles over the occupants of the room would weaken the heart of a lesser man. With few exceptions, it's a good thing a heart is something I don't have.

"Fix it. By Monday. If you have a problem with that, speak with your immediate supervisor. Otherwise, when I check in, this issue better be resolved." I toss the iPad into my bag and swing it onto my shoulder. Without another word, I stride out the door.

I'm maybe fifty feet from the conference room when I hear my name called out in a sultry tone. "Keene, don't you think you were a bit harsh on them?"

I pause and turn to the voice. I know who it belongs to—a one-night mistake.

"Your office," I growl, my foul mood turning rancid.

I see her lips tip up slightly before she turns and walks away, swaying her hips slightly. One time, I made the mistake of paying too much attention to those hips and what they had to offer. Our encounter wasn't bad, but it wasn't worth a repeat. It sure as fuck doesn't give her the right to question decisions I make for my company. Only Caleb has the right to do that, and that's because he co-owns Hudson with me.

Once I close Melody's office door, I turn, and her body is practically pressing against mine, forcing me back. Through clenched teeth, I grit out, "Step away."

My words confuse her, and she appears uncertain about her next move.

"I don't believe you misunderstood me, Melody. Step back and sit down," I order. I'm pissed and ready to read her the riot act, but I don't.

"Can you communicate your job description for me, Ms. Dempsey?" She starts to ramble, so I hold up a hand, stopping her. "Succinctly."

Narrowing her dark eyes, she sits. Taking a deep breath, she says, "Managing the successful completion of investigations without compromising the integrity or privacy of our clients."

"Something you failed at spectacularly today," I sneer. "Not only did your team"— I wave my hand at the smoky glass window separating her office from the conference room I was just in—"fail to meet the objective of a client who was paying us an exorbitant amount of money, one of them broke the privacy clause." Before she can object, I continue. "That individual will be dealt with by Hudson Legal. I suggest you stay out of it unless you want the same fate." At those words, her aggressive stance fades and fear sets in. "Moving on. I was inclined to hold you accountable for all of this, but Caleb convinced me to give you the opportunity to address these issues. However, he also agrees with me. This is a one-strike-and-you're-out scenario." The panic eases from her eyes, promptly followed by something I'm used to when dealing with both men and women who think they can get something from me.

Calculation.

Melody stands and walks around her desk, and I hold my ground. Mentally, I'm berating poor choices made while drinking. God, I must have been more of a fucking mess than I realized over my sister missing for so damn long to have ever screwed this piece of work.

"What can I do to make it up to you, Keene?" she breathes, trailing her nails along my suit lapel.

I look into the corner of the office with mild disgust, seeing the small red dot of the hidden camera flashing. I know I'm going to catch hell for this later with Caleb, but I'm glad I had the wherewithal to have him monitoring all conversations in this office for the duration of my time here due to the gravity of the situation.

"Mr. Marshall," I correct her coldly. I step back away from her, making my lack of interest succinct.

Apparently, my intentions are not clear enough for the barracuda in front of me. "I can call you that...Mr. Marshall. Are there other parts of this...improvement plan I need to work on to make sure I'm on solid ground with the company's executive staff?" Her hand reaches for me again.

Before it can make contact, I caution her. "Ms. Dempsey, I'd like to advise you this conversation is being recorded."

Her seductive veneer fades away. "What?" she chokes out, her eyes darting to the corners of the room. She knows where the cameras are, at least she should. She helped install them.

"I was not required to advise you of this in advance since, as a part of your acceptance of this role at Hudson, you agreed to one hundred percent monitoring of your activities in this office. That includes video surveillance." Her face is now chalk white.

Ah, the rush of power. I wish I could have justified continuous monitoring before this past week. I wonder what other information we might have found.

"I—I wh—" she stutters.

"With that understanding, Ms. Dempsey, let me make a few things clear. Number one, if it was entirely my choice, you would be gone. At this point, if half the analysts in that room left with you, I'm not certain that would be a hardship considering this disaster." Melody winces. I'm brutal, but I don't care. Hudson's DC reputation is on the line.

"Number two, we don't enforce a 'no-dating' policy at this company, but certain rules must be followed. No means no, whether that means being involved with someone upward or downward. Have I expressed in the last"—I rapidly calculate—"sixteen months, any desire to become involved with you again?"

She lowers her head, but not before her cheeks reveal how frustrated she's become. She grinds out, "No."

"One could also make the argument that this could be considered harassment because we've spoken about this before. I. Am. Not. Interested." I say the last words slowly, emphatically pounding the point home for what will hopefully be the last time.

I feel my phone buzz in my pocket. I'm certain it's Caleb telling me to calm down.

"How can I make this any clearer, Ms. Dempsey? Do I need to send out an intradepartmental memo to all Hudson's executive staff, advising them of a regrettable one-night stand?" I lean forward across the desk. Her anger is now emanating from her. Without caution, I continue. "Your job is to run this facility, not worry if I get my coffee each morning or if my cock has been sucked the night before. Am I understood?" I've made the issue clear enough. I'm sick of walking into this office week after week, fending off this woman's advances.

"It's your word against mine, Mr. Marshall," she warns, emphasizing my name. Her fury could light the room on fire.

"Actually, Ms. Dempsey, it's not." Leaning closer, I say softly, knowing the mics can pick up every word, "Not when you're emailing your girlfriends on company time or talking on the company phone.

We're permitted to record and review all traffic on our networks. Everything." I point to her computer, her phone, and again to the recording device in the corner of the wall as I speak.

Her face colors from crimson back to ghost white. Her hands are shaking when she leans away from me and folds them in her lap.

"You should feel incredibly lucky I'm leaving Virginia for the foreseeable future, Ms. Dempsey. But rest assured, your actions will be closely monitored." I straighten to my full height. Is it wrong to take great delight in her being so nervous? Because I do. She swallows audibly. "Excellent. Any questions about my directives in the boardroom?"

A quick negative head shake.

I think I've finally made my point, just in time to make my flight back to New York.

"Then we'll see what kind of damage control your team can do by Monday. Enjoy your weekend," I conclude and make my way out of Hudson Investigations to start my journey home.

Home. A word I haven't used in years.

"YOU'RE SUCH A PRICK. It's amazing we have any staff left in the Virginia office," my best friend, brother-in-law, and partner, Caleb Lockwood, laughs in my ear a few minutes later from the back seat of the hired car driving me to the terminal, where I'll fly the company jet into Teterboro. "For that matter, New York."

"I can't deny that I enjoyed it immensely," I say calmly.

Caleb laughs harder. "You would."

True. I can't dispute that. Melody Dempsey was a huge mistake in more ways than one, in my opinion.

First, I've found her work in the Virginia office to be merely par when we need superior performance at every turn. Her credentials and her interview were exceptional, but now that she's in the role, she's barely making the grade. That won't continue much longer, or she'll have the choice of stepping down from her current role to one with less responsibility or leave the company altogether. We can't risk her jeopardizing a recently repaired relationship with our government contract holders by allowing shoddy work to pass through.

Second, I shouldn't have gotten drunk that close to my sister's birthday years ago. My anger and guilt for failing to find her always left me self-destructive. I was tempted, briefly, into a single night in Melody's bed and didn't have the common sense to restrain myself. It crossed every moral line I had. Don't fuck around with employees. Don't fuck around with the business. Don't show weakness to an enemy. Don't show weakness, period.

But at the time, my sister had been missing for twenty-four years. The flicker of hope I carried around inside of me was slowly beginning to fade. And between a bottle of Scotch, a depression so deep it was like a crater, and the persistent seduction of Melody's curves, I threw my rules out the window.

She's been trying for a second round ever since. I've tried to shut her down, politely, until today.

Her scheming machinations to get me back in her bed and lack of attention to our work would cost us a cool million. My temper rekindled at the realization. And while I know my best friend would enjoy taking a few shots at me over the next few weeks with the things he's learned from reading Melody's emails and listening to her phone conversations, it was worth listening to him to shut that crap down. This time for good.

"I swear, if that office isn't in order by Monday, we'll run ops back out of New York and shut it down. She'll be out on her ass," I threaten, dropping my head back against the seat.

"I believe you, buddy. I've already put the team leads here on alert." He doesn't stop clicking away on his computer, saying, "Seriously, it was a massive fuckup. And if I wasn't worried about the fallout we're already taking because of the Mildred issue, I'd have let you fire her ass already. We had plenty of justification."

The Mildred issue. I let out a long sigh of frustration. I can't even take his head off for the incident he just brought up, because that burden is equally shared between us.

Thirty years ago, Caleb's mother, Mildred, and my father, Jack, were having an affair. They colluded together to abandon their respective families, including all their children, and run off together. That plan would have been fine, except my father was still sleeping with my mother. Consequently, my sister was born.

As the story goes, my father was so overcome by his conscience after my sister arrived, he decided to give his marriage another try, ignoring his lover. So, she decided to dispose of the child that took him away. For years after my sister disappeared, I despaired, wondering if she was alive. When I was old enough, I spent every spare minute searching for any trace of her, until last year, when I found her alive and living under the name Cassidy Freeman, now Cassidy Lockwood.

Amazing how we've come full circle in some ways.

Driving over a pothole on the Dulles Toll Road, I'm jostled from my thoughts. I hear Caleb still clicking away over the phone line. "Is there anything else?" I ask brusquely.

"Not on my side. Other than did you talk with Cassidy? Dinner tonight?"

I outright groan. "Shit, I forgot. It's not tomorrow?"

Caleb laughs again. "I take it you don't want me to request any anatomically correct food demonstrations tonight?"

I shudder at the thought of any of my sister's adopted family making phallic symbols out of food. "If you do, after the day I've had, I'm walking out the door," I warn.

Caleb, the bastard, continues to laugh at me, knowing there's no controlling the Freemans when they're all together.

My car approaches the Dulles VIP terminal. "Hanging up. I'm pulling up to the airport."

"Safe travels, brother. FYI, Cass arranged for your place to be cleaned and stocked. Just letting you know so you won't think that someone broke in."

I'm touched by the small gesture. My relationship with my sister is still too new for me to take such things for granted. "I'll thank her later. What time am I expected at the farm?"

"See you anytime after six."

"Later." I disconnect the call and jump out of the back seat of the car.

Grabbing my carry-on, I walk through security to the Hudson private jet. Within thirty minutes, I'm airborne, heading back to New York.

Toward home.

4

KEENE

If it wasn't for the cleaning people Cassidy had arranged, I'm certain I wouldn't be relaxing with a beer, contemplating tonight's family dinner at the farm. Instead, I'd likely be searching the internet for a hazardous-waste company that could come and eliminate the mutant life-forms certain to be left growing inside my fridge.

Taking a deep breath, I inhale the clean scent of lemon. It's good to be back, knowing I'll be staying in my own space for longer than a few days for the first time in months. I hate hotels.

Absentmindedly, I rub my forehead. A picture on the credenza of me and Cassidy dancing at her wedding captures my attention. If I'm brutally honest, I still struggle with such conflicting emotions whenever I think of her, which is often.

Thank God I no longer wonder if she's safe and happy. That, I can say is true, with one hundred percent certainty.

I can't figure out my feelings, and that annoys the shit out of me. I've been forcing myself to confront them, to get to a place where I'm comfortable around this new status quo.

For so long, my search to find out what happened to my missing sister was a mission of justice, a right to be wronged. Simple, definable, and relentless. I never said it out loud, but in the back of my mind, I imagined it would end with my finding her dead. It's why her real name is tattooed on my leg. A brutal weight to carry with me as I traveled through this life.

Now, that weight is gone.

If I had any faith left, I might conclude that my tattoo was the catalyst that brought Cassidy back to me, but I prefer to think it was something in the recesses of her mind, calling her home.

Moving toward the credenza, I pick up the picture. Cassidy looks like our deceased mother, so much so that I can't believe I didn't recognize her from the first meeting the second our eyes met. I can't believe I let my bitterness blind me to what was right in front of me.

It's next to impossible for me to reconcile that less than a year ago, I was still searching for her. And where did I find her? In Collyer, planning a wedding I was going to attend. My company was responsible for completing a background check on her siblings, their business, and her—the adopted family my company had investigated in the past.

Even more incredulous was the fact that Cassidy managed to fall in love with Caleb, my best friend since childhood. He'd disregarded all the odds stacked against him, including my own warning about the ethical compromise of getting involved with someone we'd previously investigated.

Still holding the picture, I brace my other forearm against the pre-war windows, squinting against the light flooding into my condo. The first time I met Cassidy, long before I realized she was my sister, Caleb brought her to a party we were all at. I confronted her, asking flat out if she thought it was ethical for her to see him because she was in a business relationship with his family. Cassidy, knowing her self-worth, and not devolving into my game of one-upmanship, managed to turn my words back on me. I smile, remembering that conversation.

After my initial suspicions about Cassidy's identity lodged in my brain and wouldn't leave, I practically stalked her. Hell, who am I kidding? There's no "practically" about it. I accessed data I never should have been privy to, proving my suspicions. When I read what her life had been like in the years between, I raged. I went into the darkest place I'd ever been, knowing it was due to our father's infidelity that she was even gone.

Forgiveness wasn't something I deserved to ask for and never thought I could earn. I couldn't go back and change her first impression of the big brother who was supposed to protect her.

Cassidy's so damn strong. She grabbed my hand and dragged me from my darkness. Together, we've managed to come out of that stronger than ever.

I rub my thumb over her smiling face in the photo. I was holding her during what she christened the "brother-sister" dance at her wedding. I was shocked since I fully expected her to dance with her adopted brother, Phillip.

I remember asking, cautiously, "Are you sure you want that dance to be with me, Cassidy?" I wanted it, and I struggled to be fair. It was my sister's wedding, after all, and she deserved to have exactly what she wanted. At the time, I didn't want her to include me because she felt obligated, yet it pained me when I said, "Phil has been your brother longer than I have."

Cassidy's smile softened. Sitting on her double lounger overlooking the lake her house is built on, she leaned on my shoulder and said, "Keene, honey, trust me, please?" Looking up at me through eyes like my father's, ones I never thought I would look into again and not feel hatred, stole my soul. "Phillip will be walking me down the aisle. I think he needs to know in his heart that he's giving me away to a wonderful man. That's his duty as my brother, and you and I deserve to have our moment together." Tears tangled with her dark lashes. "If you don't want to…" Her voice trailed off with uncertainty.

"I do." My voice was gruff as I choked back my emotions.

She pinched my ribs lightly. "That's what I'll be saying to Caleb, you goof."

We both laughed, taking away some of the stress of the moment, right before she gutted me.

"What was Mama's favorite song?" she wondered aloud.

"Lean On Me," I answered immediately. Our mother used to sing it all the time. Cassidy was a baby; she wouldn't have remembered.

Cassidy's face had turned contemplative. I sang to her softly, like I did when she was a baby. By the end, tears were falling down her face as she said, "That's perfect for us, isn't it? We'll have each other, and Mama will be with us as well."

I swallowed hard. Unable to speak, I clutched my precious sister to my chest.

That day, there wasn't a dry eye during the ceremony or when we had our "brother-sister" dance. The look on Cassidy's face as she held on to me during our dance is something I will hold in my heart as one of the most cherished memories of my life. Especially after finding out not long before she was pregnant with my niece or nephew.

When I realized Cassidy was my sister, I wanted to rip her away from her life with her adopted family and give her everything she missed in the twenty-five years she was away from me. I wanted to be the center of her world and make her the center of mine. I even begrudged, albeit less so, the time she spent with Caleb. But the time she spent with her adopted family, the Freemans? It ate at my gut. She was supposed to be mine to protect, but I had failed, abysmally.

The Freemans' love and acceptance of us is a reminder that I couldn't keep her safe. It doesn't matter that she was four and I was ten. The tattoo I see on her neck is a constant reminder that it wasn't me who managed to pull her out of a living hell, long before I could even start looking for her.

Setting the photo down as I walk into the kitchen, I debate on whether or not to have another beer but decide against it since I have to drive to Connecticut tonight for a family dinner—with a certain blonde who showed me what heaven was like and knocked me on my ass from the first night I met her.

Alison. What am I going to do about Alison?

My mind drifts back to the moment I tossed my keys to the valet at the Plaza Hotel where I was staying until my condo remodel was done. I'll never forget hearing someone shout, "I dare you, Ali!" followed by a husky laugh of acceptance.

I saw two women dressed in bridesmaid dresses, both gorgeous in their own unique way. But it was the leggy blonde who captured my attention. She shot a dazzling smile at the petite brunette, then walked the perimeter of the fountain in front of the Plaza Hotel in her pencil-thin heels. Just as the valet was about to go put a stop to their antics, I stepped in. "I'll handle it," I murmured quietly, absorbed by the look of nonchalance, daring, and unfettered amusement the feisty blonde gave me.

The valet was busy with a line of cars pulling in. "Thank you, Mr. Marshall. The two sisters are part of a wedding party inside. I'm sure they're just having a bit of fun, but I wouldn't be doing my job..." He had trailed off before he made his way to the next vehicle.

I walked slowly to the fountain so I wouldn't startle the two women. I watched Ali finish her lap around the fountain and stop, trying to figure out how to dismount without breaking a heel or a leg.

"Maybe I can be of some assistance?" I offered smoothly.

Devastating blue eyes locked onto mine. Stunning—the entire package. From the top of her head, to her athletically built legs that seemed to go on for miles, she was a knockout. She smiled, and I had to stop myself from taking a step back at the impact. "I think you can —maybe in more ways than one," she purred.

Game. Fucking. On.

There was a soft laugh from behind me, but I never turned around. I barely heard her speak as Ali reached out and grasped my shoulders to steady herself on the side of the fountain. I felt her hands through my shirt, all the way to my cock. Hell, it still gets hard whenever I think about that moment.

"Hello, Ali."

She nodded. "Hello, handsome."

"Keene."

"Hello, Keene. Thanks for rescuing me from the fountain. I would've ruined my new prized silver Choos." She cocked her head and smiled.

I'd never even asked for her last name, and I didn't see her again until I walked into the kitchen of Amaryllis Events, my sister's family's event planning business. She was sitting at the counter in a business suit that hugged every inch of her body, showing off her crossed legs. I was overcome by her teeming anger, even as she laughed with her family.

Standing in front of my kitchen sink, my fingers tighten on the lip of the countertop. Alison Freeman is a complication I'm going to have to figure out, but I have no idea how.

I need to remember my boundaries, of what I've always considered right and wrong. Unfortunately for me, Alison Freeman is the worst kind of wrong there is. The kind that could actually be good for me.

I need to focus on dinner and strategize how I'll handle tonight. If past experience with dinners at the Freeman farm are anything to go by, I'll need eye bleach, Xanax, or a bottle of the best Scotch money can buy to make it through the impending shit show. And that's not counting my constant pull to interact with the knockout blonde lawyer.

Walking into my bedroom to change, I decide I have enough time to shower DC off me. I make my way to my bathroom, and as the steam builds, my mind drifts to the last time I saw Alison, which was after Caleb and Cassidy's wedding...in Alison's kitchen.

Her dress was somewhere, as were my clothes. I had licked her, sucked her, and fucked her on her kitchen island. I was so damn hot to get my hands all over her body.

We were both so demanding about what we wanted.

Harder. Faster. Deeper.

If I close my eyes, I can still feel her juices flowing down my legs. That's how hot it burned.

Then she kicked me out. Still glistening from where she came, she showed me the door.

Her extraordinary blue eyes were vacant, unlike that night at the Plaza.

I never got to tell her I'd been thinking I wanted one more thing.

More.

5

KEENE

I navigate my Audi as I make my way into Collyer from New York. My tension increases as I approach the farm, the ten-acre piece of property where my sister and her siblings each restored a hovel to make their individual homes set around a lake a few years earlier.

Although I acted disinterested when he first talked about Cassidy, I never told Caleb I thought he was crazy when he started spending as much time as he was in Connecticut when they first started dating. The company Caleb and I own is in the heart of Manhattan, near Rockefeller Center. On a great day, the commute is an hour and ten minutes' drive from the farm.

Unfolding myself to get out of my car, I grudgingly begin to understand why Caleb gave up the easy convenience of his commute. The jewel the Freemans have established here is breathtaking. Holding a hand up to ward off the glare of the sun as I glance around the lake, I look at the dark green leaves of the trees that frame the carriage house Cassidy and Caleb call home.

Knowing what she built with so damned little and nothing more than her own determination, I'm filled with a rush of brotherly pride.

"Amazing, isn't it? I love this time of year here." Feeling a clap on my shoulder, I tense as I turn. Jason Ross, Phil's husband, offers me a welcoming smile as he holds out his hand. "Welcome home, brother."

I'm uncertain about his ease in accepting me into the Freeman fold, but I grasp his hand and accept a back slap anyway. I do admit, I've always held a deep respect for Jason. Not only because he's an ER doctor in a major New York City hospital, but he's the man who manages to be married to Phil on a daily basis and not smother him in his sleep.

"It's good to be back."

"Is it?" He starts to laugh, and I frown. When did I become so easy to read? "When did you get in?" he continues as if he hasn't unsettled me.

"A few hours ago." I roll my shoulders, releasing any lingering tension before I see my sister again. She'd read it in an instant and worry something was wrong. She'd fuss over me, needing to fix whatever it is she sees.

That's not the way our relationship is supposed to work. I'm the fixer, the one who solves all the problems. My role has been ingrained in me for so long, I don't know how to live without it. My rules are so structured on what is right and wrong, black and white, it's hard for me to let go of control and let others in.

I remember one of my Harvard professors writing a Sir Arthur Conan Doyle quote on the board during class that fascinated me, about logic being rare and dwelling on that. Despite what others may think, I'm not unaware of how I live my life. As a result, it's been hard to settle into the Freemans' world.

I'm dragged from my thoughts when Jason asks, "Sure you're up to a summons for a family dinner?"

I take an involuntary step back. "Is there going to be anything resembling body shots, food art, or Phil trying to demonstrate positions from the Kama Sutra?" One night over dinner, Cassidy provided me with some the more interesting highlights of her family get-togethers. I want to see my sister, but I don't need to see a live sex show. I've been privy to some of the better ones, and I know they're not hosted by Phil Freeman.

Jason laughs. "Not that I'm aware of, and I don't think anyone is actively planning."

Thank God. "Then I think I'm safe." I pause. "'Think' being key there."

Jason claps my shoulder again as we make our way to the front door of the farm, where we immediately stop dead. Through the ringing of my ears, I hear Luke Bryan blaring over the surround sound.

Before I can take a step into the room, I feel the impact of a small body, with what seems like a deflated basketball shoved up her dress, smashing into me.

"Oomph." The air rushes from my lungs as a shoulder hits my solar plexus.

"Welcome back, Keene!" Cassidy shouts in my ear above the music. Her ocean-blue eyes sparkle up at me as she leans forward to press a kiss against my cheek. My arms tighten around her. My baby sister. Even now, her enthusiastic reaction causes my heart to stutter in my chest.

I wrap my arms around her small—not so small now that she's pregnant—frame, and rock her back and forth. Over the cacophony of noise, I whisper, "Thanks," into her ear.

She beams up at me before saying, "I'll be back," and runs back into the chaos of the main room.

Luke is crooning about the country girls shaking it, and damn if all the Freemans aren't doing as he's requested. My eyes widen at the sight of my pregnant sister joining the dance party. At least she's not on top of the table or counter like the rest of her family is, or I might have to question Caleb's sanity. Cassidy has enough sense to be dancing on the floor while holding on to something, namely her husband. As I'm watching her with an indulgent smile, I see her swaying back and forth. Then I hear Corinna call out with a huge smile on her face, "Shake it, Ali!"

I stiffen. Every muscle tightens as I scan the room, trying to find

Alison. The second I do, my dick hardens, immediately. I think I'm going to have zipper tracks running up the underside of it from the blood racing to it so fast.

In a sundress that hugs her toned body, Alison's back is facing me as she raises her hands above her head, feet spread as wide as the narrow slits in the side of her skirt will allow. She does some kind of shimmy move that ends up with her rocking her sweet ass back and forth on her heels, a move I've only seen performed by professionals using a pole. Using those sleek thighs that I've memorized the taste of, she sways her sexy body back up to a standing position, to catcalls from her other family members. "Super-hot, Ali!" is yelled from a table to my left where Em is dancing. Phil whistles between his teeth like he's at an actual strip club. Holly flips her long mane of hair out of her face, sees me, and loses it.

Pointing in my direction, she yells, "Ali, you got an audience! One who can actually rate that move!"

Alison swivels around on the end table and our eyes meet. Cobalt blue to my green. Coolly, her eyes narrow in my direction before dismissing me. I hear a snort of laughter from Corinna at Alison's response.

What the fuck was that? Not even a hello?

I'm mentally running through the catalog of information Cassidy has kept me up-to-date on while I've been gone. I know Alison isn't seeing anyone. If I'm not mistaken, I'm the last person who's slid into the tight slickness of her body, feeling her muscles clamp down while her juices leaked out.

Like the first night I met her, she challenges me with a single look. On her next spin, I make certain I'm in her line of sight, sending her a predatory smile. I keep my face expressionless as she almost falls off the table.

Going to try to keep me out, Alison?

We'll see about that.

6

ALISON

That was mortifying.

I sit at our huge farm table, the spoon for the pasta salad in my hand forgotten, as Holly patiently holds the bowl for me.

I swore Keene had been looking at me in front of the family like he wanted to rip off my dress and tear my panties to shreds with his teeth. I could almost anticipate him dragging me off the table I was dancing on earlier. Knowing exactly how his cock feels driving into me probably isn't good for our family dynamic. Or the slick wetness now coating my panties. Keene looking at me like I should be gagging for it has changed everything. I'm tired of feeling the way I do when I'm around him. I'm not his easy lay.

Corinna kicks me from under the table, shooting me a look. "Heads up," she mouths and nods at Phil, who's watching our end of the table with interest. Crap. I refuse to be the one interrogated during a family dinner by our big brother. Quickly putting some pasta on my plate, I grab the bowl from Holly, who's the last to be served. Standing, I walk toward the island when a hand grabs my elbow. I look down into Keene's all-knowing eyes.

"If you don't mind, Alison," he murmurs, reaching for the spoon.

His hand slides over the inside of my arm to take the handle. I know he feels how he affects me. My heart rate trips as his fingers dance along my skin. Because of my position, no one but me can feel the back of his long finger graze lightly over my puckered nipple as he roots around the bowl with the spoon. For fuck's sake. It's pasta salad, not an archeological dig.

I cock my hip impatiently, waiting for him to finish. "Could you lower the bowl a little?" he asks, his voice innocent, his face anything but. I lock my jaw and tilt the bowl slightly away from my body. If he keeps this up, this pasta salad may end up on his head.

The minute the spoon hits the bowl, I give Keene my back as I walk away and place the bowl on the counter, before heading back to my seat at the table. I have no idea what new game he's decided to play, but it's wreaking havoc on my mind and my body. Somehow, I have to shut this down.

"That was interesting to watch," Corinna purrs as I sit.

"Shut up," I mutter back, while Holly snickers next to me.

"He's a fine piece of ass. I still can't believe you tapped that." Corinna glances down the table at Keene. Her mouth keeps moving as if I haven't even spoken.

"Twice," Holly pipes up.

I glare at her. How the hell does she know that?

Corinna whips her head around so fast, her hair whacks me in the face. Holly is outright laughing. Fortunately, there are so many of us around the table, the musical sound of Holly's laughter doesn't catch anyone's attention.

Namely Phil and Keene.

"You didn't say it was more than once!" Corinna hisses at me.

I glare at Holly, but she only shrugs.

"When?" Corinna demands, getting louder. When I see a few heads turn our way, I know I need to shut this conversation down. Can't someone spill something on the table? I look down at my wine, but before I can tip my wrist, Corinna says, "Spill it."

"I was trying to, but you stopped me."

We both burst out laughing, and Holly joins us. Not for the first time, I think of how blessed I am that Phil, Cassidy, and Em found us and got us away from the hell of our lives. Instead of being permanently scarred for what my father had tried to do, I was graced with four sisters and a brother. I adore them, even when they're being annoying.

Removing my hand from my wine glass, I reach over and touch the amaryllis tattoo on the inside of Holly's left wrist. Strong, self-confident, pride—our family motto. We strive to live up to that.

Which is exactly why I have to shut Keene down. How can I continue to disrespect myself by falling deeper into the pit of nowhere with him?

I reach for my glass again as Holly tells Corinna, "She doesn't want to talk about it."

"How do you know, then?" Corinna demands.

I'm curious about that myself. Holly merely shrugs. "I was taking a picture of her at her desk as she was reading something. She had this look on her face that was...intriguing. When I developed the picture, I zoomed in. It looked personal, so of course, I read it."

I choke. Corinna toasts Holly, smiling the brilliant smile that's dropped hordes of men to their knees. "I'm so pissed you didn't tell me, but I'm proud of your stealth and skill."

"It was only last week, Corinna. It's not like I've had a lot of time to tell you," Holly grumbles.

Ignoring both of them, I refill my wine glass. Abstractly, I wonder if I can grab a couple of straws from the kitchen and drink straight from the bottle.

Turning to face me, Corinna orders, "Start talking or I'm telling Phil." With horror, I lift the bottle straight to my lips, causing them to howl with laughter. Corinna grabs my arm before the bottle reaches my mouth. "Jesus, does he suck in bed or something?" Unfortunately, her voice carries over the lower conversations, and suddenly, all eyes are on me.

Holly and Corinna mutter simultaneously, "Shit."

Screw it.

Raising the wine bottle to my lips, I take a large swig. When I lower it, my eyes meet Keene's across the table. His face, previously flirtatious, is now remote. Raising his eyebrow in question, we engage in a brief staring match before he turns back to continue his conversation with Cassidy and Caleb. I realize I'm trying to figure out why he's questioning what we're talking about when I conclude that he thinks I've slept with some random guy after him.

Fuck you, Keene. I'm a woman, not your possession or some client brief you file away and take out when you want it. I'll do whatever the hell I want.

Under the humored glances of Corinna and Holly, I grab the bottle of wine and take another swig before attacking my meal with a vengeance.

I've had enough of men trying to control me to last a lifetime, starting with my father.

I sure as hell don't need an ex-lover trying to do it.

After a while, dinner settles down to some semblance of normalcy.

Caleb stands, tapping his dessert fork against his wine glass. Smiling at Cassidy, he asks, "Are you ready?" Cassidy, her face alight with happiness, nods. She stands beside him, placing her hand on her protruding stomach.

Phil drawls, "Wait, let me guess? You're pregnant?" We all break out into laughter. Typical Phil, the smartass.

Cassidy says, "Just for that, I'm not going to name one of them after you."

Em spews her drink right into Phil's face and chokes, unable to catch her breath. While Phil's recovering from having Bailey's spat in his eyes, Em jumps up and screams, "One of them? One of them? Holy shit, Cass!" She runs into Cassidy's arms, and the two of them start dancing around and talking over one another as they do with news of this caliber.

I'm not far behind. My chair clatters to the floor and I leap over the legs as I run around the table, adding my voice to the increasing volume of my two older sisters. Soon, our bodies are slammed into by

Holly and Corinna. We're a weeping huddle, talking over one another in sheer excitement.

Not just one baby we're welcoming into our family, but two. I'm overwhelmed. I hear Em say, "This explains why you look like you've swallowed a basketball overnight."

Corinna says, "I thought it was all the chocolate she was craving. I was making quadruple batches of icing between her and Phil." Another wild burst of laughter erupts.

Holly joins in with, "I thought my cameras were going all screwy because she was glowing. I kept having to change my settings when I'd approach her office. I thought I was going to need a solar eclipse filter soon."

We're still joking and wiping away tears of joy when I realize the men haven't joined in. Twisting my neck, I find myself captivated by the look on their faces. I quickly elbow Holly, who squeezes Corinna to get her attention.

Phil has tears cascading down his face, his shoulders shaking. His hand, held up to his mouth, is trembling with the force of his emotions. Cassidy, who has always been the little girl he protected from the world, isn't only becoming a mama, but she's doing it in a huge way the first time around.

Caleb is standing with a look of complete tranquility on his handsome face, his arms crossed over his chest as he watches his wife. She survived unimaginable horrors to become the woman at the center of his universe. I never thought I'd see it again, but the look on his face is a deeper, more intense version of the one they shared on their wedding day a few months ago. Pure, undiluted love.

Knowing the hell they went through to get to where they are today, I couldn't be more thrilled that my sister and brother-in-law found the happiness they so richly deserve. And I wouldn't be human if there wasn't a small part of me that didn't envy the depth of devotion the two of them have for each other.

I catch Caleb's eye and mouth, "Congratulations, Daddy." His smile broadens as he mouths back, "Thanks, Aunt Ali."

God, I'm going to be an aunt two times over. My eyes mist again, and I beam back at Caleb.

The girls start chattering about the babies again, when my eyes finally make their way over to Keene. I expect his cool exterior to have thawed, for him to be as ecstatic as the rest of us are. The sister he lost for so long is pregnant with not one, but two babies. More love to fill the missing spaces, right?

What I see on his face guts me, and not in a good way.

Sure, he has a smile on his face, but even from a distance, I can tell it's strained around his eyes.

How can Keene not be thrilled with this news?

I watch as his eyes scan Cassidy's body from head to toe, lingering on the babies nestled safely in their mother's womb. A look I can't describe crosses his face before he masks it.

Does anyone else notice? Em is joking with Cassidy, Holly, and Corinna about horrid baby names, so no help there.

The guys are now in a small huddle, slapping Caleb on the back or upside the head, as it were in Phil's case. Keene is holding himself back per usual, but it allows me to observe him.

Keene's jaw clenches. Shock, anger, and...disgust, maybe over Cassidy's news? Then, as if he can feel the hole I'm drilling into his head, his face snaps to mine. He shakes his head, conveying without words that this isn't my issue.

The hell it isn't. I won't allow Keene's disinterest or heartlessness to touch Cassidy the way it did when they first met. He was such a douchebag to her. He had his shot at distancing himself, but he decided to become a part of this family.

That means he pays for his mistakes, just like everyone else.

In this family, you show expressions of pleasure, love, and joy over other people's fortune, even when your heart might be dying a little inside. You curb the need to rage your off-the-charts anger when a man messes with someone you love. It means saving your temper tantrum for a time when you're not in a room full of people.

Keene's sister taught me that.

Tears of frustration blur my vision. My temper continues to edge out of control, but I don't let Cassidy see. She pulls me to her side and squeezes me against her for the first time in forever, likely misinterpreting my tears for emotion over the babies. I relish the closeness, savoring it.

Burying my head in my sister's neck, I make a promise to protect those babies from anything that might hurt them, including an uncle who apparently has an issue with them. Over Cassidy's shoulder, I see Keene's face twist into something painful.

I turn my back. I can't care.

I won't.

7

KEENE

Why is Mommy bleeding? It's staining the tile as I walk in, clutching my bear to my chest.

She's sitting on the floor of her bathroom, holding her rounded stomach, her face pale. Her long brown hair is matted to her head like she's been running. Her green eyes have so many tears in them.

"Mommy, what's wrong?" I walk to her, my feet squishy in the goo as I get closer.

"Keene, you shouldn't be here, sweetheart," she rasps, her tears falling harder. Her face is so warm when I reach out to touch it. "Where's Daddy?" she asks me.

I shake my head. I don't know. Even so young, I recognize the agony crossing her face.

"What about Mrs. Tilly or Dawson?" she questions. I shake my head again. I don't know where our housekeeper and the driver are.

"Okay, my brave boy. I need you to do something for Mommy. You have to get the phone from my side of the bed. Can you go do that?"

I nod. I can. She runs her hand over my hair and face. It's so warm and sticky. I touch her where she's touching me. Why does Mommy feel so...wrong?

"Okay, baby. Get the phone and come back here with it. We need it to *help the babies.*" She and I both look down at her stomach, where I know the babies are sleeping.

"*Okay, Mommy.*" *I turn to her bedroom but first hand her my bear.* "*Hold on to this until I get back. It will make you stronger and help the babies, Mommy.*"

Tears run down her cheeks as I duck out of the bathroom, slipping a bit, before I grab the phone.

I shake myself away from the memory. Standing outside the farm, I gaze at the star-studded sky over the lake. Cassidy's announcement has everyone inside celebrating with loud music and laughter. All I want to do is curse the heavens for putting her in such danger. Her body is just like our mother's was—too petite to handle two babies in it at one time. I can't imagine the sick hell she and Caleb will feel when she loses them. My fists are clenched tightly in my pockets, and my shoulders are rigid beneath my shirt. Haven't they been through enough to last three lifetimes? I'm so lost in my dark past colliding with the present, that I don't hear the door open behind me.

Until her voice berates me, crashing me back to this reality.

"I somehow knew you were selfish, standoffish, and a general prick about our family, but not congratulating your sister and best friend on their joy? That takes a special kind of resentment, doesn't it, Keene?"

I don't bother turning around. Her words are like a knife slowly piercing the layers of my skin.

"What? Nothing to say? Why am I not surprised? Any man who can sneak away without even bothering to put on his pants is one hell of a coward after all."

My jaw tightens and my fists open and close inside my pockets.

Alison continues. "At least she has the rest of us who love her and those babies unconditionally."

My temper is about to boil over. I wish Alison would walk away and leave me alone. I remain silent, not engaging the blonde warrior behind me. But I feel her. I feel the emotions she can't hide. And what I feel is nothing but crashing waves of disappointment and fury.

"I'm grateful Cassidy still has the illusion that her brother gives a damn about her. I hope you can keep up the façade for the rest of her pregnancy before you break." She steps up behind me, so close I can feel her breath through the back of my shirt. Turning slowly to face her, it's her next words that snap my control.

"Because if you can't, if Cassidy feels one ounce of your repulsion for the lives she and Caleb created, know that all of the Freemans will create a barrier around her so tight, you'll never get close to her again. No one will ever make her feel that kind of pain again."

She turns to walk away, and my hand shoots out of my pocket involuntarily, grabbing her upper arm.

Sneering at my hand with distaste, she composes her features before saying coolly, "Not the first time I've been manhandled, Keene."

I'm so surprised by her statement and by my own actions, that my fingers immediately slacken. Before I can find words to explain, Alison strides back into the farmhouse, her back ramrod straight as she closes the door behind her.

"Not one of your finest moments, Keene?" a voice says behind me. Shit. I scrub my hand down my face. I don't need any of this right now. I turn around to face Phil and Jason. Phil looks furious, Jason thoughtful.

"Not now, Phil." I wave at the air between him and Jason. "Please."

Phil opens his mouth, but Jason beats him to it. "Give me a few minutes, babe. Keene and I have a few things to discuss."

Phil turns to his husband and asks incredulously, "Are you kidding me, Jace? You heard everything Ali said to him, and he didn't contradict a word she said."

"I heard, but there's more going on here. Isn't there, Keene?" Jason turns to face me. His insight as a trauma doctor has given him the ability to cut through people's bullshit over the years. There's no way to take back what just happened inside, but I have to tell someone what I know to protect my sister.

"I..." My voice cracks. Phil's anger is evident. His mouth opens, and Jason calmly places his hand over it to shut his husband up.

If I was in any other frame of mind, I'd applaud that move.

"Take your time, Keene," Jason says.

Taking a deep breath, I try again. "All I can remember is the blood." Phil's sharp intake of air could be heard a mile away. My whispered words are almost ripped from me. "She was pregnant with twins, and she was screaming out in pain. It woke me from my sleep. I must have been three? Four?"

"Oh, sweet Jesus," Phil whispers. I concentrate on Jason, who nods encouragingly.

"Of course, my father was off somewhere with another woman. My mother was bleeding on the bathroom floor when she miscarried them at barely seven months. I remember visiting her in the hospital later and overhearing the doctors saying it was a fluke, that there was no reason she couldn't have more children. When I read her medical records years later, I found out that her placenta detached from one of the twins, and the rupture caused too much blood loss. She spontaneously aborted one baby, and the other was too premature to survive."

Phil is perfectly silent. Jason inhales deeply and lets it out. "I wish I could say it's a one in a million chance, Keene, but it's not completely uncommon." He nods as if he's understanding, finally. "That's why you're out here and not—"

I cut him off. "Celebrating? Yeah." I laugh bitterly. "I stepped in my mother's blood to hand her my teddy bear. I called 911 because my father was nowhere to be found." Phil flinches.

The reality of my baby sister having twins has rocked me to my core.

"There's another good thing about tonight, then," Jason says, no-nonsense.

A good thing? I look at him as if he just told me he got his medical degree at a Holiday Inn Express rather than Yale.

"None of the girls, or Phil, know anything about their family medical history. Now that we know about your mother's difficult pregnancies, we can proactively monitor Cassidy." Jason shifts to doctor mode, focusing on the tangible fear that drove me into the night. The potential of my sister going through what our mother did.

"We'll get Cassidy scheduled for extra scans to monitor for placenta previa, make sure she watches for the warning signs of a placenta abruption, and consider the options of her delivering early. Keene, you may want to donate blood to store up in the event of an emergency, though I don't think we'll need it. But with your and Cassidy's blood type being so rare, it doesn't hurt us to have it ready. If we don't use it, it can be donated."

A plan. Something Cassidy would appreciate. Analytical thinking.

Something I do as well.

Phil lets out a shaky breath. "Jesus, Keene. I was an ass."

I turn to him. "Frequently." It isn't up to me to provide him absolution. I learned long ago no one could do that. Everyone lives with their mistakes. I've been living with mine for a long time.

My eyes dart to the door that Alison stormed through.

Phil runs a hand down his face as he catches my train of thought. "The girls will talk about this after Jason tells Cassidy, so Ali will know."

My face is carved in stone as I state, "All Cassidy needs to know is the potential issue I identified to Jason as a medical concern, not that we lost two siblings before she was born. She doesn't need that burden during her pregnancy."

Phil starts to object when Jason cuts him off. "Keene's right, Phil. The less stress Cassidy has, the better. However, Phil is also right, Keene. You'll likely be hearing from Ali. Regardless if she knows the whole story, knowing the little she'll hear will send her into a tailspin," Jason surmises. "You have to decide between now and then on what you plan to do once you hear from her."

There are so many reasons I should leave what Alison and I shared in the past. Forget about what she makes me feel. Let her think it was a no-strings hookup and that the nights we spent together meant nothing. Then I think of the disgust in her blue eyes when I touched her just now and a lead balloon of regret settles in my chest. Even if I can't have her, I can't let her believe those things.

She has to know I think more of her than her father, who tried to sell her when she was a blossoming teenager.

I hear Phil and Jason shuffle farther away as I contemplate the evening sky with only the smallest spark of white in it. I feel like it represents my life—so little light to offset the darkness. But it shows me clearly the contrast between right and wrong, and why my rules work in my world.

I throw up my emotional defenses and walk back inside. I choke down the end of this family night, pretending I'm happy for my sister and best friend and ignore the daggers being shot at me from across the room.

Because I'm surprised to find her daggers hurt.

8

ALISON

A few days later, I'm putting the final touches on the monthly profit-and-loss analysis when I hear Cassidy say, "So if it wasn't for Keene, I swear we would never have known about the potential for this," as she walks past my office door.

"Does your doctor think it's going to be a problem?" Em asks her. Doctor? What? I jump out of my chair and follow them around the corner to Cassidy's office. It's super cute the way her stomach is starting to lead her around.

"No. They've run the scan a few times now at Caleb's orders. But knowing I'm the same size as my mother, and that she had placenta previa, changed my doctor's approach for now until delivery. Caleb's ensuring we take all sorts of precautions." I turn into the doorway and walk into Cassidy's office. She looks up at me, and I pretend to not notice her smile dimming. "Hey, Ali. Sit. I was going to tell you this later anyway."

"What's wrong? Is it the babies?" I demand.

"Chill out, Ali. She's fine. She's taking all precautions," Em says on a laugh.

"What is it?" I know this is important, and somehow, not just to Cassidy and the babies.

Cassidy sighs as she mistakes my nerves. "It turns out Keene was upset about our announcement concerning the twins." She shakes her head compassionately, while my thoughts turn snide at that understatement. "I wish I'd told him in advance because he doesn't handle surprises well. At all. In this case, his reaction was for a good reason. A condition called placenta previa occurs in the women in my family, particularly if they're pregnant with twins. After we shared the news, Keene immediately started worrying about the medical issue."

Suddenly, I'm nauseated. "What does that mean, placenta previa?"

Em answers for her. "It's when the placenta, which feeds the babies, implants itself in the wrong place. Without monitoring for the condition, it could lead to bleeding and possible detachment. It's harmful and can lead to the loss of one or both babies. Cassidy could also lose so much blood she bleeds out," Em states matter-of-factly.

Oh. My. God.

"And it's a condition that occurs in your family?" I ask softly. I feel like I'm about to throw up between worry for Cassidy and the guilt for my harsh words to Keene.

"Keene told Jason about it after dinner the other night. Apparently, my mother was pregnant with twins before she had me. She lost both babies," Cassidy says softly. I look at her with my eyes practically popping out of my head.

"How can you be so calm?" I yell.

She laughs. Laughs! "Because the minute Caleb heard about it, he was on the phone with my OB/GYN and paid an obscene amount of money to have a scan done yesterday. They fit me in when I didn't have an appointment. The ultrasound focused on locating the placentas. They're in a good location. Caleb even had pictures printed out for Keene to help alleviate his worry."

Even I see the humor in that. I can totally imagine Caleb doing that, and it makes me smile. "Everything looks good, then?"

"Right as rain. We'll go in every month for visits until delivery, ultrasound each time, no exceptions." Cassidy shrugs. "Gives me more pictures of the babies to show off."

I stare at her in amazement. "I have no words." I sit in the chair across from her desk, astonished.

Crossing one leg over the other, I shake my head at Em. She smiles at me, and despite her laughing at my reaction, she's relieved. None of us could handle it if something happened to Cassidy or the babies.

"Like I was saying to Em, I can't believe Keene held it together as well as he did at dinner. I feel guilty," Cassidy admits.

The insensitive words I said to Keene come crashing back to me. This explains why he acted like he did. His reasons weren't selfish; he was buried in past grief and current worry. What have I done?

I begin to chew on my thumbnail, a sure giveaway to my sisters.

"What?" Em demands, as Cassidy shakes her head. "What happened?"

"Well..." I drag out the word in three syllables, my tempered Southern accent finding its way out of the box I bury it inside. "I might have had words with Keene for his behavior." Cassidy tilts her head and waits for me to explain. "To be completely honest, I had the words. He didn't say anything." I drop my chin to my chest as my sisters let out simultaneous sighs of disappointment.

Silence falls for a moment before Cassidy asks me, "Do you know if this was before or after he spoke to Jason?"

"I don't. But the things I said? I don't think that matters," I admit, feeling ashamed.

"Damnit, Alison. This is hard enough to navigate for all of us!" Cassidy yells. She struggles to pull herself to her feet before gravity and anger have her leaning forward to place her hands on her desk. Her next words are lethal. "Can't you get over riding his cock, if only to help for once instead of driving a further wedge into this family?"

Whoa. Wow. I'm having difficulty breathing. I stand to leave the office, but before I reach the door, I say, "You didn't see his face."

"When, Ali?" Em asks.

I turn around and open my mouth to speak. No words come out.

Cassidy sits down. She and Em exchange inscrutable glances.

"At dinner the other night. Everyone else looked so incredibly happy. Thrilled. There was so much love surrounding you, yet Keene was so withdrawn, detached. I was afraid he was going to say something to hurt you, Cass. Knowing what I do now, I know his discomfort was coming from a place of fear. But that night...?" I shake my head as my words trail off.

Em stands and walks to me. "Ali, you can't always be the one to protect us."

I focus on a spot on the refinished floor. "I guess you all don't need me to." Despite the fact that it's my job and what my heart tells me to do.

Cassidy shakes her head and says, "Come here, Ali. I'm not standing up again."

I shake my head.

Cassidy sighs, her frustration evident. "I know it's part of your nature to protect us, but Keene's not going to hurt me. He never will. We need to figure out a way to make this family work, but you don't need to be my bodyguard."

I nod, emotional to the extreme. I'm turning to leave when Cassidy's voice stops me again.

"Ali." I keep my back to her because I know what's coming. I brace myself for it by placing one hand on the doorjamb. "Do you still have his number, to call him to apologize?"

"This one requires a face-to-face, Cassidy. I wasn't only harsh, I was borderline cruel." I drop my head in shame. "I'll rearrange my schedule. I'll meet him tomorrow to apologize in person."

"Why not today?" The disappointment in her words is clear. She's upset this won't be resolved immediately.

Exhaling, I turn. "Because I have an event in the city I'm attending with Jared. I made this promise a long time ago, and since I've already let one side of this family down, I'd prefer not to let the whole family down in twenty-four hours."

Turning away, the pounding in my ears prevents me from hearing them try to call me back.

I have a party to get ready for, even though I'm not in a party mood.

I THINK I'm a bit starstruck.

Holding on to Jared's arm loosely, we glide through the 600 people in attendance at the Fair Harvard Annual Reunion at the Plaza Hotel. There are even faces in the crowd I recognize from the news. I nod as I pass by someone whose wedding we'd helped plan. He squeezes his wife's arm, and they wave me over. I give a helpless smile over my shoulder and walk farther into the fray. Unfortunately, I don't look where I'm going and end up running into a chest full of ribbons.

"Oh, excuse me," I blurt out, embarrassed.

"You should look where you're going in a crowd like this, Ali," the chest underneath the ribbons rumbles, sounding amused.

I look up into a set of warm gray eyes. Surprise causes me to drop Jared's arm, and I'm immediately engulfed in a one-armed embrace by Major Colby Hunt, an old friend from college. "Colby! What are you doing here? It's wonderful to see you," I murmur in his ear.

Colby's breath tickles my ear when he responds. "You too. I wish I would've known you were going to be here. Makes work more interesting."

"You're working?" I ask, confused.

Keeping his arm wrapped around my waist, he nods in the direction of a political figure so prolific, so revered, her name hits the front page every time something newsworthy is mentioned.

"Temporary assignment," he says quietly, still close to my ear to prevent being overheard.

"Since when does she require protection?" I murmur back.

"The answer to that is on a need-to-know basis only," Colby reprimands, gently.

I push the rebuke aside. "Does this mean you will be stateside long enough to come visit?"

"Yeah. Unless someone does something to cause a scandal, we've been assigned to assist protective services. The plan is to be around for the next six years." He pulls back and gives me a huge smile.

My returning one is so large, it must look deranged. "No way. And you haven't called any of us? Boy, are you going to hear about that." I feel Colby's body shake with suppressed laughter against mine.

"Rein it in, Ali. I need to cover the chairman for another hour." He snags two glasses of champagne from a passing waiter, handing one to me.

"Cheers, my friend." The clink of our crystal glasses rings out as we each take a sip.

It's at that moment Jared realizes I'm not next to him, and he saunters up to Colby and me. I introduce them, and after handshakes are exchanged, Colby slips his arm back around my waist as he nods at Jared. "Is this a date where I get to tell all the embarrassing stories I've saved up over the years and kept from Phil?"

I roll my eyes at Colby.

Jared says, "There are stories about Ali that Phil doesn't know? Hmm, this could be valuable information." Demonstrating his own quick wit, Jared counters with, "Ali, why don't you just stop breaking hearts all over the place and find a nice man like the major here to settle down with?"

I want to remind Jared it's because I have no intentions of ever settling down with any man since they could crush me like an ant, like his friend Keene did. Instead, I go with a non-answer. "Hmm, me?"

That sends Colby and Jared into guffaws.

When Colby stops laughing, he says mockingly, "Are you collecting a harem these days, Alison? Making up for lost time since UConn?"

I elbow him. "Jerk. Just for that, let's see if I invite you out to the farm while you're stateside."

His eyes gleam down at me. "You already did. Besides, it was you who enticed me after half a bottle of Jameson that you'd set me up with one of your sisters. Now that I heard Cassidy's off the market, I'm trying to figure out which sister I want."

I have nothing to refute. I think Colby would be great for a specific sister, but she's not ready yet, and neither is he for that matter.

Colby's arm tightens before he grins down at me. "Let's see. You're in a bind with your date already? You've been here for"—he checks his watch—"twenty minutes?" Colby leans back, giving me a critical look from head to toe. "Must be the dress."

Jared's lips are twitching, his amused smile about to break.

"Might be the date," I return.

Jared pipes up, "Hey, I take offense to that."

We laugh again. I so needed this.

The lighthearted banter continues for the next few moments before Jared excuses himself to speak with his partners. Jared drops a kiss on my cheek and tells me to have fun.

Colby and I catch up on what he's been up to. He's telling me hysterical stories about guys who I knew when I was in law school. I can't stop laughing.

Shaking my head, I surmise, "It sounds like some of them never grew out of their frat boy ways, Colby."

"True words, Ali." He grins.

A short time later, Colby's relief signals that he's off duty. Taking both of our glasses of barely touched champagne and passing them to a harried waiter, his smile turns genuine.

"Let's eat." Pure Colby. All Army, but he can bear so much pomp and circumstance.

I toss my hair. "Such a rush, Major. What's the hurry?" My eyes widen as I hear his stomach rumble. He barks out a laugh. "You've convinced me. Let's find Jared and bail. And not for nothing, I'm not eating nachos in this dress. You're eating real food."

"Oh, come on. I have a craving for them," Colby whines.

"You always have a craving for them after a formal event," I retort.

"You liked them in school," he counters.

"I still do when I'm wearing a T-shirt, but the dry cleaning bill for this dress would suck." I strike a pose to show off the beaded number I'm wearing.

Colby admits, "Ruining that dress would be a tragedy, Ali. Okay, we'll let Jared pick."

Sliding his hand from the center of my back to the curve of my hip, he guides me out of the ballroom.

Colby and I make our way through the throng of people. "What a crush. No wonder we all needed to be here tonight," he mutters. I shoot him a sympathetic look. I know crowds aren't exactly his favorite thing.

"Oh, my wrap!" I exclaim. "I need to remind Jared to stop and grab it at the coat check on his way." Pulling my phone from my clutch, I turn it over and quickly text him.

I didn't forget. I'm standing in line. Send Colby over. He can probably get it faster and we'll be out of here. Otherwise, I'll be waiting forever.

With a laugh, I show Colby my phone. Clicking his polished heels together and snapping me a salute, he says, "Never fear, Ms. Freeman. All in a day's work. Run five miles, shoot some guns, retrieve silk wraps."

"Bite me," I retort.

As he's walking away, he tosses over his shoulder, "There's certainly enough real estate showing in that dress!"

Laughing, I back up a few steps and bump into someone for the second time in one night. "Oh, I am so sorry!"

"Hello, Alison." The deep timbre of Keene's voice causes shivers to race up my exposed back.

Crap. Crap. Double crap.

I turn around and face him. The bottom drops out from my stomach.

In jeans, Keene can make your mouth water. In a suit, he'll turn your head.

In a tuxedo, he's every woman's fantasy.

Taking in a deep breath, I slowly let it out. "Hello, Keene. Lovely to see you."

"Is it really?"

I avoid answering. Instead, I focus on the displays around the outskirts of the lobby.

"You didn't answer my question, Alison." Keene steps closer, picking up my hand as he does. Bringing my fingers up, he grazes his lips over them. "Are you really happy to see me?"

Brazenly, I toss my hair. The movement has every glass bead on my dress shimmering in the overhead light. "We're family. It's always lovely to see family." Lovely. For me, lovely ranges in meaning from "bullshit" to "full of crap" to "oh, hell no."

All of which seem to apply to my present situation.

I'm not ready to face Keene yet. I have no idea what to say. I knew I wouldn't be ready to face him all superior-like when I forced myself to go to his office tomorrow.

His face darkens. "We're not family."

Swallowing hard, I try to remove my hand. "I realize my behavior the other night may have caused you distress, Keene, but I didn't realize you were so disturbed by my comments that you've already disowned me. I only wanted the chance to say, had I known—"

He interrupts me, snarling, "What the hell are you talking about? I have a general rule that I don't slide my cock inside a woman who's related to me."

The people walking by us are shocked into silence.

Mortification stains my cheeks. I open and close my mouth, but no words come out.

He pulls me closer to his body, away from the flow of people coming and going from the ballroom.

9

KEENE

Up close, her dress is illegal, and so is her body.

After catching up with a few former classmates, I wandered around the room, looking for Jared. Caleb had mentioned in passing that he was bringing Alison as his plus one.

I saw her almost the minute she entered on Jared's arm.

Across the ballroom, I caught glimpses of her crystal-encrusted dress skimming her luscious curves from where I was. Every time she moved, the crystals on her dress shimmered, brightening the room almost as much as her smile.

My reaction was visceral. I wanted to pick her up in my arms. I wanted to find a private corner to be alone with her. I wanted to pull the front of her dress down with my teeth and see what she was wearing underneath. Hopefully, nothing.

Now that she's standing in front of me, part of me wants to break her damned neck for how little there actually is to that damned dress. The straps holding it up could be snapped with a quick yank. Her entire back is exposed. Any finger—hell, a full hand—can trace her smooth skin from her shoulder to the top of her tailbone.

I decide it's time to stop playing. I've asked myself some serious questions about the delectable Alison Freeman, and I decided the answers were simple.

For as long as it lasts, we'll check our tempers.

For as long as it lasts, we'll balance our family and the fucking.

No more trying to second-guess wanting to bury my cock in her so deep she'll scream my name. I want to squeeze her ass in my hands as I'm pounding into her dripping pussy from behind. And those tits. They're mine too. I'll flick her nipples and make her moan.

I don't deserve Alison Freeman, but I can't deny myself anymore.

She's the kind of woman that makes a man beg for forgiveness.

It's too bad. I don't plan on asking for any.

You'd never know those thoughts were running through my head as I step forward, controlled, after she bumped into me. I've been observing her for too long with the unknown Army major. Observing their intimacy, their familiarity. I'm not pleased with the conclusions I've drawn. Alison knows him intimately, if I had to guess.

I want to dole out a little punishment for that.

I realize she doesn't know I've decided that we're not done, despite her throwing me out at the wedding, and our blowup at dinner the other night. She's mine. Another man should not touch her with such familiarity. Then again, it was his mistake that he left her alone.

I slowly shake my head back and forth in frustration as I look down at her. This woman drives me out of my mind in more ways than one. It's been like this from the moment we met outside the doors of this very hotel a few years ago. Nothing has changed, from the push and pull between us, or the urge to grab her and fuck her while pushing her away to keep her heart whole. I know the man I am and the man I come from. Her presence pulls me in like no other woman I've been with before or met since. I can't help my attraction to her.

Everything around us falls away until it's just the two of us. Her glossy lips are slightly parted. I know the color has intensified not only on her face, but down the column of her neck and in between her remarkably luscious breasts. I'd also bet my last dollar her nipples are puckered beneath her square-cut dress. My dick hardens when I find her sexy cobalt-colored orbs peering at me. I feel seared, scored.

"How's my sister?" I ask, trying to appear casual. I'm hopeful that talking about the impending additions to the family will lighten the mood. I expect her to bathe me in her glow as she goes off in a montage of all things baby related, but I'm shocked when the light in her eyes dies. It's like I struck her. The glow that was there moments ago shut down. Extinguished.

What the hell?

Her color fades. "Cassidy is wonderful, Keene. When I saw her earlier today, her baby belly was leading her into the room. It's adorable. She mentioned you two spoke recently, and that she's been keeping you up-to-date on her and the twins' health."

Alison's worrying her ring around her finger, twisting it so hard, I fear it's going to either pop off and hit someone in the eye, or she'll lose it forever in the hotel lobby. She stopped to rub her hands up and down her arms, taking a small step away from me.

Her awkwardness hits me like a boulder between the eyes.

Guilt. She heard what I shared with Jason and Phil, and now she's berating herself for the way she spoke to me, trying to protect her family. Sighing heavily, I raise a hand to the back of my neck and rub it vigorously.

God, what a fucking mess.

She's throwing up her walls for defense, but she's not fast enough. There's unspoken agony on her face.

"Alison, don't." The words are out of my mouth before I even know I'll say them.

She bites her lower lip and shakes her head, her mouth opening and closing as she shifts back and forth in her pencil-thin stilettos.

This won't do.

Pulling her closer, I slide my hand around her back. Even in heels, the top of her head only grazes my throat. My fingers trail over her exposed lower back as I lean down, putting my mouth next to her hair to inhale her scent. Chanel. "Alison. Eyes on me." I lower my head and say softly, "Please." A word I rarely use does the trick.

I watch as her head slowly lifts.

There's so much sadness behind her eyes. What the hell put it there? "Baby, what's wrong?" I ask quietly, cupping her chin. Her head drops. "Huh-uh," I admonish gently. "Look at me." And that's when I see it, resting on her lashes, trapped and held captive, but waiting for release.

A tear.

How much does this woman in front of me feel and hide inside?

How much is the real Alison?

She takes a deep breath and opens her mouth to speak, but I hold up a hand. Gently, I sweep my fingers under her eye to capture the tear before it can mar the perfection of her face.

Alison stands there like a statue. Her long lashes blink before she whispers, "I need to apologize."

"Alison, listen to me. You don't have to apologize." I move my hand from her back to her arm—the one I grabbed her so roughly by the other night—and rub my thumb over the sensitive skin there, and she flinches. If I bruised her, she must have covered it with makeup. "But it appears I owe you one."

She shakes her head.

I capture her jaw in my hand. "Now's not the time, but we need to talk about this. You. Me. What happened. Not at dinner, but before."

Over the last few days, I've realized I want more as long as we can have it. The million-dollar question is, does she?

There's only one way to find out.

I go to open my mouth when I hear a deliberate cough close by—too close. My hand tightens on her face before she pulls away.

I step back, only to meet a protective stare narrowed in on me over her shoulder.

"Major," I greet calmly, respectfully, even if I feel neither. What I want to do is rip off his arm that's now extended to Alison and drag her someplace where we can talk, alone. Instead, I watch as he holds her wrap out for her to bundle under.

"Hello." He regards me intently. "Ali, do you want this gentleman to stay and have a drink with all of us? Jared says the car's ready." He's affable and protective around Alison. I still want to shove him into a wall.

Seriously, who the fuck is this guy? My temper, barely held beneath the surface on a good day, is about to let loose when Alison speaks.

"Colby, that's sweet of you, but I'm sure he has other plans. This is Cassidy's biological brother, Keene. He's family." She smiles up at him, giving him my smile. His dark head lowers toward her with the same genuine smile I saw across the ballroom.

They make an attractive couple.

I think I'd enjoy killing him.

"Then it's time to go. Thank you for looking out for our girl, Mr. ...?" Major Cockblock asks, holding out his hand.

"Marshall. Keene Marshall," I growl, shaking his hand in return. "Thank you for your service."

Major Hunt, who's now close enough for me to read his name-plate, smiles as he turns Alison away. Before they move more than a few steps, she glances back at me, offering me the same vacant smile she did before.

I have no idea what was said between the Freeman siblings, but whatever it was just sent her spiraling away from me and into the arms of another man.

The only thing preventing me from causing a scene is knowing that Jared's with her and will keep her safe. Meanwhile, I stalk toward the exit, already pulling out my phone to text Caleb to find out what the hell happened in Connecticut today.

10

ALISON

In the middle of the night, New York City shimmers like scattered diamonds on velvet from Ryan and Jared's rooftop deck.

It wasn't long after Colby and I left, we got into the car to find Colby some real food. After my unexpected run-in with Keene, all I really wanted was to find a quiet place to think.

The three of us ended up at an all-night deli with sandwiches the size of my head. I only picked at mine, too distracted by my thoughts.

I tried to show Jared and Colby the Ali they expected, while mentally, I was replaying every moment of my conversation with Keene in my head.

I pull my knees to my chest and rest my chin against them, blindly staring out into the cityscape. Sighing, I reach for my glass of wine and take a gulp. Maybe I can drown my thoughts tonight and have a better perspective tomorrow.

It's always been easy to let men come and go, compartmentalizing my feelings for them. I never let anyone other than my adopted family get too close to me. After all, men, with a few exceptions, have always been after the same exact thing—my body. Just like dear old Dad.

Fortunately, mine didn't want to rape me, and he didn't allow his drug buddies freebies. He sold me off like I was a piece of mismatched furniture to pay back his drug dealer and maintain his habit.

Setting the glass down, I run my hands through my hair, when a thought I rarely allow pushes to the forefront of all the others.

God, Mama. I miss you.

Giving up, I put my face in my hands and let my tears fall. It's all I can do whenever memories of my delicate blonde mother come to mind. Her death was senseless, caused by a four-time drunk driver running a red light. Fate took her away from us before it was time.

My father raced to the MUSC emergency room with me trailing behind him, with only a sweatshirt thrown over my nightgown. His face had been frantic before sliding into hysteria. He had collapsed to his knees on the ground and grabbed on to me, burying his face into my hair as he sobbed.

I remember that exact moment because it was the last time my father held me or showed me any love or compassion. While he lost my mother that day, I actually lost both of them to that damned car wreck.

Scrubbing my eyes, I let out a long sigh. I know I come off as a sharp-edged cynic. My armor has been carefully honed to deflect the pain from having my world shattered over losing something so precious and beautiful. Instead, I was left with a broken father who forgot I was alive until I was worth something. I was stripped of the things I needed to survive, such as people who loved and took care of me.

I've learned to stop blaming myself, mostly. I can't help but look back and wonder was he addicted before Mama died? I could find out if I wanted to, merely by asking to see the details of my file at Hudson Investigations, but does it matter? I know he's alive and still in prison, but I've had no contact with him, and I haven't seen his face since watching his sentencing on TV. I recall watching the news broadcast while I was at law school and feeling...nothing. I'd never felt so alone, even with the happiness of my new family cloaking me. I was on the edge of two lives, fitting into neither one with ease.

I still don't fit in—that's evident by my behavior over the last few months. At least, according to my older sisters.

God, when will I learn?

When Cassidy first got involved with Caleb, I opened my mouth to defend her and didn't choose my words carefully. Then there's the issue with the prenup. The result has been catastrophic to our relationship. With rare moments of normalcy interspersed, I've been treated like a pariah by her ever since.

And here we are again, with me opening my damned mouth to defend Cassidy, only this time to Keene. And, once again, I'm the troublemaker, the misguided one, exercising poor judgment because I couldn't hold back what I thought a little longer.

Why isn't loving me enough? Why does it have to come with so many conditions? Am I so terrible?

A memory of my father screaming at me as he was being carted off by HTU and ICE plays in my head like it happened yesterday. I pull the blanket I have wrapped around my shoulders tighter.

"Louise! You tell these damn officers you asked to be up there, you hear me? You're my damn daughter!"

When he got no reaction from me, his face contorted as he gathered the spit in his mouth and hocked it at me. It landed about ten feet from where I was still chained to the stage.

"You're nothing but a whore like the rest in that damn container! No better than any of 'em. You hear me, Louise Rae?" he screamed as he was dragged out the door.

Because of that hellacious experience, I never let any man get too close, managing to never let them past the surface. It's why I never expected that first night with Keene to latch on to the part of my soul that I thought was buried and gone. A part I thought didn't exist anymore.

There's no way Keene understands what he made me feel before he pushed me toward the shower that night. For a few hours, he made me feel like I was whole. For the first time in years, a man made me feel intelligent, beautiful, cherished, and worthy. And that's why it hurt so much when he tried to sneak out without saying anything. Making everything I felt that night seem like a lie.

I'm never enough.

My phone lights up with a text. With a small sigh, I hope it's not Corinna getting drunk and deciding to text everyone on her phone list. She's done that before, resulting in disaster.

Picking up my phone, I unlock it and almost drop it when I see the text from Keene.

Keene: Why are you sad, Alison?

I quickly type out a response.

Alison: Do you guys have this place wired or something?

Keene: No. I live close by.

Stiffly, I stand. I allowed my shields to drop because in a city of eight and a half million people, I thought I could lose myself and be alone. I scan the darkness of the rooftop deck where I felt so cocooned just a few moments ago. Suddenly, I'm bitter because he can see me.

My thumbs fly across the keyboard.

Alison: I hope you enjoyed the show and that I provided enough entertainment. Good night, Keene.

Quickly, the message bubbles start. I collect my things and turn to make my way back downstairs. I'm halfway across the large expanse of the deck when my phone lights again.

Keene: Damnit, Alison. I didn't want you to think you were alone.

I pause. Does he mean he's here for me, or does he mean that people can see what I'm doing? Likely the latter. This is Keene after all.

Alison: Thanks for the PSA, Keene. Next time, I'll save my moods for the country where I can hide myself amongst the trees. Didn't mean to disturb you dignified city folks.

His reply is much faster this time.

Keene: Now you're taking your embarrassment out on me. Stop it.

Alison: No. I honestly have no idea why you care. I mean nothing to you.

I type out the reply and hit Send.

Seconds later, my phone rings and I answer it. "You honestly believe that?" Keene's voice, normally so cool and modulated, is incredulous.

"Yes," I reply without hesitation. My voice is huskier than normal due to my tears.

"Alison, that's...not even close to accurate." His voice is strong. Determined.

Too bad I can't believe a word out of his mouth.

"I appreciate the call and your clarification, Keene, but I'm going to bed now. I'd rather not wake my hosts."

Placing my hand on the knob, I stop when he sighs into the phone and says, "Talk to me."

I blank. Then, I laugh harshly. "About what? About work? About our family? What else could you possibly want to talk with me about? Let's end this conversation before we say anything we'll regret."

There's a pregnant pause; then Keene's voice turns husky when he says, "That's not all we've talked about when we've seen each other."

And like that, the final thread on my sanity snaps. "You know what? You're right, Keene. You ignore me, walk away, or we have sex. And I'm tired of being nothing more than a hole when your cock needs a place to bury itself. You want to know why I thought you'd hurt Cassidy? Because you don't seem to have a shred of humanity in your skill set." I laugh bitterly. "But then again, maybe that's only with the whores you fuck. We're probably not worth that effort. Never mind. I see where my error was. I hope you'll accept my apology for assuming you'd hurt your sister. Now, leave me the hell alone."

I hang up the phone, pull open the door, and run down the stairs. I wipe the tears running down my face as I quickly make my way to the guest room. Chucking my phone on the bed, I pad into the bathroom. Brushing my teeth and splashing cool water on my face helps me to regain my composure.

I crawl into the massive bed and curl into a ball. Snagging my phone, I reach for the charger when I see a number of new text messages. Sighing, I unlock my phone.

I know this is going to be bad.

Keene: If it wasn't the middle of the night, I would be over there so fast. You can be damn sure of that, Alison. And I'm on the fucking approved list to enter that condo, so there'd be no escaping me, baby.

Keene: DO NOT TRY TO LEAVE WITHOUT TALKING TO ME!

Keene: And I swear to God, if you ever call yourself a whore again, I don't care what time of day or night it is, I'm coming for you.

I look at the clock—3:23 a.m. With a sigh, I set my alarm for six. I want to be out of the condo and well on my way back home before Keene thinks of pounding on Ryan and Jared's door.

11

ALISON

I feel like hell. Crawling out of bed after less than three hours' sleep so I could avoid Keene completely sucked. The only thing that kept me going was knowing I would soon be able to pull on a pair of sneakers and hit the road.

I *need* this run.

It's a good thing I'm a seasoned runner. I would probably have puked long before now or passed out from fatigue. Between the few drinks I had last night, the lack of sleep, the small breakdown, and my intense conversation with Keene, I have a pounding headache. The persistent ringing of my cell phone over my tunes the last thirty minutes isn't helping either.

Keene. Cassidy. Keene. Em. Keene. Colby. Keene. Keene. Keene.

Seriously, people, I don't just want my run this morning. I need my run this morning. Stop calling!

I pause to turn on the Do Not Disturb function. If it's an emergency, Corinna can break through by calling. Since everyone in the family knows she loves her sleep, waking her ass up had damn well better be an emergency, or she'll likely gut you with a kitchen knife. If Corinna's calling, emergency or not, it's for a good reason.

Once back on the road, I perform a check of my body. I need to be careful not to pull anything or push too hard today, even if I need this run more than I need food. What I don't need is to risk an injury that will put me out of commission for weeks or months because I was stupid, upset, and didn't get enough sleep.

As my feet slap the pavement, I think about last night.

Groaning aloud, I get angry. At myself.

What the hell was Keene thinking?

Why is he suddenly in my way?

Fueled by anger, it's time to wrap it up and finish my run. I'm deciding if I want to veer directly home or head toward Main Street with my emergency twenty for a mocha when my phone rings.

It rings.

Shit.

"Corinna, what is it? What's wrong?" I demand as I stop running, my breath coming out in huffs.

"Sister, drama has shown up at your door. And I do mean that literally." Corinna's drawl flows effortlessly through the line.

My heart rate slows as I lean my back against the crosswalk sign. I wave a few cars on who were waiting on me. "I've been ignoring calls all morning. Is this an emergency?" I snap, frustrated. If gossip about last night has caught her ear and she's calling to get the dirt directly from the source, I may scream. Literally.

"Oh no, Ali. I mean drama has shown up at *your* door. Tall, hunky, brown hair, green-eyed drama. And he looks mighty pissed off because you're not answering your door and your car's in the driveway. He's rung your damn bell a million times and was pounding on your door, waking me up. You understand? Now he's just sitting on your doorstep." She pauses for dramatics. "Waiting."

My heartbeat increases so much, it sets off the heart rate monitor on my wrist. Muting the thing, I clarify, "Are you telling me Keene is sitting in front on my doorstep? At my house?" Because that seems ridiculous.

"I am indeed, sister dear. It seems like there's a story here." Corinna, always up for a good story, is about to bargain for the details. I know it.

I sigh as I stretch my legs. I do not need a muscle cramp while I'm negotiating. "What do you want?"

"I want to know what happened and to go shopping." Corinna is adamant about what she wants for once. While I mentally thank God for it, I have no idea how we'll pull this off. I'm a hot mess right now.

"Cori, I stink!" I laugh into the phone. "How do I get back to the house, change clothes, and shower?"

I can almost hear the wheels spinning in her head while she's silently thinking over options.

Finally, she asks, "Where are you?"

"Not far from Main Street." I refuse to give up my exact location in the event Keene has figured out a way to bug my phone. I decide to power the sucker down when I'm done with this call.

"Get coffee, and then shower at the office. I'll meet you there in an hour with clothes. We can grab food and you can talk. We'll hit the mall after," she says definitively.

Bless her determined, conniving heart. I love this plan.

"Done. I'll meet you there within the hour."

I hang up and turn off my phone before taking off in the direction of The Coffee Shop.

CORINNA and I decide to make a day of it and head to Orem's Diner in Wilton for a monster breakfast before driving to the Danbury Fair Mall. Corinna, showing mad stealth skills, snuck into my back door using my extra key, nabbed my purse and a pair of shorts, a T-shirt, flip-flops, and other necessities. After sneaking back to her place, she made enough noise to wake the dead, stomping to her back deck and then to her car, waving at Keene as she drove off.

Sneaky bitch. I love her. I'm totally treating her to breakfast.

After catching her up on the events of last night, she's silent. "You must be excited that Colby will be stateside for a while," she says.

"Aren't you? You and Holly were closer to him than I was. He mentioned last night that he might visit everyone at the farm. I can't remember the last time he was there," I muse.

"When does he plan on coming?" Corinna questions.

"I don't know. Want to FaceTime him to find out?"

Her mouth turns down, and her head turns away. That's unusual. "No," she says softly.

I frown. "Why not? You guys get along great."

She plays with her fork for a few minutes before taking a deep breath. Something's not right here. What did I miss between her and Colby?

"I don't think he likes me that much." She fiddles with her coffee next, stirring it repeatedly.

I frown. Where on earth is this lack of self-assurance from my man-eating sister coming from? Did Colby do or say something to make her feel that way? Before I can try to contradict her, she takes another breath and continues.

"It's just that...a long time ago..." Her words trail off. Taking a deep breath, she sits up straight. She's completely unaware of how much her luscious figure captures more than one set of male eyes around us, I note absentmindedly. "Ali, can we just leave it by saying there are things Colby did that make me realize that I'm not the kind of woman he'd ever go for?"

I burst out laughing.

"It's not funny!" She falls back into her seat, frustrated and miserable.

Whoa. Hold the hell on.

"Where is all this coming from?" I reach for my sister's hand and squeeze it, hard.

She shakes her head. "I don't want to talk about it. It's just something I overheard him say at school." Decisively, she shoves her food away, her face a picture of misery.

I'm in shock. "What did he say to you?" I tread cautiously. I don't want to hurt her more.

"It wasn't him directly," she states. I'm ready to find Colby and kill him. "But let's just say a long time ago, I learned very definitively what Colby Hunt thinks of me. Let's add that I won't be going down that path anytime soon, and that's all I'm saying."

I slide out from my side of the booth and move over to hers. She immediately rests her head on my shoulder. "It's so hard to be as perfect as all of you. I've given up trying." I sit with my sister for a few moments, both of us lost in our own thoughts. Hers have to be vastly different from mine, which are running along the lines of murder and mayhem. She interrupts my plotting by saying, "I think I'm going to join a nunnery."

Cori in a convent? I burst out laughing.

She giggles, squeezing me harder.

"I miss you, Ali, so much. It used to be you, Hols, and I against the world." She runs her hands under her eyes while I look at her in astonishment. How did I not realize I was contributing to my sister's unhappiness? "When I realized you were avoiding Keene, I figured something had happened. I hoped maybe you'd talk to me like you used to."

I'm quiet, absorbing the impact of the blows she just threw at me.

Corinna has always been known in our family as the happy-go-lucky sister. Have a Christmas surprise you want to spring on someone? Don't tell Corinna. She wants all the joy to happen immediately. Having a bad day? Walk into her kitchen and get a hug. She can't keep a smile off her face. She's the one who believes the world is meant for no boundaries and there's no such thing as a bad day. To know that this has been building up inside of her, worming its way into her enormous heart, is making me bleed inside.

I turn to my sister and say some of the most important words I think will ever come out of my mouth.

"No matter where I am, where I live, who I'm with, or where I work, there is nothing in this world more important to me than family, Corinna. I would give up my life to protect, nurture, and love it. I would give up friendships, relationships, anything for it. I would even walk away to protect it, and I mean that. Nothing will ever break the bonds we have. Nothing." I shake her hands that I'm holding. "Do you understand that?"

She nods before lifting our joined hands to wipe away her tears.

"I don't know what was in Colby's mind." If I can find out, preferably with a meat cleaver in my hand so I can chop up valuable body parts, I will. "But you're sensational. All of us have our special skills. Do you not think I wish I could hold a camera like Holly?" I'm not lying about anything I'm telling her.

She laughs a watery laugh. "Don't we all. Remember that selfie we took and one of us had our thumb over the camera?"

I snort at that memory. "We showed Holly and she got us PopSockets for Christmas so we couldn't do that again."

We giggle.

I reach over for my coffee and take a sip while admiring my sister. Corinna is sexy, smart, funny, sweet, and Lord love the girl, she sparkles. And damn Colby for causing an ounce of pain and doubt in her.

I'm mad at myself. Our family has been through so much together. The pain we've suffered is the glue that holds us together day after day.

Wrapping my arms around her, I cuddle her close and admit, "I don't know why, but I feel like I'm not enough anymore."

She shifts back in order to look at me. "What do you mean?"

It's my turn to fiddle with the utensils on the table. "I mean, what do I bring to this family, Cori, except disappointment? Honestly?" The burn hits, and I blink rapidly to prevent my tears from spilling over. "Please don't say anything..."

"I'll take this to the grave," she vows.

I nod, knowing there's no greater promise from her. "I'm a disappointment to everything I touch lately. To Cassidy and Em, and to Phil. God, it started so long ago, I don't even know how I haven't been voted out of the family." I press the heels of my hands into my eyes to stop the pain.

"Where is this coming from? You're not a disappointment, babe. Look at you! You graduated at twenty from law school. Twenty, Ali. You've managed our business and helped us grow. Why do you think you're anything but what you are—which is amazing?"

"Oh, maybe because you haven't been there for one of the many lectures Cass and Em see fit to give me about my behavior. Cass is permanently pissed at me about Caleb and recommending the prenup. About Keene. Most recently because of how I was up in his face at dinner because he was an ass after she and Caleb told us their news. I was ordered to play nice and apologize. I know if I wasn't family, I would've been fired from the company. At this point, I'm so far in the doghouse, maybe I should resign." I don't realize how bitter and broken I sound.

It's quiet next to me. I should have taken her silence as my warning.

"Are you kidding me?" she explodes. "Forget the prenup. That was a mistake and you apologized. That's over. But why the hell do you have to apologize to Keene? He looked like he had a pineapple shoved up his ass the wrong way when they announced their news."

I contemplate briefly if there's a right way to have a pineapple shoved up your ass before I turn to face her. She's now the one breathing fire. "Cass feels this is too much with her trying to navigate everything—" I start to explain before I'm cut off.

"Then let Cass get on the phone and tell her brother he needs to get a lobotomy or something after he's removed the pineapple, Ali. I swear to God, if you apologize to him, I'm going to hit you," she threatens.

I hesitate to answer. "I kind of did last night."

Whack!

"Damnit, Cori!" Rubbing my arm in the same spot where Keene grabbed it, I glare at her.

"You don't apologize to him! He should be on his knees apologizing to you, for this and so many other things, starting with Phil's wedding. He may be the best lay you ever had, he may make you feel things you never expected, but I'm still waiting to see a soul in those eyes." Corinna hesitates. "I don't want you breaking your heart over him."

My lips part. "Why haven't you said anything?" I didn't realize she had seen this much. I thought I was the only one who had.

I thought I was all alone. Always alone.

"Because you keep too much to yourself. Going on runs and trying to work crap out in your head. Now, if we'd figured shit out over chocolate, we'd talked before now and I would've told you what I thought."

Even as I'm laughing, I'm curious yet hesitant to ask. "Don't you like him?"

She tilts her head to the side. "I like how he is with Cassidy now, but he has wounds he has to be willing to heal. If he doesn't, he's never going to open his heart." Her hand covers mine and gives it a squeeze. "If all you want is to screw him again, then go for it, honey, but if you find you want more, and if he's not willing to go one hundred ten percent with you, then get out. Fast. Whatever you have to do." She takes a deep breath. "Even if it means leaving."

"Christ, Cori, I'm not planning on falling in love with him."

Her eyes turn sad and discouraged again before she says, "No one ever does, Ali."

I wrap my arms around her. "Whoever falls in love with you and gets you to love them in return is going to be the luckiest bastard in the world, Cori. You know that, right?"

With a small laugh, she squeezes me back and says, "Let's see if I live to see that day."

$\sim$

BEFORE LEAVING THE MALL, Corinna's managed to score some super cute Chucks in neon pink that will look adorable while she's working. She's smiling, laughing, and singing, which I realize I haven't seen her do for way too long.

I did even better. I repaired my relationship with my sister. Leaning back in the seat as she drives her Volkswagen through the back roads to Collyer, I absorb the magnificence of Corinna belting out Kelsea Ballerini's "Yeah Boy." Her hair is blowing in the wind, her eyes covered with sunglasses, a gorgeous smile on her face.

Suddenly, I'm overwhelmed by how much I love her.

We pull up to a stop sign, and I touch her arm. "Hold on."

I'd turned my phone back on a while ago and was doing a great job of ignoring it. I pull it from my purse and scroll to the camera app. Flipping it around, I take a selfie of the two of us. I show it to Cori before she starts driving, then send it to the family in our group text with the note, "Out with Cori. We'll be home whenever."

I read what I'm typing aloud. Corinna lets out a delicate sneer. "That'll piss off the assorted people trying to reach you."

"Let it. I'm done trying to be anything but what I am. Today, with you, reminded me of that."

"Good." She reaches over and grips my hand. "I was worried we were losing you, Ali. I'm not ready for that."

Does she expect me to leave one day? I wonder if Corinna doesn't have a bit of magic behind those eyes. "What do you mean?"

Sighing, she keeps a hold of my hand while she downshifts. "You, me, and Hols. Of the three of us, you've always been about ten paces ahead of us. We thought you were pulling away because you were ready to leave Collyer. We didn't even come close to thinking it was because of crap Cass and Em are dishing out."

Jesus.

"Cori, you know if I ever decide to leave, I'll tell you. And I promise I'll tell you if it's for a specific reason, okay?"

Taking her focus off the road for a second, she sends me a baleful look. "You better. At least I can tell Hols then."

I laugh, knowing everything I shared with Corinna today will at some point be shared with Holly, as it should. "I promise. And I'm telling you the truth: I have no immediate plans to leave Collyer, not even for a vacation."

"Good." She drives quietly, looking thoughtful. "If you decide to head to Washington to kick Colby's ass, I want to go with you. I might enjoy watching."

I throw my head back and laugh. I'm so glad some of what I said to her got through.

She smiles at me and cranks the volume on the radio.

IT'S ABOUT six in the evening when we pull into the farm. I've never been so glad for summer as I am right now. Corinna is driving super slow, trying to mask our attempt in making the mile-long drive to my house unnoticed. We're hoping the sound of the early-evening birds will cover up our giggling as we sneak past Em's house and slowly drive past Cassidy's. We're like schoolgirls sneaking in past curfew.

Keene's car has moved from my house over to Cassidy's, and that's fine. His focus should be on his sister, not me.

We pull up to the outside of my house, and Corinna idles her car. I give her a huge hug. "Thank you," I whisper.

"No thanks needed. We both needed this."

"We need this more often," I suggest. I forgot how much time with my sisters recharges me.

"Done. Next time, let's bring Hols too."

I beam at her before I slide out of her car. She toots the horn before driving away. I stand there for a few moments, holding on to my phone and purse. The events of the day are running through my head when I'm interrupted by a furious voice.

"Are you done running so we can finally talk?"

AFTER STORMING PAST KEENE, I throw on the lights as I enter my house. I'm infuriated he's here and show him zero hospitality as I head through my kitchen, throw open the sliders, and point. "Outside."

"I'm not a lapdog you can just order around, Alison." Keene's hands are on his lean hips, and he's smirking. "Generally, people like it when they're asked to do something nicely."

After Corinna spent so much time boosting me up today, Keene's snark grates.

"And generally, people wait to be invited over and don't stake out someone's house. I've decided you're going to get the attitude you cultivate, and to hell with what anyone thinks about me for giving it to you," I growl back. "I didn't ask you to come here. Let's make this quick so you can go back to visiting your sister."

Keene doesn't say anything. Instead, he silently walks past me until he's outside, standing on my deck. "Does my sister realize your temper is this ferocious?"

"Yes." There's no need to tell him we're usually arguing about him.

"Interesting." He leans back against the railing, waiting for me to speak.

The silence between us continues. The only sounds are those of the wildlife around us on this early Connecticut summer evening. I can hear the birds calling from the lake that Cassidy's house is built on. Birds in my trees answer before I hear the brush of the branches as they prepare to take flight.

I turn around to confront Keene and find him standing directly in my space.

"Please step back."

"Alison, we need to talk."

"I agree, but I had a wonderful day today. I'd rather not taint it by ending it with someone who prefers to spend his time insulting me. My lack of response should have made it obvious whether I wanted to see you or not. You should have respected that. You didn't, and now I'm asking you to leave."

"I've done a lot of things wrong with you. Intruding on your personal moment last night was another mistake. I would truly like the opportunity to discuss all of them with you, but you're right." His expression doesn't change. I almost feel sorry for him, but his apology seems rehearsed. Practiced. "This goes both ways, Alison. I come to the table with my apology, and you come to it with your issues."

What the hell? I let out a bark of laughter.

"Are you kidding me? What table? We only have to get along well enough to suffer through family events together. Nothing more than that," I inform him haughtily.

He steps into my space again, his hands quickly and gently clasping my cheeks. I grip his wrists to pull his hands away, desperate for him to let me go.

"Tell me you're not as lonely as I am. Tell me you don't wonder late at night what it would have been like if I'd stayed. Tell me you don't wonder if we would have fought or fucked our way through our inevitable arguments. Tell me you don't wonder if we would still be together." He growls the words next to my ear.

"Stop, Keene," I say hoarsely. I can't prevent the full-body shudder his words have on me. Because I have wondered this so many nights.

"Tell me you don't want me. Us. Tell me you don't want my lips on yours right now. Tell me you don't want my hands sliding all over your skin. Tell me you don't want my fingers and my cock inside you. Tell me you don't want any of that, Alison, and then I'll tell you there's nothing for us to figure out."

He lowers his chin. I can almost feel his lips brush against mine when he whispers, "See what we could've been working out all day?" before he pulls away and walks through my kitchen and slams my front door.

I'm frozen where I stand, unable to make sense of Keene's latest hit-and-run.

12

ALISON

Monday morning, I'm at my desk when the inquisition begins. I'm surprised it took this long. They must have been pissed I didn't return their calls.

I was too busy hearing Keene's voice over and over again in my ear all night long.

Phil strides in with new customer intake forms he wants me to review, something Cassidy assigned to me ever since he failed to list some key information during Ryan and Jared's wedding on theirs. He plops down in one of the chairs in front of my desk. "And?" His Southern drawl is as pronounced as Corinna's.

"What?" I hope to deflect him by playing dumb.

His response is sharp. "Better start talking, Ali. There's a line behind me."

"For intake forms? Did you decide to add to your job responsibilities?" *Keep the ball bouncing, Ali.*

"Very funny, Alison. I do my job just fine," he huffs.

The laughter from the other offices tells me our conversation is not only being overheard, but actively listened to. I quirk my brow at him.

"Shut it, y'all! It was one small mistake!" he yells out the door.

"You forgot to tell me your husband was previously engaged, Phil. That's kind of a big deal." Cassidy's voice floats down the hall.

"Worked out just fine for you. You're married to the groom's brother and having his babies, so hush your mouth!" he reprimands her.

As irritated as I am, I manage to hold in my laughter. Phil not telling Cassidy that piece of information was a huge issue at the time.

Holly's howling can be heard coming from her office down the hall.

Cassidy, however, is quiet. I hear her chair rolling back from her desk, and then she's muttering something under her breath. Moments later, she's in my doorway, glaring at Phil. She's been actively trying to make her way down the hallway to my office this entire time.

Phil winks at me. "The doctor said it's good for her to move around often. I'm just helping out where I can."

Cassidy throws him the middle finger before waddling to my corner easy chair, which has an ottoman in front of it. Longingly, she strokes the arm. "If I sit down in this thing, I may never get back up."

Choked laughter escapes me before I can control it.

"And for that, you can be the one to haul my ass out of this thing when it's time for me to leave," Cassidy declares as she sinks into the chair. Lifting her legs onto the ottoman, her smile is pure bliss. After a contented sigh, she turns to Phil. "Please, continue. Now I have a better view for the show."

My stomach roils. They planned this? They're going to grill me at the office? What the hell? There are rules about this kind of shit. We save it for family dinners when we won't possibly be interrupted by, you know, clients.

Oh, wait. Now Keene is at our family dinners. Consequently, why this ambush is going down in my office.

"Anyone else you want to invite?" My voice drips with venom.

Cassidy flinches slightly, but Phil takes no notice.

"No, Em is with a client. Corinna said she refuses to take part. Hold on. Holly, are you coming?" Phil yells out my door.

My face is burning as I fume in silence. Holly's quick footsteps make their way down the hall. "Should have done this in the conference room. More chairs," Holly claims as she walks in.

"Close the door. Em has a client," Phil urges. Holly quickly shuts the door and then leans her back against it.

I'm trapped and cornered in my own office.

And it's all Keene's fault.

"What do you think you're doing?" My voice is low and lethal. This should indicate I'm past upset and edging toward infuriated. In Cassidy's condition, I don't want to add any undue stress to her, but damn her. Damn all of them. They're bringing this on themselves.

"Why did you avoid Keene all day yesterday, Ali? He was over at my place worrying about where you were. Apparently, you two had words, again. I thought you were going to resolve that," Cassidy says reproachfully.

"Ali, you can't have an ongoing war with Keene. He's a member of the family now," Phil adds.

Since I can't direct the full blast of my anger at Cassidy, I unleash it on Phil. "Oh? And what would you call what you and he have, Phillip? A mutual admiration society? Maybe we can get Keene on the phone to tell us all about how he feels about his other brother." I reach for the button on my speakerphone, when Phil's hand reaches out and grabs mine. I pull mine away violently. "Not willing to let bygones be bygones just yet? Then shut the hell up, Phil." I dismiss him.

The sharp breath I hear is his only response. Then I turn on Holly.

"And Holly? What's your stake in this? Do you really care, or are you just planning on handing out more of my personal information again? You know, despite the fact we're siblings, this is a place of business, and there are laws around data privacy in this state."

Holly's face pales. The only person she's given that information to is Corinna, and I didn't care at the time. Now? I care. A lot.

"And Cassidy? It might be nice if you actually asked me if I apologized to Keene before jumping down my goddamned throat. Because

I tried to when he accosted me at the party I went to with Jared the other night. He told me I didn't need to. This, of course, was not long before he implied he wanted to fuck me again for the third time, and I told him I was tired of being his whore." Watching Cassidy's face pale, I feel no remorse except for the two little beings inside her who might have felt a blip in their oxygen supply. "That's right. And last night, did he tell you he snuck up on me at my house? Do I have nowhere that's safe anymore?" I laugh bitterly. I stand and begin pacing back and forth behind my desk. I see Cassidy struggle to sit up, but I wave her back down. "I am tired of being your brother's plaything. It took my sister pointing that out to help me realize that. And I'm damn glad she refused to come upstairs to participate in this joke of a conversation." My eyes sweep the room. "I deserve more from all of you, despite what you might think of me."

I stop pacing. Quickly, I shove my laptop into my bag and walk around my desk, directly in front of the door. Holly's face is filled with a wordless, beseeching plea. I narrow my eyes at her. "Move."

She scurries out of the way.

I open my office door and turn around. Everyone is in some state of shock. Holly is now leaning against my desk, her face chalk white. Phil is facing me, his jaw set. Cassidy's face is one of self-flagellation and devastation, a look I'm already familiar with. I see it in the mirror every damn day.

"I trust you'll be able to let yourselves out of my office. I'm heading to New York to file the real estate paperwork with Jared."

I turn before the first hot tear of anger falls down my cheek.

I blindly head down the grand staircase of the mansion as Em's clients are finishing their appointment and are leaving her studio. She opens her mouth to say something to me, but I shake my head and head out the back door.

Reaching my car, I connect the Bluetooth before peeling out of the lot. Using the hands-free, I say, "Call Jared Work." I tap the wheel impatiently while I wait for the call to connect.

"If you miss me, you should have stuck around for breakfast the other morning," Jared teases.

"The meeting we were supposed to have later in the week? I have all the signatures. Are you busy today?" My voice sounds strangled even to me.

Jared's quiet on the other end. "How long will it take for you to get here?"

"I have no idea," I tell him honestly.

"There's a nasty storm coming in, Ali. I'll see you at the office when you get here. Drive safely." Jared hangs up the phone.

Almost immediately, my phone starts ringing. Glancing at the caller ID, I see it's Corinna. I answer wearily. "I'm going to deal with some legal matters. I don't know when I'll be back."

"If I were you, I'd go shopping, leave my car at the airport and board a flight for a beach." Corinna's fuming.

A broken laugh escapes. "Thanks, Cori, but that's not going to help right now."

"Let me know when you get there. I'm concerned about the storm, okay?"

"I will."

"Love you, Ali."

You might be the only one who does, Corinna. "Love you too, sis."

13

KEENE

"Keene Marshall," I answer the phone brusquely.

"I am so pissed off at you right now, I don't know what to do with all my feelings. I want to yell and scream, but I have two other human lifeforms currently taking up space inside of my body, Keene. Tell me what the hell I'm supposed to do, because I'm trying to stay calm," Cassidy yells at me over the phone.

"First, stop yelling at me," I tell her, my voice softening. Swiveling in my desk chair, the painting I had commissioned from a photo of us as children is perfectly in focus. I smile as I kick back, because even through the phone line, Cassidy is taking deep breaths to control her temper. "Why don't I call your husband and put the call on speaker to calm you down?"

"Oh, go ahead and do that, Keene. Please." Cassidy's voice is vicious, the likes of which I haven't heard since the first night we met.

What the hell did I do?

I'm mentally running through the possible scenarios when another voice comes over the line, this one definitely not as beloved as my sister.

"We're going to play twenty questions, Keene. You will answer these." Phil's annoying Southern drawl gives him away immediately.

"What makes you think I'm going to answer a damn thing you ask me, Phil?" Arrogantly, I turn my chair back to overlook the Manhattan skyline.

"Because you're the reason we caused Alison to storm out of the office. She's no longer speaking with any of us," Cassidy replies. Her voice is a combination of anger and resignation.

Shit.

"You couldn't leave her alone, could you, Cass?" I mutter into the phone.

"Hmm. Apparently, I'm not the only one. It seems you were desperate to see her yesterday, Keene. Don't talk to me about leaving her alone," Cassidy snaps at me.

I rub my hand against the side of my head. Direct hit.

My office door opens without warning. Before I can react to the intrusion, Caleb walks in. He immediately walks over to my phone and hits the speaker before sitting down across from me. "Okay, Pixie, I'm finished with my call. You can start asking."

"Thank you, my love," Cassidy says.

"I think I'm going to be sick," I mutter loud enough for apparently everyone to hear.

"Not as sick as you'll be after some of these questions," Phil says. I hear quiet crying in the background. Holy hell.

"Who's crying?" I demand.

"That's Holly. You've managed to cause a complete upheaval here, Keene. Ali's gone. We only know she flew out of here to drive, upset. She's supposedly headed to Jared. I have no idea if that's true, when she'll get there, or when she'll be back. The storm of the summer is hitting, and I'm about to freak out!" Like I couldn't tell that from her escalating screech. Cassidy takes a breath. "Now it's our turn. Did Ali try to apologize to you?"

I close my eyes and rub my hand over my forehead. I remember her gorgeous dress on Saturday night, and her attempt to apologize for misunderstanding my concern about Cassidy and the twins. I stopped her before she could, but I have to give the facts. "Yes."

There's a harsh intake of breath on the other end of the line.

"Did you proposition her again? Sweet Jesus, I can't believe I'm asking this— afterward?" Phil asks.

I don't want to answer his question. I shove away from my desk and pace, then turn to Caleb. His lips are pressed together as if he's trying to keep from saying something he might regret. He also knows me better than anyone, including my sister.

Finally, I say, "Not exactly a proposition. More an...invitation."

"Oh God," Cassidy stage whispers, followed by a groan.

Caleb shakes his head at me.

Cassidy takes a few deep breaths. "Final question. Did you say, imply, or indicate that you wanted Ali as your plaything or that she was a whore?"

Holy hell. What happened at that office today? "No!" I yell. "I have no idea where she got it into her head that I thought of her as either of those things."

"Gee, Keene, maybe it was when you snuck out of her hotel room the first time you slept with her," Phil suggests. "I mean, you didn't even bother to put on your pants. Leaves a girl with an impression that's hard to get over."

"Maybe I know how that feels since she kicked me out the second time," I roar.

That silences everyone.

Caleb breaks the silence. "I'll deal with this, Cassidy."

"Okay." Shit. She's crying.

"Cassidy..." My voice cracks as I try to console my sister.

"Not now, Keene."

The phone line disconnects abruptly.

I growl, turning to Caleb like a lion stalking fresh meat. "Don't you even dare lecture me about starting something up with Alison. Not when you met and married my sister while owning this company."

Leaning back in his chair, he locks his hands over his stomach. "I wouldn't say a word about that."

Surprised, I sit down. "Good."

"If what I thought you meant to start with her was an actual relationship and not you getting your rocks off," he continues, as if I hadn't spoken.

"Seriously, what does it matter what I want to do if it doesn't hurt anyone?" I ask my best friend. I'm actually puzzled by this. Why does anything I do matter to anyone? It never has before.

Sighing, Caleb pushes to his feet in front of the floor-to-ceiling windows that overlook the Manhattan skyline. I remember when we took over these offices after forming Hudson Investigations. We got lost in the beauty of the view, but now, it's another landscape to use to think, as Caleb's doing now.

"We don't talk about it," he finally says, interrupting our mutual introspection.

"Talk about what?"

"What happened in Warsaw." His voice has already gone back to the night where he was almost shot. The night I was shot.

"Probably because we're not supposed to. National security and all that." I try to deflect the discussion. I don't want to get into a conversation with Caleb where he expresses his thanks for saving his life. He's already thanked me a million times.

"I've thought about it a lot recently," he continues. I brace myself for the gratitude, but what he says surprises me. "I would have spared you the pain of taking a bullet for me for certain. It was my distraction that got us into that hot mess, and for that, I will always be sorry. But now, I'm equally certain it had to happen that way for you to find your sister again."

Whoa, what? My shock must speak for itself without words because Caleb continues.

"Other than with me, and occasionally with Ry, you'd forgotten how to be a member of a family, Keene. Even adding Cassidy to the picture, for the most part, you've still forgotten."

I feel like Caleb just punched me in the chest. I'm hardly breathing. I tip my head to the side as I wait for him to continue. It doesn't take long.

"Your father is a complete asshole. Your mother was murdered, and you've never dealt with that. Your sister was kidnapped and brutally assaulted for years before she escaped with the help of a stranger. For twenty-five years, she was presumed dead. She built a life with people who are closer to her than blood."

Even though hearing this recount causes my blood to simmer, I reply calmly. "And I have nothing."

"And right there is the problem. What you have is me. Your brother growing up. Your brother-in-arms. And your brother now through marriage. And you still refuse to lean on your family."

His answer rocks me to my core. My mouth falls open slightly, and I take a step back. My mind scrambles with this newest piece of intel tossed in, altering the picture of my reality.

I thought when my mother died all those years ago and I'd been left to be reared by nannies, I had no one. My father wandered the world with his latest conquest. I shut down, feeding off the only thing I could to keep myself putting one foot in front of the other each day.

Control.

But I'd forgotten I had one other thing. A brother.

I hang my head in shame.

Caleb has been by my side through all of my fucked-up shit. Never letting go, even when I pushed him away. Hell, even when I tried to shove him away. In the darkest of hours, when my mask slipped and despair had me by the balls, he never let me fall. Taking a bullet in the thigh for that kind of friendship was a small price to pay to keep the one good thing in my life alive. And without question, I'd do it again.

"It's not easy," I murmur.

He steps closer, clasping my shoulder. "What isn't?"

"Leaning on...people. Trusting them. Learning how to live after so many years of darkness. It's not easy. It's easier to keep the shield up," I admit.

"I'm not saying to let the world in, Keene. Just try trusting a few more people. Give them the benefit of the doubt. It's not always wrong if you can't figure it out right away."

That's something he's been saying for years, and easy for him to say, I think nastily. Then again, my mind reconciles that it isn't.

Caleb's life was a lot like mine. Cold, embittered. He lost his father and had one of the worst human beings for a mother. Until he fell in love with my sister, he was content to remain fairly distant—except from his brother. Brothers, I amend in my head. And I let the small warmth of that feeling spread through me.

"What are you thinking?" I know Caleb's curious, not malicious. Which is why I give him the real answer.

"Like I'll be overexposed if I do. Like I'll lose control. Like I'll hurt someone."

"Like Ali."

"Like Alison," I confirm.

"You're not going to hurt someone who's already touched your heart," Caleb says confidently.

"I don't think I have one anymore," I admit.

"A heart?" he asks incredulously.

I hesitate before nodding.

His response is to laugh. Uproariously.

I don't respond. I don't even flinch.

"If you didn't have a heart, you would never have searched for Cassidy for so damned long. You wouldn't have been worried about her mental health when you began to suspect she was your sister. You never would have danced at our wedding with her. You would have made sure she was alive and slipped silently from her life." He pauses. "Your problem is that you care too much, and you're afraid to because of obstacles you may not be able to protect them from." Shooting me a wry look, he says, "As a future parent, I understand that. Now."

I quietly absorb the impact of Caleb's words, filing them away to think about later when I have time to apply them to my situation, not only with my sister but with Alison as well, because he's right. There's a pull between us.

My problem is going to be figuring out how to untangle the mess I've apparently now made in Alison's life.

After I go to Jared's law firm looking for her.

14

ALISON

Fortunately, the weather gods hold off passing their judgment
until I'm on West 56th Street. I'm minutes from Jared's office
when the storm's full power unleashes. The incessant rain
pelting my windshield makes no difference in my visibility, as I've
been crying on and off since I left Collyer.

I've denied every call that's come in unless it's from Jared to track
my progress. I'm racing against time. Not only to get these papers to
Watson, Rubenstein, and Dalton so Jared can leave but to get this one
task done before I completely lose what is left of my sanity and
crumble into myself.

Brushing my hand under my eyes to wipe away the trickle of tears
escaping, I make the final turn onto Avenue of the Americas, slowly
pulling my car beneath the awning of Jared's building. As the
doorman rushes to open my door, I slide out of the car, gripping my
briefcase. Pausing once I'm inside, I fire off a text to Corinna as
promised. I'm determined to finish company business before I find a
place to lay my hurt down for just a few hours.

I'm so focused on the task at hand, that I don't even notice the
man who jumps out of the cab behind me and stands in the lobby,
watching as I make my way into the building.

~

"Is everything in order?" I ask Jared. I'm hiding the crater in my heart behind my professional demeanor.

Even though I'm a barred attorney, my specialty is not commercial real estate. Thank god it's Jared's and I can lean on this family connection. Heavily. Though instead of charging me his regular billable hours, which are outrageous, he pushed me to do all of the work which is why I'm sitting here dripping in the partners' conference room of Watson, Rubenstein, and Dalton.

Robert Watson and Bryan Rubenstein are both reviewing the documents to ensure I didn't miss anything. Jared nods, even as he signs his name and notarizes the next set of paperwork, before passing it along to Robert. "Yes. You did a tremendous job, Ali. In an incredibly short amount of time, I might add."

The compliment does little to soothe the hurt inflicted on me earlier, but it does make my professional vanity preen just a bit. "I appreciate the compliment."

Watson looks at the papers again and shakes his head in appreciation. "We have members of our team who couldn't have pulled this off. I'm impressed. What tactic did you use, Ms. Freeman?"

Sitting back in my chair, I cross my arms over my chest. I respond with two words: "Persistent nagging."

The two older partners bellow. "Jared, she's just like you, isn't she?" Rubenstein chuckles.

"In many ways, she's better. Stronger," Jared acknowledges. "She's too modest though." His last comment is directed at me.

"Why have you never tried to recruit her to the firm?" Watson asks Jared. I straighten a little in surprise.

Jared pauses in the act of signing a document. "She's loyal to her family. If I saw that waning, perhaps she could be tempted. Ali knows we have offices all over the U.S. if she ever wanted to find out if corporate law was for her." He tips his chin at me.

He believes in me, to the point that he just went to bat for me with his partners. The barest of smiles begins to cross my face.

Jared passes the last document over to Watson, who quickly scans it before scrawling his signature across it. Rubenstein reviews it as well before signing in his more precise script. Handing the document back to Jared, both men stand up. I join them, straightening my skirt as I rise.

"A pleasure, Ms. Freeman," Rubenstein says, extending his hand. I shake it firmly.

"For me as well, sir."

"And please, consider this an offer, Ms. Freeman. If you would like to get your feet wet, we have a few cases where we could use some temporary assistance starting up in the next few months." Watson turns to Rubenstein for confirmation. Rubenstein nods. "Might be an interesting way to push your boundaries on a trial basis."

If you'd have asked me a few weeks ago...hell, a few days ago, I'd have politely turned these legal giants down, knowing nothing could possibly take me away from my family. With the despair I feel after today, I leave them with, "I'll keep that in mind, gentlemen. I'll keep Jared in the loop on any decisions I make."

"Excellent," Watson declares before both men leave the room.

Jared silently gathers the stacks of papers and slides them into a folder. We make our way out of the conference room into his office before he speaks. "Just the idea of you entertaining their offer tells me how bad things are. Do you want to stay with Ry and I tonight? Talk it out?" he says quietly, curling his arm over my shoulder.

I shake my head and let out a bitter laugh. "I booked a room at the Hilton Midtown. I'm heading there once we're done. There won't be any problem with leaving my car though, right?"

Jared waves his hand. "None whatsoever. But I don't think you should be alone, Ali. Come with me, and let's figure this out together. Let Ry and I pamper you for a bit."

I shake my head. "I need to be alone tonight, Jared. I think I'll order room service and crash." And maybe drink myself into oblivion.

"You'll be doing all of that from my place, Alison," an unwelcome voice says from the door. Jared's arm tightens around me.

We both turn to see Keene standing there. He looks infuriated and determined.

I turn around to face Keene straight on and say, "They said it was the summer storm of the century, Keene, not that hell had frozen over. What are you doing here? Where did you get that ludicrous idea?"

Keene leans against the doorjamb. "I came for you, baby, and after what I just overheard from Jared's partners, apparently not a minute too soon."

I laugh dismissively. "Right, like you give a shit whether I stay or go." I turn to Jared and touch his cheek briefly before murmuring, "I'll call later."

"If you can find the phone," Jared responds, not leaving me with confidence. I stride past both men and out of Jared's office, intent on making my escape.

Keene catches up while I'm waiting for the elevator. I press the button, then press it again.

"Pressing the button won't get it here any faster."

His calm logic infuriates me more. I ignore him and lean forward to press the button again. This time, with more force.

"It's an illusion of perceived control, Alison. A psychology professor at Harvard did a study on it."

"Maybe the effort isn't futile in this case. Maybe pushing the button six times will make the elevator arrive six times faster. Maybe Jared's firm is smarter than your professor's study. After all, he went to Harvard," I snap.

At that moment, the elevator pings, notifying us of its arrival. I don't bother throwing a triumphant look at Keene. I want to be as far away from him as I can get. I press the button for the lobby, and Keene manages to slip in before the doors close. As we descend, calmness overcomes me. The walls I had begun to erect around my heart crumble. What's left is a mass no man, no human, can penetrate. I feel the comfort of numbness, the beauty of nothing. No pain. No wounds. No hurt.

I've learned something this week. Words are as violent to the heart as a punch is to the body. Words wound as much as they heal. But broken promises are worse because it's where you base your dreams, and when those promises die, so do those dreams.

The budding promises I had with Keene died the same night they were born years ago. Tonight, the promises I made with the rest of my family were destroyed.

I'm left floundering with nowhere to drop an anchor for my dreams.

I guess my father was right. I'm nothing. I was a fool to think I could ever change it. Stepping from the elevator, I don't acknowledge Keene as I make my way toward the lobby doors. Getting out of this building is my priority, despite the raging storm outside.

Escape. Run. Get away.

I'm lengthening my stride when Keene's hand shoots out and grabs my wrist.

Facing him, I try to shake it free. His hand tightens more. "It's been a long day, and I would like to retire to my hotel room. If you or your family have questions about the business conducted tonight, contact me in the morning."

"You're not going to the hotel, Alison," Keene bites out, stepping closer to me. I feel nothing. Nothing but numbness from my pain. There's a freedom in being numb.

I carefully step back. "I'm leaving to check in at my hotel. I would appreciate if you'd let me go."

He steps forward, closing the gap I've made between us. I step back. Again. The narrowing of his eyes tells me I'm not going to get much farther.

Then, the expression on his handsome face softens. "Alison, please. Don't be stubborn for no reason. If you need to be alone, my place is certainly large enough for you to have your own space." I open my mouth to refuse again, but he cuts me off. "The guest bedrooms are on the opposite end of my condo. You can have your solitude."

I reach down to where his hand is still holding my wrist and pry his fingers off. Leaning toward him, I whisper, "Right now, if the difference was between sleeping in my car in the middle of the storm or staying at your place, I would roll down the windows and welcome the rain." Turning, I walk to the doors.

The doorman jumps up from behind his desk. "Miss, do you have anything to cover yourself? Do you need me to call you a cab?"

Offering the poor man a wave, I stop in the door. Turning slightly, I see Keene standing where I left him. As the whipping wind catches my hair, I reply for both of them. "Don't worry about me. I'll survive."

And I hurry off into the torrential rain.

HOURS LATER, I've checked in and settled into the Hilton's presidential suite.

Because I'm in one of their premier rooms, the bellman who escorted me up assured me there was nothing they wouldn't get for me. Putting in my request for something to sleep in, I change out of my soaked clothes and into one of the two robes hanging behind my bathroom door. While there might be no rest for the weary, I figure that has more to do with my soul. Tonight, my physical self is going to try to relax in a tub overlooking the New York skyline.

I hand the bellman my laundry and a large tip, knowing it is well worth whatever cost I'll see on the bill in the morning, knowing I will wake up to dry and pressed clothes for my trip home. After he leaves, I waste no time in calling room service. While I'm in no mood to eat, I know the bottle of wine I plan to consume will go down better with something on my stomach.

After my order is delivered and set up, I pour myself a glass of pale, gold Sancerre, grab some cheese and crackers, and make my way into the bath. After filling the tub with water slightly cooler than scalding, I drop in a bath bomb. Watching it fizzle and sink, I find it an appropriate analogy for my relationship with my family. Even if it were to be pulled out now, it would never be the same.

I sink into the fragrant water, knowing I can't avoid my family forever. I work with them. We live on top of each other. As much as I hurt, I know I'll forgive them, because while the steadfastness of their love may have changed, they did save me from life decisions I wasn't ready to make at sixteen.

I sigh. I know I need to call Corinna.

I reach on the side of the tub and pick up my phone. Not surprisingly, I find eleven missed calls and six messages. Ignoring them for the moment, I scroll to Corinna in my favorite numbers and press Send.

It barely rings once before she picks up.

"All tucked in safe?" she queries. The noise in the background when she first picks up dies down immediately.

"I'm fine. You're at the farm?"

"We all are. Have you heard from Keene? He was supposed to call Cassidy, and he hasn't. Of course, she's freaking out," Corinna says.

"What do you mean you haven't heard from Keene? He followed me into Jared's office for God's sake!" I snap.

"What? Hold on. I'm putting you on speaker." Before I can tell her not to, Corinna's already hit the button and announces, "It's Ali."

Cassidy immediately asks, "Have you heard from Keene?"

Suddenly, the organ in my body I swore was a stone earlier tonight begins to crack and seep blood, hearing the worry in her voice. My sister, Keene's sister—does it matter? All that matters is I left him a few hours ago, pissed off, and no one has heard from him.

"I'll apologize in advance because we exchanged words." My voice is empty, even to my own ears. There's a hush on the other end of the line. "He wanted me to go to his condo with him, and I refused. However, as his lack of communication is likely my fault since I last saw him at Jared's office, I'll begin looking for him immediately." I stand up out of the tub. The water sluices from my body, the splash echoing inside the tiled room. Holding on to my phone with one hand, I step from my bath and reach for my robe with the other.

Right then, the en suite phone rings.

"I have a phone call, I'll call you back," I tell my family. Disconnecting them, I answer, "Alison Freeman."

"Ms. Freeman, this is Thomas, the bellman, with your requested items."

"Yes, Thomas. I'd like to request a few more things." I'm already imagining going out into the storm to find out if Keene is home.

"That's fine, Ms. Freeman. The problem is that I went to deliver the items and there's a man sitting outside your door."

I tie the robe tightly around me. "Can you describe him?"

"I didn't get a good look, ma'am, but he's in a business suit, dress shoes, and he has dark hair." Keene wouldn't sit outside my door...would he?

"Hold on, Thomas." I walk barefooted through the suite, my hair still dripping. I reach the doors of the suite and hope, if only for Cassidy's sake, that Keene is stupid and arrogant enough to be here.

I open the door and find him sitting there, his back against the wall. He turns to find me standing in my robe.

Sagging against the doorjamb, I hold the hotel phone to my ear and tell Thomas, "It's okay. I've got this."

"I'll bring your items to your door, then."

I thank him and hang up the phone. Then I sigh, relieved that I won't have to deliver bad news tonight. Keene stands and moves toward me. He opens his mouth to speak, but I beat him to it.

"Before you say a single thing to me, call your sister. She's worried sick about you."

After he crosses the threshold to my room, I slam the door behind him.

15

KEENE

The outer door of the suite was the first of three to be slammed shut with such force, I swore the windows rattled. When the hair dryer turned on, I exhaled slowly. Alison hasn't said another word, but she's made her feelings clear with regard to my presence.

Pulling out my phone, I scroll through my contacts and push my sister's number. Before it even has a chance to ring, I hear a frantic "Where are you?"

Damnit. As I'm explaining to Cassidy that both Alison and I are safe for the evening, I hear a knock at the door. I open it to accept a bag full of sleepwear, as Alison was obviously not expecting to be in the city tonight. Cassidy is talking in my ear, worried about Alison. I'm half listening as I walk around, holding the smallish bag.

I'm about to place the bag on the table when I hear the hair dryer cut off. I interrupt Cassidy mid-sentence to say, "Hold on." I walk to the double doors protecting the master bedroom suite. I knock loudly and wait.

Within seconds, the door flies open to reveal the Alison I've been searching for.

Her hair is untamed, and her face is flushed from the heat, leaving her cheeks rosy.

"What?" she snaps. Her temper hasn't abated much in the few moments we've been apart.

I hold up the bag between us. "Dropped off by the bellman."

She glares and then mutters, "Thanks," right before she slams the door in my face.

Again.

Pulling the phone back up to my ear, I hear my sister laughing on the other end. "Is there something funny?" I growl into the phone.

"I'm just hoping your room is soundproof because when Ali lets go of her temper, which it sounds like she is, it can get pretty loud." Now she's cackling. While a part of me is pleased the worry has left her voice, I still have the rest of the evening to get through.

"Cass—" I begin, before my sister interrupts. What is it with these Freeman women not letting a man get a word in edgewise?

"Keene, just deal with the part of her that has to do with you. Don't try to fix anything having to do with us." She takes a deep breath and lets it out.

The door opens behind me, and my brain stops functioning. That's the only way I can explain my lungs seizing at the sight of Alison in an electric-blue satin sleep shirt, carrying a glass of wine.

Muttering, "Gotta go," I disconnect the call and focus my attention on the woman making her way over to the table, perusing the pitiful remnants of her meal. She tops off her wine before moving away.

The silence between us is broken only by the thunder and lightning outside the massive floor-to-ceiling windows of the suite. Alison watches the storm, each flicker illuminating her golden hair as she sips her wine, pretending to ignore me.

I wait. I'm good at this game, better than her. I'll wait for her to break, to ask me what I want, why I'm there, what I'm thinking.

Her.

It's been Alison I've wanted, craved, and needed since that first night at the Plaza too damned long ago. It was the wrong time with what could have been. And I ran to protect us both from what was sure to be a self-destructive failure of a relationship. Then I found my sister and realized who Alison was. To Cassidy. To me. And the chasm between us seemed to widen because, unlike me, Alison doesn't play games. With her body, heart, or her mind.

Instead, she closed down. She stepped back. She escaped.

I feel her doing it now.

I step closer to her, studying her for any kind of change in her body, her face, her movement. Had I not been trained to watch people as closely as I had for years, I might have missed the minuscule tightening of her hand on the stem of her glass. Her face remains blank when she turns to me.

"Why are you here?" Her voice is flat, and that's disturbing. Disturbing because Alison is electrifying. Energy. Being around her is what I imagine orbiting the sun is like; you're drawn in despite knowing its danger. "You have what I assume to be a lovely condo. Why were you sitting outside my hotel room?"

"We weren't done with our conversation," I declare, shrugging out of my suit coat. My tie follows. Both land on the back of the sofa as I make my way toward her.

She snorts derisively. "What conversation? The one where you want to use me to get off when you're bored? Nope. What else do we have to talk about?" She's glaring at me.

I'll take that any day over the blank mask I've recently been privy to.

Moving closer to her, I see her hand tighten even further on the stem. She shores up her mask before turning to look at me. It's in her eyes though. I see it. The weariness, the pain, the fatigue. The desperation she can't quite hide anymore. At least not from me.

And it makes me feel like the biggest asshole, knowing I'm the reason she feels this way.

I clear my throat. "I meant our conversation around copyright protection and fine arts that we began discussing at the Plaza, Alison. I still want to hear the impact that case has on Emily's work."

Her lips part. She's surprised I remember, but I haven't forgotten a thing. Not even those damned shoes she was wearing—her prized silver Jimmy Choo sandals.

The meager food choices she ordered for her dinner, along with a half-finished bottle of wine sit on the table. My chest hurts knowing this woman was going to console herself curled up in a hotel bed surrounded by nothing but the storm to keep the pain away. And at the heart of it, I was the reason for it.

I offer a detente. "Come on. That was a decent appetizer. Let's order real food, and we'll talk."

She gapes at me like I've lost my mind. And maybe in some ways, it's true.

She turns back to the windows, her body slumping in defeat versus the defiance it normally holds. My insides twist as shame washes over me.

My selfishness might have been what ultimately broke this strong woman. I thought I could demand her to give me a chance, explain my reasons, share my secrets that were weighing me down in time. Suddenly, I have nothing. No reasons. No explanations. Nothing good enough to explain taking the light away from the sun.

I turn away from her and rub the back of my neck. I'm defeated too.

Suddenly, she throws me a lifeline, offering, "This is what looked best on the menu." She's guarded, wary, and wounded. The acid in my gut is rising. "I didn't care about eating earlier," she admits quietly.

It's hard not to let her quiet comments increase my agitation, but she doesn't need anger at myself misinterpreted. I reach up and gently push a lock of hair away from her face. Just as I imagined, it's soft.

"How about now? Think you might want something a little more substantial?" I coax her to meet my eyes by bending down a little.

She shrugs. Her noncommittal response is disquieting. Quickly thinking, I come up with, "How about some mac and cheese instead of this crap?" I gesture behind me.

She shakes her head sadly. "It wasn't on the menu. I already looked."

I smile at her. "Oh, ye of little faith, Alison. This is New York." Pulling up my phone, I look for the phone number for Butter Restaurant Midtown. Within minutes, I confirm they have their infamous gnocchi mac and cheese on the menu and arrange, with a hefty delivery fee, for it to be delivered to the presidential suite of the hotel. During my conversation with the famous restaurant, I watch as Alison's posture relaxes a little.

Hanging up with the bar at Butter after giving them my credit card, I ask Alison, "How about some more of that"—I nod at the half-finished wine bottle—"while we wait? And you can explain to me again why Em has to copyright all of her dress designs when they're all basically white dresses." I cock my brow and wait for her response.

Her lips twitch as she raises her almost empty glass to them. "Don't ever let her hear you say that."

She walks over to the wine and pours herself another glass. "Make yourself useful, Keene. Order more wine."

"What? Tracking down mac and cheese isn't useful?" I toss back, thrilled to see her more animated.

She's thoughtful for a moment. Tipping her head to the side, her hair brushes against the satin of her sleep shirt. "Are you eating some of it?"

I scoff, playfully. I paid close to a hundred dollars for delivery to make her smile. I'm getting a forkful at least. "I'd planned on it," I answer with amusement.

"Then it wasn't completely useful. It was self-serving. So now it's time to be useful." There's a smile hovering on the edge of her lips that makes me want to pump my fist in the air. I'd forgotten what it was like to spar with her and her smart mouth. "Order the wine, and I'll once again try to school you on the importance of copyright law and design."

At that small smile, my muscles relax. Somehow, I managed to pull her back tonight from the abyss of her thoughts with simple gestures and words.

Walking over to the phone, I remember something my mother said to me long ago as she held my head in her lap.

"Don't underestimate the power of honesty, Keene. Sometimes it hurts and sometimes it heals. But if you want it, you have to give it. Honest words may make a life-changing difference."

Ordering more wine and two fresh glasses, I watch her. In profile, her beauty is stunning, but it's the daredevil, the brilliant mind, the warrior's soul living beneath the beautiful face that has captivated me since our first meeting.

One battle at a time, Keene, I tell myself, dropping onto the couch. First, I have to get her to trust that I just want to know her as Alison again. And even while I'm waging war with my own body because I want her so desperately, Alison needs to know I'm not just looking for her as a one-night stand.

But as more.

16

ALISON

When the knock came at the door, first for the wine and then shortly after for the gnocchi, Keene jumped up both times to answer. After he plated the food, he presented me with a dish of gooey, rich, buttery cheesiness that had me moaning aloud at the first bite. Hearing him mutter, "This might have been a mistake," had me throwing my head back and laughing.

And it came to me. It was the first laugh we've shared since our night together at the Plaza.

The same thought must come to him because his full lips turn into a smile before he lifts his glass of wine. "A toast. To more laughter."

Quickly swallowing a bite of heaven, I tip my wine glass to touch his. The ping echoes in the quiet room. "This mac and cheese is incredible. Thank you." I inhale another bite. I didn't realize how hungry I was.

He acknowledges my words with a small nod, a smile playing on his lips.

I pick up my glass and twirl it by the stem. We're both silent; I'm not certain if asking what I need to will shatter the calm we're operating under. I place my glass on the table and reach for my fork when I feel his large hand cover mine.

"You can ask me whatever is going through your head. This is the beginning for us." His warm hand engulfs mine, squeezing.

I sigh. "What do you mean the beginning of us? There is no us." My voice is sharp, but my heart is damaged from the feelings this man has dragged to the surface.

His emerald eyes narrow on my face. "Is that what you want? For me to walk out that door and not give this a chance?"

My head is blank, and the spot where my heart used to live until a few hours earlier is aching at the thought. I croak out the only words I can. "I need time, Keene."

He nods slowly, his expression cautious. "I understand. And I want you to know everything before you make any decisions anyway. So, tonight, let's keep it light and easy?"

I tag my wine glass as I sit back in my chair. "Okay, but can I ask what I was going to ask?"

He tenses a bit before he says, "Fire away."

"How did you know mac and cheese was my go-to comfort food?" I'm dying to know.

What I don't expect is to see him roar with laughter. "Oh, please. In the months since I found out Cass is my sister, I've dropped by your office how many times? Have you counted how often Cass has pleaded with me to pick up food for everyone? More often than not, you want pasta with cheese."

Somehow, him noticing such a simple thing about me warms me more than the wine. "Then we shouldn't let such an incredible example of it go to waste," I answer quietly.

Keene leans over, topping off my wine and then his own. "Agreed. And while you're doing that, let's go back to that conversation we had about the difference between copyright and intellectual property when it comes to fashion, because I'm still confused." He pauses mid pour. "Then again, this could be because I buy clothes and frankly don't care."

A giggle escapes me before I realize it. Suddenly, I'm in a heated debate with a man who probably couldn't care less that Em copyrighted her own pattern of lace for her wedding gown collections. He's intrigued that Em turns rabid when someone blatantly steals her design and that I have to issue cease and desist letters threatening lawsuits when we catch mass-market reproductions of her work.

Soon, we've finished dinner and more wine, and we're lounging on the couch. The stress of the last few days takes its toll. My eyes drift shut for just a minute. The next thing I feel is Keene removing my glass from my hand. I murmur a quiet "Thanks" before snuggling up against the soft satin of my pajama sleeve.

He sighs deeply, and then his finger runs along my cheek where my hair rests. Somewhere in the depths of my subconscious, I think I hear him whisper, "This was how it was supposed to be that first night, Alison. You warm and sleepy, and me enjoying this peace with you."

He slides off the couch and lifts me in his arms.

I murmur sleepily, "Keene." Just his name.

He kisses my forehead. "Go back to sleep, baby. Tomorrow will be here soon."

I'm so exhausted, I don't remember him carrying me into the bedroom and tucking me into the bed, and I don't remember saying something in my sleep that changes things irrevocably between us.

THE SUNLIGHT STREAMING through the windows of the hotel bedroom tells me the storm has passed. The storm inside my head has also subsided, despite not being quite certain of how I ended up wrapped in the luxurious sheets of my hotel bed. I realize I feel better than I have in weeks.

Maybe a timeout was what I needed.

Maybe a reset with Keene was what I needed as well.

I begin to wonder how my clothes faired at the hotel's laundry. Stretching, I realize I need a good run. I need to put the last few days into perspective.

My hurt floods back, as do the tears. I turn my face away. He doesn't get this part of me.

Keene pins me down to the bed and forces my head toward him. I refuse to let it turn all the way though. "Listen to me, damnit. I couldn't let you, us, happen then, Alison. I had to walk away. I hadn't found my sister. I swore to myself I wouldn't let myself feel anything until I found her." He drops his head next to mine on the pillow, breathing harshly. "I felt it that night too, baby, and I had to walk away. I swore I couldn't...wouldn't...allow myself to care for anyone until I found her." He swallows harshly next to my ear. "And then I met you." His voice breaks. "I couldn't stay. I had to run. Otherwise, I knew I would never leave."

No, he can't be saying all of this. He can't mean it. It's some kind of game. "Stop it. I don't need to hear this now." I'm pathologically adamant in my refusal to listen to him.

He forces his weight to bounce the bed. The uncharacteristic move has my eyes jumping to his. "It's not a game. If anyone's been playing, it's you. What was with that crap at the wedding? I felt the spark between us, again, and you kicked me out without a chance to explain. Didn't you want to know why I left after our first time together? Christ." He rolls off me and runs his hands through his thick brown hair. "Is that how we're going to be? Constantly at war with each other?"

My jaw opens and closes several times while I process what he asked. Do I want to give the man who helped shatter the remains of my heart the key to the fortress I swore only last night I would store it in? Without thought, I say the first words that come to mind—"No, I don't think we'll always be at war with each other"—right before I lean over and gently press my lips to his.

Keene's arms tighten half a second before he rolls me over onto my back deepening the kiss.

17

KEENE

Alison's lips on mine is enough to send my senses reeling anytime. She initiated this kiss, forcing me to forget my anger at the mistreatment she's been absorbing for both of us.

It's primitive, my need to be with this woman.

Easing her deeper into the bed, I stretch out on top of her. Breaking our kiss, I take a deep breath just to absorb her. Her golden hair spread out around her head is like a halo. Her cobalt-blue eyes are sultry, her skin reddened from where they met with the stubble on my face. Her lips are parted, waiting for mine to descend upon them again.

They say there are none so blind as those who refuse to see. That's me. For not seeing her, for not seeing her pain. For not understanding why she would pull away from these feelings between us. Instead of moving heaven and earth to figure out why, I let personal issues push her further away. I want to...no, I have to see where this leads us.

Starting now.

Alison writhes on the bed, deepening my desire. I can't help it when I pivot my hips, pushing my rock-hard cock against her soft-ness. Her legs part, one wrapping around my back to pull me closer to her body.

Fuck. This might have been a mistake.

My head drops forward to trail kisses over her neck, exposed by the V-neck of her nightshirt. I can smell the natural scent of her skin, and I can't help but trail my tongue against the edge where the satin of her pajama shirt meets her silky skin.

She whispers, "Keene." Her voice is throaty, sending another bolt of urgency to my already needy cock.

This has to end soon, or we're never getting out of this hotel room.

I trail my lips back up to hers. Alison sinks her hands into my hair, pulling and tugging on the ends as our mouths fuse together.

I'm drowning. I'm lost. I have no way of saving us.

Fortunately, someone else does.

Knock. Knock. Knock. "Housekeeping!"

When we pull apart, Alison's eyes have gone comically wide. She's pushing at my chest, saying, "Did you set the chain last night when you followed me in?"

"I honestly can't remember," I tell her.

"Shit!" She stands on the bed, shaking out her nightshirt so it covers her luscious ass. I'm momentarily distracted by the visual when she hisses, "Get up. You need to put your clothes on," before she leaps off the bed and runs into the other room, closing the door behind her.

I blink my eyes a few times before I fall back on the bed with a roar of laughter. I know I'll pay dearly for that later. As housekeeping calmly assures Alison her dry cleaning is in order, I'm sure her emotions are anything but. Deciding I'm probably in enough trouble, I decide to play along.

For now.

Rolling off the bed, I reach for my clothes where I left them in the chair last night. I shrug into the dress shirt, buttoning up but not bothering with the cuffs. I don't plan on going into the office today. It's time to put my life in order.

Pulling up the zipper to my pants, the door to the bedroom flies open, and Alison comes scurrying in with her dry-cleaned suit. She's flushed from her conversation with the housekeeper or my kisses, I don't know which.

"Baby, calm down. They're not throwing us out of the room." I saunter to the bathroom where she's staring at herself above the mirror, a panicked look on her face.

"Keene, she almost walked in on us." She's mortified.

Sliding my arms around her, I grin. I can't help it. "If we only spend time together in hotels, I'm pretty sure it's bound to happen again."

She swats at my arm before turning in my embrace. Leaning against the vanity, her head plants into the center of my chest. She's shaking. My arms tighten protectively.

The next thing I know, her head is tossed back in laughter. "I was literally getting ready to slide my hand down your boxers, and all I heard was 'Housekeeping.' Got to admit, I'm not sure how long it's going to take to get over that."

I growl. Literally, growl. Boosting her up onto the vanity, I step in between her legs and push. "Soon would be preferable, baby."

"Whoa," she breathes.

I let out a breath of air that ruffles her fine hair. "Okay then. Plan of action. Get dressed—let's go shopping for some clothes for you to wear while we figure out what we want to do with our day."

"Not for nothing, Keene, but"—she lifts my hand with my Tag Heuer on it—"isn't it a workday?"

"Not anymore. Get dressed. I'm texting our people to tell them they can handle any emergencies." I slide my hand up her jaw.

Her earlier embarrassment forgotten, she slides off the vanity in front of me and turns on the taps before reaching for facial wash. "If you plan on being this autocratic, you can text my siblings to let them know I won't be in as well."

That answer is so much better than what I was expecting, I mutter, "For that, you can pick where we go to dinner."

Her laughter and happiness radiates around the room.

Right here, right now, she's back.

I sigh with relief.

"I WANT to see all the dresses, Alison."

"I'm not living out some little fantasy you've got, Keene. You'll get what I give you."

I clamp my lips together to suppress the laugh that's trying to escape. Saks isn't incredibly busy on a midday Tuesday. Most of the people who are in the store are either tourists who aren't paying attention or the few that are truly shopping couldn't care less. I raise my brow at her.

She stomps off in bare feet toward the women's dressing room. I take the opportunity to pull aside her sales assistant. "Please find her shoes for whichever dress or dresses she chooses. But make sure Jimmy Choos are included." Her silver strappy pair from that first night flash in my mind.

"Yes, Mr. Marshall." The assistant quickly scurries after Alison, and I make my way over to the couch to wait for the first dress. Dropping to the plush softness, I pull out my phone and scroll through messages that have been plaguing me all morning, I deflect some of them to Caleb and some to my assistant. Suddenly, hands clasp over my eyes from behind. I'm about to flip the person over my shoulder before I hear a breathless "Guess who?" from behind me.

Fucking hell.

Melody.

"Ms. Dempsey. What the hell are you doing in New York? Aren't you supposed to be, I don't know, working at your job in Washington?" I say in my coldest voice, shoving her hands away from me as I stand.

"I heard through the office grapevine you were off today. I thought I'd try to catch you so we could fix that silly misunderstanding from the other day." Her face is a mask of false innocence. She knew where

I was going to be. She reaches out to touch me as I step back. "I didn't expect to find you here when I was picking up a few things to surprise you with later." Her smile is both coy and sullen.

I am so beyond infuriated, I'm afraid I'm going to crack my cell phone before I have a chance to call Caleb to relay what's going on. Not only does this mean we have a leak at Hudson, again, but it means we have a crazed lunatic running our office in DC. Not to mention, I finally have a chance to work things out with Alison, but I have to deal with someone I wet my dick with one time.

Fucking hell.

I hear muttering behind me. "Keene, I swear to God, I am not coming out after every dress, but if you tell me this one works..." Alison's voice trails off as she spots Melody. "Hello." Walking right up next to me, she demonstrates exactly why she's meant to be in my arms, my head, and maybe if I'm lucky, my life.

Correctly interpreting the set look on my face, Alison walks between Melody and me and spins around in a slim-fit sheath that fits from just over her breasts to just below her knee. Two straps angle off each shoulder to meet in the lowered back. Glancing down, I see she has on a sexy pair of delicate heels as well.

She is perfection. My vision of it. My hope for it.

Stepping forward, I slide my arm around her waist and pull her as close as I can. "Are you sure we need to go out?" I murmur. Her husky laugh appeals to me.

"Down, boy. One dress down. How many do I need?" Her blonde eyebrow arches at me.

"Get a few, baby," I say loud enough for her to hear, as much as I do for the woman staring at us both, her mouth agape.

"You realize I need other clothes too, don't you?" Her voice is practically a purr. With her hand, which had been steady on my shoulders, she writes something out on my chest. It takes me a moment before I realize she's spelling out W-H-O.

I shake my head in the negative. At some point, I'm going to have to explain this. Alison won't take me completely brushing this off, but for the moment, she nods playfully. God, she would have made a great agent back in the day. "What else do you need, baby?"

She makes a big production of leaning forward and getting closer to my ear before whispering, "Running gear."

I can't help the smile that breaks out across my face. Nuzzling my nose against hers, I whisper, "We'll have better luck at Lululemon."

Alison steps back. Walking away, she says, "You say the sexiest things."

I outright laugh.

Adding a little more swing to her step, Alison smiles over my shoulder at Melody and makes her way back into the dressing room. I follow every thrust and sway until I hear Melody say behind me, "Fucking slut."

The ice that had been slowly thawing in my veins returns in full force.

Before turning around, I engage my phone to call Caleb's directly. Knowing the line is open, I hold the phone in my hand. I turn my attention from the woman who snared it with nothing more than a smile to the woman who is trying to hold it hostage.

Her bullshit ends now.

"Ms. Dempsey, I'm at Saks in New York City. My first question to you is, again, why aren't you at your post in DC at Hudson when you're under review for poor job performance? Additionally, we have pending investigations. And lastly, do you want to repeat what you just said about my woman to me?" My jaw is clenched. I'm fairly certain my dentist is going to have a field day telling me I need a mouth guard or some bullshit like that.

"Keene, I told you, I heard you were taking a free day. I want to be where you are. You know that together we can do anything, and we'll have so much fun doing it too." Melody's voice has dropped back to its seductive tone.

I'm not sure how I missed it in her background check, the crazy with the extra helping of batshit she has going on, but somehow, all of that slid through. And not only that, I compounded that error by breaking my own rule. But until Caleb gets this, I'm essentially fucked.

"And what about the DC office, Ms. Dempsey? Didn't we just have an issue with your job performance there?" My head is aching from dealing with her bullshit.

"I thought you said you wanted me in New York, sir? I honestly didn't think I was making a mistake." Her voice is pure innocence.

"You're not dressed for work," I fire back.

"Neither are you."

While Ali finished getting ready and checked out of the hotel, I ran by my condo and changed from yesterday's suit to casual clothes. Now, I'm wondering if Melody followed me from there.

The smile that crosses my face doesn't come close to reaching my eyes. "But I'm not working today, am I? I'm also not under review for poor work practices."

Her face reddens, but that doesn't help me on the phone with Caleb.

"Let's get back to the problem here. Why are you here in Saks, Ms. Dempsey?" I press.

"Well, I..." Her voice trails off.

"Ms. Dempsey, right now your answers need to be clear and succinct. Why are you in this department store?" I wait, tapping my finger on my phone.

"Your office said you weren't coming in. I...did a little tracking...on your phone and found you here," she huffs. "I didn't expect to find you with some skank picking out clothes."

Bingo.

Melody continues her rant about Alison, but I know it's only a matter of minutes. Soon enough, my phone is vibrating, alerting me of a call waiting. Reading the caller ID, I see one of our office numbers. With a smirk, I switch over and answer.

"Yes?"

"I don't care what you have to do to get her ass in this office, Keene. She's done," Caleb growls in my ear.

Apparently, Caleb answered my call and had been listening in. He called from one of our office lines to end this.

Once and for all.

I hand the phone to Melody and say simply, "It's for you."

I can only imagine Caleb's tone while ordering Melody into the office. If I had to make a guess, I'd say he plans on canning her ass for failure to perform duties as assigned and walking off the job site. I have to remember to tell him the bit about the cell phone. Melody had effectively stalked me. And let's not forget that Caleb loves Alison.

Within moments of listening to Caleb, Melody leaves Saks.

Shortly thereafter, Alison reappears in a new dress and flats. She's carrying a dress bag and a bag brimming with cardboard shoeboxes. Her suit and shoes she wore here are nowhere to be seen. The smile on her face brings an echoing one to my own, restoring my good humor.

Just as I'm about to open my mouth to suggest we head to Lululemon, she says, "Want to tell me about that crazy bitch who thinks she still has a claim on your cock?"

Stunned silent, I gesture her forward. I follow, admiring the way the silk of her new dress encases her ass and outlines her legs. I wonder what she has on underneath.

She stops dead in her tracks in the middle of the store.

Waving her hand to get my attention, she says, "Crazy first, Keene."

I snap out of my lust-filled haze. Cocking my head to the side, I say, "Agreed. And while we're on the topic, can we get Major Cock-block from the other night out of the way too?" The tic in my jaw becomes pronounced.

I stalk ahead of her to hold open the door to Saks, where she sails by, laughing. "Sure. Let's talk about Colby."

Just his name makes me want to rip his head off.

"Because you know, Keene, he and I have never fucked, never dated, never kissed." She lifts her finger to her lips, pondering for a moment. "I guess that's technically not true if you count the cheek.

Do you count that?" Her tone is angelic innocence, but she's mocking me.

"Depends on which cheek it was, baby," I mutter as I take the bags from her arm. I pull her toward me on the crowded city street, grab one of her ass cheeks, and lay a kiss on her laughing lips.

18

ALISON

Daniela Trattoria in New York City has to be my favorite restaurant of all time. Their Ravioli Amatriciana is my downfall. I'm not above begging them for the recipe to recreate it at home. I would literally run ten miles a day to not gain an ounce from eating that dish for breakfast, lunch, and dinner.

I remember the first time I ate at this restaurant. Phil wanted to celebrate Jason getting his full-time ER job in the city. Between the seven of us, our table took up a large portion of the balcony area overlooking the seating in the trattoria and the killer view of Eighth Avenue. The house sangria flowed like buckets as we celebrated the man who would become our brother-in-law.

Little did we know that right after Phil's congratulatory speech, Jason would drop to his knee and ask him to marry him. My heart stutters as I think about the tears shimmering in Phil's eyes when he said, "Yes." Our celebration became even rowdier.

"I want to know what's putting that smile on your face," Keene says as he sits next to me, instead of across from me. He had stepped away to take a call from Caleb that he didn't want overheard by the other patrons.

"Memories," I reply softly.

The smile doesn't leave my face when he reaches for my hand. Playing with my fingers, he says, "Tell me."

I look down at our hands. His fingers are long and strong. My gaze moves up to his wrist, where the first sprinkling of dark hair that dusts his body begins. His hand tightens on mine.

"You're hesitating. Why?"

"Because I don't know how much of our past Cassidy has already shared with you, and I don't know how much you want to know. Sometimes, I just don't know what to say without making a difficult situation more painful for you." I let my fingers explore his.

His hand tightens again before he releases mine. Disappointment sets in, but then I feel his hand slide up to my elbow, his thumb strumming back and forth. That simple touch causes pleasurable chills to erupt across my body. My lips part because the sensation is almost overwhelming.

"Baby, I don't want you to hold back what's happened in your past. Any of your past," he adds with emphasis. I know he's not only referring to my adopted family. "If there's something you want or need to share, I want to hear it. And I promise that if I can, I will as well."

That sounds promising, but— "What do you mean by if you can?" I ask softly.

We're seated against the aging brick wall, with patrons to either side of us. He leans closer and murmurs, "Has Cass shared what Caleb used to do for a living?"

I nod. Keene nods slowly.

Holy crap. I knew Keene had been in the service, but he was also part of the intel community? Now his comment made a hell of a lot more sense. It wasn't that he didn't want to share his past. It meant he was legally unable to share certain pieces of information for the rest of his life.

His thumb is still moving back and forth. I expect he felt the jump in my pulse. He's patiently waiting for my reaction, so I reach for my glass of the homemade sangria and take a small sip. "I'm fond of this drink," I offer.

He smirks. "I couldn't tell, as we're already on our second pitcher and our appetizers haven't been delivered yet." His thumb is still stroking. He's waiting.

"I remember the night we celebrated Jason getting the job at the ER here. He proposed to Phil that night too. We all enjoyed the sangria more than our fair share. I think we drank three, four pitchers each? Granted they're small." I laugh at the details of that memory.

"What you're telling me is that Jason was impaired the night he proposed to Phil?" Nodding, Keene lifts his glass and takes a sip. "That explains so much."

"Oh stop! Phil isn't that bad."

Keene's smile slashes across his face. "Please, I've heard from both sides how he thought Caleb was actually marrying his brother."

"That is so not how it went. Your sister is who thought that."

Keene almost drops his glass. "You learned that from Cassidy."

My smile offers no apology, but it doesn't look like he expects one.

"*Bueno*! Calamari fritti...*Bella*! I didn't see you sitting here!" The manager beams. "You save room for my tiramisu, yes?"

I laugh out loud. "Always."

"Good, good." He frowns at our pitcher of sangria. "I get you more to drink."

I'm laughing by the time Georgio leaves our table. "You can see how we ended up drinking so much the night Phil and Jason got engaged."

But Keene hasn't been watching Georgio. His focus has been on me.

"Tell me another reason this place is so special, Alison."

Taking a deep breath, I let it out and tell him. "This was where we celebrated after we became Freemans legally. After our name changes came through."

His hand slides from my elbow, and the loss I feel is almost immediate. Gone is the easy camaraderie.

"Why did you bring me here?" His voice is neutral.

It was stupid...so stupid why I brought him here.

"Why, Alison?"

I should have known better.

"Alison, tell me why," he bites out.

"Because every good beginning in my life has been celebrated here. From my acceptance to law school to graduation. From proposals to jobs. And I wanted ours to start the same way." My words end softly.

His breath comes out in sharp bursts. He abruptly turns to me and grabs my arms so I'm facing him, our knees bumping in the small space.

Keene's nostrils are flared as he pulls me closer so that I'm nose-to-nose with him when he says, "Great answer," before crushing his mouth to mine.

I raise my hand, brushing it against his jaw when I hear Georgio say, "I'll come back."

Ripping my mouth free from Keene's, the laughter falls effortlessly from me.

What's better is when Keene lowers his forehead to mine and does the same.

BETWEEN BITES OF MAGNIFICENT FOOD, Keene asks me more about the times we celebrated here at the trattoria. I truly don't think I've talked so much in one sitting since I sat for the bar. Every memory I bring up leads to a new one. Big or small, Keene wants to hear my thoughts. Like the first night we met, he is attentive and asks questions about all of my stories. What surprises me is that he isn't focused on my memories with Cassidy, but he is genuinely interested to learn about the cake that won an award for Corinna, or how we felt when we were named Connecticut's Vendor of the Year.

While the pieces of my heart had been shattered the day before, blood still flows through those pieces. Some of them are fitting back together, trying to remind me to ask myself if I'm letting my guard down too soon.

When our entrées are delivered, we stop speaking, and after the first bite, I let out a soft moan.

Keene's fork clatters to his dish. "Alison," he utters hoarsely.

I find his hands are clenched into fists. His jaw is tight, his cheeks flushed. Heat hits my own cheeks as I fork another bite. "It really is terrific," I murmur.

"Are you willing to give me a taste?" he rasps out. And somehow, I know we're not talking about ravioli.

I scoop a forkful of my ravioli and offer it to him. My pulse is leaping when he reaches for my hand to guide my fork into his mouth. Chewing slowly, he nods his approval. "You're right. Delicious. One of the best things I've ever tasted, but the best was a lot... sweeter. The best thing I've ever tasted has a certain flavor I can't quite describe." He reaches for his napkin to wipe his mouth, his implication clear.

I feel the flood between my legs, my panties soaking from the charge of his words.

He cuts a piece of his chicken piccata and offers it to me, and I lean forward to accept it. The flavors of lemon and capers explodes on my tongue, melding together with the sweetness of the chicken. "Hmm. Delicious."

"You like the flavor?" he asks mildly.

Two can play his game.

"It reminds me of one of my favorite things. Salty, briny. While I'm not sure I could ingest more than a few shots of it at a time, it truly has a magnificent taste." I lift my napkin to my lips to dab.

Keene shakes his head, a small smile playing about his lips.

After a few more bites, Keene asks me out of the blue, "What do you have planned for the rest of the week?"

The week? I sit back in shock. "You do realize I have to go home, right? I have a job. I can't stay here."

"Do you have to be in your office to do it? Could you work from here?" I'm not surprised to feel his hand brushing my leg when he reaches for mine. "Just think about it. If you could work from here this week, would you want to?"

Would I want to? Am I willing to open myself up to the potential pain again?

"I don't know." I hesitate. His face closes off. "I told you earlier, I need some time."

"Don't you think it would be prudent if we take time to work through issues together?"

"Maybe? I don't know, Keene." I press my lips together. "You have no idea what the last few weeks have been like for me."

His other hand, not touching me, slaps the table. "Then tell me! For Christ's sake, Alison, I'm not a fucking stranger."

"I thought you said you wanted to start over?" I challenge.

"I do. That doesn't mean we toss out everything we already know about each other. It means we use it to see if there's something more between us. If there's not..." He shrugs. "We part much more amicably than we did the first time."

I shouldn't be surprised that Keene's already foreseeing our end before we even have a conversation to start. Somehow, it gives me the strength to pull back. "Like I said, I'll see. I have to review my commitments." And I need to decide if I want to go down this path again.

His eyes bore into mine before he gives a hard shrug and continues to eat. Silently.

All of our earlier camaraderie disappears as if it never occurred.

19

ALISON

Bidding Georgio a good evening, Keene guides me out onto the quieting streets of Eighth Avenue. The theater crowd has slowly dissipated while we were finishing our meal due to the misting rain.

I open my mouth to ask Keene where he'd like to go, when he starts talking. "You made it fairly obvious during dinner that you're not interested in pursuing anything further between us." His face is closed off. "I wish I had understood earlier your intentions were truly to establish a familial dynamic between us."

Is he out of his ever-loving mind? Who the hell kissed him back in bed this morning?

"I think it would be best if we limited our interactions for a while to those with other individuals around. I'm not entirely certain I can be completely cordial," he continues.

The anger I've held back since the first time Keene walked out the door after our first night together claws up from the bottom of my soul. It's crueler than knowing my father sold me for drugs. It's more potent than the wine I just drank.

My chest heaves as he takes his first few steps away from me. I'm over his shit. His back-and-forth emotional yo-yo. He wants to walk away? Fine. Not without me having my say this time.

I walk quickly and reaching out, I shove him.

"What the hell?" he snarls at me.

"Fuck you, Keene. Seriously. Fuck. You. This is all about *your* issues. Your issues, not mine. You're the one who walked first. Physically, emotionally, every which way there could be. What was it?" I shout into his shocked face. He's still leaving, but I refuse to live one more second with this festering in my soul. I gesture angrily between the two of us. "You know, I was hopeful about tonight. Excited. I was ready for the challenge." I step back, my fury receding. Instead, I'm left with disgust at both of us. Shaking my head, I say, "Keep running, Keene. You're even better at it than me," before I turn on my heel to head down the street toward Jared's office, where my car is still waiting for me. I stop a few steps away, turning back to sneer, "It's too bad you're such a coward, too afraid to reach for something you might actually want in this life before it walks away. You're too busy looking for all the ways to make it wrong in your perfect world, so you dispose of it."

I turn and continue walking down the street when I hear Keene call out, "You're wrong, Alison."

I don't even stop to acknowledge him.

It takes me about ten minutes to reach the offices of Watson, Rubenstein, and Dalton. I briefly greet the doorman as I walk in, and he hands me the packages I had delivered from Saks earlier that day. Making my way to the elevator, I pull out my keys. I see my phone light up with what I'm sure is a text from Keene. The man just hates not having the last word. My phone has buzzed repeatedly in the last few minutes, but frankly, my anger has burned out, leaving only the ash behind.

Tossing my purchases into my car, I slide into the driver's seat, resting my head on the steering wheel, allowing myself one moment to grieve what could have been before I pull all of my emotions together and start my car.

I refuse to let one asshole be the reason I wrap my car around a tree on the Hutch.

I'm backing up my car when I hear something slam into the trunk. Slamming on the brakes and whipping my head around at the sound, my heart pounding, I meet the volcanic look on Keene's face. Putting my car in park, I jump out.

"Are you out of your damned mind? What if my reflexes had been off? I could have run you over with the car!" I shout at him.

"I think it's time we establish some boundaries, Alison." His face is pure fury; his voice is ice. "If we're in the middle of an argument, you don't walk away from me." He rounds the trunk of the car, stalking toward me.

"We weren't in the middle of anything. We're just a brother and sister having a little spat. Don't worry. You'll get the hang of them again. We have them with Phil all the fucking time." My voice, already loud, rises further. My hands are clenching and releasing at my sides.

"And you know that's a fucking lie."

"Yeah, I could tell when we—" I can't finish my sentence because Keene has backed me up against my car, his hands fisted in my damp hair. Without warning, he slams his lips down on mine.

My senses are overwhelmed when his tongue passes my lips. My nose is filled with the scent of the rain mixed with his cologne. My arms immediately wrap around his sinewy muscles, trying to pull him closer.

This kiss is like no other Keene and I have ever shared. It's a declaration, a statement, a demand. I'm no longer the warrior forced to hold a shield and sword; I'm a woman in the arms of a man. His arms make me feel like this spot is where I should have been all along.

This kiss obliterates every hurt, every pain, everything from my mind, except for one thing.

Him.

Keene.

For the rest of my life, I'll never forget this kiss.

Long moments later, it's the glare of headlights shining directly in Keene's eyes that have him lifting his head. Muttering under his breath, he curses the offending vehicle.

A choked sound escapes me as my head crashes into his chest.

Tipping my head back, Keene brushes his thumb under my jaw. "I was prepared to apologize until you called me a coward. Now, I figure we're even." His face hasn't changed, but I look closer. The ticking in his jaw. The arm banded around my waist. The darkening of green eyes to almost a midnight-green hue. And suddenly, it dawns on me. Keene's not angry, he's hurt.

I try to push him away.

"Keene, you emotionally walked out on me in the middle of dinner because I didn't agree with you. All I tried to say was this is new and I'm not ready to take a week off and jump into the deep end. I'll also have you note, *counselor*, I didn't say no. I just said I needed more time to adjust. You were the one who already had a backup plan in the event we didn't work out," I throw at him accusingly.

Keene rocks back about six inches before he's right back in my space, his face slightly menacing. "You mean to tell me after you were sweet all day, *counselor*, I'm back to you being a viper because I perhaps misspoke at dinner?"

Wow, that stings. "You don't misspeak, Keene. This conversation proves that."

How many times had I laid in bed wishing he had misspoken when he walked out of the room at the Plaza?

"Wrong, Alison. I do. I just don't always have the luxury of correcting myself," he counters, scrubbing a hand down his face.

"You had the chance tonight and you chose not to. Again." I turn in his embrace and move to open my car door, but it's slammed closed from behind. Keene steps against my back, his arms tightening. I smile sadly to myself before I pull his arms away.

I open the door again and slide into my seat. He immediately leans down.

"Don't go, Alison."

Without looking at him, I say, "I need to sleep in my bed, wake up, and go for a run. And I'm doing that alone. I'm telling you this so you won't harass me tonight."

He flinches.

"You see, this is what I mean when I say I need to ease into this. You've admitted it yourself; you view things in black and white, but you also treat people that way. Did you know that? Since we met, it's been nothing but dark with a few moments of bright pure white—light so blinding, I forget what it's like to be in the dark. The things you said this morning? I felt like I'd never know darkness again." His body relaxes slightly before I continue. "Then I'm plunged in the dark again. By you. By comments like you made outside the trattoria." I shake my head. "Why don't *you* take the rest of *your* week to figure out what you really want. I'm driving home."

Still crouched beside my car, he says, "This wasn't how I planned for the night to end."

Turning my head toward him, I respond with, "I'm sure you didn't, but then again, I'm just your *sister* now, right?" His unguarded wince still doesn't cause me to blink. "Thank you for a lovely day, Keene. Thank you for trying to defend me to *my* brother and sisters. I just wish, I truly wish, the dark didn't have to come."

I roll up the window as I hear him call my name, but I need my space.

Alone.

I back up the car, this time without interruption. Somehow, I make it out of the city. It isn't until I turn off I-684 that the first tear falls.

What had started as such a lovely day with so many possibilities ends with me in tears again over Keene Marshall.

PULLING into my driveway in Collyer is almost a comfort, despite how I left yesterday. It's close to midnight, and all I want is my bed. My body hurts, and I'm so emotionally drained from the events over the last several days. Sliding my legs from the car, I barely have the energy to move.

It takes me so long, the overhead light in my garage blinks out. It's likely why I notice my phone lights up with a text.

Surprisingly, it's from Caleb.

Caleb: I figure you don't want to talk to anyone right now, but Keene's been blowing up my phone for the last hour to keep an eye out for when you got back. I want to know if it's okay to give him the high sign you're here.

I'm alternately pissed Keene worried Caleb with our issues, and touched that Caleb even asked.

I debate on what to type back. Finally, I answer with, *You didn't need to wait up. Sorry for the inconvenience. Thanks for letting him know.*

His response comes immediately. *Ali, I've been worried since yesterday. We all have been. The only thing that stopped the others from following you was me sitting on them.*

Don't worry about me, Caleb. Take care of Cassidy.

His response makes my heart hurt a little. *Ali, you're family. We'll always worry.*

Sure. Thanks.

I see the little blue dots moving and stopping as Caleb starts and stops typing. Finally, he sends his message. *Just because Cassidy's my wife and Keene's my best friend, doesn't mean I haven't seen what they've both done to you.* The blue dots blink again. *I never thought I'd see the dazzle die out of you. Until yesterday. All of them were wrong on so many levels. And Keene didn't inconvenience me. We were awake. Honest to God, I don't think anyone on this property will sleep, wondering if you were coming home. And they all had every reason to worry. Everything is wrong right now.*

I'm in shock. I start to text. I stop. I start again. I stop. What the hell am I supposed to say to my sister's husband who just took my side? The blue dots on his side move again.

And now, I've said what I needed to say. I'm going to sleep. Good night, sister.

I respond. *Good night, Caleb.*

While his words are comforting, I'm so drained, all I want to do is sleep. Pulling my bags from the car, I close the garage door and enter my home. Not even pausing to drop my purse, I make my way through the moonlit rooms to my bedroom, where I strip and fall on the bed.

I'm out within minutes, but my sleep is filled with nightmares.

I'm bound, chains around my arms and neck, holding me naked to the auction block again. I stare unseeing into the hellacious unknown. How did my father get out of jail and find me? The familiar chains on my wrists are held by simple padlocks. My head bows in shame.

Suddenly, cool metal slithers over my skin to wrap around my body. Around my wrists, around my neck, crossing in front of my heart. My eyes follow them as they bind me. They're different. They're not as heavy, but I can tell they're infinitely more dangerous. From the quick perusal of them without lifting my head, I know two things: I can't find where these chains end, and they're the gleaming green of Keene's eyes. I frantically struggle against them as the old chains break away.

Leaving me bound to the new ones.

Captive.

I can't escape.

I can't run.

As I'm being led off the auction block, I can't see him, but I can hear his voice clear as day saying to me, "Stop running, Alison. It doesn't solve anything."

I wake up with a start, feeling just as drained as when I'd gone to bed. Reaching for my phone, I find only a few hours have passed. Turning off my alarm, I say to hell with it.

I feel a sick day coming on.

20

MELODY

Hmm, that didn't last too long.

I giggle from where I'm watching down the alley. The blonde with the long legs storms off. Keene just stands there, infuriated.

Sliding out of the alley and exiting on Seventh Avenue, I make a decision to head over to his place later to let him make this up to me.

It's the least I deserve.

KEENE

Everything she said was right.

Everything.

I take a large sip of amber liquid from the crystal tumbler in my hand.

She was laughing with me this morning. We spent the day together. And because she wanted to slow things down a bit, I crushed her. I wrecked her. Again.

She was right.

I bailed on her in the middle of dinner.

She never got her tiramisu.

I swallow more Scotch and look at my phone.

Nothing from Caleb.

Fuck, where is she?

My home phone rings, and I frown. No one has this number but Caleb, and he knows to call my cell. Before I answer it without thinking, I check the caller ID. Blocked. Lovely. Probably some telemarketer. I wait for it to go to voicemail and resume pacing.

Back and forth.

I take another drink.

My home phone rings again, and I pause. This number never

rings. Please, for the love of fuck, don't tell me some dumb twat gave out my number to a drunk asshole at a bar. Ignoring it, I resume pacing. Has to be a wrong number.

When the hell is Caleb going to ping me about Alison?

I check my cell. Did my battery die? No. It's still got a decent charge. As I'm studying the condition of my phone, it lights up with a message from Caleb. *She's home safe. We'll talk tomorrow.*

I quickly send a message back. *Thanks, buddy.*

Okay. At least she's back in Connecticut and not in a ditch. I can fix this. I can. I have to. I have to show her I'm serious about getting to know her, being with her, wanting to know her.

Caleb knows how to run our company, but I'm the one who knows how to plan a siege. Attempting to get Alison to give me another chance after tonight is going to be just that, especially since she's back in Collyer.

My house phone rings again. Shit! Again, I check the caller ID. Blocked.

A chill races along my skin.

"This wasn't how I'd planned for the night to end, Alison."

I grab my cell phone and call my house phone voicemail. Punching in the password, I wait.

"Hey, baby, I saw you sent *her* on her way earlier outside the restaurant. No great loss." Melody's voice comes out over the phone. "I know if you're not home that you will be soon. I figure I'll give you an hour, then I'll head your way. Hope you're ready for a big night." She ends the call by blowing a kiss into the phone.

My hands are shaking. I'm hanging up on the voicemail and dialing Caleb as I race down the hall to my room to pack.

"Jesus, Keene. I just fell asleep. Cassidy's been a wreck all day. The idea is that we're supposed to get sleep before we have kids," he grumbles.

"Call my house voicemail. Password is your birthday and Cassidy's birthday, in that order. Listen to the messages, and get someone up to scramble the tracker we have on my vehicle."

"Huh? What the hell?" Caleb's awake now.

I've already hung up.

Quickly changing into a dark T-shirt and jeans, I pull down bags and toss in clothes to last me a while. In the second bag, I toss in anything of meaning in the apartment that can't be replaced. Pictures of my mother and me together, a box of old photos, my mother's jewelry, a couple of laptops, and critical papers.

I also clip the holster of my Glock to the back of my pants and pull my shirt over top of it.

I ignore the constant ringing of my house phone. I'm not certain if it's Melody or Caleb calling to try to track her.

I can't care.

She's obviously lost what's left of her marbles, and I know better than to confront her alone.

Grateful the majority of my mother's possessions are still locked in a storage unit in Connecticut, I'm lacing up my boots, just about ready to go when my phone rings again. This time, it's my cell. Caleb.

"I'm on my way out the door," I warn.

"You're clear to leave driving your car. The analyst assigned your tag to one of the parked cars in the corporate garage. Right now, we can see Melody's car parked downstairs from our office. It's just... idling. When you pull out, a black Volvo will follow you to the city limits. It's one of ours." Caleb is in full operations mode. "You need to switch to a burner until we can get you on a new cell."

"Jesus, Caleb. How did we miss this?" I'm locking my door as I make my way to the elevator. Pushing the button inside, I look up. "Do our guys have eyes in here?"

"Yes. They're watching right now."

I slump against the elevator. "I got your text, by the way."

"I saw. I take it your night didn't go as planned."

"I fucked up."

"On a scale of flowers to...?" Caleb inquires.

"There is no scale. I lost my temper when I couldn't get my way and was an unmitigated douchebag."

Caleb's sigh expresses how close I am to being disavowed. "If I seriously didn't think we were dealing with a chick who would tie you to a chair and break your ankles with a sledgehammer right before fucking you, I might leave you to clean up your mess—both your messes." Caleb is pissed, an emotion he rarely shows.

"Yeah. I have no clue how to fix it," I admit. I'm hopeless.

"Not getting caught by your stalker is a good way to start."

As I step off the elevator, I suddenly freeze. *Stalker.* I have an honest-to-God stalker. "Where should I go?"

"First to your car, then you turn it on, and then you put it in drive." Caleb's words are as condescending as it gets.

"No, I mean once I get out of the city. Where should I drive to?"

There's silence on the other end of the line. "You really swallowed a bunch of stupid pills at some point today, didn't you? Get your ass here. You can't fix shit from hundreds of miles away."

"Caleb, I have a fucking stalker after me. I don't want to bring that to the family," I argue as I walk around my Audi, searching for bombs. I wouldn't put it past Melody to plant one.

"And who else is going to have your back? In a town this size, we'll have an advantage. Besides, you can work on removing your head from your ass while you're here. Though that may require surgical intervention."

"Fuck you," I say, with a distinct lack of heat. I start my car. Good, it didn't explode. There's a plus for the evening.

"Don't get caught by a psycho on your way here," he says optimistically, right before he hangs up.

Dick.

Soon, I'm on my way to Collyer. I can finally breathe.

Not surprisingly, together, Caleb and I managed to plan a near-perfect op in less than five minutes, just like when we were in the Army. A slash of a grin crosses my face and then quickly fades when I realize Alison could have been with me when things went fubar tonight. Even though I'm completely at fault, and I have a shit ton of work ahead of me to get my foot in the door again, I can't help but think this was the way it was supposed to be. With me in Collyer.

At Alison's pace.

On Alison's turf.

With Alison calling the shots.

I wonder how she's going to react to seeing me. My guess? Not well at all. I laugh darkly at the irony.

I realize I never told her the story about Melody, and I groan. I don't need a fucked-up one-night stand getting in the way of repairing what I want with Alison. Caleb needs to know that Melody remains Hudson business and doesn't extend to the family. There's no reason why this should impact the Freemans.

I rest my head back against the leather headrest. She has to give me this chance, this last chance.

I won't hurt your heart again, Alison.

22

ALISON

"What the hell do you mean Keene's here?" I screech at Corinna on the phone before flopping back into my bed.

"I swear it on my red velvet cake recipe, Ali. He and Caleb walked into Amaryllis this morning. They're working from here for the, and I quote, foreseeable future. So, back to you. What the hell happened?"

I groan. "Too much for a phone call. Do you want to go for a run later?"

"Do I look like I took a stupid pill instead of my gummy vitamins this morning?"

"Cori, come on," I whine pathetically.

"No. If you want to talk, I'm willing to do so over chocolate. I'm even willing to bring said chocolate to your house and you can continue to rest on your sick day. What I am not willing to do is sweat outside when it feels like it's over a hundred degrees in the shade."

"It's only supposed to be ninety today," I mumble.

"You work in a kitchen filled with ovens, sweating your ass off all day, and then argue semantics with me, sister. Do you want chocolate?" Corinna counters.

I give in, albeit reluctantly. I need to run, but Corinna is right—it's too humid to be putting in miles right now. I'll likely lace up after dark.

"Yes. When can you get here?"

"I'm leaving now." Corinna hangs up.

Dragging myself from my bed, I take care of all my bathroom essentials before making my way downstairs. Starting a fresh pot of coffee, I wait.

"ARE YOU KIDDING ME? He said what?" Corinna screeches with a mouthful of triple chocolate cake she made earlier today.

I nod. "And that was before I walked away. I haven't even told you what happened when I got back to the garage." I take a bite of a cake I've dubbed over the years as Corinna's Chocolate Sin. "God, Cori. Had to bring the whole cake, didn't you?"

In between her own bite of cake, she smirks. "Everyone deserves an I'm-falling-for-an-asshole cake. This one is yours."

My fork hits the side of the plate. "I am not falling for him, Corinna." Screw the fork. Picking up a large piece, I shove the whole thing in my mouth. I must look like a chipmunk with my cheeks full of chocolate, but I don't care.

"Uh-huh," she mumbles around her next bite.

"I'm not!" My protest warbles as I talk around the moist cake.

"I'm not arguing with you," she says calmly.

Grabbing my coffee off the counter, I take a sip and slam it down. "You didn't agree either. You think I'm falling for him. For all that is holy, why would you think that?" I ask accusingly.

Corinna calmly places her fork along the side of her plate. She takes a sip of her coffee and wipes her mouth before she speaks.

"He's been in your thoughts since that first night, and you haven't been able to let him go. You compare every man you've slept with to him. And they all fail."

I start to protest, but she holds up a perfectly manicured hand, something I still don't know how she pulls off while baking all day, when I can't keep a manicure to save my soul.

"Ali, for women like us"—she points her dark pink fingertip between the two of us—"men are a game until they're not. This is tearing you apart inside for one reason. You care." She shakes her head. "You stopped playing about two years ago when Keene entered your life and blew out of it just as fast. You don't remember how destroyed you were after your wedding hookup, but I do. It was the same way you're acting now." She pauses. "Before you were wounded. This time, you're afraid to give him a chance because of what could happen."

My back snaps straight. "I'm not afraid." I'd told myself long ago to never give a man the power to make me afraid ever again.

"Ali, you're so petrified of letting your heart break, you've enclosed it in a tomb, sealed it with a lock, and put it inside a castle on top of a mountain. You won't even give a man a fair chance," Corinna tells me bluntly.

I recoil in shock.

"What your father did to you, what my family did to me, and what Hols' did to her can't be the measure of how we judge men. Otherwise, they win. After all these years, is that what you want? For those bastards to be sitting in a jail cell knowing they still won, even after all they've done?"

"You've been thinking about this a lot," I mutter, shoving my cake away.

Corinna nods. "More and more lately. Yes, we're all damaged by what happened to us, but I think you still hang on to that pain."

"What?" I choke out.

"It wasn't my body on display on that auction block, Ali. It wasn't Holly's. We've been able to let go of things from our past easier. It wasn't our fathers in that room when it all went down. Trust isn't the mountain I have to conquer if I want to accept love."

Her words strike too close to home. "Are you saying I shouldn't be freaked-out, Cori? With Mr. Hot and Cold? What possible inkling do I have that Keene might care enough about me to treat me with anything close to respect when every other word out of his mouth is tantamount to the opposite?"

Her exasperation comes out on a long, slow sigh. "Have you considered that like our families, his was decimated too? That maybe he's as unsure of things as you are? Maybe he's just as clueless as you? I swear, you two are a certain kind of special."

I wince. With Corinna's new perspective, I realize I haven't. I haven't looked at any of this from Keene's point of view. I've been filled with so much pain.

I let out a rough sigh.

"Hey, I didn't say this to make you feel worse, Ali. I said this to make you understand that there are two sides to every story, and we know all truth and lies fall somewhere in between. Unless it's the crap our families did to us, then they're completely wrong, and we reserve the right for vengeance."

My mouth quirks in a smile, but my mind is still locked on what Corinna is saying. How much am I fulfilling my father's prophecy about me, sabotaging my own happiness because I refuse to look beyond myself? "What do I do, Cori?" I whisper. "How do I fix this?"

"Blehhhh." Corinna sounds like a braying sheep. "Wrong answer. This is not solely on you, Ali."

Color me confused. Didn't Corinna just spend the last hour trying to make me look at things from Keene's point of view?

"That man has a temper a good ol' exorcism needs to get out of him. Keene needs to do some begging to get back into your good graces, and not while he's anywhere near your—" Her finger makes a circle near my vagina.

I burst out laughing.

"His mouth sounds awfully good, but his lips need to work well when they're not looking for some sugar."

I topple off my stool from laughing so hard. Only Corinna.

"It can't be anything after dark. I've already decided he's a vampire when the sun goes down. That's when his inner prick emerges," I manage to get out.

Corinna gapes at me for one second, two, and then shoves her cake plate forward as she face-plants onto my kitchen counter, laughing. "Only you, Ali." She leans down to give me a high five.

I grin as our hands connect, but it slowly fades as I slide to rest my back against the kitchen cabinets. "I'm constantly fighting to be me when I'm with him, Cori. Like being me just isn't good enough."

"Is that you picking up on things from him, or your own doubts pushing at you?" she probes.

I pick at a loose string on my ratty UConn T-shirt. "If I'm being honest, I don't know." Her eyes are sympathetic. "I didn't think asking for time to take things slowly and not agreeing to spend the week with him was blowing the whole idea off."

"It wasn't, and that's why my next stop is the office to smash a pie full of whipped cream in his face," she says smoothly. "That was a total dick move."

"I know, right? And this is why I'm so confused...wait, what the hell do you mean you're going to shove a pie in his face?" I demand.

"Did you really think he was going to be sitting in our offices all week and I was going to watch you here, broken, without exacting some sort of revenge?" Her honeyed voice is smooth. And hard.

"He didn't break me, Corinna," I say sharply.

"You sure about that?"

I raise my chin. "Positive."

"Did this family break you?" she demands.

I inhale roughly, my breath shuddering. That one is harder to answer. Cassidy, with all of her demands to play nice or face her displeasure. Em's constant support of Cassidy. Phil and Holly watching from the sidelines. And all of it circles back around to... "Keene. It's all about him." I drop my head.

Corinna slides off her stool and joins me on the floor. "What they did to you Monday was just wrong."

"And you know that was only the portion of the iceberg that was visible. I've been dealing with this for months."

She quirks her head. "What pushed you over on Monday?"

I think back. "The feeling even work isn't a comfort anymore. They trapped me in my office—Holly included. That hurt. Killed.

Like nowhere is safe." I rub a hand over my chest where it aches. "I feel like I don't belong anymore. Nowhere I go is a place for me to think. My house isn't safe. Keene was waiting for me the night we got home. Work is out. I get questioned about him all the time. The only place I'm safe is when I'm running. If I could run all the time and never stop, I would," I admit.

Corinna reaches for my hand. "What can I do?"

I squeeze hers in return. "You're doing it. You're giving me faith I'm not completely lost."

We sit like this for a few minutes in silence when Cori's phone goes off. She reaches for it, makes a face, and flips it toward me to see who's calling. Cassidy's name appears on the screen.

"What?" Corinna snaps out. I huff out a giggle. Corinna disengages our hands to hold a finger to her lips, so I hush and listen to her end of the conversation.

"I'm with Alison. Why?" Her face becomes pinched. Suddenly, her head snaps straight. "No. No way in hell. Are you crazy?"

The acid begins to churn in my stomach.

"No, I don't think it's a good idea for you to drop by, Cassidy. No, nor Em, or Phil. Even Holly. Keep everyone away," Corinna rasps.

"You know what? I can't believe I'm about to say this, but y'all are being a bunch of bullies. Right now, Ali doesn't need your crap. The last time she talked to you, you accosted her in her office." A myriad of emotions cross Corinna's face as she listens to Cassidy. They range from resignation to irritation, to flat-out anger. "No, this isn't one of those times when talking it through will make things better. I remember not too long ago when you froze people out too. No, I am not making comparisons to the situations, Cassidy. What I'm saying is that people take time to process things, and you have to respect that."

Corinna rolls her eyes at me, like what she's saying should be fairly obvious.

"Hand me the phone, Cori," I say quietly. Before I can change my mind, I want to get a few things out of my system.

Corinna covers the mouthpiece. "Are you sure?"

I nod. I'm exhausted, and I just want to sleep.

She puts the phone on speaker. Taking a deep breath, I open my mouth, and no words come out because Cassidy is still talking.

"...I just want to talk with her, Corinna. So does Keene. That's all. Just talk," I hear Cassidy plead.

"What makes you think I want to speak to either you or Keene right now, Cassidy?" I say coldly.

"Ali?" Cassidy chokes.

"You have no idea what you and your brother have managed to do to me in a few short days. Not a clue. You both took something from me, and I'm not quite ready to forget that." I feel Corinna's hand squeeze my shoulder.

"No, honey, that's not the way it was meant," Cassidy tries to convince me.

"That's the way it felt. And right now, that's all I care about." I run my hand over my face. "As for your brother, while it's none of your business, it was scary and exciting to see that place you claim he has. You know, a heart." I laugh, but it's harsh. "Apparently, he took offense to my caution. Since it was his way or no way, I chose the easy solution—my way." Hearing nothing, I check Corinna's phone to make sure the call is still connected because Cassidy isn't responding. "You'll excuse me if I don't want to play his games anymore, or yours. I'm worth a hell of a lot more than that."

"Alison..." Cassidy cries, but I'm ruthless as I hang up Corinna's phone, right before I collapse in her arms in tears.

"I shouldn't have had to say all that, Cori."

"I know, but tell me you don't feel better for getting it out."

I do, and I don't. I'm glad my family finally understands where my head and my heart are at. I'm so vulnerable, I don't think I can take another hit or blow without breaking. When I say as much to Corinna, she asks, "Who originally said that quote you love so much about strength, courage, and confidence?"

"God. It comes from the book of Isaiah in the Bible," I mumble. The quote is about not being put to shame over our pasts because the humiliation of our youth will disappear.

Corinna rolls her eyes. "Not the one from the Bible. The other one."

I sigh, sadly. "You mean Eleanor Roosevelt?"

"Yes, that one. The one where you gain more from every experience where you stop letting yourself feel fear." She cups my face. "Stop being afraid. Don't run from life."

I nod, not able to do much more, hampered by the pain and doubts that enslave me.

Corinna helps me stand, pulling me to my feet. "And know I always believe in you. Who else was strong enough to hold my hand and get me through nights full of dark?" She puts her arm around my shoulder. "Come on, let's get you back upstairs. You look like you're about to collapse."

After sitting with me in bed for a while, hoping I'll fall back asleep while she strokes my hair, Corinna admits she has to head back to the office to get a cake completed for a sixteenth birthday party tomorrow.

Brushing her lips across my cheek, she makes her way downstairs and out the back door of my house, closing it softly behind her.

After she leaves, my mind refuses to let me rest, wondering what to do, how to feel. I stare at photos of me with various family members that I can see from my bed. I'm unwillingly pulled into memory after memory when finally I can't take it anymore. Tossing aside the covers, I pull my shirt over my head.

Within moments, I'm on my way down the long drive at a fast clip, searching for my escape.

23

KEENE

I leave Cassidy, Phil, and Em devastated in Cassidy's office. While normally I'd have sooner had someone shove raw bamboo under my fingernails than listen to the rehash of Cassidy's conversation with Alison, I have a new appreciation for what is holding her back.

The bedrock of this family is strength and pride, and here I've been doing nothing but undermining Alison's confidence. I don't even know why.

Thundering down the stairs, I'm about to go out the front when I hear the back door slam shut.

It has to be Corinna. No one would dare enter Corinna's sacred domain that way.

I hesitate, my thumb still on the latch of the door, ready to fling it open. Deciding it's worth a shot, I make my way back to the kitchen.

"Corinna," I call out. I don't want to scare her, and announcing my presence might get me a moment's grace.

Big mistake.

As I enter the kitchen, a platter full of whipped cream comes flying with unerring accuracy at my face. Red-tinted, strawberry-flavored whipped cream splatters all over my pristine white button-down and all over the wall behind me. The remains clatter loudly to the ground.

"W–what in the fuck was that?" I sputter, wiping my eyes so I can get a clear look at Alison's deranged sister.

Corinna smirks, completely unrepentant. A quick glance around the room shows the cake she's baking is pale blue, with graham cracker along the edge to resemble a beach. It's remarkable, truly a work of art. What it doesn't have is the color red anywhere near it.

That means her attack was planned and deliberate. I was ambushed. Gee, I wonder why.

"Are you crazy?" I bellow. I hear footfalls and quickly surmise we're about to be joined by at least one member of the Freeman family.

I couldn't be that lucky.

Instead, it's Caleb who pokes his head around the door. "Corinna, is everything okay? What the hell happened in here?" Opening the door into the kitchen, he carefully steps around the mess surrounding me. "Going for a new look instead of industrial clean?"

She merely shrugs and says, "The cleanup will be worth it. Hell, I was tempted to chuck a bowl full of red food coloring, but I was feeling gracious."

"What?" I yell, incensed.

"Yes, indeed. Food coloring is made up of food dye that can damage your eyes, causing stinging and burning. By diluting it with the whipped cream, it was slower to fly at you and permitted time for you to close your eyes. I couldn't give a shit if your face looks like a clown." She turns back to the cake in front of her, dismissing me.

"What the hell did I do to you?" I stomp over to the paper towels attached to the wall. Ripping them out, I run them over my hair and clumps of the red whipped cream fall to the floor.

Caleb chokes back his laughter.

"Oh, it's a buddy system—all for one, sister from another mister kind of thing. I'm sure you understand. It's like...Oh, wait, you might not understand that. It involves things like thought and having a heart. Dear me, should I apologize?" Snickering, Corinna resumes her decorating.

Her hands are moving so fast to add depth to the layers with the flat of her knife while she slowly spins the cake, I'm dizzy. Turning away, I stomp over to the sink. Without moving, Corinna says, "Farthest sink to the right. The first two have a sanitizing solution in them for the dishes."

"Thanks," I mutter. Even though I'm a hot mess, at least she wasn't trying to physically injure me. She only wants to humiliate me.

Caleb gives in to the laughter he's been holding back. "As long as there's no emergency."

Corinna looks up and offers him a beatific smile. "No, but while you're here, can you take out the trash?" She shoots me a meaningful look. "It stinks."

"Damnit, Corinna. I just wanted to—"

"Talk to me about Ali? I'm never going to do that with you. I have never, and I do mean never"—she slams the decorating knife down on the table; I'm pleased to see a small splatter of blue icing land somewhere she probably didn't intend for it to go—"have seen my sister in such a state. Over a man? Over you? What have you done to make it worth it?" Dismissing me, she picks up her knife. Turning the cake this way and that, she locates the splatter and immediately begins to work it into the frosting, as if it was an intended design and not an error. "Now get out of my kitchen. As a result of your crap, I'll be here forever making up time."

Caleb's hand grabs the soggy elbow of my dress shirt before I can respond. "I'll get him out of your hair, Corinna."

"I'd appreciate that." She returns her attention back to the cake.

I open my mouth to respond when Caleb mutters, "Don't make it worse," as he drags me out of the kitchen.

Walking me all the way out of the foyer and onto the porch, he holds his tongue before he lays into me. "What were you possibly thinking going to Corinna?"

I was thinking Corinna could give me some insight on how to fix things with Alison. Maybe tell me how Alison was feeling. Maybe she might be able to give me some hope.

"Obviously, I wasn't, Caleb." I rub a hand down my face. I touch something soft and pull away some more whipped cream. Touching it to my lips, I savor it. The taste is light, sweet, and if the price I paid for my stupidity was looking like an extra on a Halloween set, at least it had some fringe benefit.

"I hope she didn't put ipecac in it or something," Caleb mutters.

Even as I'm mentally berating myself for not thinking of that, I say, "Thanks for the advance warning, buddy."

Caleb sighs. "You've actually got bigger issues, Keene."

Shit. Melody. I mentally brace. "What did you find out?"

"Melody charmed her way past your doorman last night. He'll need to be taken care of when this is over." Caleb's tight expression reflects what I'm feeling. "She sat outside your condo the entire night. When you never showed, she went downstairs and hit up your super. Fortunately, he does know how to do his job." Caleb takes a deep breath. "We found out after talking with him that he tried to call the office to verify the cock-and-bull story she dreamed up. The minute his hand touched the phone, she cold-cocked him with her P938, grabbed his keys, and entered your place." Caleb takes a deep breath. "As you know, we have eyes in there."

I pace back and forth under the portico of the deck, trying to get some semblance of control over my emotions. "And?"

Caleb shakes his head back and forth, not in refusal, but in regret.

"Tell me!" I seethe.

Caleb looks away and swallows. Whatever he's about to say, I know it's bad. My hands tighten into fists at my sides.

"Melody started in your bedroom. After she stripped off her clothes, she crawled onto your bed and proceeded to..." Caleb's voice trails off. His throat convulses. "Take care of things on your bed. Multiple times. Then she went into your closet and got one of your shirts before she walked around your place and proceeded to destroy anything that had the appearance of a woman in it." He's silent as I absorb the implications. "We have it all on camera, Keene. We've already gone to the judge to order a warrant for the breaking, entering, and destruction of property. We'll review the tapes to see what else we can tag her with. We've also obtained a restraining order against her for you. Because of the nature of what she did, and the visibility of the pictures, I obtained one for Cassidy too." Caleb's voice is filled with barely suppressed fury. "Unfortunately, the rest of the family is vulnerable."

"Did you contact judges here in Connecticut as well?" I'm a lawyer, but I'm not certain about reciprocity in this area of the law.

Caleb nods. "The order is good anywhere in the country, but there's a glitch."

There always is. "What?" I'm weary already, and this has barely begun.

Caleb moves over to the porch railing and braces his back against it, facing me. "She's not around to serve the order to, Keene. Right now, what the processors have is an empty piece of paper. We've got someone camped out at your place. The analysts are trying to use facial rec to find her, but for fuck's sake, she knows how to find the wind and stay there. When she's not fucking crazy, she does know how to do her job. It's why she was recruited in the first place." His frustration is palpable. "Which means, not only are you in danger but so are my wife and kids. So is this family."

Rapidly running through possible scenarios in my head, I ask, "Do you want me to leave?" I don't want to. I want to stop this crazy bitch with my bare hands. I have to fix what's left of my home and take a good look at my life. I want—no, I need, to fix what's between Alison and me.

Caleb shakes his head. "No way. First, we're stronger together. Second, I think she'll end up coming to us." His dark eyes meet mine. "And this bitch gets no mercy."

"None whatsoever," I agree.

Caleb nods toward the mansion that houses Amaryllis Events. "How much do we tell them? We can't keep them in the dark completely, Keene. Right now, Cass assumes I'm here because of what happened with Ali." Throwing me a hard look, he continues. "I assume that situation isn't going to last forever."

Even though I know Caleb has good intentions, the last thing I want to do is add fuel to the Freeman rumor mill. "I'm working on it."

He snorts. "Obviously, it's going well. Red is your color." He grins, referring to the whipped cream Corinna threw at me.

I give him the finger. "Like I said, I'm working on it. I fucked up." Caleb's lack of response is all I need to know that he agrees with me. We sit quietly for a few minutes before he says something completely asinine.

"Personally, I'm all for honesty in this situation. The more eyes, the better," he announces.

"Are you crazy? Telling my sister's family we brought a stalker to their doorstep? When she's waddling around pregnant with your kids? They'll stake me out in the front yard," I say cynically.

"Not everyone," Caleb disagrees.

I raise an eyebrow in challenge.

"Cassidy wouldn't," he argues.

"And she would be the only one who wouldn't," I say amenably.

"If you'd just fix what went wrong with Ali," Caleb starts.

I finally lose it. "Don't you think I'm trying? I fucked things up so badly, I don't even know where to start."

"The question is why?" Cassidy says from behind me.

"Hi, baby," Caleb greets her. He holds out his arm to his wife, and she moves beneath it, wrapping hers around his waist.

"Why did you fuck things up so badly, Keene?" My sister's eyes are troubled.

"Look at what I did to her before. I felt more with her than any other woman...hell, more than any other person in my life, and I snuck out the damn door while she was in the shower. I've acted like a spoiled two-year-old whose favorite toy has been taken away when she doesn't do exactly what I want her to. I've never been the guy looking for forever." I'm suddenly ashamed. "What if I'm just like him, Cass?"

Saying it out loud lifts this burden from my shoulders. I've been living under this cloak of pain, shame, and fear from what my father did to my mother, and by extension, me. And the hell of it is, if I was honest with myself, those are the same reasons I keep myself from truly connecting with any woman.

I'm stiff as a board, waiting for the condemnation when I witness it.

My sister's laughter. Cassidy is practically falling over from it. If it wasn't for Caleb's arm around her waist, I think she might be on the porch floor.

I'm about to blast her, when she holds up a hand and wheezes out, "Hold on, Keene. Let me get my breath."

Figuring my future nieces, nephews, or combination thereof need oxygen, I hold my tongue. Barely. No one ever said patience was my strong suit.

Once Cassidy regains her breath, she balls her fist and sucker punches me in the stomach.

"Jesus Christ, Cass. What the hell was that for?" I yell.

"For being such a horse's ass. Who the hell was it that looked for me for close to twenty years?" Before I can open my mouth, she answers her own question. "You. Who walked into gunfire and took a bullet for his best friend? You. Who got my name tattooed on his leg? You. So now you're trying to tell me that part of your problem with Ali is that you don't want to be our father? Keene, honey, you never could be our father." She shakes her head. "That's ridiculous for you to think that's possible. From what I understand, he only looked out for himself. You look out for everyone but you. So cut the crap, admit you have feelings for my sister, and stop jerking her around or you will lose her. Of that I'm sure." Cassidy takes a deep breath. "I should know. I'm flailing alongside you with no oars, trying to get back to shore to fight for her."

Caleb brushes his lips across Cassidy's temple. "You'll find a way to get through to her, my love. I know you will."

I watch them stand together and grapple with the emotions battering me from every side. Pleasure and pain equally battle for space before they splinter in two, leaving me with something completely unforeseen. Envy. It pours through me. I can't escape it.

It took my sister and my best friend to show me I carelessly threw that chance away for no good reason. I need to get away to think.

Clearing my throat, I ask, "Is there a place around here I can work out? I need to do something. Clear my head." Normally, I'd hit the gym at Hudson, but since Caleb and I won't be back there for the foreseeable future, I'd better get the lay of the land in Collyer.

"There's the workout room at the farm," Caleb comments. "It's not bad for weights and universal. I hate running in that room though. I feel like I'm going to fall through the damned floor. That treadmill was obviously not purchased for someone our size," he says wryly.

Knowing the powerhouse equipment we have back at Hudson, I mentally groan. That means I'll be running in this blasted humidity.

I wonder if I should shower off Corinna's "gift" before I work out?

"I'm going for a run." No need for them to worry when they don't find me back at their house for a few hours. I need to find some place I can think without prying eyes.

"You should drop by Tabor's Sporting Goods in town," Caleb says. "They know the best trails around Collyer. Some might give you more of a challenge than others."

I nod. Good idea. I don't need to be lost in the wilderness when I can use a trusted trail the locals know about.

"Leave your GPS on," Caleb warns, reminding me of the inherent danger we brought to Collyer.

"Copy that." Squeezing my sister's arm and tossing a two-finger salute to Caleb, I jog to my car and roar out of the parking lot.

Soon enough, I'm out of Tabor's with a decent trail that will keep me busy for the next hour, with a promise of a vista overlooking the town that should be perfect to clear my crowded head. After changing into running gear, I leave my car at Cassidy and Caleb's and take off.

Finding a comfortable pace, I think about everything Caleb told me about Melody. Fury drives my legs faster. Everything in my place destroyed. I make a mental note to get my super a bonus and to have my place gutted. I also note I should beef up security around my storage unit here in Connecticut.

Not surprisingly, my thoughts move to Alison and everything Cassidy said before.

Do I have that in me? That same ability to fight past the legacy of our father when I see his face in the mirror every single day? Is it possible for one woman to go to war against my demons, give me hope, and bring out the feelings I've suppressed for so long?

Turning toward the tree line, I pull out the directions Tabor's gave me. I begin the incline to the summit after giving Caleb a ping to let him know I'm safe.

24

ALISON

There's something magical about the time right before dusk. The honeysuckle bushes I brush up against have had all day to warm in the sun, and the scent they release almost drowns me. Deer come out to graze in the open fields, easily leaping over the white post and rail fences lining the horse farms around the edges of Collyer. I hear laughter, smell barbecues and charred meat, and one thought passes through my mind. I hate how at odds I am with my family.

I've just reached the stone steps and head for the summit. This run was needed, and seeing Collyer from this view gives me time to just breathe.

I climb up to the ledge, just like I did a few days ago. It seems so far away. How did my life and my heart become such a mess in such a short amount of time?

I curl my knees to my chest and sit in the shadows of the darkening sun, trying to figure out when we all stopped trying when I hear the snap of a branch. My head whips up to search my surrounds, looking for an animal. It's not unheard of to see a fox in these hills.

But then I hear his voice, and anger takes over my sadness.

Is no place sacred anymore?

"I swear, Caleb, you have to see this vista to believe it. I can't believe you haven't run this. The sunset from up here is amazing. No, I'm just going to sit down for a while and think about everything that's happening." Keene's voice goes quiet as he listens to my brother-in-law. "No, I wasn't followed. I can't imagine how I would have been followed unless she went into the store to get the trail map, but my GPS is on just in case." He pauses. "Right. Later."

Long minutes pass where I stay in the shadows, and Keene stares out over Collyer, looking like a king staring down over his fiefdom. As I watch from my perch above him, emotions play over his face. It's like watching a film noir. He's the weary warrior, racked with guilt and overthinking.

Keene moves near the edge. "Jesus, this is breathtaking." His whisper carries over the distance between us. "Alison would love this." I watch him raise his camera and snap a picture before ducking his dark head.

A minute later, my phone buzzes against my hip. Warily, I pull out my phone.

Keene's text weakens me. *I can see the first star over the sunset. If I believed in such things, I'd wish for you to talk to me. Please, Alison.*

I look over his head. He's still facing Collyer, his arms crossed. He's right. Right over where the sun is dropping, you can see the first star. Damn him for being right. Damn him for being sweet. Damn him for being here where I have no resistance.

Before my brain can connect with my fingers, I begin to type. *Then move away from the edge before my urge to kick you off really takes over.*

I see the phone light up against Keene's arm where he's been holding it. He quickly reads the message and turns. "Where are you?" he rasps out.

"On a ledge about forty feet behind you," I say quietly.

He starts to take a step forward and then stops. "I swear, I didn't know you were here."

I nod before I realize he can't see me in the shadows. "I realize that."

He hesitates. "I don't want to interrupt your peace more than I already have."

Okay, coming from Keene, that's actually...sweet. "I'll come down." I slowly make my way off the small ledge until there's about ten feet between us. I clear my throat and say, "Hi."

Keene takes one step forward and then another. Finally, a third. He's in touching distance. "Hi." He reaches up and pushes some hair that's clinging to my cheek away from my face. He frowns. "You've been crying."

I shrug. "Letting off some steam."

"Not ready to share?"

I shake my head emphatically. Definitely not.

Surprising me, he says, "Okay." He hesitates. "Can we sit?"

Crossing my legs, I immediately drop down Indian-style at his feet. He blinks at me a few times before he chuckles.

"Keene, you do realize I'm the resident smart-ass of the family?"

Still chuckling, he maneuvers down next to me and says, "I think that title passes between you all, depending on the day."

"Eh. Maybe, maybe not. Cassidy's still learning her way. Particularly when we talk about sex." I shoot him a small smile. Maybe this is how I need to navigate it, one small conversation at a time.

Chuckling, he throws an arm around my shoulders. "Nope. You're not going to distract me with a discussion about my sister and sex. Especially since her babies were conceived by immaculately. Caleb hasn't touched her."

Laughing, I lean into his shoulder and jostle him. "Keep telling yourself that, buddy. I've heard stories."

Keene groans.

The pain around my heart is different now. Keene's a good guy. No, he's a great guy if he'd let himself be one. Yes, there's this crazy, stupid attraction between us, but maybe not for this life. I take a deep breath and speak at the same time he does.

"I owe you a huge apology, Alison."

"It's okay you decided we're just family."

I'm proud I got it out. I'll be all right, eventually. We'll be one big happy family and move on. Keene will always hold a place in my heart.

And then I feel his arm drop as he starts laughing hysterically.

"What the hell?" I snap.

"Back at ya, babe. I told you already, there is no way you'll ever be my sister." His voice is laced with amusement.

"And then you acted like a dick last night, remember?"

"Which is why I was apologizing." Keene leverages himself in front of me on his knees. "You deserved exactly five percent of what happened after we left the restaurant."

"Which part is that?" I sneer, my anger coming back in full force. I jump from sitting to my feet in about point three seconds.

He stands as well. "The part where I kissed you. The rest was self-protective bullshit I dished out because I'm scared as hell of what I feel when I'm with you." He laughs, and the bitter sound isn't pleasant. "You've never met him. Did you know I look just like him? What if I inherited his shitty behavior too?"

Well, crap.

"You're not your father," I say carefully.

"How would you know?" he lashes out.

"Jesus, I swear it's just like I told Cori. You turn into an asshole the minute the sun sets. Cool it with the vampire dickness and I might tell you!"

"Vampire dickness?"

"Yes! Every time we've been together when the sun's gone down, you've turned into an asshole. I'm about to stop talking, texting, seeing, or speaking with you unless the sun is in the sky."

He steps forward and wraps his arms around me, his body shaking.

"It's not funny," I warn.

"It really is." I can hear the laughter in his voice.

"Keene."

"Alison. First, I'm pretty certain I can be a dick all the time.

Second." He never gets the second item on his list out as he doubles over laughing with me in his arms.

It's such a great feeling, I give him a few moments before I repeat, "You're not your father."

His hilarity sobers up quickly. "I hope I'm not, but I was never willing to try with any other woman. With you, I keep screwing up by being myself. Who knows what will happen if I let things get deeper between us."

There's no way he can't feel the erratic thump of my heart at his words. Still, I do my best to deny it, and him. "I want to tell you there's no way things are going to get deeper between us, but I guess that ship has already sailed?"

"And that, right there, is one of the many reasons I can't deny this anymore. You're honest, even when you don't want to be." His arms tighten slightly.

"I can't do this hot and cold, Keene."

He doesn't respond. Verbally, that is. Instead, he pulls me tighter. "Do you know what I felt tonight?"

"No, what?"

"Envy. Pure envy at what my sister has with Caleb. I was watching them together, and it blew me away, realizing what they've found." He's quiet while he gets his thoughts together. "I resented Cassidy on so many levels when I first met her." I knew this already but keep quiet while he continues. "I tried to stop Caleb and Cass when they first got together. Later, I hated myself for not recognizing her as my sister. But you know the thing that still gets to me the most?" His hands brush up and down my arms. "It's that I was more interested in knowing I finally knew how to find you. When Cass slid that fucking phone with your photo across the table, she proved I was a sanctimonious asshole. I didn't recognize my own sister after looking into her eyes, at her hair, and her face. I didn't realize she was the sister I'd been looking for almost twenty years. All I could see was you."

Whoa. "Seriously?"

"Alison, I can barely see other people when you're in the room with me. I can barely control the urge to toss you over my shoulder

and find the nearest flat surface half the time. The other half, I want
to wrap my arms around you and dare someone to come between us.
Does this in any way sound rational? Logical? That's what's been
between us since the night we met. And if I hadn't promised myself
I'd find my sister before I ever fell in love with a woman, do you think
I could have walked out of the Plaza that night?"

The twilight is outlining the planes of his face. It's harder to make
out his features now. I can't see the truth or the lie in his eyes, even
though his words are binding me to him through the shroud of darkness. "You don't need to say that," I whisper.

"I know I don't." His voice is harsh through the air. "But it's time
for some truths between us. It's the only way you'll give me a chance."

"Why? Tell me that, Keene," I challenge him. "I have a father in
jail for trying to sell me..."

"And I have one who should be in jail for failing to find my sister,"
he interrupts smoothly. "Your point is?"

Well, crap. When he puts it like that, I don't have an argument.
Keene's right. My father was a direct perpetrator of his crimes. His
father is just as guilty of the crimes against Cassidy as the monsters
who took her, at least in our eyes, because he forgot about her. The
bastard.

"You scare the hell out of me, Keene." He stiffens. "I never know
which you I'm going to get. One minute, you're the concerned lover
lambasting your sister over the way I'm being maligned at work. The
next, you're dumping me in the middle of Eighth Avenue. Do I need a
crucifix and garlic?"

He sighs. "No, but—"

"If I give you this chance, Keene, this is it. No more crazy. I can
deal with fights. Look at my family. Hell, you're a part of it, so you'd
better get used to them. What I won't deal with is being made a fool
of a third time."

Breath whooshes from his nostrils as it releases. "I never meant to
make you feel like a fool the first time, Alison."

"No, just yesterday," I say with saccharine sweetness.

"Yesterday, I was being a spoiled child," he admits.

"Excellent. We're in agreement."

"We're us. We're going to disagree."

"Quite a bit." I smile. "I imagine it'll be fun to make up once we get to that point."

There's a delicate pause. "Once we get to what point? Sex?" His voice is a mixture of outrage and disbelief.

I want to howl laughing. Oh, Keene, you poor, poor man. Better get ready to enjoy your hand for a little while longer. "Yes."

"You realize that horse left the barn a long time ago." Now he sounds like Keene— irritated.

"Yes. And I feel like we need to have a couple of dates under our belt before we jump back into bed," I calmly explain.

His teeth must be clenched. I'm freaking delighted. "How many?"

"Dates? I don't know." I pause to think. "Thirty?" I wait for the explosion.

He doesn't disappoint.

"Thirty? Thirty separate dates? Not a date that lasts thirty hours?" His voice is so loud, I imagine they can hear him back on the farm.

I'm biting my lip to keep my laughter contained. "What's your negotiation, counselor?"

"Three," he says firmly.

"I don't think so. Fifteen."

"Five." His arms slip around my waist.

I like his idea, but I don't want to give in too quickly. "Does that include the family dinner this week?"

"Absolutely." His voice is firm.

"No, I don't think so. That's more like a coming out party. Besides, you're basically giving Phil an opportunity to harangue me all night. Ten, plus the family dinner."

"Five plus the family dinner, or I swear to God, I'll end up bending you over in front of your entire family and let Phil take pictures," he threatens.

I finally lose it, laughing hysterically.

He grumbles, "I was so had."

"Not for five more dates," I singsong.

Smack! The slap Keene delivers to my ass, wearing only running shorts, feels almost as good as it does as when it's bare. I can hear the taunt in his voice when he says, "Think about that when you're using your fingers later, baby."

"Asshole," I mutter. "Ready to head back?"

He looks down the way he came up. "Those steps should be interesting in the dark."

I pull him over to the beginner's trail. "Please. I'm not a complete idiot."

Swiftly dropping a kiss on my lips, he starts down the trail, using his phone as a flashlight. "I never, ever thought you were, Alison."

"Good. While we're walking home, why don't you tell me why you and Caleb are really working out of Collyer?"

25

KEENE

Damn, I forgot I was on the phone with Caleb when I reached the summit. I keep walking when I realize Alison isn't following behind me. She's waiting for me to respond.

"Caleb and I have a small problem," I start, wondering how much I should tell her. Do I tell her that I'm being stalked by an ex-lover? Not only that, it's a woman who worked for my company and was caught on film masturbating on my bed? The same bed I'd hoped to take Alison home to last night, right before Melody destroyed my place?

I don't think so.

"Really? You both have an office and you've decided the scenery around Collyer is just so spectacular in the summer, you want to enjoy it from our boardroom? Or was it the suits that were getting to you? Not that your ass doesn't look delectable in one, but I can appreciate how the coat might get hot as you're skulking the halls at this time of the year," Alison drawls as she walks beside me.

Sweet Jesus, that mouth.

I reach out an arm, hook her around the waist, and drop a hard kiss on her lips. "How'd you know we'd taken over the boardroom?" I'm amused, despite the gravity of the situation.

Alison chortles. "Please. That was the first of many things Corinna told me this afternoon when she dropped by."

I reach for my crusty hair and say, "Corinna, yeah..." in my most menacing tone of voice.

It's Alison's turn to pause on the trail. "Uh-oh. What did Cori do?"

"You mean you didn't notice the new red streaks in my hair, or did I manage to get them all out? I still feel them." Slapping my hand against the back of my neck, I start walking. "And apparently, the bugs like them too."

She starts laughing. "What did she do?"

"I'm sure you'll hear about it."

We've reached the end of the mountain trail, and Alison grabs my arm and points to a worn pathway. "See over there? That'll take us right to the fence behind the farm. Cuts about two miles off our walk."

With the gnats and mosquitos starting to think my whipped-cream hair is their personal snack, I'm all for shortening the distance. "Lead on."

"Now that's two things," Alison comments as we cross the dark-ened field.

"Two things, what?" I'm finding the nearest shower the minute I can. Along with a bottle of rubbing alcohol so I don't scratch these bites all night.

"Two things for you to tell me. Pick which one you want to tell me first. Why you're in Collyer, or what Cori did to you that's making you the newest hive for every mosquito and gnat in a fifty-mile radius. Because while the first is intriguing, the second is making me want to smear you with it every time you're with me. My own personal bug trap." Even through the darkness, I can hear the smile in Alison's voice.

I inhale deeply and manage to swallow some kind of flying bug.

Coughing, I choke out, "She flung a platter of red-dyed whipped cream at me when I went to talk to her today in the kitchen."

"Oh my God, Keene! Are you okay?" Alison exclaims.

"Yeah. She didn't throw it very hard, but it was seriously messy." I'm pleased she sounds concerned.

"No, I meant about the bug you swallowed. Be glad she diluted it with whipped cream. Red food coloring stings like a bitch if it gets in your eyes."

Before she can move away, I pull her closer into the cloud of bugs swarming around me. "What, no sympathy for the mess?"

Even in the darkness, I can see her head cock to the side. "For Cori, sure. Whipped cream is a pain to clean. You, on the other hand, totally deserved it."

I touch my still-sticky hair to hers. "Seriously?" I don't know what I was expecting. Maybe a little sympathy? Then again, knowing what I put her through last night, taking a platter of whipped cream to the face was a small price to pay and I know it.

"Yep. I only wish someone had taken pictures. Or video. We like to get that kind of stuff made into T-shirts for the holidays," Alison sighs regretfully.

"Your family is crazy, baby," I tell her honestly.

"It's your family now too, Keene. No take backs."

It's an amazing feeling to realize I wouldn't want to.

We start walking again. "What's the other thing that happened?" She hasn't forgotten.

I'm quiet, at a loss for words, thinking about how to explain the situation with Melody. A few minutes pass and I'm surprised when we reach the fence that cordons off the Freeman farm from the property that surrounds it. Directly behind the fence are the lush pine trees that stand tall behind Alison's house. Looking around, I don't see a break in the miles of fence. I watch as Alison contorts her body between the middle and lowest rails. That hot little move pulls the back of her running shorts up so I can see the cheek of her ass.

"Jesus, Alison, what do you wear under your shorts?" Of its own volition, my finger drags across the exposed skin where her cheek meets her thigh.

When she pushes to her feet, she's on the other side of the railing. Leaning against it, she says, "Nothing. It causes too much chafing."

My mind blanks. When my hand smacked her ass before, it really was like touching her smooth, perfect skin. I growl right before I place my hands on the post and hop over the top rail.

She backs up, applauding. "Impressive. What's your next act?"

"Stop moving and I'll show you," I bite out.

"Nope. Five dates, remember?" she taunts.

"Doesn't mean I can't do this." I grab her, spinning to push her against the nearest post, and slam my lips down on hers.

Every time my lips touch hers now, my heart stops and restarts to a new rhythm. Sometimes the blood flowing through it pulsates with despair, sometimes with longing, but always with desire. Always with need. Always with passion. Tonight, her kiss almost brings me to my knees.

I hear her soft moan as she breathes into my mouth. I swear that moan ignites a fire along my skin.

I know I could make her forget this asinine five-date rule simply by touching her very visible skin, but I want to show her I can be a better man and live up to the things I say.

I need to rebuild her trust in me that I seem to shatter over and over again.

Tearing my mouth away, I press her head into my chest, and what comes out of my mouth surprises even me.

"We have someone targeting the business. Me specifically. Someone who used to work for us."

Alison pulls back. "Are you in danger? Is the family?"

I don't know. How dangerous is a stalker who wants to tie you up and fuck you until your dick falls off? "Caleb and I don't think so, or we wouldn't have come here," I say neutrally.

She nods. "Thank you."

"For what?" I'm confused.

"For being honest and telling me the truth. I also suspect that's part of what has had you on edge the last several days."

"Part of it. Come on, let's keep walking." I grab her hand, but she holds still.

"Do I owe you an apology?" Her voice is quiet in the dark.

I could seriously kick my sister's ass right now. If she wasn't a hundred months pregnant with twins, I likely would. "You didn't do anything wrong. Crazy ex-employees set me further on that edge. I owe you the apology, which I would like to give you over a series of dates and other courting rituals I will likely suck at, as I have never attempted them before."

Her burst of laughter is a balm to my ragged senses. "You have so dated. Caleb tells stories of the two of you in college all the time."

Note to self, schedule appointments to interview for a new best friend this week. "That was a long time ago. I haven't dated a woman beyond one, maybe two dates, in about fifteen years." She's still not moving. "Baby, at the rate we're moving, what's left of Corinna's whipped-cream massacre is going to fossilize in my hair."

She smirks and starts walking through the maze of pine trees. I see the security lights shining from her back deck. Good girl.

Walking her to the back door, I turn to her and run a hand over her blonde hair. "How about we finish this conversation over breakfast tomorrow when I pick you up for work?"

She swallows nervously, causing my brows to lower.

I thought we had already agreed on seeing where this was going to lead, and then I hear her whisper, "I'm not sure if I'm ready to go into the office yet. I'm not entirely certain they want me back."

Now I really want to kick my sister and the rest of her family in the ass. Except for Corinna. I'd welcome the whipped-cream ambush every day if I could eliminate the uncertainty out of Alison's voice.

"Baby, they are way more uncomfortable about what happened than you are." I shake her slightly. "You did everything right with the way you handled me. You did everything right to maintain your self-esteem. They were wrong, and Caleb agrees with me. Corinna agrees with me. You need to get past this. It isn't you."

"Cassidy thinks I was wrong." And hearing those whispered words pulls out my protective instinct full force.

"Right. We can go over to Cass's house and deal with this tonight." Her appalled face answers that for me, so I continue talking. "Or we can go to breakfast, get you some of your favorite coffee, go to the office tomorrow and basically tell them all to shove it. And since I'll be in hearing distance, I can jump in if they try to pull any bullshit." I wait for her to respond, and when she doesn't, I tack on, "And if it gets too bad, we can enlist Corinna to make more whipped cream."

Alison grins. "Option B."

I relax. "What time should I be here?"

"What time do you need to start work?" she counters.

I think for a minute. "My first call is at nine. Is seven too early?"

She snorts derisively. "Please, Keene. I'm the one who normally gets up to run well before that. I'll see you at seven."

She walks away.

Just as she hits the door, I call out, "Alison?"

She turns back. "Yes?"

"Right now, it may not seem like it matters a lot, but it does."

"What does?" She looks at me quizzically.

"Taking this chance with me." I step backward slowly. "I'll see you in the morning. Sleep well."

"You too, Keene." She steps out of sight and closes the door.

Walking around the front of her house, I feel anxious and hopeful, despite the bugs that have been attacking me since the sun went down.

Almost cheerfully, I swat at my neck as I approach the converted carriage house my sister and Caleb have made their home. As I'm about to open the front door, my phone lights up with a text. Hoping it's Alison, I unlock it, and I'm visually assaulted by pictures of Melody fucking herself with objects she's stolen from my home.

I'm disgusted.

I'm appalled.

I want this over.

26

ALISON

"Is this life or death?" Corinna mumbles when I call her early the next morning.

"I don't know. Does a breakfast date with Keene before I go into the office count?" I say sarcastically.

"Holy shitballs! Yes, it does!" Corinna is clearly awake now. "When did all this happen?"

"After you threw a massive quantity of whipped cream on him, and before I woke up this morning," I reply dryly. I'm standing in my closet, trying to determine what to wear. I have the phone on speaker while I search through the racks.

"Should I apologize for that?" Corinna asks.

"Not to me. I only wish it was daylight so I could have seen the red and not just heard about it." Corinna's infectious giggle erupts on the other end of the phone. "I told him he should be grateful it wasn't straight-up red food coloring. Not like you did to me in college."

"True. But you got a new hairstyle out of it."

I can't help but agree. Silently. Back then, waking up to a third of my hair dyed red because of Corinna's fury was not pleasant. "Can we get back to the matter at hand before I demand full restitution for not eating the birthday cake you made for Colby?"

Ignoring me, she instead asks, "Did you call just so I don't come after him with a different color today?"

I laugh. "Partially. That, and I have no idea what to wear to the office."

"You're going to the office? Whoa, forget balls, it's your tits I admire, Ali."

I roll my eyes. "Let's give the credit where credit is due. Keene's practically dragging me. He wants to be there in the event someone says something nasty. That way, he can play savior."

"I guess your theory about him being a vampire wasn't entirely accurate?"

"No, and he didn't appreciate it when I told him that either."

"You did not," she laughs. "Did you?"

"I sure did. I called him a vampire dickhead," I say proudly.

Our mutual hilarity is warming my soul, but not my ass as I stand in my closet with no clothes on. "Cori, I promise I'll tell you all about this later, but what the hell do I wear today?"

I hear the rustle of her sheets. "Where's breakfast?"

I shrug before I realize she can't see me. "I'm assuming The Coffee Shop, since he mentioned my favorite coffee."

"Smart man," she mutters. "He'll hit you where you're weakest."

"Bite me," I retort.

"I'll tell Keene where to bite you instead."

"He already knows. Oh, one thing about last night. I got him to agree to a five-date, no-sex rule."

"Shut the hell up! You didn't!" She's screeching, she's laughing so hard. "Damnit, now I have to pee."

Thank God there's a dressing table in the middle of my closet that I can lean against. I'm laughing to the point I might fall down, while Corinna's losing it in my ear. I can hear the swooshing as she kicks her legs back and forth in her sheets. "I'm dying, Ali. I swear it." Her drawl is pronounced. "You are my damn hero."

"Back at ya. Now..." I spin around in my closet. "What. Should. I. Wear? I have—" Shit. "Thirteen minutes to be downstairs."

"Is your magenta silk suit clean?" I love that my sister knows my clothes as well as she knows her own.

I walk right over to the suit in question. "I'm holding it right now."

"Black pearls, black heels. Pops your coloring for your date but says don't mess with me at the office. Shows you made an effort on both fronts," Corinna says decisively.

I scan the suit for all of about two seconds. "Will I be safe if I come down to the kitchen wearing this today? I heard the red went everywhere."

She yawns. "Why do you think I'm hanging up on you in about thirty seconds and going back to sleep? I was there forever cleaning it up. I'll be in around lunch. Tell Keene or Caleb to pick up Genoa for lunch."

Genoa is a little Italian restaurant in nearby Ridgefield. It's also one of our favorite places to eat. When anyone is near the restaurant, they pick some up for everyone.

"I'll mention it at breakfast. Thanks, Cori. Go back to sleep. Love you."

"Back at ya, Ali. Knock 'em all dead." Corinna disconnects the call.

Dressing quickly, I walk over to the full-length mirror in my room. Corinna's choice of color does add a punch of color, making my eyes appear bluer. The suit's trim fit and my sky-high heels show I mean business.

Pressing a hand to settle the butterflies dancing in my stomach, I grab my black briefcase from the closet and make my way downstairs. Peeking out the window, I find Keene's Audi is already parked out front.

I open the door, saying, "I just need another minute to finish transferring my bag."

"Hold on a moment, Alison." Keene steps over the threshold then stands back before circling around me.

I start to feel anxious when he doesn't say anything. "What?" I demand in my most pugnacious voice.

"We're in agreement that this is date number one, right?" he asks.

"We are."

"Good, then I'm doing this here versus at the office." Reaching for my hand, he tugs me toward him and pulls me into his arms. In these heels, his head doesn't have as far to descend before his lips land on mine. I'm already lost in him, and he walked in the door a little less than a minute ago.

Pulling back slightly, I nibble on his lower lip. "I'm hungry."

He thrusts his tongue back into my mouth for another foray. "So am I."

I push at his chest, and he pulls away reluctantly. "For food, Keene. And I'm desperate for coffee. I need to get my bag."

He gestures with his arm. "Lead the way."

Walking in front of him, I add an extra little sway to my hips, causing him to groan. "In case you couldn't tell, baby, I really like the suit. Sexy, powerful, and delicate. It's perfect for you."

I beam at him, right before making my way over to the kitchen counter to finish transferring my briefcase. Soon, we're in his Audi and on the way to The Coffee Shop.

On our first official date.

"She seriously did not dip your hair in food coloring." Keene is astonished. He drinks his coffee and asks, "How did you not kill her?"

"First, it was Cori," I explain. "Second, I got a kickass haircut out of the deal." I toss my hair back and forth.

Keene smiles slowly. "I always wondered what makes women decide to have long or short hair. Now that's one mystery of the world solved. Psychotic sisters."

Cracking up, I reach for my mocha—extra chocolate, of course. Taking a sip, I put the cup down and try to explain. "It's not that I wasn't pissed—I was. Completely. But it wasn't like she poured it over my head or brushed it in stripes. She just dipped the ends in. If I wanted to, the ends were easy enough to snip off and I could've grown it back."

"Do I ever get to see pictures of you with long hair? I'm fascinated by the concept of this." Keene forks a bite of his eggs, lifting them to his full lips.

I grin. "Just ask any of the family when we're at the main building of the farm. There are closets filled with photos of all of us. However, remind whomever you ask that I get to pull out the albums as well."

"Some pretty bad ones?" Keene's grinning as well.

"At one point, Em thought Aqua Net was her best friend. Her hair used to reach out to here"—I gesture to my shoulder width—"pretty much every day. Phil tried every color of the rainbow at least once. Holly tried to work dreads for about two weeks before the lack of washing her head got to her."

Keene's deep laughter booms off the walls of The Coffee Shop.

Ava scurries up with a coffeepot at that moment. "Keene, do you want me to top you off? Ali, honey, do you want a cup to go today?"

I glance over Ava's shoulder at the clock. Just after eight thirty. "Yes, please. I'll take one to go." I look over at Keene.

"Same for me, Ava. Actually, can I get a second one for Caleb as well?"

"Not a problem. You two keep talking and I'll get your check ready, or should I put it on the business account?"

Just as I'm about to open my mouth, Keene responds to her with, "I got it." He reaches into his back pocket and pulls out his wallet. Removing a few bills, he hands them to her. "Keep whatever's left for the fundraising you're doing for K9s for Warriors."

Ava and Matt keep a fundraising bucket at the front of The Coffee Shop. In lieu of keeping Ava's tips, they donate them to various local, state, and national charities. This month, the lucky recipients are K9s for Warriors—a nonprofit dedicated to providing service canines to veterans suffering from PTSD, traumatic brain injury, or who experienced sexual trauma during their military service. Matt, Ava's husband, was a VA psychiatrist for a number of years and helped any number of people in Collyer with their own personal issues.

A small smile plays on my lips as I look at Keene. "That was nice of you."

"I'm hardly ever nice, Alison." Keene's voice is mocking. It's funny, now that he and I have actually spent time talking, I can see past that condescending tone. I look at his face where the blush lies along his cheeks under the neatly trimmed scruff he wears.

"Hmm. Really?" I pick up my coffee. "I know the chocolate used in my mocha is imported from France, but I didn't know the eggs were imported from Antarctica. How do penguins taste for that price?"

His cheeks burn bright red.

Gotcha.

"I...it's just..." Keene lets out a deep breath. "They're doing a good thing for an amazing organization. I'm in a position to help." He tries to oversimplify the fact that he just paid ten times what he should have for our breakfast.

"I see."

I smile as Ava walks by, leaving our to-go drinks on the table. She brushes Keene on the cheek on her way past. "You two have a good day at work!"

"We will, Ava. Thanks!" I call back. I look across the table at Keene, who looks like he's ready to bolt. "You ready to head in?"

"Funny that fifteen minutes ago, I thought I'd have to drag you in," he grumbles as he stands. Picking up his and Caleb's coffee, he steps back to let me precede him through the door.

"Funny, fifteen minutes ago, you'd have been right," I concur. We get outside of The Coffee Shop and start to cut down the alley toward Amaryllis Events when I turn sharply toward him. "Then again, generosity, benevolence, and a kind heart wrapped up in a sexy package seems to do something to me."

I press my body into his before I give him a kiss to last us both until the end of the day. Keene's unable to move, as each of his hands is filled with scorching hot coffee. But boy, can his lips move—sliding over mine, taking control of the kiss. I hold my mocha away from us as I run my free hand from his hair down his shirt, feeling each ripple of his delicious abs.

A few moments later, I step back and wipe my lip gloss from his lips. "Like I said, there's something about that combo." I turn on my heel and keep walking.

Catching up to me, he rasps, "That was a hell of a way to end a first date."

I laugh. "Please. That wasn't the end of the date. The end of the date is us walking through those doors. It's like meeting the parents for the first time."

He stops dead in his tracks. "Oh, hell no."

"Don't worry about it. I don't let Phil scare me, and neither should you." I pat his cheek condescendingly.

"It isn't Phil I give a crap about, it's my sister. I can't be a jackass to my pregnant sister." He honestly looks like his eyes are about to roll back in his head.

Hmm. "She might not be able to make it downstairs," I point out. "She is moving slower these days."

"She's about to become a mother. I swear those hormones release some kind of special sense because she was practically waiting by her front door when I got back to her place last night."

"We could ignore them," I say as we approach Keene's car. He places the coffee on top to reach for his keys. "Cassidy tried that when we were grilling her about Caleb. It sorta worked."

"I heard about that night from Caleb. Apparently, it involved you all making food penises and drinking bottles of wine. Not happening." Keene is adamant.

"Did Caleb ever show you the pictures?" I bend over to reach into the back of Keene's Audi, grabbing my briefcase.

He groans but recovers quickly.

"Of food dicks? Why the hell would I want to see that?"

I try, but I can't control my laughter anymore. Keene's expression is too much for me to handle. "Babe, I meant the ones of me, Cassidy, and Em. We totally drunk texted him. The pictures are a riot. If I'm not mistaken, the next day is when he and Cassidy—"

"Stop. I can't listen to this. You're killing me." He pins me against the car.

"Then shut me up," I taunt.

With a wolfish smile, he does. A few moments later, he says, "Now let's see if Cassidy can make it to the foyer before you make it to your office since she was looking out the window just now."

Oh. My. God. "Jesus, you're such a vampire dickhead!" I stomp toward the porch steps.

"It's daylight, baby. You have got to get this idea that I'm a vampire out of your head. Like I said, I'm just a regular old dick." The laughter is back in his voice.

My annoyance carries me up the porch to the stained-glass door. I take a deep breath. With everything we've been joking around about, I've been pushing aside all the reasons I ran out of here a few days ago.

I feel Keene's warmth behind me, and his mouth brushes against my ear. "No matter what, you put yourself out for them every day, every way you can, Alison. Don't think just because I've been on the outside I haven't seen it. You slay me with your devotion to them." He nuzzles my ear, causing my heart to trip. "You're their warrior and their fighter. They may say things they regret later, but nothing is worth losing you. I should know." He straightens. "Now, walk through that door and show them who you are, what you're made of, and how bad they hurt you. They need to know."

There are so many things I want to say, but my throat is clogged with emotion. Nodding slowly, I open the door.

And chaos erupts.

27

ALISON

"You two walking in together? Should we assume you've worked out your churlish behavior, Alison?" Phil drawls from somewhere to my left.

My chin lowers so Phil can't see the pain his words inflict on me, but I remember what Keene said on the portico. Sharply, I turn to my brother. "Are your reports complete and on my desk?" Keene moves away quietly with a squeeze of my arm.

Phil looks taken aback. "What? Well, no. I haven't had time this morning to complete them."

"Because you've been spending company time gossiping about me. Don't worry, I'll be sure to deduct that from your next paycheck." Phil's mouth is opening and closing like a fish. I step forward into his space, a lash of power whipping through me. "You all taught me this is a place of business, and yet you've made it impossible for me to work. That ends now." Without remorse, I continue. "Your reports on my desk in two hours. If you'll be kind enough to excuse me, I have a large amount of work to catch up on." I hold his stunned gaze for a few more seconds before I turn and climb the stairs to my office.

I pass Holly in the hallway. "Ali, do you have a minute?" she asks hesitantly. She's gnawing on her lower lip anxiously.

I squeeze her arm briefly before I say, "Not here, I don't. I just explained to Phil that this just became a nonpersonal zone for me. It's work." I hesitate. "We do need to talk though, Holly. I'm not happy with you." I pause to give my words more credence. "At all."

"I know." She's biting her lip so hard, she's going to draw blood. She takes a deep breath. "I uploaded something for you on your drive for you to look at later." She wrings her hands together.

Remembering the way those hands would do that beneath mine in the darkness of the shipping container, I reach out to cover them and squeeze, the only sign that I hear her through my anger and pain. "Later, okay? I can't right now."

"Okay," Holly whispers. "Ali, I'm..."

I cut her off before she can apologize. I have to accept, but I'm not ready to do that just yet. My hurt is too fresh. "Later, okay?"

Her face deflates, but she nods. I walk quickly to my office.

I drop my briefcase on top of my desk when I hear her voice. "You and Keene? I was hoping you would get along, but this is so much better than that."

I don't turn around from the wall of photos I'm facing, my eyes seeking out one in particular. When I find it, I don't take my eyes off it. It's of me and Cassidy on the day I graduated law school. Her arms are wrapped around me, squeezing the life out of me. My cap is askew, and we both have crazy smiles on our faces.

Before meeting Caleb, it was one of the few times that glorious smile graced her face. I was flying high that day, a twenty-year-old law school graduate. A few months later when I passed the bar didn't live up to that moment of unadulterated pride emanating from my family as they all sat watching me accept my degree. It was the first time anyone ever had.

Even if my family is never the same going forward, the memory of that day will never be tarnished. I turn around.

"Do I have any meetings today, Cassidy?" I ask, sidestepping her question.

She waves her hand in the air, almost knocking over my desk

lamp in the process. "We'll talk about that in a minute. I want to hear about you and Keene." She smiles at me, the first real smile I've received in weeks. Months.

And I want to shatter into a million pieces.

"No, Cass," I say gently. "We won't be talking about Keene and me. This is work. You're the one who laid down the rules about not bringing family matters into the office. We have a reputation to uphold, clients to see to, and a company to run."

She laughs. "I think I decimated that rule the night I had sex with Caleb in my office. So, we're okay to talk about whatever you want."

Internally, I'm giving myself a high five. I just won a massive bet against Phil and Em. Cassidy just confirmed the sounds we heard from her office the night before our largest wedding to date was her having sex with Caleb. Externally, my face is blank. "But what if I don't want to?" I ask quietly. "What if I don't want to talk about Keene anymore because no matter what, I can't win with you, Cassidy? And I'm tired of seeing the disappointment in your eyes."

Cassidy looks as if I'd just slapped her. "Ali...no, it's not like that at all."

"Yes, it is," I counter. "Every. Single. Time." I count to five. "I've ceased to be your sister, and I've become the enemy. I've tried to figure out why. I've tried to explain. I've tried to make you understand, and you don't want to hear me. You want to hate me." I shake my head, missing her face, which goes wild with despair. "So be it. I can't be anyone else but me. Love me, hate me, that's for you to decide." I pause. "Now, if there's nothing pressing on the docket today, I have a number of things to catch up on and projects I need to start that I've been putting off." Sitting behind my desk, I move my briefcase to the floor and remove my laptop.

Cassidy is still standing there, stunned.

"Is there something else?" I ask politely.

"I...I guess not. I'll see you later." She smiles weakly.

"I'll likely be working straight through the day, but buzz me if you need me for signatures," I say.

She hesitates at my door. "Actually, I was hoping we could all grab lunch. We haven't done that in a while."

I'm already shaking my head no before she stops talking. "As I had to take a few unexpected days off, I need to catch up. Another time, maybe." Maybe when I feel like a member of this family again.

"Oh, okay. I'll leave you to it." She pauses another time.

I sigh, and Cassidy flinches.

"Was there something else, Cassidy?"

"I don't say this often enough, because I assume you just know it. I'm so impressed by what you do here. By who you are as a person," she says softly.

I snort. I can't help it. "Yeah, I can tell."

Her expression is laced with pain. "I mean it, Ali."

"Right now, I'm sure you do." My voice is, gratefully, still void of the bitterness desperate to seep through. "Though I wonder how much of this VIP treatment I'm receiving from you this morning is due to my actual work performance versus what you saw in the parking lot. Or is it the job offer I received from Watson, Rubenstein, and Dalton?"

What little color was left in Cassidy's face leeches away. "You're thinking about leaving?"

Well, crap. I guess Jared hadn't spread that info to the family. "Actively, no. But with the way things have been going here lately, it's nice to know I have alternatives. Now, if you'll excuse me." I stand up and make my way to my door.

She takes a step back, her blue-green eyes glassy. "I'm sorry, Alison. For so much." And before I can reach the handle, she quickly nabs it and pulls it closed behind her.

I can hear her muffled sobs as she makes her way to her office.

Rubbing my hand along my forehead, I feel a tension headache starting to build. I root around in my desk for medicine, pop a few tablets with some coffee, and boot up my laptop, ready to get to work.

∽

THERE'S a knock on my door hours later.

"Come in," I call out. I'm fighting with the questions Phil has asked about the intake process. So much of what he's asking could be done before the couple walks through our door if they're willing to sign certain privacy waivers. I'm tapping a pen against my desk, trying to figure out the solution, when Keene slides through the door and closes it behind him. He's holding a bag that permeates my office with a delicious aroma, reminding me that I haven't eaten anything since breakfast this morning.

"I thought you might be hungry since you didn't come downstairs." I listen for any censure in his voice but hear nothing.

Relaxing, I lean back in my chair. "What time is it?"

"Close to two. You've got to be starving by now." There's the gentle rebuke.

I roll my eyes right before my stomach growls. My cheeks flame and I can't help but laugh at myself as I reach for the bag he's holding out toward me. "What did you bring me?'

"Cassidy subjected your siblings to Subway because she was craving their chicken teriyaki." Keene's words are laced with humor. "Phil was horrified. He proceeded to lift his shirt and explain he didn't get his abs by eating Subway like their spokesman did. Cass countered that he didn't get them by working out either, as the only workout he did on a regular basis was sucking Jason's cock."

I burst out laughing at the terrified expression on Keene's face.

"I'm traumatized. I don't know whether I need eye bleach or noise-canceling headphones if we work here much longer." Keene's serious tone and stoic face is full of crap. His eyes are dancing.

Still amused, I reach over for the covered bowl and find chicken and dumpling soup with homemade biscuits from Frances—amazing Southern food. I dive in.

"You learn to adapt," I mumble around my first bite. "God, this is so good. Thank you." I take another few bites before I look to find Keene staring at me. "Did you eat? Are you hungry?"

His laugh is low and rough. "Yes, I ate. And right now, I have four dates before I can satisfy what else I'm hungry for unless this ticks another date off?" He nods toward the soup.

I had just taken a bite of biscuit and promptly choke. Shaking my head, I reach for my bottle of water. "No, this doesn't count," I manage to get out.

Keene tips his lips. "I didn't think so, but I had to ask. Where do you want to go for our second date tonight?"

Unfortunately for him, I had just taken another sip of water. It arcs beautifully across my desk, all over his dress shirt as I spit it at him. Unrepentantly.

Keene looks down at his shirt before standing. He starts to round my desk, and I get up out of self-preservation. I back up slowly when I see he isn't stopping. "Listen, Keene," I begin, placating.

He doesn't stop until I'm backed into the corner of the room. My face is about four inches from his wet chest, and I can't help the snicker that escapes.

"Think that was funny, do you?" Keene's breath moves my hair. I want to see his face, but I'm distracted by the springy mat of hair underneath his white dress shirt. It's even more potent now that it's wet. I reach up to touch his chest before it's caught in his grasp. Keene raises my hand to his lips before placing it along his jaw.

"What am I going to do with you?" he whispers, his eyes now roaming over my face.

"I have no idea. I think that's what worries me," I reply back honestly.

Something flashes across his face before he leans closer into me. His dark lashes lower, and I watch as his head tips, telling me his lips are about to fasten onto mine. My head tips in the opposite direction as I anticipate his kiss.

And then, my office door flies open.

"Ali, we have got to talk about the number of emails you sent out that require a response by the end of the day. There is no way I can get to them all tonight. Jason and I—well, well, well." Phil's voice goes from panicked to all-knowing in one breath. "Did I interrupt something?"

He knows he did, the ass.

With a sense of calm I didn't imagine he possessed, Keene asks Phil, "Do you know what a closed door means, Phil?"

"Yes, Keene, I'm not two," Phil counters.

"Then start acting like it. Close the door," Keene orders before turning back to me. I hear the snick of my office door closing before I lift my face to Keene's. "He's such a buzzkill," he grumbles.

"You'll get used to him. I promise."

Keene lowers his head to mine and brushes his nose along my cheek. "Not making promises, Alison. Phil's a pain in the ass."

"He's charming."

"He's annoying."

"He's funny."

"He's obtuse."

"He's—" I counter, when Phil cuts in.

"You both know I can still hear you, right?" my pain-in-the-ass, annoying, obtuse brother comments.

Pushing Keene aside, I stomp over to him. "What the hell are you still doing in here?" I screech. "Keene told you to leave!"

"No, he said to close the door," Phil counters. "I did that. I didn't think I was going to get a front-row seat to all that chemistry. Phew." Phil waves his hand in front of his face. "It's like watching Caleb and Cass all over again. I almost started perspiring."

"Killing you would be too much of a gift for Jason."

Keene snickers behind me.

I turn on him like he's fresh meat. "Seriously? Now is not the time to point out you were right. You might not make it to five dates."

Phil chooses then to pipe up. "Speaking of that, Keene, I feel for you, man. She's a hard negotiator. Always has been."

Keene's voice is laced with humor when he drops into my chair before pulling me into his lap. "Thanks, Phil. Right now, you're not helping me though."

"Oh!" Phil jumps up. "Right. Got it. I'll send you an email, Ali. It's just Jason and I have this thing he's been planning for months."

I rub my hand across my forehead from my perch on Keene's lap. I can't with him right now. "Fine. Whatever. Just go."

Phil dashes around the desk to drop a kiss on the top of my head. Keene lets out a low growl. "Right. Sorry! Leaving. Bye!" And this time, Phil closes the door with him on the correct side of it—in the hall.

That's when my head literally hits the desk with a thunk.

Keene is shaking with laughter behind me, stroking my back where it's flattened out. "You'd be bored anywhere else."

I wave a hand at him, shushing him, even though I know it's the truth.

Still stroking his hand up and down my back, he asks, "Any preferences for our second date?"

I turn my head and gape at him.

"Because for me, it could be as simple as grilling on your back deck, watching a movie, or eating one of those freaking amazing hot dogs from that guy in Ridgefield." Keene's expression is thoughtful for a moment. "If we do one tonight and the other two tomorrow, then we'd be up to four dates. Then we'd just have breakfast left," he muses.

I laugh, and then something remarkable happens.

Keene's entire face changes when a smile breaks fully across his handsome face. This isn't his trademark smirk or a grin. This is a smile that shows his teeth, lifts his cheeks and crinkles the corners of his eyes. It transforms his face from a dark cloud, and it causes my heart to thump erratically in my chest. I knew I was in trouble before, but until this moment, I didn't realize just how much.

"No answer? Good. I'm taking silence as agreement," he declares. He pulls me up from my flopped-over position and readjusts me in his arms. I gasp at my heart righting itself in my chest. Keene's face becomes more charged, more alert. "Alison? What is it?"

My mind is racing. When did it happen? What changed? When did he slide in? When did I surrender to feeling...more for Keene, when I swore my heart wasn't going to get involved with anyone, ever? How did I unknowingly give power over to a man who might be as damaged as I am?

The lashes of my eyes graze his cheek as I close my eyes in defeat. It doesn't matter if it's one more date or four. This man is indelibly written on my soul.

"Nothing. It's nothing. Just tell me, who's actually doing the cooking?" I counter lightly.

Keene laughs as he squeezes me. My heart clenches.

God, what am I going to do if it all ends?

28

MELODY

W hy the hell isn't he at Hudson? I've wasted my time there the last few days, but none of my contacts would tell me a damned thing until yesterday.

He's with *her* in Connecticut.

Fucking cuddling in her office.

I could send a bullet right through her window, taking that smile right off her face.

I want to blow that building, and every occupant in it, sky-high.

But no, Keene wouldn't like that. His sister is in that building. Think about what your man wants for once, Melody, and you might not be in this predicament.

Picking up the binoculars next to me, I see him lower his face down to her. He's brushing his nose back and forth across hers, his look tender.

He was never tender with me.

"Argh!" I cry out.

The price for his betrayal must be paid.

29

KEENE

I arrive at Alison's after the late-summer sun sets, with a bottle of wine in each hand. Uncertain of what we're eating, I'm prepared for anything.

I'm about to lift my hand to knock when the door opens. I'm glad I pull my hand away, or I would have tapped Corinna right on her forehead. "Sorry," I offer.

"Put 'em up," Corinna demands.

"Pardon me?" I'm confused. Does Alison's sister want to have a boxing match? I'm guessing I outweigh her by a hundred pounds, and I have two bottles of wine as weapons.

"The bottles, Keene. Let's see what you brought."

Ah. I lift a bottle of red and a bottle of white. Reading both labels, Corinna snags the bottle of white out of my hand before gliding past me. "I know what you're having for dinner. I'll consider it payment for having to clean my kitchen from the food coloring."

My mouth falls open. "You threw it at my head!" I couldn't care less about the wine, but the idea that I owed her for a mess of her own making is ludicrous.

"If you hadn't been a jackass, we wouldn't have to go there. But you do apologize so well." Corinna waves the bottle of wine in the air as she skips down the steps, making her way toward her house, which is the closest to Alison's. "Have a good night!" she calls out.

Using my free hand, I rub my head. "Did that just happen?"

Alison is standing next to me now. "Cori can totally turn anything into someone else's fault when it comes to making her do more work than she needs to. It's best if you learn that now." She leans against me and hooks her arm through mine. "Thank you for the bottle—I mean, *bottles* of wine. Even if we're only drinking one of them." Her voice is dripping with laughter.

Like me, she's changed into shorts, but hers show the toned legs she's earned from running thousands of miles. The shorts barely skim the curve of her ass. She's paired them with a body-hugging tank and flip-flops in electric blue. "You're trying to kill me, aren't you?" I groan while giving her body a full perusal.

Her eyes widen. "What? I'm dressed."

"True. But baby, I have a great imagination and an even better memory." I tug her close and press a kiss to her smiling lips.

By the time I let her up for air, it takes a moment or two for her to open her eyes. All the humor has been chased away and replaced with desire. Once our bodies are joined together again, and they will be, we're not coming up for days. She'll be begging me to stop laving up her sweetness. To stop pinning her to the closest flat surface. And there's no way I will. I'm that hungry for her.

I want to memorize this moment, this second in time. There's Alison in my vision, my lungs, my mouth.

"Are you hungry?" she asks me.

"For food, not especially." I pull her tighter against me so she understands my meaning. A slow smile graces her lips.

"How about a little drive before dinner? I've got everything we'll need all packed up." She gestures into the kitchen, where I see a cooler packed. "I don't think we'll be able to bring the wine though."

"We'll have it after we get back." I'm immediately intrigued. "Where are we going?"

She gives me a small smile. "You'll see."

I'M surprised Alison doesn't ask me to take her to the mountain, but instead, directs me to New Fairfield. Following her directions, we end up at Squantz Pond, which is surprisingly empty for the beautiful summer evening. Jumping from my car, Alison reaches for the bag she packed before leaving the house. Stopping to kick off her flip-flops, she looks up at me. "You don't mind?"

She's practically dancing to get her toes in the sand.

"The only problem I have is that you're carrying the bag. Hand it over," I demand.

"Might want to kick off your shoes first, babe. Sand's a pain to get out."

Not a bad idea. Kicking off my shoes, I dump both sets in the trunk of the Audi before relieving her of the bag. "So, what are we having for dinner?"

"You have no patience. Do you know that?" she admonishes.

"It's been mentioned a time or two," I mutter.

"Then give me a few minutes to get everything out and I'll show you."

Alison guides me over to one of the picnic tables. "I love the beach, but I hate sand in my food. Now, the bag please, fine sir," she says with mock courtesy.

I place it on top of the table and let her do her surprise dinner reveal while I absorb our surroundings.

The public beach almost appears to be private for the number of people on it. It's almost remarkable how it appears to be carved out of the cavernous hills lined with thick lush trees. Despite the heat and humidity, a mild breeze kisses our skin.

It's so peaceful here. You could almost forget the rest of the crazy world just waiting to intrude.

"It's beautiful here," I murmur.

"I know. I found it a few years ago when I was out driving. It's crazy insane during the day, which is fun too. There are boat launches, kayaks, families. Inevitably, someone brings a volleyball net and sets it up, and someone gets whacked with the ball." I'm captivated listening to her. "But at this time of night? This is when the true lovers of the beach come, just to absorb the essence of the water in their soul." She shakes her head. "Sorry. It must sound silly."

"Who taught you to love the beach that way?" I have my suspicions. In all the time I've known her, I've never heard her talk about her.

Alison fidgets with the plastic utensils a few moments. "Alison?"

"My mother. We used to go whenever we could in Charleston." She lets out a deep sigh. Leaning her chin on her hands, she appears captivated by the water. I'm stunned when she quietly says, "Today would have been her fifty-seventh birthday. She would have loved this beach." Reaching up, she wipes a stray tear from under her lashes.

"So, in honor of my mama, we have some good ol' Southern favorites for dinner. I hope that works for you," she drawls in such a way I've so rarely heard when she speaks.

"That sounds perfect. What did you bring?"

"First, we have to give thanks to Cori for running to Frances for all of this today." Alison shoots me a baleful look.

I dutifully oblige. "Thank you, Cori." Also, thanks for not flinging more whipped cream at me today.

"No, you don't understand, Keene. This isn't on the menu." Alison reaches into the bag, and suddenly, the smell of homemade barbecue assails me.

"Gimme." I reach for the container with both hands, but she smacks them away before I can touch it.

"I haven't been back in eleven years, and this is still the closest taste to Melvin's Barbecue I've had since I left. Good food is probably one of the few things I miss about that place," she murmurs. Alison also pulls out containers of homemade mac and cheese, collard greens, and baked beans.

And cornbread. Sweet Jesus. If Corinna can get Frances to cook like this, I need to get on Corinna's good side.

Once the bag is unloaded, Alison looks down at her plate and closes her eyes briefly, her hands clutched together.

I've never seen her pray before a meal was served. Respectfully, I bow my head.

When I raise it, it's to find a sweet look on her face. "I don't normally pray over my food. I was just wishing my mama a happy birthday. But I thank you for that."

I relax, but there's something I've been wondering.

"What happened to your family, Alison?" I ask bluntly. "I know what I read in the reports at Hudson when I was trying to find out if Cass was my sister, but it's not the same as hearing it from you."

Alison stills.

Shit.

"What do you want to know?" she asks quietly.

"Whatever you're willing to tell me."

Silence stretches out between us, and despite our physical closeness, I feel a chasm looming. I regret bringing up the topic and ruining our evening until she starts talking.

"It's easier to talk about my mother than my father," she says quietly. "My mother was...amazing." She's spooning food onto a plate before handing it to me. "I'm supposed to be more eloquent than that, I suppose. But when I think about my mom, it's the everyday things I remember the most. How she'd ask me about my day at school. How she'd pack my favorite things for lunch. What she was like the first time they told me I was a gifted student." Alison smiles at me wryly. "And that will be the only time I'll ever talk about that."

I smile back at her, encouraging her to keep going. Alison picks up her plate and starts spooning out her own food.

"I was so immature emotionally when she died. I barely had my nose out of a book. Mama encouraged me to learn everything, read everything, absorb everything. She didn't want me skipping too many grades because of my maturity. It was the right decision then. I was a late bloomer, and I worried about it. Mama kept telling me not to, though, that God had his reasons for it, and in the meantime, it just meant she got to keep me at home longer. I was always more connected with Mama because I looked just like her." Alison pauses, and I let her words sink in.

I reach over and pick up her hand, lifting it to my lips. "She must have been beautiful, then."

"Keene." Alison's voice trembles.

How is it possible I surprised her so much with such a simple truth? "What do you think she would say if she could see you now?"

She bursts out laughing. "Oh, are you sure you want to know?" Alison's expression is pure wickedness.

"Bring it on, baby." I lift a forkful of collard greens to my mouth.

"After she asked me about twenty million times if I planned on marrying you? I guarantee you, Mama would have called me, scolding me something fierce over my five-date rule." Alison wipes her eyes as tears of laughter stream out. Just as suddenly, they turn to tears of pain.

I can't handle it anymore.

I grab her hand and move her onto my lap to hold her. She rests her head in the notch of my neck and continues to weep quietly. "Let it out, baby. Let it all out." I'm beginning to understand more about Alison's pain. Her mother wasn't just her mother; she was full of life and sass. She was her best friend. And not only was her death a tragedy, she wasn't even able to be mourned by her daughter since her father bulldozed their family apart.

I let her cry for a little longer before I ask, "Would she want you crying this much?"

Sitting up and wiping her eyes, she says, "Oh, hell no. You are so, so, so right, Keene. She's probably watching us, going, 'Let's get past the tears to something good before I change the channel on the two of you.'" Alison's smile could illuminate the sky.

"Well, we wouldn't want her to do that, baby." I curl my hand under her jaw and kiss her soundly. Alison tastes of barbecue, mac and cheese, and summer nights.

In other words, perfect.

ALISON STUMBLES A BIT and falls into me as I'm folding our blanket. "You okay?" I ask, concerned.

"Yeah, just lost my balance."

"Do you have everything? Do we need anything on the way home?" I ask.

She shakes her head in the negative, and then she looks at her texts. "Better check your phone. Looks like there was an impromptu family dinner."

I mutter, "Like I give a shit."

That sends her into a giggling fit. "Why, Keene, if I didn't know better, I'd think you don't enjoy our family get-togethers." I reach out and take her hand as we make our way back to the Audi.

"Truth?" I ask.

"Of course."

"They scare the hell out of me."

Alison bursts out laughing.

"There she is," I murmur, stepping closer to her as I drop the bag into the trunk. Leaning against the side, I pull her between my legs. "How are you feeling, baby?"

Alison's honesty floors me. "It's never going to change. It's never going to have a closure that leaves me happy, but today you helped, so thank you."

I rub my nose against hers before kissing her languidly. My heart rate picks up. "Then I'm glad we came."

She rubs her lower body against mine and sasses, "Well, not quite yet."

I groan. "I still have three more dates, Alison. No teasing."

She cups my jaw. "In the last few days, you've been different. You've been there when I didn't know I needed someone and were the first person when I absolutely did. You listened when I needed an ear and not a lecture, or a million opinions, and gave me space when I needed that too."

I can feel my jaw tic under her hand. "What are you trying to say, Alison?"

"I was ridiculous and we both know it. I just needed reassurance this wasn't another fly-by to you, especially after the way you spectacularly tried to start us up." Even as I cringe, I feel her hand stroke through my hair. "I'm trying to say that we were never over, and I needed my brain to get the message the rest of my body was sending it. It's taken a while for me to be ready for more, but I'm in."

Suddenly, I'm marauding her mouth. One hand is traveling down toward her rear, while the other is driving deep into her hair and pulling her head back. Our mouths mate against each other as if it's been years since our lips connected, since our tongues tangled, since our breaths mingled instead of minutes.

Finally, I pull back and mutter the one thing that comes to mind. "Thank God we missed that fucking family dinner."

Alison doubles over, laughing.

WE ARRIVE BACK at the farm and see everyone's cars still at the main building. I have no desire to go in, but I want to make certain Alison feels the same. When I ask her, she lets out a slow breath.

"What is it?" I reach over the console and place my hand over hers. I don't even realize she's been worrying them since we turned onto the property.

She tries to find the right words. "I love them all, I do. Really. But Keene? This date is always a huge deal for me, and the only one who remembered was Cori."

"Right," I clip. "We're going home."

"I'm sure they're expecting us."

"Then I'll send a text later, once we get back to the house. Right now, I'm going to run over to Caleb and Cassidy's and grab a few things. Any problem with that?"

Alison ponders for a moment. "Do you think she's going to turn into a crazy stalker and start looking in my windows?"

Her choice of words is eerie. "No, I highly doubt that."

"Then no, I don't have a problem at all." I hear a hesitation in her voice as I pull into Cassidy's driveway. Stopping the car, I turn toward her. Gnawing on her lower lip, she asks, "Are you bringing everything over?"

"I had planned on a few days. Why? Should I?"

"Why don't we try the few days and go from there?" She's still cautious. I can work with that.

"I'll be back in a few minutes." Jumping out of the car, I run inside and throw a couple of days' worth of stuff in a bag. Within minutes, I'm back in the car, putting it in gear, and heading toward Alison's. "Not to alarm you or anything, baby, I can work with what I have in the bag, but I suspect by the end of the weekend, the rest of your closet is going to have clothes in it."

When I pull into her driveway, I glance over. The small smile that plays on her lips tells me the idea isn't entirely unwelcome.

Before we can get out of the car, a figure approaches us from the side. I catch a glint of metal and my instincts kick in. I slam Alison back in her seat, and then the moonlight catches the warm red-gold of the approaching bogey.

It's Holly. And she's holding a metal pan.

"BET CASS LOOKED like she sucked a raw onion after that text," Holly offered.

After my heart rate returned to normal, Alison jumped out of the car to ask Holly what she was doing there. Turns out, Holly hadn't forgotten Alison's mom's birthday. In fact, she made Southern-style banana pudding (which she apparently makes better than Corinna) to celebrate.

Yelling from the upstairs bedroom that Corinna's car was inbound, soon Alison's kitchen was full of sweets and chatty women.

Corinna came in with the bottle of wine she confiscated earlier. I got a wink, along with a muttered "Goes better with banana pudding."

I tried to make myself as absent as possible by disappearing to the deck and dealing with my own sister, who wasn't pleased that I didn't answer her summons to a family get-together earlier.

I hear Alison let out a sigh. "Great. Another reason to put me on the shit list."

Holly says, "I don't think that's it, Ali. I think she feels out of control right now. You know how she craves control." She pauses. "She's putting up a super brave front about the twins, but she's scared."

"I got called into her office the other day too. Don't worry, you're not alone anymore," Corinna says to me, right before yelling, "Keene, you'd better be worth it in bed!"

I roar with laughter.

"Bitch," Alison mumbles.

"Slut," Corinna says back cheerfully.

"Not yet," Alison rejoins.

"Damn, that sucks," Holly says. "Who's holding out? You or him?"

"You three realize there are doors open and I can hear everything you're saying, right?" I offer. "Even without the yelling?"

I hear a loud thump. I turn and spy Alison's head down on the countertop. I can't help but laugh.

"And to answer your question, Holly, Alison put me on a five-date rule that was recently rescinded. Consequently, eat and get out," I call out before turning back to my phone.

An incoming text arrives from an unknown number. Fuck. Not tonight.

There's silence. Then, "Was he like this the first night at the Plaza?" Corinna whispers.

"Yes," Alison hisses.

"Shit, no wonder you fell into bed with him," Holly mutters.

With dessert finished and all the dishes put away, we've walked Corinna and Holly to the door.

I chuckle as I'm locking up. "Tonight's the first time I've spent much time with them. Are they always that funny?"

"Yes. Holly does better with smaller groups. Otherwise, she'll have a camera in her hands. Corinna does well with people she's comfortable with, or you get the fake version of her, which is all dramatic bombshell." Alison flings her hair and strikes a pose.

I crack up.

"I know, right? I do bombshell so well." I'm still laughing as she walks to the kitchen to toss a dish towel on the counter. Within seconds, I've scooped her up and her ass lands on the counter.

"You do bombshell by breathing, baby. You don't need to strike a pose to do it." I drop my head to nuzzle at the space between her neck and shoulder.

A low moan is all she can manage. Her fingers come up to thread through my hair.

"While I have very fond memories of this kitchen counter, Alison, tonight I want you spread out across your bed." My lips travel up her neck, making her arch her back. "Tell me that's what you want too."

"More than that. I need it, Keene. I need you," she rasps.

I reach over and flick out the lights. Then, quick as lightning, she's in my arms and I head toward the stairs.

30

ALISON

Keene carries me across the threshold to my bedroom, looking at me the entire time. Somehow, I know deep within me that when we touch this time, it's going to be more than sex.

It's going to be us laying claim to one another's souls.

I tremble with the force of it as he lowers me to the floor beside my unmade bed.

He brushes my hair away from my ear. "I didn't expect nerves, baby." His head dips and he nibbles on my ear, sending shockwaves down my skin. I sway in his arms, unnerved, even as I reach up to grab on to the only steady thing in my world.

Him.

"I didn't either," I admit. Every time with Keene has sent fireworks through me, cravings, longing for more. I expected all of those things. But what I didn't expect were butterflies.

He lets out a low laugh, even as his dark head pulls back a bit. "I didn't mean you, beautiful, though I have to admit, it helps mine to know it." His hands still from where they'd been roaming across my bare shoulders, squaring me off against him. They meet behind my neck and tip my head up, forcing me to meet his eyes. My breath gets caught somewhere in between my stomach and my throat.

"Why?" I manage to croak out.

"Because we both know we've stopped running. The minute our bodies meet on those sheets, there's no turning back from the path we're on. I'm afraid too, Alison. I'm afraid I'm going to fuck this up somehow and there won't be another chance." Keene's making me a vow I'm not entirely certain I understand. "But I promise I'll try every day we're together to never give you the chance to regret us."

"Okay," I whisper. I take a deep breath and let him know something he should already know. "It was always more for me, even from that first night."

"I know." His head bows. "Alison, I can't say there haven't been…"

I lift my finger to his lips to silence him. "Neither can I." We both thought we'd never see each other again. Who would have thought of how we'd ever end up finding each other again? My hand drifts to his shoulder.

"The last woman I was with was you. And even before that, it was more than six months," he says quietly. "The minute I knew where to find you again, I knew I couldn't touch another woman again. No one could compare."

"The last man I was with was you. And before that, it was more than a year. Even before I found you again, I was tired of searching and never finding what I had with you in one night. I'm tired of comparing every man I meet to a ghost."

"I'm not a ghost, Alison." He takes my hand and places it over his heart. "I'm right here."

"Then make me feel again, Keene. Take me where only you can," I plead.

His kisses me, driving me to the point of insanity. He backs me up until I'm against my bed, and without releasing my lips, he sweeps me into his arms and places me diagonally across my mattress before crawling on top of me.

God, this feels so right.

Keene, in my bed.

Keene, obliterating my mind.

Keene, infiltrating my heart.

I gasp on the last thought. He pulls back slightly and uses the break in our kiss to whip my tank over my head. The sheer, nude-colored bra I was wearing beneath does little to camouflage my breasts and everything to incite the man before me. With a growl, Keene's head drops and captures one of my protruding nipples between his teeth. He begins sucking, using the fabric between my nipple and his tongue to drive me even closer to the edge, where control is a memory.

I arch my back, pushing my breast closer toward his mouth.

Pulling back, he reaches for his T-shirt with one hand. When it's gone, he lowers his body back onto mine, and I immediately rake my nails over the skin covering the sinewy muscles of his back. He lifts his head from my breast, moving to the spot under my ear that drives me insane.

Soon, I'm writhing on the bed, my hands slipping down the back of his shorts, pulling his hips deeper into mine when he rolls off and says, "No."

The flush that hits my body must travel from head to toe. Embarrassment and shame make me want to gag. Tears hit the back of my eyes. I have to get out of this room. I'm just about to scramble off the bed when Keene's arm hauls me back on top of him.

"Where do you think you're going?" He's pissed. I struggle to get away from him before the tears I'm holding back fall. "Alison, stop moving." He rolls on top of me again, and I turn my head. I'm not going to be able to hold the tears back.

"In the conversation I was having in my head, which apparently you weren't privy to, I was saying I wanted to... Hey, baby. No. No tears." He has to forcibly turn my face, but I refuse to look at him, no matter how much he pleads. I finally feel him hold himself up on his arms, and I brace for it. This is when he leaves me. Again.

His weight redistributes on top of me, and slowly, I feel him kissing away my tears.

"Baby, please give me your face," Keene says quietly. His mouth brushes my cheek to capture another tear as turn my head.

"I wasn't saying no to us. I was saying no to how fast we were going. I need to savor you, devour every inch of your skin. I want to taste the parts of you I never had the chance to before. I want to hear you moan when I touch you somewhere you've never been touched, somewhere no one has ever touched you. I want to bring you to the brink of pleasure and start all over again. I want to give you more than I've ever given anyone. Say yes to that," Keene whispers. My mouth falls open. He uses his wicked mouth to deliver a slow, languid kiss before he murmurs, "Don't just fall. Drown with me, Alison. Dive into oblivion with me."

I can't catch my breath enough to speak, so I nod instead.

A hint of a smile tips his lips. "I've dreamed about this for so long, I almost don't know where to start. I'm afraid I'm in my bed at home, still dreaming."

I roll Keene to his back and straddle him. "At any time in your dreams, do I get a chance to savor every inch of you?" Keene's not the only one who's dreamed these long, lonely years.

"About the fifteenth or sixteenth time, baby. I have a lot of territory to cover." His eyebrow quirks, and I laugh.

"Now I know I'm not dreaming. You never laugh in my dreams."

My laughter subsides. "Keene," I whisper as my mouth lowers to place my lips over his heart.

"And that never happened," he chokes out. "Come here, baby."

I slide up so our bodies align and our lips are even. Our breath mingles. Our heartbeats, so frantic, slow until they're in tandem. The soul I felt shatter inside of me years ago when he walked away begins to piece itself back together as Keene rolls me to my back. Slowly, his fingertips trail down my leg, over muscle and bone, over tendon and skin. When he hits my knee, I bend my leg. He smiles but doesn't kiss me again.

His fingers trail all the way down to my toes, then back up. His fingers map my leg outside and then in. By the time he reaches the apex of my thigh, my panties are soaked and I'm shaking with want, just from him touching my leg with his calloused fingertips.

"So strong. So beautiful," he murmurs. Finding the button of my shorts, he quickly undoes it, then pulls the zipper down. I raise my hips to shimmy them down, but he surprises me when he doesn't dive between my legs and feast. Instead, he finds my tattoo on the arch of my foot with his lips. My back arches and my hips lift from the bed in reaction.

Running his eyes up my body, he whispers, "Every inch of you will know my lips, Alison. Every inch will burn before you feel my cock slide inside of you. This night will be seared in your mind forever." As his lips move over my ankle, he mutters, "It already is in mine. I've lived it a thousand times in my dreams."

I clench my thighs together. Raising my hands to my breasts, I whisper, "Keene, I don't know if I can take much more."

He laughs roughly. "Oh, you'll take it all, baby. Every. Single. Inch. And you'll be begging for it."

I moan as I push my breasts together—something, anything to alleviate the ache he's building layer by layer.

Quick as a cat, his body covers me as his mouth plunders my mouth voraciously. I'm as helpless to his taste now as I was the night we met. It's more potent than any alcohol, more decadent than Corinna's richest cake. It's Keene.

And then I feel the ridge of his hardness through his shorts, rubbing up against me, and I know I'm not going to last. "Keene..." My voice is high-pitched, warning him I'm already there.

"It's calling out to you, baby. Fall into it." When he bites down on my lower lip, I spiral off into ageless space. Gripping his shoulders tightly, I leave half circles with the marks of my nails. I don't even realize I call out his name as I shatter or that I beg for more.

But he does.

After I come down from the first crest, Keene has my bra off. I feel like I can finally breathe. I nuzzle my face into his shoulder before I take a small bite.

He lets out a feral growl. "Baby, I'm holding on by a thread, and I want to give you more."

Sliding my hand down the back of his opened pants, I hear him pant before he regains control of himself. "Give me more. I'm going to be giving it back at the same time."

"Is that so?" Keene says as his mouth drops to my nipple. He tongues it slowly before latching onto it with his teeth, flicking his tongue back and forth over it. Switching to the other one, he torments it the same way. When he lets it go and begins making his way down the front of my body, I lose my grip on his. Using his advantage, he pins my wrists to the bed while running his lips across my abdomen, which ripples from the sensation.

When he reaches my barely visible curls, he releases one hand to drag a finger from my clit, down my slit and back up.

"I've never seen anything in my life as beautiful as you." Keene's voice is filled with awe and something else. It sounds like regret over our lost time.

"We're here now." I regret the time I contributed to it as well, with my stubbornness and refusal to listen.

"I'm not quite certain I believe it," he admits. Separating my folds with his finger and thumb, I feel the cool air rush over my clit, making me quiver. His face displays his fascination. Slowly, torturously, he blows gently across it again. I squeeze myself tight, trying to keep myself from having another orgasm.

"I need a taste," Keene says, right before his mouth lowers to suck at my clit. One finger slides inside, followed by a second, into my slick channel. His other hand releases mine to hold my stomach as I try to arch into his mouth. Oh, the pressure. The delicious pressure building up inside of me.

"I need you, please. Not without you again." I'm begging him to take me. Fill me. He looks at me from between the V of my legs as they shift restlessly on the sheet. He's as relentless at eating me as he is with everything he does.

I can't say I don't appreciate it. But more than that, I want him inside of me. I want to tighten around his cock when I fly away. I want to ride into our oblivion with him.

He takes a final lick and releases me as he pushes up to his knees. He shoves his shorts and boxer briefs down, and there it is—his thick cock surrounded by dark hair. My hips lift in an ancient rhythm of anticipation. "Please. Now," I growl.

"Protection, Alison," he rasps.

"Pill." I gasp as I feel him crawl back over me, his cock dragging over my leg. His precum leaks on my leg as I shift below him restlessly.

"Be sure, because once I take you with nothing, I'm never going back." His voice holds both warning and promise.

This is more than just one night.

Thank God.

"Come home, Keene. I've been waiting for you a long time," I whisper.

He needs no more encouragement. Rolling his hips against me, he rubs his cock up and down against my entrance to ensure he's wet enough to slide in fully on the first drive. He's also driving me insane with want.

Finally, he notches himself against my entrance. "No more running, Alison. You're mine."

"Yours," I whisper back.

He thrusts inside, and I immediately wrap myself around him. My legs go around his lower back, and my walls clamp down on him. Letting out a long moan, my hands find his ass as he kisses me, while waiting for me to relax. He drags his hips back slowly before thrusting inside of me, over and over, until I'm incoherently tossing my head back and forth, begging for him, for something—for anything.

Keene knows what I need. He leans down, nips my ear between his teeth, then says, "Give it to me, baby," right before his hips hit mine for the final time, and his seed spurts hotly into me.

My orgasm hits seconds after his, and I clamp my teeth on his shoulder as I shudder my way through it.

I tighten my arms and legs around him, silently telling him not to move. He buries his head in my neck, his breathing taking time to even out.

Long moments later, Keene shifts his weight without disengaging us. I feel the wetness dripping between my legs. It's a beautiful, complicated mess. Not unlike my feelings for the man lying on top of me.

Slowly, he pulls out before murmuring, "I'll get a washcloth to clean you up. Be right back." He rubs his chin against the side of my temple.

I think I murmur something in kind, but I let the allure of sleep pull me under, knowing I won't be alone tonight, or for any night I can imagine in the future.

31

MELODY

I *hate her.*
That cunt dared to take what's mine?
Mine?
She has no idea of the lengths I'm willing to go to for my man.
I'll get Keene back soon enough.
Keene Marshall is mine.
He'll never forget it again.
Never.
Somehow, someway, I will show him that.

32

KEENE

Caleb throws down his pen. "I'm never going to get used to the commute back to the city when life returns to normal and I have to start working out of the Manhattan office again."

I chuckle, but not without some sympathy. It hasn't been a hardship to trade a twenty-minute subway ride for a five-minute drive to the office.

More importantly, the mornings lately have been better since I've been waking up next to Alison.

It's been a month since I was able to touch her, taste her, take her again, since Alison and I became an *us*. During that time, we've gone out for breakfast at The Coffee Shop too many times to count, gone out for long runs, and found a mutual addiction to all things related to Sherlock Holmes, be it books or movies. We've spent countless hours in front of her television, arguing about watching the original movies or RDJ on Netflix. Sometimes, I'll hold her in my arms as we read our favorite books on our e-readers. Later, we'll argue about what Sir Arthur meant in a certain passage.

There's something comforting about that.

I've also found out Alison can recite most country songs like they're Bible verses, has actually taken pole dancing classes to strengthen her core, and would rather kill a spider than ever see a snake. When we saw a snake running one Saturday, she screamed with her hands waving in the air as she sprinted away.

The snake was a black garden snake, no more than a baby. I fell into the grass next to it laughing.

Alison's a constantly changing kaleidoscope. She's warm, unapologetically intelligent, and has a heart ready to take on the world with the right encouragement. She's also fearless, daring, and easy to love.

If it wasn't for the burden hanging over my head, I'd have already handed over my heart to her.

Caleb and I are no closer to finding Melody. There are no distinguishable patterns our analysts can identify. There's no trace on the burner phones she's using. Fuck, the whacked-out bitch must have a storage unit filled with them. She'll call one day, telling me all the ways she plans to punish me for ignoring her, and then she'll send a picture of herself masturbating in another one of my stolen shirts, with a dildo in her snatch or in her ass. Sometimes there's video.

Then there are her constant texts.

Unknown caller: Who the fuck is she, Keene? She can't have what's mine.

Unknown caller: What, more than one? I guess I'll have to be creative in how I deal with them. Then again, if you like them, maybe they'd put on a show for us.

Unknown caller: You got one of those fucking sluts pregnant? Are you fucking kidding me? I'll cut it out of her. No one can have your child but me.

Getting the restraining order wasn't hard. It's serving it that's fucking impossible. That's what keeps me awake at night after Alison's sated body has fallen asleep beside me.

She's out there. Somewhere close.

She's seen me with my sister, Alison, and the girls.

Caleb won't say it, but he's worried. I'm close to offering to leave again to lure the crazy away from Collyer, but there's more that holds me back. I know Caleb would come with me. I know it would leave our women vulnerable, and who knows what Melody would do in her psychotic state to them if we left them unprotected?

And then there's Alison. While I refuse to drag her into this mess I brought to her doorstep, I can't leave her.

I finally have her, and I can't walk away.

"Keene," Caleb says sharply. My head snaps his way. "I was asking if you got anything new from the psycho in the last day."

Sighing, I slide my phone over to him. Quickly linking it up to his machine, he downloads all the texts.

I'm beyond ready for this to be over.

"Me too, buddy," Caleb answers.

I didn't realize I had spoken out loud.

Caleb's perusing the texts, and his thoughtful "Hmm" gets my attention.

"What is it?" I'm suddenly alert.

"Where was your car yesterday?" he asks.

"I assume the garage. Alison and I came into the office together." While my heart wants to jettison back to the memory of the wild laughter Alison and I had experienced driving around in her convertible, just his question has my spine tingling.

Caleb flips my phone around.

Melody has sent a new picture. It's my car, her half-naked ass on it this time. Fury roars through me at the thought of her at our home. Our home? When did Alison's house become my home?

Probably the minute I sank myself back into her body, I admit to myself.

"Fuck!" I roar. "She's been to the farm?"

"Calm down, Keene. I'm checking something." I pace back and forth in front of Caleb while I watch his fingers fly across the keyboard. For as much as he's taken over his role of CEO and owner of Hudson, his skills haven't slacked much, I note absently.

He grabs his cell to make a quick outbound call. "I need the VIN on Keene's car, and I don't want to go through the analysts." He holds the phone up to his shoulder as he types. "Got it." A pause before he smiles. "Yeah, Charlie. Cassidy and the babies are fine." Looking over at me, he smirks. "Ali's doing okay too. I'll have the girls call you. Thanks." He sits back and laces his hands over his stomach. "It's not your car."

"How do you—" My question is interrupted by a knock at the door. Caleb clears the screens in front of him before calling out, "Enter."

Alison comes in with a bouquet of roses and a huge smile on her face. Placing them on one of the smaller conference room tables, she moves directly to me. "They're beautiful, and I love them." Her arms move around my neck, still holding the card. Before I can say a word, she continues. "Of course, I'd love to spend the weekend at the inn with you." Without a thought that Caleb is also in the room, she brushes her lips against mine and murmurs, "I didn't know you had that in you."

I didn't. Because I never sent them.

"Let me see if they got the card right," I cajole her. Giving me one of her dazzling smiles, she hands it over.

You're looking so stressed. How about we work on us this weekend? Let's stop playing games and meet at the inn?

Flipping the card over, I see the seal on the back. MD. Melody. She sent the flowers. But they were meant for me, not Alison.

Fuck.

I have to think fast.

"There's only one thing they got wrong about the card, baby," I say softly. Her smile dims.

"What's that?"

"I wanted to take you next weekend. I was waffling about it over the phone because I couldn't remember if you had a wedding. The florist probably got sick of uncertainty and put the wrong date down," I bluff.

"I could get out of it," she whispers.

"Don't, baby. Things are starting to get back on track for you and the family. I already have the reservation for next weekend anyway." The lie keeps expanding.

Then again, what are a few lies going to cost me when it means protecting this woman from danger?

"Okay. I'll put it on the planner so everyone knows we're out of town," she breathes. Her eyes are still sparkling. "Can I have my card back?"

No. "Right after I call the florist. I want to talk with them about the mistake. This could have caused an issue, and they need to be aware of it."

She grins. "Of course you do." After one more quick kiss, she turns to walk to the door. She opens it and reaches for her flowers.

Shit. The flowers.

"Babe. Let me bring them down once I have a chance to talk with the florist." And after I make sure my crazy stalker didn't put any hidden cameras inside. "This way, I can see where they are in your office."

Alison's smile could light the darkest corner of my soul if I didn't have such foul things running through my mind.

The door closes, and Caleb springs up from behind the conference room table. "Shit. You don't think..."

I hand him the card. "I know. They weren't meant for her."

He reads the card, flips it over, and sees the embossed MD on the back. "You have to tell Ali, Keene."

"I will once I'm certain she's not still traumatized by the way we started or how her family treated her." I shoot Caleb a look. "Do you think she can take much more right now?"

He lets out a deep sigh. "She's stronger than you're giving her credit for."

"I know that. I also know her fears about me run deep," I admit. I inhale sharply. "I can't lose her again, Caleb." My hands skim over the delicate roses in the vase. I'm cursing, as I know this will kill them faster. I make a mental note to send Alison flowers after our trip to the inn to make up for this.

It's on the fourth bloom that I find the first camera.

The seventh, I find the second.

Amid the greenery, I find the third.

None of them are turned on, and all of them appear to be visual only. I take great enjoyment in crushing them beneath my booted foot.

Meanwhile, Caleb has already been to the supply room, finding the closest cardstock to the one the flowers were delivered with. He replicated the card and silently hands it to me. I attach it to the plastic thingie sticking out and am about to make my way out the door when I stop.

"What did you mean when you said it wasn't my car?"

"Close the door." I do so quietly and wait. "I called Charlie for your VIN because I was able to get a clear shot of the drivers-side window, and then I pulled up the cameras we had installed at the farm. After her little stunt," he says in disgust, "I also wanted to see if I could get a clear shot of her getting back in and get the VIN on the inside of the car door for confirmation." He leans back smugly. "And I did."

"While she was on the farm property, she didn't break into the house?" I ask, letting out a relieved sigh.

"Confirmed. It's an exact replica of your car, Keene, but all it does is show more of her crazy. The good news is"—Caleb flexes his fingers—"I have something tangible to track her on. Cars of that price don't come cheap. She had to pay for it somehow."

"God, I knew there was a reason I kept you around," I breathe out reverently.

"What, as your best friend?" he snorts. "No one else wanted that job."

I walk over to the door. Picking up Alison's now debugged flowers, I say, "No, in the Army. And trust me, plenty wanted that job."

His laughter follows me into the hall.

I HAVE to tear my mouth away from hers, or I'm going to lock her office door and take her against it.

"Alison," I warn, my breath coming out raggedly.

The impish smile shining up at me almost makes my control crumble and reach for her again. Fortunately, the knock on the door behind my back, where Alison pinned me the moment I arrived inside her office with her flowers, interrupts us.

Stepping back away from me, Alison flips over at the waist, and her short hair falls back in place perfectly from where I had buried my hands in it. Smoothing a hand over her dress, she calls out, "Come in."

I shoot her daggers as I quickly move away from the door. Cassidy and I collide. I almost fall over as I run into my sister's protruding stomach. I can't help it. The "Oomph" escapes me.

"Keene!" two very feminine voices snap at me.

Alison looks at Cassidy. Cassidy looks at Alison, and they both burst out laughing.

"And on that note, I'm out of here," I mutter.

"Actually, Keene, you're welcome to stay. I just popped by because I heard about the flowers." Cassidy looks over at Alison hesitantly. Their relationship has been mending, but it's going to take time for Alison to feel like Cassidy won't hurt her again.

"Aren't they beautiful?" Alison turns to Cassidy and reaches for her hand. Cassidy stiffens for a second before she moves closer and wraps her arm around her younger sister.

"They are, honey. They are so beautiful." Risking a lot, she squeezes the younger girl. "I am so happy for you."

Alison throws her arm around Cassidy's shoulders and squeezes back. I watch as a tear trickles from my sister's eye that she tries to unobtrusively wipe away.

For the moment, two sisters have united once again.

Courtesy of my stalker.

As my feelings of self-loathing skyrocket, I realize I need to find Melody now to get her poison away from my family.

Moving toward the doorway, I grate out, "I have to get back to work."

As I move out the door, I hear Alison say to Cassidy, "This is why the flowers were such a shock. You see how well he does sentimental."

Then I hear my sister respond, "Tell me about it. The first time he hugged me, I thought I was going to roll into a ball weeping."

Pausing a few feet away from the door, I listen to the beautiful sound of their laughter, something that hasn't been heard in way too long. The two women who own my heart laughing together.

God, I wish my mother was alive to have had a chance to have heard it.

I make my way down the hall to the conference room and slam the door as I enter it.

33

ALISON

I t's been two months since Keene and I...well, since Keene and me. I'm petrified to put a label on it, truth be told. We just are.

He's moved out of Cassidy's house completely, and his clothes are now hanging up next to mine in my closet. Looking at all the casual wear, I asked him one morning where all of his suits were. He got an uncomfortable look on his face when he responded, "Back at my place in Manhattan."

He never gave any indication he would have to go back and get them, nor did I ask if he wanted to. It's still early days, and it's still new. For right now, Keene is with me. That's all I can ask for.

That, and to get rid of this damn bug. God, I feel like utter crap, and if Keene tries to pour any more chicken soup down my throat, I'm going to find a live chicken and shove it down his to make up for all the mutilated ones he's forced me to consume over the last few days.

I don't know how much longer I can tolerate feeling like this.

Chuckling at that thought, I realize I must be feeling better. My mother always used to tell me I'd always get whiny at the end of whatever illness I had as a kid. As an adult, I typically curl into a ball and growl at anyone who tries to take care of me.

Now Keene's here, and I pretty much don't have any choice in the matter. He refused to let me kick him out of our room for fear of getting him ill. Whenever he'd catch me retching over the toilet, he'd hold my hair back from my face before wiping it down with a cool washcloth. And last night, when I couldn't take the scent of myself anymore, he drew a bath for both of us and held me while I got clean in the warm water.

I can't say I haven't enjoyed seeing this side of him—this nurturing part of him. I've spent too much time throwing up over the last few days to think about it much. It's another piece of the puzzle of Keene Marshall that fits so beautifully into place. Maybe one day, I'll finally see the whole picture.

I bet it's going to be devastating.

I'm still weak, but I'm finally up to heading downstairs. I need a change of scenery other than the four walls of my bedroom or my bathroom. Besides, I need to find my purse to locate my pill packet. I have to figure out when my cycle is supposed to start, so when I feel better, Keene and I can talk about the need for condoms until I can get back on my cycle. Sighing regrettably, I know I'm going to miss the wonders of feeling him skin on skin, when I pause.

Wait, when was my last cycle?

I count backward before another bout of nausea hits. At the sluggish speed I'm moving, I barely make it to the downstairs powder room. My head hanging over the bowl, I start counting again.

No. It's not possible. I didn't miss a single pill.

Finishing, I wipe my mouth and flush, waiting for more nausea to rip through me. My heartbeat is thundering through my chest. Pushing myself to my feet, I grab on to the vanity with weak hands and look at my reflection in the mirror. Don't panic before you know, Alison. You have a bug, and it's likely throwing everything off.

Including your brain.

Passing through the kitchen, I grab my purse and a bottle of water. Suddenly, my room, our room, which I was so eager to escape from a few minutes ago, offers a necessary haven.

It's also where I keep my pregnancy tests.

Dragging myself back up the stairs, I pause partway up and lean against the rail. What am I going to do? What will the family say?

What will Keene say?

Whoa, Ali. First things first. Take the test.

I climb the rest of the way up the stairs and go to the linen closet in the hall. Reaching blindly in the back, I grab one of the pregnancy tests I keep back there. Scanning the expiration date, I let out a sigh. It's still good.

I trudge through my bedroom and into the bathroom, holding the test in one hand and my purse in the other. Sitting on the toilet, I unwrap the test. Right now, I'm grateful I went for the easy ones. A plus sign if it's positive; a minus sign if it's negative.

Uncertain of how long Keene will be gone picking up groceries, I quickly pee on the stick. Placing it on some tissue, I wash my hands, grab up the trash, stuff it into the original box and wait.

I wonder if Keene's going to laugh with me later when I tell him about this.

I glance down at the test.

The longest three minutes of my life just turned into a responsibility lasting at least eighteen years.

I stumble backward and hit the cool glass of the shower. The door reverberates loudly in the silent room.

I don't have a bug. I'm pregnant with Keene's baby. I start shaking. This isn't some happily ever after. This is my life. His life. And I don't know what part of his life he wants me to have. And now, we're going to be tied together permanently in some way for the rest of them.

Right now, I wish there was someone, anyone, I could reach out to who could keep this a secret. I love my family, but God, they are a bunch of gossiping biddies. Keene would know sooner than I could manage to tell him.

Telling Keene. Shit. Nausea hits again, and I head to the toilet just in case. "Little one, you're already a pain in the ass and you're not even here yet," I murmur. "Taking after your daddy already?" My hand smooths over my flat stomach. "It'll be so easy to fall in love with you, just like I did him."

My heart clenches and tears prick my eyes. God, between trying to figure out when I got pregnant and when I fell in love with the baby's father, I'm a wreck. It could have been any of the numerous times we've laughed and loved, sliding our hands over each other's warm, slick bodies.

I could have made this baby and fallen for its father at any of those points.

The fact is, I did both. The question is, what do I do?

I hear the garage door go up and know I have mere moments before Keene comes up to check on me. Quickly grabbing the pregnancy test and box, I race into the closet. Opening up my safe, I put everything inside and close the door as I hear Keene come up the stairs.

I walk out as he enters the room.

"Hey, baby. I thought I'd find you downstairs." Sliding an arm around my waist, he pulls me toward him. "What's your purse doing up here?"

"I was looking for my pills," I tell him honestly.

He nods. "I thought of that too. We need to figure out what to do about it after you're feeling better."

In eighteen years? Mentally, I'm laughing, but I calmly tell him, "I want to see the doctor this week anyway. I was too weak when I went downstairs. I need to be cleared to run again." Especially while pregnant. I don't mention the last part.

He runs a hand through my hair and drops a kiss on my forehead. "Probably not a bad idea, baby."

Every time Keene calls me baby, I want to shout at him to stop. I want to lean on him to panic. I want to know his reaction, but I need to have the pregnancy confirmed by the doctor before I do anything irrational. It could be a fluke due to being sick and a messed-up cycle. Right?

"Okay, if you're still feeling shaky, you know what that means." Keene leans down and sweeps me up in his arms before walking over to the bed.

I groan. Anything but more sacrificed chickens. "Can't I just have crackers and some other kind of broth?"

He smirks. "If you can keep it down. When I was a kid, the only thing I could handle was chicken soup."

Of course. Because this child is going to be just like his or her father.

That is, if I'm pregnant.

A WEEK LATER, I have no choice but to accept the news.

Dr. Donnelly looks at me kindly. "You have this incredibly blank look on your face, Ali."

Blank. That's an apt way to explain how I'm feeling. "How do I tell him I'm pregnant? I took the pill every damn day?" I whisper.

"These things happen." The OB/GYN pats my hand. "Even if you're perfect taking the pill, there's always that small chance it can be ineffective."

I drop my head back against the exam table. "Let me guess, less than a percent?" My voice is dripping with sarcasm.

Dr. Donnelly laughs. Laughs. I might kill him. "According to the literature, yes. However, the reality is actually closer to nine percent of the time oral birth control fails when used as the only form of contraception."

"Have you ever thought of freaking saying that as your statistic? Maybe women would be less likely to saying yes to going bareback, then!" I snap at him.

The good doctor chuckles, shaking his head. "Probably because it also requires your partner to have some pretty strong swimmers."

Keene. My thoughts turn to cutting off his dick. No, I like it too much. I wonder if I can have it bronzed afterward. When I say as much to Dr. Donnelly, he guffaws. "Okay, Lorena Bobbitt. It's a baby, not the end of the world."

Suddenly, all my bravado fades away. "But what if it's the end of my world with him?" And I break down into a sobbing heap.

"Oh, Ali. You have to calm down. Do you want me to call some-one? Maybe one of your siblings?"

"No. No one can know, Dr. Donnelly. Especially not them."

"Pretty soon, you won't be able to hide it from them, unless you're going to seek out other options, Ali," he says seriously.

I place my hand on my belly protectively. "I have no plans beyond being the best mother I can to this baby, but it's a complicated mess right now." I bite my lower lip. "I just need time to adjust."

He squeezes my hand a final time before letting it go. "Then let's finish your exam to see how far along you are."

My eyes widen. I never even thought about that. "You can do that? Today?"

He chuckles. "We're going to get a nurse in here, and you're going to see your baby in about five minutes."

I gasp, my hand pressing down harder. "You hear that, angel? I get to see you in just a few minutes," I whisper.

"Okay, Alison. Based on how far along I suspect you are from the information about your last period, strip from the waist down. This is going to be a transvaginal ultrasound."

Looking up at him from a haze of euphoria and fear, I ask, "What does that mean?"

"Well..." He pauses as the nurse knocks. Opening the door, she pushes a portable ultrasound machine into the room and approaches me with a sheet. "It means we stick this"—he holds up a phallic-shaped probe—"inside. Then we'll be able to hear the baby's heart-beat and get some pictures. Maybe that will help make it easier to break the news to Daddy."

Keene. Just the thought of him not being here right now hurts. I should have told him. Suddenly, an idea comes to my mind. "Dr. Donnelly, can you give me a minute?"

He looks down at his watch. "How about three of them? You can get changed, and then we can get ready."

Perfect. As he and the nurse walk out of the room, I grab my cell phone, and I quickly call Holly.

"Hey, Ali. What's up?"

"Listen, you know it's Keene's birthday next week, right?" I rush out with this idea. I don't know why I think he'll be thrilled over the news of our child. I just feel it deep in my soul.

"Yep. What the hell are you getting him? I have no freaking idea," she grumbles.

"That's why I'm calling. I need your help." Quickly, I tell her what I'm looking for—a bunch of photos I know she's taken, simply because she's Holly—of Keene and I put together in black and white in a matted frame. "What do you think?" I ask anxiously.

"I think it's perfect. What are you doing in the other blank spots?" she asks curiously.

"That's part of the surprise. Keene gets to know before everyone else does." I'm adamant that I'm not telling my siblings about how I've finally fallen in love, or about the baby until I tell him.

Holly laughs in my ear. "I think I can guess. And if I'm right, he's damn lucky to have you. I'll have it ready in a few days."

Perfect. I hear a knock at the door. "Gotta go. The doctor's about to clear me for running." Which he has to do once I know our baby is okay.

"Sounds good. Love you," Holly says.

"Love you too," I repeat.

Suddenly, the panic of telling Keene is gone, and all I feel is the excitement burning in my soul. This may be soon, way too soon, but this is right between us.

"You ready to see your baby, Ali?" Dr. Donnelly pokes his head around the door.

I shimmy out of my shorts and panties, letting them drop to the floor. Snagging the sheet, I wrap it around my waist. I feel euphoric. "I can't wait. Let's see the little bean."

He laughs as he comes back into the room. "A little larger than that if I'm right. More like a grape."

I'm confused. A grape?

"Wait just a second and I'll explain." After rolling a condom on the probe and lubing it up, he hands it to the nurse before typing some information into the ultrasound machine. Pulling on gloves, he asks me to slide forward.

I do.

"This is going to feel a bit odd." Understatement. "Now reach down and take the probe and insert it for me, Ali."

I do, and the next thing I know, there's this whooshing sound in the room. "What's that?" I whisper, awed.

"That, Ali, is your baby's heartbeat. Perfectly in range for an eight-week-old baby. Or as I said before, a little grape."

I look down at my stomach in awe. "That's how big he is?"

Dr. Donnelly and the nurse laugh. "Or she," he says. He moves the probe around.

"What are you looking for?" I ask curiously.

"I'm making sure there aren't two sacs." My face must show my confusion. "Two babies," he clarifies.

Holy shit.

"One," I croak. "I think that's all I can handle right now."

Laughing, he pulls the probe out slowly and removes his gloves. Hitting a button on the ultrasound, he turns back to me with some wipes. "Then you're lucky all I found was one sac—baby," he corrects himself.

I close my eyes. One is going to be hard enough to tell Keene about, but remembering how he reacted when he heard about Cassidy's twins? No. Just no.

"Here's your pictures, Ms. Freeman," the nurse says to me kindly. "You need to make an appointment every month while you're pregnant, and then at twenty weeks for another ultrasound." Her pretty face gets excited. "If you want to know what you're having, that's when they may be able to tell."

I can hardly catch my breath with all of this being thrown in my lap at once. "Thank you," I say softly.

She smiles reassuringly before she turns to leave.

Holy crap, how could I forget? "Wait! I forgot to ask about exercise!" I call out.

Dr. Donnelly ducks his head back in. "Yes, you can run, but don't push your body. Drink a hell of a lot more fluid than you are now, and watch out for your joints. There are some brochures on exercise that we'll give you." He pulls his head back out.

I slide from the table and move over to where my panties and shorts are. Absentmindedly, I put them on.

I'm having a baby. I'm having a baby with the man I love. I want to shout it from the rooftops, but I only have to hold it in for a week.

Keene is going to have the most insane birthday ever; I can guarantee that.

34

KEENE

y phone rings on the conference room table. "Tell me you've got good news," I bark at Kevin, one of our lead analysts.

"Sir, I have better than that. We have a lock on where Ms. Dempsey is staying. I just sent over two men to track her." Kevin's voice sounds half-exhausted and half-relieved at the news.

Thank God. I rub my hand over my forehead. Finally, this nightmare is coming to an end. "Do they have the processor with them?" I ask wearily.

"They do, sir. Ms. Dempsey will be served with the restraining order within the hour. Hold on, sir." Kevin types on his keyboard. "I just received word she's been served. I can upload the video to you and Mr. Lockwood in the next few minutes."

"Do that. And Kevin—" I hesitate. Even though it was a personal attack against me, our team treated it as a threat against the entire company. "I appreciate everything. All the extra overtime all of you have done to resolve this problem."

"You'd do the same for any of us, sir" is his swift reply. It's no less than the truth. Caleb and I built the company based on the same basic principle we learned in the Army; these are more than people you work with. This is your extended family, and you put your life on the line with them day in and day out.

They proved that to me over the last two months.

"Still," I say gruffly. "It's been noted."

I hear the smile in his voice when he says, "I hope you don't mind my asking, sir, but do you have any plans to celebrate? The rest of us are planning on going out for a few beers tonight."

I'm not surprised. At the end of any major op, the team typically gets together to celebrate its success. "Keep the bill to expense it, but I already have plans." I'm standing and reaching for my car keys.

"Good ones, I hope." Kevin's voice is full of success.

"The best kind. I'm finally able to go home." And I know just the beautiful blonde I want to bring with me to see it for the first time.

CALEB LETS out a huge sigh of relief when I call him from the car after I stop off to pick up a bouquet of flowers for Alison. "It's over."

"It looks that way," I say.

"Finally, things can return to normal around here. I can actually tell my wife what I'm working on again," he grumbles.

I feel a huge pang of guilt, realizing the added stress this has put him under. Not only is Cassidy just a few short months away from delivering their children, he's had to help me clean up my colossal fuckup. "If I haven't said it before now, Caleb, thank you. There's no way to repay everything you did for me the last few months."

"You'd do the same for me in a heartbeat. Oh, wait. You already did, remember? In fact, you've done it twice."

"Twice?" I say, confused.

"The first time when you stepped in front of a bullet for me, and the second time when you saved Cassidy's life. Either way, I would have died, Keene. The way I look at it, I still owe you." His voice chokes up.

Neither of us says anything over the open line, both lost in our memories of those awful days.

"So, I guess you plan on going into the office tomorrow?" he asks.

I frown. I hadn't thought beyond taking Alison home with me for the first time and making love to her in my newly refurbished condo. "I guess so," I say slowly. "We haven't stepped foot in the office in months, Caleb. We should probably go in." Even to my own ears, I sound less than enthusiastic. I know why. I want to be away from Alison about as much as he wants to be away from Cassidy.

Caleb sighs. "I guess so. Especially as we get closer to Cassidy's due date, I'm going to work from home more often."

"Understandable." I rap my knuckles on my steering wheel. "I was thinking of taking Alison into the city tonight. We haven't been more than a few miles away from Collyer since this started."

Caleb lets out a bark of laughter in my ear. "Going stir-crazy?"

I scoff. "No, I just want to show her my place." And maybe explain to her this relationship of ours is more than limited to my time in Collyer. After all, the last time we were in New York together didn't go well.

"I think it should be fine, but let me send some people by," Caleb says.

"Pretty certain they're all out celebrating," I tell him wryly.

After the laughter dies down on the other end of the phone, he says, "Okay, but I'm going to remote in to watch your place until I know you're in it and you're secure."

I swallow hard. "You don't have to do that."

"You're taking precious cargo with you. Pretty sure you'd feel more comfortable if I did."

Precious cargo. That's the understatement of the century. He's talking about my Alison. The woman who showed me that falling in love was absolutely the right thing to do when it was with someone you can hand your heart to and know it won't be rejected.

"Thanks, buddy. I mean, for tonight to be pretty special," I tell him.

"Finally plan on telling her you've fallen for her? About damn time if you ask me," he says before hanging up.

I shake my head before pressing the button on my steering wheel. "Call Alison Home."

The phone rings before she answers with a breathless "Hello?"

I smile. "What were you up to, baby? You just got over being sick."

"Wrapping your birthday present, if you must know," she smarts back at me.

Jesus, my birthday's next week. I'd completely forgotten about it in all of the chaos of trying to find Melody and flush her out. "You could just tell me what you got me," I suggest.

"And spoil the surprise? Not a chance. I've been working on this for a few days now." I hear the excitement in her voice.

I can't wait for it, no matter what it is.

"As long as you're a part of it, I'm sure it will be perfect," I reassure her.

"I hope so," she murmurs. Then louder, she asks, "Did you just call to check in?"

I decide to play with her a bit. "What if I was calling for phone sex?"

There's silence on the other end of the line. "Aren't you at the office?" Her voice isn't refusing the idea out of hand.

"Hmm." My response is noncommittal. "What do you have on, baby?"

I hear her breathing pick up through the phone. "A tank, shorts, and panties."

I judge my distance between where I am and the house. Pushing down on the accelerator, I say, "Lose the shorts."

"Keene!" she laughingly exclaims.

"You heard me, Alison." My voice is stern. "Unzip those things you call shorts and kick them down your legs."

I listen carefully for the metallic sound of her zipper teeth releasing. When I hear it, I say, "That's my girl. Now tell me, what room are you in?"

"Bedroom." Her voice is husky over the car speakers. I can feel my cock swell behind the zipper of my jeans.

"Even better," I purr. "Lift your hands to your breasts. Cup them for me, but don't touch the nipples." Her raw groan is the sexiest sound ever heard through this sound system. I wish I could record it. I'm minutes away from the farm, so I don't want her coming before I get there.

"You're killing me, Keene. I hope you know that." Her voice is pure sex. My woman is turned on. Turning down the farm's main road, I smile wickedly.

"Not yet. Besides, you love what I do to you," I say confidently. "Put the phone on speaker, baby."

"Done," she says breathlessly. Her voice sounds farther away, even though I'm less than thirty seconds from the house.

"Pull off your top." I wait for her to comply. Then, "Suck on your fingers. Start rubbing them over those beautiful nipples." I park outside so she won't hear the garage door open. I switch the car off and let the call switch back over to my cell. Sliding out, I let myself in the front door. I hope she's so involved in what I'm saying to her that she'll ignore the telltale sign of the chime. "Are they hard yet?" I can hear my voice from the bedroom over her speakerphone.

"Yes." Her voice is shaky. "What now?"

Pausing by the stairs, I give her one last order. "Take one hand and slip it down your panties, Alison. I want to hear how wet you are." I wait until there's a slight hitch in her voice before I say, "Don't you dare come."

She lets out a mewl of protest. She has no idea I want to be thrusting inside her, feeling her clasp around me when the eruption of her orgasm hits.

Quietly, I make my way down the hall. "How bad are you, love?"

"Bad, Keene. So bad. I need something." Her groan reaches me through the bedroom door.

I whip off my clothes and stand there, stroking my aching cock. It's leading me like a compass, guiding me to where I should go. Opening the door, I see my woman writhing on the bed. She's just let out a breathy "Keene" when I disconnect the call. She groans, dropping her head back in frustration.

"Yes, love?" I taunt from the doorway where I stand, still stroking my cock.

Alison's head snaps up, and she hops up on all fours. Her eyes are almost feral with heat. God, if I could take a picture, I'd take one of her like this.

This woman owns my soul. There was never one who did before her, and there will never be another after.

"What are you doing here?" she whispers as she blows her hair out of her eyes—eyes so magnificently blue, they look like they drained the sky to feed their color.

If I'm lucky, one day our children will have eyes that color.

Shaking the runaway thought from my mind, I drop my hand from my cock and prowl over to her. "We finished the case."

Much to my surprise, her face freezes. "Does this mean you're leaving?" she whispers.

"No, it means we're going into the city to celebrate. I just decided to start a little early." Seeing her head drop in relief, I tug her toward me and notice the fear easing. "Hey, what's this? Alison?"

She shakes her head. "Nothing. Just a little leftover insecurity, I guess." She gives me a smile. "Where were we?" She reaches for my cock, but I stop her hand.

I don't think so. "I think we're going to go somewhere different than what I was originally planning."

She tilts her head. "No sex?" Her voice is now rich in amusement.

I pull her close to me as I lean her back on her bed. "No sex. I plan on taking care of you, and then I want to take my woman for a night out."

And as I drop my head toward hers, I proceed to use my mouth, my hands, and my lips to drive Alison out of her mind. Soon after, she reaches her peak and falls over the edge. I pull her close into my side and let the relief of the day wash over me. Holding her tight, our breath synchronizes, and within minutes, we're both dozing in the early-afternoon sun.

Holding on as if we'll never let go.

35

KEENE

"I can't believe I'm finally in your place," Alison hums as she walks around. She reaches the picture of Cassidy and I dancing at her wedding, which I replaced after Melody trashed my condo. Smiling at it, she moves to the next one. She stops at a collage of photos in a window-paned frame. Looking over her shoulder, she asks me quietly, "Your mother?"

I put down the spoon I was stirring the pasta with and walk up behind her. Sliding my arms around her waist, I confirm, "When she was pregnant with Cassidy. I figured it was appropriate they were next to each other." Her arms resting on top squeeze mine in support.

I need her to know that now and forever, her heart is the only one mine will ever need. I don't need a harem of women like my father. I won't walk away again. What we have between us is all that matters.

Looking at the pictures of my mother, I know how.

"Come on, dinner's just about ready." I squeeze her one more time before letting go. She smiles at me before sliding onto one of the new high-back barstools.

My decorator tried to find as many pieces that resembled my old place as possible when I explained I'd had a break-in, even down to frames and photos. Unless you were a frequent visitor to my condo, you'd be hard-pressed to tell there had ever been an incident in here.

It still doesn't feel like home anymore. Home is Alison's house.

Stirring the sauce into the pasta, I wonder if she'll let me hang up some of my frames with the ones in her place when we eventually merge homes. Whistling to myself, I pick up a bottle of red wine and turn to where Ali's holding the picture of me and Cassidy at her wedding.

Her face looks sad.

"What is it, baby?" I ask. Walking over to the counter, I hold up a bottle of red wine. She shakes her head. "Still feeling off from being sick?" Alison merely shrugs. I reach in the fridge for a bottle of San Pellegrino, pour each of us a glass, and hand her one before I plate the pasta. Carrying the pasta around the bar, I sit next to her and nudge her knee with mine, encouraging her to continue.

"I miss her. I miss Em and Phil too, but Cass was more like a surrogate mother to me," Alison says quietly. "Being hurt because of the way they treated me at work has led to this rift I just can't quite close." Putting her fork down, she turns toward me. "I feel like I just don't belong there anymore." Alison shakes her head and turns back to her plate. Stabbing her fork into her pasta, she swirls it around before she takes a bite.

I haven't noticed anything at the office. "It's been fairly quiet. Maybe they're just trying to keep things professional since Caleb and I were there," I offer as an alternative.

She snorts. "Please. If everything was the way it normally was, Phil would have been sending us penis balloons or some crap."

I put down my fork. "Is it acceptable to take a hit to my manhood and admit I'm glad penis balloons weren't delivered to the office while I was there?"

Alison scolds me. "Stop it. You make it sound like Phil scares you."

"Phil scares me," I joke. "I'm afraid he's going to start modeling marshmallow fetishware at the next family dinner."

I said that right as Ali took a drink. Somehow, she manages to hold it in and swallow before she lets loose a peal of laughter. "If I were Em, that would have ended up in your face."

"Why do you think I try to sit on the same side of the table as her during dinner?" I say lightly, trying to keep her mood lifted.

Alison grins. "Come sit down by me. We're too far for her to reach."

Tagging the back of her neck, I squeeze. "Deal."

Just then, Alison's cell phone rings, causing her to jump in surprise. "It's Cassidy." She quickly answers with a smile. "Hey, your ears must have been burning. We were just talking about you."

It takes less than a moment for the light I had been watching in her eyes to slowly fade. "I didn't make a mistake drawing up the contract, Cassidy." She pauses. "No. I didn't. Those were the terms I was given on the client sheet." There's silence while she listens. "Yes, I checked. When did you discuss adding Holly's services? This afternoon? And did you bother to tell me before I left the office?" Alison pinches the bridge of her nose between her fingers. "No, Cassidy, I didn't check my email after five. I've been busy."

"Alison," I say softly as she slides off the barstool. She shakes her head at me.

"Cassidy, I understand you're feeling a lack of control. I get it, trust me. Taking it out on me isn't going to help though. If you needed changes, I would've been happy to have put them in immediately. But you should have called me." She stands stock-still. Her voice crackles with bitterness. "You know what? You're absolutely right. Before I fell in love with your brother, I was much more available. Now that I have someone who I spend my time with outside of work, you're pissed at me because I'm not at work's beck and call. Or are you pissed because it's Keene? Hello? Hello? Damnit!" Alison hurls her phone onto the couch.

Moving swiftly to her, I pull her into my arms, holding her patiently while she crumbles. I'm mentally seething at my sister. Bending at the knees, I pick up Alison and carry her over to the couch, not far from where the phone landed.

"You didn't do anything wrong, love. You're not expected to read her mind," I assure her.

She sniffles into my shoulder. "I know. I'm just so tired of defending myself, Keene. It makes Jared's offer look more and more appealing."

One night, while we were lying in bed, I asked Alison what she would be doing if she weren't working for the family. She told me about the offer she received to work for Watson, Rubenstein, and Dalton. I had whistled long and low, knowing the prestigious firm didn't hand out offers to just anyone. "Is it something you're considering seriously now?" Maybe I should be wondering if Alison's photos would be joining mine on the walls of the condo.

She shrugs. "I don't want to. I was happy, Keene. I..." Her hands flail helplessly. "I just don't know what to do anymore."

Her phone rings again. Cassidy. "Let it go to voicemail," I suggest.

She shakes her head. "I can't. Not with her as pregnant as she is."

"Then put it on speaker. I want to hear what she has to say," I demand.

She bites her lip before nodding, even as she's pressing the speaker button. "Was there something else?" Alison's voice is quiet.

"It turns out the email never left my inbox. It was a computer glitch. I'll see you tomorrow, and we can fix the contract then. Have a good night."

Alison's thumb moves, but before she can push it, I say, "Are you fucking kidding me, Cassidy? My woman is sitting here in tears because you're having some sort of personality displacement disorder, and you think you can get away without a damn apology? I think not."

"Personality displacement? It's called being pregnant with twins, Keene. Try it sometime," Cassidy snaps back.

Alison bites her lip and looks away.

"It's called being a human. You made the mistake, not Alison. Not me. So be one and apologize. After all, you've forced your sister to apologize to any number of people before when she hasn't wanted to, haven't you?" I add silkily.

"Completely different, Keene. I was trying to help this family adjust to everyone being a part of it. This was work," Cassidy argues.

"And it was your mistake, not Alison's. So, lose some of that damned righteousness and apologize before you lose your attorney," I tell my sister.

Cassidy laughs. "Where would Ali go? She loves working with us. We're her family."

"Oh, you'd be surprised, sister dear. Have a good night." I disconnect, leaving her to stew on that thought. Now it's my turn to throw Alison's cell phone. "God, she can be so damn stubborn."

Alison laughs in my lap.

"I'm so glad that amused you," I grumble, even though I'll gladly stand on my head to make her laugh instead of cry. "What's so funny?"

"Can you imagine you two as teenagers if you do this much fighting now? It was probably best for the northern hemisphere you two grew up apart." Alison lets out another giggle before slapping her hands over her mouth.

Astounded by her train of thought, I stare at her. The next thing I know, I have Alison flipped on her back and I'm tickling her for all she's worth.

"Stop!" she screeches. "I can't take it!" I pause momentarily to allow her to get her breath back before I pin her with a wicked smile and get her right behind the knee. She's rolling back and forth on the couch, squirming. "You have to stop, Keene! I swear, I'm going to pee all over your couch!" Her face is red from laughing. I've never seen anything more beautiful.

I frame her face with my hands. "God, I love you." The words just come out, but I don't care. Her laughter, her tears, her heartbreak, her happiness, it's what I live for now.

Her lips part. "Keene." Just my name on a gasp, and then silence while tears fan out from her eyes.

I hear her murmur, "I hope I never forget this moment."

"Why is that?"

"Because I want to be able to look back one day and remember every single thing about the moment when the man I fell in love with told me he felt the same way. From the look on his face, to the smell in the air, to the feel of his body on mine." Alison's face is radiant. "And I want him to know what's in here"—she presses her hand against my pounding chest—"is just a mirror of what's in here." She touches her own heart. Her eyes never leave mine when she says, "I love you too, Keene. I love you for everything you are, everything we've made, and everything we will be."

My forehead drops to hers. I'm unmanned by her words.

We sit like that for a few minutes before I murmur, "I want to make love to you." Feeling her nod against my head, I slide off her body and push myself to a standing position. I reach down and pull her into my arms.

For just a moment, we stand there, framed by the window—two people who felt the sparks of love the first night they met, but who never had the chance for it to catch fire. Until now. Lifting her hands to my lips, I pull her behind me toward my bedroom.

When the door closes behind us, I forget about everything but the fact that I'm holding my heart in my arms.

Much later, I move from the bed, and Alison makes a mewl of protest when I lean down. "I'll be right back."

She gives me a tender smile. I love that look. Hell, I love all her looks.

I grab up my jeans by the side of the bed and find the flat jeweler's box inside. I snag it and walk back to her. "Come here, baby. I have something for you."

Alison makes a sleepy protest. "I don't need anything."

I drop a kiss on her swollen lips. "I know you don't need it, but I want you to have it." I hand her the box, but before she can open it, I place my hand on top of hers. "There's a story that goes with it."

She swallows and nods.

"When I was growing up, there was one piece of jewelry I could always remember my mother wearing. No matter where she went or what she was doing." I nod to the box. "I knew I would eventually give that to the woman I fell in love with one day, because it would be my way of showing her I know my mother would have loved her as much as I do." I smile tenderly when I see the first tear hit the worn velvet, then the second.

Alison hands me the box. "Put it on me please."

I choke out a laugh. "You haven't seen it yet."

"Like I care about that, Keene." Her eyes blaze with beautiful certainty. Her lips curve as she rises to her knees to straddle my lap, gloriously naked. "Put it on me."

I take a deep breath and open the box. Inside is a long platinum chain with a carat-and-a-half diamond on the end. Picking it up, I shake it out. "Lean over, baby."

Alison ducks her head.

I slide the chain over her head with ease. Picking up the end, I give it a quick kiss before it drops between her breasts. "It looks beautiful on you."

"Your love looks beautiful on me," she responds back. She's not wrong. Since we laid our hearts bare earlier, something shifted within Alison. She sparkles, even without the addition of my mother's diamond. Slowly, I pull her head down toward mine.

"I love you," I say hoarsely.

"I love you too, Keene," she whispers in the darkened room.

The diamond lands in between us as our hearts align, right before our lips and then our bodies meet to communicate that love.

THE NEXT MORNING, I'm adjusting my tie when I catch a glimpse of my world in the mirror above my dresser. Alison's sprawled across my sheets, wearing nothing but the diamond I placed around her neck in the early hours of the morning. She's clutching my pillow tightly to her, a small smile on her face.

Everything is exactly as how it should be.

A feeling of unease spreads through me. My future is wrapped in thousand-thread-count sheets. I want to spend the day solidifying the promises we whispered in the dark. I want to figure out how we're going to make the complexity of being an hour apart work on a day-to-day basis. Nothing has ever held more appeal than stripping off my clothes and crawling in next to the woman I love.

The absolute last thing I want to do is to go into the office.

But like I told Caleb last night, we haven't shown our faces because of Melody in months. We need to stop being absentee owners of Hudson.

It's time to go.

Walking over to the side of the bed, I brush Alison's hair away from her face. Her smile grows wider. "Hmm. Time for me to wake up already?"

"Were you planning on running before heading home?" I trail my lips along her jaw.

"Yes. I want to feel what it's like here in the city." Sleepy blue eyes roam over my face. "I figure there are nights we're going to want to be here instead of the farm."

I lean down and kiss her. "You figure correctly. I have to go, love."

Alison shifts in bed, putting her perfect breasts on display, and I groan. "Maybe I'll see you later."

"Drop by if you can before you leave the city." I kiss her languidly before I stand and make my way to the door.

"Keene?" I poke my head back inside. "I love you." Even in the shadows of my condo, Alison's words light the deepest part of me.

Sending her a smirk, I wink at her before I head out the door.

If I had known it would be the last time I'd be able to speak to her for the foreseeable future, I would never have left without her knowing exactly how much I loved her.

A SHORT WHILE LATER, I make it to our office near Rockefeller Center. Taking the elevator up to the executive floor, I greet a few employees who enter and exit on the elevator. I get off to find Caleb and my admin, Tony, huddled together. Tony's holding an ice bag to the side of his head. All it takes is one look at Caleb's face for me to know shit has hit the fan and is splattered across the office walls.

The feeling of unease has spread to complete dread as I approach the two men.

"What is it?" I ask without preamble.

"Brace, brother," Caleb says. His fury and disgust are palpable. "Crazy landed in your office after she clocked Tony in the parking lot for his key card."

Melody? Here? Panic flows through my veins. "Alison's supposed to be coming by before she leaves the city. Fuck!" I explode.

"Then I suggest you deal with her quickly. Because when I checked the feed, she was lying naked on your desk." Caleb is pissed. "And I don't take it you finally told Alison about what was going on?" He gauges my reaction, and I have the good grace to flush. "Yeah, I didn't think so. That lunatic isn't leaving unless her ass is dragged out by cops or she gets the fucking she's been asking for."

I hand my briefcase to Caleb. "You're going to monitor and record everything?"

He nods.

I turn to Tony. "Cops have been called to pick her up for violating the restraining order?"

Tony nods. "They just needed you to be in the office, Keene. I'll go down and escort them when they arrive."

I take a deep breath. "No one lets Alison in, understood?"

Caleb mutters, "Boy, did you fuck this up. You should've told her."

"Do you think I don't realize that right about now?" I roar. "What the hell am I supposed to do?"

"Fix it, Keene. Get us the hell out of this mess." Caleb storms off to his office and slams the door.

I look at Tony, who nods at me and sits down behind the desk. I take a deep breath before crossing to my office door. Opening it the narrowest amount, I slide in. Inside, I find Melody laid out on my couch beneath the portrait of my sister and me. Her fingers are sliding in and out of her cunt, juices dripping. I'm repulsed and can't hide my look of disgust. A snarl comes from deep inside. "What the fuck are you doing here?"

"Hello, lover. I thought it was time for us to play since I got your note yesterday. You've been a bad boy, Keene," Melody purrs.

I feel like I'm going to be sick from seeing Alison's sweet beauty tangled in my sheets to Melody's crazy draped across my office couch.

This is what Hell looks like.

36

ALISON

I step out of the elevator on the executive floor of Hudson Investigations, absorbed in my cell phone. I'm texting Corinna about everything and nothing. She's probably flat-out laughing as I'm blathering on about how the sky seemed brighter today when I was out on my run. How the flowers seemed brighter. Smelled better. In New York.

It must have been how well I slept after Keene finished making love to me because that is exactly what it was.

Love.

Fingering the diamond Keene placed around my neck so reverently, I kiss it. I shiver in memory at the way my heart swelled in my chest. The way he laved his tongue around it before raising his head and sipping away at the tears on my cheeks.

It's heady.

It's nerve-racking.

It's forever.

I think I'm going to tell him early. After seeing all of those black-and-white photos in his condo, I just want him to know. I can picture the collage of us up on his wall so easily, especially with the spaces that have the pictures of our baby in them.

I smile to myself when I reach Keene and Caleb's receptionist's desk but find it empty. Sailing past, I reach for Keene's office door-knob. It turns.

And I freeze.

Everything freezes. Except for the naked woman in front of me who's kissing my man.

Or the Keene I thought was my man.

I don't know what triggers their separation. Is it just a need to come up for air? Do they sense they're no longer alone? Is it a sound I make as my heart bleeds out on the cream carpet of Hudson Investigations?

There's one thing I know I'll never forget though—the look of triumph on her face.

I whirl for the door.

"Alison!" Keene roars. The brunette steps in his way.

I never thought I'd have a reason to thank her as I fly through the executive suite.

Suddenly, Caleb's office door opens, and I hear him shout, "Alison, wait! Keene, hold on a damn minute. Let me get her!"

I run through the glass doors into the foyer, just as the elevator doors open. Charlie steps out, and with one quick scan of my face, his turns murderous. Holding the elevator for me, he whispers, "Ali, what did he do?"

"Just let me go, Charlie. Please, please, let me go," I beg. The tears are falling hotly. I need to go before Keene makes it past Caleb.

Charlie holds the doors for another second, two, three. He glances over his shoulder and sees Keene shove Caleb out of the way. "I'll be in contact, baby girl," he whispers before letting the doors go.

I won't be, I think as my heart pounds out of my chest, waiting for the doors to close. Come on, faster. Faster.

They close just before Keene gets to them, but not before he can miss the ravaged look on my face.

The elevator is moving so fast, my head is spinning. Maybe I'm motion sick. How did I never notice how fast it moves before? Or is that the floor that just dropped out from under me? Suddenly, I'm heaving so hard, I turn in the elevator corner and vomit everything from last night's dinner.

Oh, God. What do I do?

Exiting the elevator, I burst out into the lobby. Quickly reaching the street, I step into the hustle and bustle near Rockefeller Center and slam into a hard wall.

"Excuse me" I barely manage to get out.

"Alison?" The voice asks incredulously.

No, please don't let it be someone I know. I focus through my tears and pain to see Colby's familiar face.

"What happened?" He demands.

I shake my head. I can't talk about it. Not to him.

I'm not sure to anyone.

"I have to go." It's all I can manage.

"You shouldn't be going anywhere but home in this condition." He retorts.

I don't have a home anymore. I have nothing. No one. Except this precious life growing inside me. Even as I shake my head wildly, I manage to get out, "I need Jared."

Jaw tightening, he mutters, "You can't walk there in this condition."

Colby, you have no idea what condition I'm in. As he tries to wave down a cab for me, I fire off a text Jared.

Alison: Do you have time to see me?

Jared: Of course.

Alison: I'll be there in 15.

Jared: Everything OK?

Alison: No.

Jared; Booze or more?

Alison: More. Much more.

Jared: Shit.

Well put, Jared.

Gathering what little strength is left in my body, I slide into the taxi Colby miraculously manages to wave down. I'm too numb to care when he slips in beside me telling me he has business in that area of the city. Whatever. After I give the driver Jared's office address, I watch the city pass by me through a flood of tears.

I stagger out of the car at Jared's office, I don't remember saying goodbye to Colby. Or thank you.

I don't remember much of anything.

"Are you sure you want to do this, Ali?" Jared asks quietly. The contracts are laid out on the table before us.

I'll be gone at least a month, maybe more. Charleston, South Carolina. The last place anyone will think to look for me. The root of all my hell.

Or so I thought until an hour ago.

It's amazing how much perspective life can provide to you when you have no blood going to your heart.

"Yes, I'm certain. How many days do I have to be there?" My voice is void of emotion.

He sighs. "Three. That barely gives you enough time to go home and pack, Ali."

Actually, it suits my purposes perfectly.

"That actually works just fine, Jared. I plan on leaving today," I say.

Jared's phone buzzes. He looks down at it. "That's reception. Should I hazard a guess who's down there?"

"I imagine it's Keene," I reply flatly. "That's why I asked about the protection clause of the firm, Jared. I need to know if that kicks in immediately."

"It does," Jared says.

"Then please, ask security to have him removed from the premises, as I am in a conference. He's not a client of mine, and he's here to harass me."

"Jesus, Ali. What did he do?" Jared's clearly in shock.

"If you want to deliver that message in person, why don't you see if he still has another woman's lipstick all over him? They seemed to be enjoying themselves in his office this morning when I dropped by." The cold in my voice could freeze an inferno.

Jared's only outward reaction to what I just said is the mild flaring of his nostrils. "I'll call down to security from my office. You have some files to review, and I'm sure you want to make some phone calls. You're welcome to do both from here." Jared gestures around the beautiful partners' conference room.

Standing, I hold out my hand. "I also have a resignation letter to draft."

He shakes my hand. "Not a leave of absence?"

I shake my head. "No. I'm confident my services are no longer needed at Amaryllis Events." Especially after last night's phone call with Cassidy.

His hand tightens over mine in compassion. "After your initial assignment, you're welcome to stay on with us, Ali."

Tears of gratitude well. "Thank you, Jared. For everything."

"Ali, if you weren't half the attorney you are, I wouldn't be able to do this. Be proud of who you are and what you do." His lips tip up sadly as he leaves the conference room, closing the door softly behind him.

Dropping back down into the soft leather chair around the table, I pull the legal pad closest to me to begin making a list longhand.

I don't realize I've stopped until the tears hit the hand holding my pen, and pain from my clenched jaw radiates out. There's no way this is going to be any easier waiting any longer.

I know I'm right. I can't stay with Keene anywhere in the vicinity.

But the person who has stood beside me throughout is going to be brokenhearted when I ask her for the largest favor of a lifetime–to let me go. Slowly, I pick up the phone and dial the kitchen at Amaryllis Events.

One ring. Two.

"Please tell me it's you calling, Ali, and not Jared."

"It's me," I say. And on those two words, I break. The sobbing starts again harder than before.

How did I think I could hold on to my emotions once I heard Corinna's voice?

"Thank the Lord you're calling me. They're going crazy looking for you. And I mean crazy." Corinna's drawl is exaggerated.

"Cori, I can't talk long."

"Sister, it doesn't sound much like you can talk at all. If it's that bad, he better not walk in my kitchen." Her viciousness on my behalf sets me off on another round of crying.

"Cori, I have to go," I manage to get out.

"I know, babe. What are you going to do?"

"No, Cori. I have to *go*." My emphasis on the last word and silence penetrates.

Corinna's soft reply is, "Oh, Ali. No..."

"Cori, I have to. You have no idea what I walked in on..." I can't allow my mind to go there. I swallow hard and try to continue. "I have to leave, Cori. I need your help."

There's nothing but silence. I'm afraid she's about to start yelling when I hear her husky "What do you need?"

"I can't be in the house long. I have to be gone tonight. I need to send you a list of things..." My voice trails off. "Screw it. I'll just buy new stuff."

"No, Ali," she interrupts fiercely. "I can do this for you. Send me what you need to the kitchen fax."

Sobs rack my body. This is what my family was supposed to be about. The unconditional love and understanding. The absolute faith in me, my decisions. The knowledge I was a part of something bigger. Instinctively, I shy away from the simple word describing why Corinna is doing this for me because right now, there is no such thing as love in a world blurred with this many tears.

"Ali, honey, you have to stop. Do you want me to call Jared?" Corinna's voice is wrecked with concern.

I wipe the snot on the back of my arm. "No, then he'll know his newest employee is a nutcase."

There's an eerie silence that's filled with a simple "Oh shit." I don't know which one of us said it. That wasn't how I planned on telling my sister I was leaving.

"For how long, Ali?" Corinna's voice is awash with pain.

"I don't know. I just don't know I can't be here. I can't be anywhere near here," I whisper.

I hear her breathing on the other end of the line, muttering things like "Okay" and "I've got this" and "Don't go for the knives."

I'm visualizing the perfection of Corinna's face, taking a mental snapshot for all of the cold, lonely nights ahead, when she suddenly says, "Okay, enough about me. What do you need?"

I swallow hard. "I hate even asking this."

"This is what we do, Ali. We're here for each other."

Oh, God, the pain. "I just need you to go to my house and pack my shit. Then, I need you to bring it to me."

"Where?"

"I'll let you know on the fax. I'll be sending it over from Jared's office shortly."

"You mean your new office," she corrects me.

"Only for a few hours, Cori. Now, let me get you that list. And I'll see you soon." I need to hug my sister one more time before I go.

Soon, the fax is on its way with instructions to meet me at The Coffee Shop in a little over two hours. A few minutes later, Jared walks in on me drafting my resignation letter to Amaryllis Events to tell me Corinna received the list and is heading to my house. Keene, after being escorted out of the lobby by security, is apparently being kept at Hudson by Caleb for some reason.

Good, it makes my escape easier. Besides, after I leave Corinna, I still have one more errand to complete. Something only I can do at my house.

"How long do I have, Jared?"

Glancing at the clock over my shoulder, he replies, "You and the courier need to be on your way within the hour." Hesitating, he says, "Ali, are you sure you don't want to fly?"

"Absolutely. Once these"—I tap the legal pads in front of me—"are delivered, I don't want to be traceable for a while."

Moving closer, Jared crouches down next to me. Reaching for my hand, he squeezes it tightly. "Right now, I want to give you whatever you need. What I don't want is a call in the middle of the night waking me up to tell me you've wrapped your rental around a tree. Right now, I want to get you somewhere quickly so you can have a place to let go the way you won't right now. Right now, you're leaving me powerless to do those things. And I hate it," he concludes.

I swallow hard to keep the tears at bay. Jared, with his quiet strength, has become so much a cornerstone of my life this last year. This is hurting him as much as me. Not only because my pain is so all-encompassing and vicious, but because someone he admired has plunged to the depths of depravity beyond which Jared sees no redemption. And by doing so, he's losing me.

"You're doing more than you know, Jared. You've given me a safe haven all afternoon. You're giving me a rental so I can't be tracked. You're giving me time to say goodbye to Corinna before I leave." I see pain flicker across his face. It hurts him to know everything now. "And you're giving me time to figure out what to do next by giving me a job. You gave me power when I had none walking in here." Leaning forward, I brush my lips against his softly. "I just need you to give that kiss, my thanks, and my goodbye to Ryan and everything will be the way it should be."

He blows out the breath he was holding. "Okay, Ali. You have thirty-eight minutes to wrap it up."

I nod my thanks and keep drafting the letter longhand, trying to figure out how to end not only a business relationship with no notice, but also sever ties with a family whose love I crave right now with every fiber of my being.

Whose mark I'll bear on my heart and my body until the end of time.

37

ALISON

The darkened windows of the car the courier is driving keep the blue of the sky at bay as we pull off of the Saw Mill Parkway and make our way through the winding roads toward Collyer. I memorize the leafy, lazy green trees as they lounge over the reservoirs that line our route.

I'm wrapped in my world of nothing, relishing the weight of it. I wish I could suffocate under the burden, be submerged and never come up, just so long as I never have to feel ever again. I wish I could go to sleep and never wake up if I never have to experience the pain that ripped through me today watching Keene with another woman.

Absentmindedly, my fingers are clutching the diamond he placed around my neck so reverently last night. If the diamond wasn't his mother's, I'd have ripped the damn thing off and thrown it into the traffic racing up Eighth Avenue. However, knowing the hell Laura Marshall had lived through in her short time on earth, I have more respect for the woman than that.

At this moment, I feel a deep kinship with her that I'd hope I'd never feel. A Marshall man proclaiming his love, swearing fealty with diamonds and fucking around with another woman right under your nose.

All while you're pregnant.

What a fool I was to think that saving my early pregnancy test and adding the sonogram pictures, along with a series of framed photos Holly had taken of us as a birthday gift for Keene, would be looked upon with joy? What did he care about being a father? He cared about getting his dick wet with any variety of holes.

And I was just another one.

I mentally add an STD test to my list of items to ask my new OB/GYN about once I arrived in South Carolina. First, I have to get my pregnancy test, leave the diamond somewhere safe, and leave Collyer in my rearview mirror.

"Ms. Freeman, we're here," the Watson, Rubenstein, and Dalton courier announces. "Do you see your sister so we can transfer your bags?"

I was so lost in my thoughts, I didn't realize we'd already driven down Main Street. We'd passed the local jewelry store, the local boutiques, the chocolatier, and even the Amaryllis Events office. We've pulled down the side street where The Coffee Shop is located, and I see Corinna's delivery van. "There." I point to the driver.

He pulls in next to her, and she jumps out. Together, they transfer three large suitcases and a few smaller ones to the back of the SUV I've been riding in. I slide out and face Corinna.

"It's worse than I thought, isn't it?"

I swallow and say, "Call Jared. He'll fill you in. I can't talk about it right now. I have to drive soon." A tear trickles down her cheek. "Don't cry." I smile sadly. "This is how it's meant to work out."

"Oh, Ali. One day, you'll find the person willing to go to the ends of the earth for you," she counters.

"I already did. You," I whisper. "Now, give me a hug to last me a while. Then you have to go back to the office. This isn't over yet." Not by a long shot.

She opens her mouth to ask and then closes it. The next thing I know, her body crashes into me and she's sobbing. All I can think is, you can't collapse yet, Ali. Not yet. Tomorrow, maybe. I stroke her hair to comfort her, and whisper, "I promise I'll try to figure out a way we can talk, okay?"

"Promise me, Ali, this isn't goodbye forever. Just for now," Corinna mumbles into my neck.

Knowing I have a lot of thinking to do before I make my final decisions on forever, I can make that promise with honesty. "I promise."

She steps back. God, she's so beautiful, it aches just to look at her. I want to beg her to come with me. If I was going anywhere but Charleston...

"I've got to go, Cori."

"I know." Neither of us makes a move to leave.

It's the coughing of the courier that finally gets our attention. "Ladies, it's time. Ms. Freeman, if you could join me in the car?"

I lean forward and kiss Corinna quickly on the cheek. "Remember, I'm always holding your hand, Cori. Always. Tell Hols I'm sorry. I'm so sorry. I just couldn't figure out a way to see both of you, and you were the only one I could contact." I slide my long legs back into the SUV and close the door. Rolling down the window, I watch Corinna's face jerk.

"Wait, Ali! I got you these!" Corinna reaches into the van. "I wasn't sure how far you'd have to drive, and I thought you might not want to stop."

In her hands are two of The Coffee Shop's extra-chocolate mochas.

I look at them, look at her, and a single tear escapes. Just one.

"After today, I didn't think I could say this word so soon, if ever. But know I love you, Corinna. Hols too. Always. Forever. That will never change." I take the drinks from her and put them in the cupholders in front of me. I'll have to drink one today and one tomorrow to watch my caffeine intake because of the baby.

I reach my fingers out and capture hers briefly, as the courier backs the car up. Our hands gradually pull apart, and Corinna's face dissolves in tears as he turns us toward the street.

"Ms. Freeman, you need to roll up your window. We can't have you caught on any cameras," the courier, Greg, says.

"Thank you, Greg. For everything." I watch the trees pass as we drive a few minutes down the road.

Pulling into the private rental agency, Greg makes quick work of picking up my keys and transferring my bags. He checks to make certain I'm comfortable with my navigation system and the temporary phone I was given by Jared earlier, and have all of my papers.

I'm finally in the car, ready to head to my house to get my final items from the safe and leave a message for Keene when Greg's face fills the window. "How much time do you need at your home?"

"Twenty minutes, tops," I answer immediately. I know what I want to say and how I'm going to say it.

"You'd best be on your way, then. I have letters to deliver." He raps the roof of my car, and I pull out of the small private rental lot that Jared paid an obscene amount of money for, for me to not have to register the car under my own name, allowing me more time to run.

I'VE RETRIEVED what I needed from my safe. The pregnancy test is tucked safely in my purse, and the sonogram pictures have been removed from the unwrapped frame.

I wrote my message to Keene in bright red lipstick on the mirror over my vanity. I figured it was appropriate. It matched the color he was wearing after he kissed that—woman. I then took out a velvet necklace holder from my closet and placed it on the vanity after plugging the drains.

Carefully taking off Laura Marshall's necklace, I drape it on the holder. Staring at the glinting diamond with my hand on my lower abdomen, I whisper, "I'll teach this little one that the price one pays for love includes respect, Mrs. Marshall. I learned that from my mother too."

Turning away, I walk back into my room and pick up the mostly framed collage of pictures Holly had put together of Keene and I.

Moving back into the bathroom, I put it into the bathtub. Using another frame from my room, I raise my hands over my head and land the first hit right on top of his lying, cheating face.

Repeatedly.

Fortunately, the glass is tempered, so I'm not concerned with flying shards landing all over me. The dent over Keene's face is immensely satisfying though.

My chest heaving, I drop the extra frame in the tub and survey the damage. There's no way to look at this frame and not understand the full ramifications of how I feel about Keene Marshall.

Now, it's time for me to go.

I stand and quickly strip my clothes, dropping them carelessly on the floor of my bathroom. I never want to see them again. Walking naked into my closet, I grab a pair of extra running clothes from my still-overflowing wardrobe that Corinna didn't pack.

I'm out the door and on the road twenty-one minutes after I entered my house, heading south. Heading back to where it all started.

Fortunately, the traffic gods are on my side, and I don't hit any major hiccups until just south of Delaware. I'm a little over three hours into my six-hour drive for the night. My goal is to hit Richmond tonight, Charleston tomorrow.

My body aching, I decide to stop and stretch at the Chesapeake House rest stop when my new phone rings.

Jared.

I still answer cautiously. "Hello?"

"Are you out of the vicinity, Ali?" He sounds tired. I hate that I left him to deal with the family, but there was no other choice.

"Do you want a specific location or general hours?" I know Jared's now my attorney and business partner, but family loyalty has got to be pulling him in two.

"Hours," he says immediately.

"I'm three and a half hours out, Jared. Why?"

"Because apparently, Greg held the letters an extra hour," he says tiredly. "When he handed them over, Keene, Caleb, and Jason had just made it to Amaryllis. If the screaming I heard through my phone is anything to go by, the family is in an uproar."

"That's nothing new." I only speak the truth.

"Fair enough, Ali, but apparently, whatever you did at your house sent Keene into such shock, he called Caleb over. Do I want to know?"

I think about it. How much of what I scrawled across the mirror does Jared need to know? "Let's just say, I left him a message asking if she was worth it. If he wants you to know more, he can tell you." My voice is hard.

"Right," he mutters. "Now I know why you sent Corinna there first."

I let my silence speak for itself.

"How much more do you have to drive tonight?" Jared's change of subject tells me he's done with his updates.

"Another few hours," I say vaguely.

"Just promise me you won't drive all night."

Already drained from the events of today, I acquiesce easily. "I won't."

"Okay. We'll talk more tomorrow. Safe travels, my friend."

"Bye." Hanging up the phone, I hold it to my chest for a second before I make my way back to the rental. I'm well on my way again before I give thought to what Jared said.

"Apparently, whatever you did at your house sent Keene into such shock, he called Caleb over."

Good. It's nice to know I'm not the only one who had to deal with a few shocks today.

Pushing the accelerator, I follow the signs for Richmond and look for a decent place to sleep.

Around 8:00 p.m., I check into the Little Swan Bed and Breakfast in Blackstone, Virginia, about sixty miles southwest of Richmond. If anyone is looking for Alison Freeman, this isn't going to be where a computer search is going to find her. Since I used Jared's company card to secure the reservation, it takes a few moments for the innkeeper to call and confirm it's an acceptable charge. Moments later, I'm escorted to a room that's rather reminiscent of the room my mother decorated for me when I was a little girl.

Done up in white wicker, with a thick blue bedspread and pale blueish-green walls, the space feels like the arms of my mother are wrapping around me and squeezing me tight when I most need it. After thanking the proprietress again for accommodating me, I strip down to nothing and crawl in between the sheets.

I can't hold back any longer.

Tears scald my cheeks, and I use the pillow next to me to muffle my sobs.

The dam I've been holding back finally bursts.

Images from this morning play through my mind like a rapid-fire movie. Keene's hands on another woman's hips. His head bent. Her naked body pressed up against him, one hand wrapped around his tie. The clenching of her hand in his dark hair. Lips fused together.

I quickly roll to the side, reach for the trash pail, and vomit. Bile rises in my throat again, and another burst comes forward. Managing to get my nausea under control, I reach for the tin of ginger Altoids and pop one in my mouth, hoping it will settle my stomach. Clutching the pillow to my chest, my tears subside to a consistent trickle. The question that's been burning in my heart all day pushes to the forefront of my mind.

Mama? Why am I so unlovable?

Daddy tried to sell me into slavery.

My new family essentially gave up on me.

And Keene? I rub my lower stomach, feeling the slight hardness that has nothing to do with my persistent workouts.

Why, Mama? Please, help me to understand?

With that thought, I fall asleep, knowing my heart will never rest easy again.

38

KEENE

C aleb and I are standing in Amaryllis Events, quietly discussing the business side of this morning's disaster. What Melody pulled in the office was more than enough to get her arrested for criminal stalking. Now, all I was focused on was finding Alison to explain.

No matter where I seem to look for her, I can't catch up with her. Not knowing what was going on, she sought asylum from Jared within Watson, Rubenstein, and Dalton. It's now late afternoon, and I have no idea where she is or what her mental state is. The only thing I know is that her cell and her car haven't left New York.

She may be somewhere in the city hiding from me, but I'll find her by tonight and have the discussion I've been avoiding. That I, someone trained to protect others, had a psychotic stalker who had threatened her, Cassidy, and me.

She has to understand. She has to. There's no other option.

I'm pacing back and forth, running my hands through my hair, when the stained-glass door to Amaryllis Events opens. Phil, who had been standing off to the side talking quietly with Cassidy and Em about Alison's whereabouts, asks, "Can I help you?"

"Yes. I'm looking for Cassidy Lockwood and Phillip Freeman-

Ross. I'm a courier from Watson, Rubenstein, and Dalton in New York. I have urgent messages to deliver," the man, dressed in a charcoal gray suit and black open-collared shirt, says. His eyes scan the room until they land on my sister. "Mrs. Lockwood," he says respectfully. He's obviously been briefed. He turns, and I get a good look at his face.

The courier, who I know from performing his background check through Hudson, is actually Greg Anderson, the head of New York security at Watson, Rubenstein, and Dalton. Whatever he's delivering isn't good news. Anderson steps forward, hands one letter to Cassidy, which is formally addressed to Cassidy Lockwood, CEO, Amaryllis Events, and another to Phillip. "These are to be opened in a particular order. Mrs. Lockwood, if you would, please?"

Cassidy and Phil look at each other, and Caleb and I do the same. Cassidy uses a nail to slide her finger into the tamper-evident envelope. When she pulls out the papers and begins to read, a choked gasp escapes her. Caleb rushes to her side, and it's a few moments before she's able to say, "Oh my God. She resigned." Her eyes meet Phil's first, then Em's. "Ali resigned from the company."

"What? Don't be ridiculous!" Phil snaps, but he sounds nervous. He stalks over to Cassidy and rips the papers from her hands. His own start shaking. "Sweet baby Jesus." His voice is a whisper.

"There's no reason? No notice?" Em's voice is clinging for something. Anything.

Phil's frantically flipping through pages. "No, nothing. Just instructions, her logins and passwords, briefs on pending cases, operating procedures—that's it."

I hear Anderson clear his throat. My head turns incrementally toward his, and that's when I feel it. This was just the first lobby. The bomb hasn't hit yet. He nods to the other letter in Phil's hand, the one with the instructions written in her beautiful penmanship, which simply says, *Read aloud when the entire family is present.*

Showing his empathy for my sister's condition, he suggests, "Mrs. Lockwood, is there a better place for this to be read? Perhaps a place where you can sit down? When I last saw her, Ms. Freeman suggested you may want to retire to the conference room."

Meaning whatever is in that letter is going to hit hard.

"Someone get Corinna and Holly," Phil demands. Em turns away to call them.

I hear Cassidy mutter, "I think I'm going to be sick."

Caleb tells her soothingly, "We'll find her, Pixie."

"You don't know, Caleb. Maybe it was the things I kept saying to her. I was such a hormonal bitch." I hear my sister crying in her husband's arms.

It wasn't you, Cass. I did this. Because I couldn't bend my pride enough to tell Alison the truth.

Em comes back and says, "They'll be upstairs in just a moment."

We all make our way upstairs with Phil leading the way, holding Alison's letters like they're the most precious and dangerous things he's ever touched. Em's not far behind him, clutching her phone as if it's a lifeline.

Caleb is leading my sister up the grandiose staircase, murmuring in her hair, likely telling her they'll figure it out together, the way they have since practically the moment they met.

I'm following behind, fear creeping into every step I take away from the door. I know every minute I'm here, I'm not out looking for her, making her understand that what she saw wasn't what she thought it was.

That I'm not that kind of man. I'm not my father—I'm not a cheater.

I would never do that to someone I like, let alone someone I love.

I feel alone, even as I enter a conference room full of people. Within seconds, I feel a blast of heat. I look up frantically, wondering if Alison is in the room, ready to lambast us all. Instead, I meet Corinna's red-rimmed, hate-filled eyes.

I lower my head in shame. It seems Alison had a moment to speak with her younger sister before she wrote her resignation and whatever is in the second letter. Now I know I need to leave. Just as I start to rise, I hear Phil ask if he should call Jason.

Anderson says the letter can't be read until everyone is in the room.

Phil says, "I'd like him to listen to the letter. Can I call him on speaker?"

I want to rail at Phil to get on with it, but I know if the situation were reversed, I'd want Alison's support.

Anderson hesitates, then turns and makes a quick call. "A Mr. Jason Ross will be arriving in less than five minutes."

Phil's relief is evident by the way he physically sags in his chair.

The grandfather clock ticking back and forth slowly is the only sound indicating the passage of time. Then the front door opening and closing, and light footsteps running up the staircase, announces the arrival of Jason.

Phil jumps up from his chair and goes running into his husband's arms. "Jace, Ali..."

"I know. Jared called me in the city. Ali asked him to."

I want to be infuriated with her for causing her family such pain, but I can't. She's taken every care to ensure their mental and physical well-being before she delivers this blow. Something I didn't do with her. Even if that wasn't what I had intended. Jesus, what am I going to do?

"Can we get on it with it?" I snap. "Everyone's here now."

All eyes turn toward me.

"Oh, if you have something to do with this, Keene..." Phil threatens.

"He has everything to do with it, Phil. But not for nothing. None of you gave a damn about Ali's pain, not only about Keene, but about anything these last few months. Just read the damn letter so I can go back to work and mourn the loss of my sister," Corinna declares. Everyone's heads swing toward her, but she doesn't back down. She meets each shocked look head-on.

For me, at least, I know for certain she knows everything. Maybe even where Alison is? I have to hold on to that little bit of hope.

"Phil, honey, it's time," Em gently encourages him. Jason, standing behind him, squeezes his shoulder. Phil sighs and tears open the back of the letter, the sound causing all of us to flinch. He unfolds the yellow legal pages and begins to read. "Hello, everyone." Phil scans the letter a few lines. Visibly swallowing, he continues.

I never imagined the day would come when I no longer worked for Amaryllis Events or considered myself a member of the Freeman family, but here it is.

First, I need to apologize for the things I've done to anger you all over the last several months. Hell, years. I was only trying to protect everyone, always. My actions were driven with that goal in mind—protecting the goodness of our family. I was determined to do so, even if it cost me my own happiness. I should have just bowed out sooner. Phil, Cassidy, Em, from the moment you found Corinna, Holly, and I at that home, I knew my time with you was limited, but that was all right, so long as you took in the sisters of my heart and protected them for the eternity they deserved. I was willing to be cast out if necessary to spare them an ounce of pain. Each time I had to deliver bad news over the years about the business, about the house, or getting angry over the actions of Jason, Caleb, or Keene, I knew the length of time my usefulness to the family was being reduced. Rapidly.

I was trying to make you all fight for what you knew to be right in your heart of hearts. I was trying to be the voice of reason and keep us from falling into the traps of our parents, even when we weren't sure who they were. In some ways, I guess I succeeded. In others, I ostracized myself from everyone. Except for Corinna. And Holly in the end.

My desire to leave started some time ago. I refuse to say when, but when I first thought of going, I thought I'd go with my family's blessing, to stretch my wings a little bit. Not under the avalanche of pain I find myself in now.

I can't say the pain I feel is worse than my childhood because it's different. The pain on the block was because my father was strung out on drugs. The pain I feel today was the deliberate cruelty of a man who I can honestly say I fell in love with of my own accord, who said he was in love with me in return. I can't say the shame is less because it cut deeper and will be felt longer. I can say I'm better equipped to deal with it. I'm not sixteen. I'm twenty-seven. And it's because of the beauty of the last eleven years with you all that I can make decisions instead of reacting blindly.

There may be no open arms where I'm going, but that's all right. I don't think I'd trust them right now anyway.

Maybe someday we'll meet again. Maybe someday you'll forgive me for needing to go.

Please know everything I did, every decision I made, including this one, was with the intent of protecting your hearts first, last, and always.

Even though I'm no longer yours, you will always be my family forever where it counts the most.

My heart.

Always,

Ali

After Phil's voice cracks on her name, a horrified silence fills the room.

Cassidy's voice urgently says, "Call her. Call Ali. Call her now."

Phil dives for the phone in the center of the conference room table. He quickly punches in her cell phone number from memory. The phone starts ringing. Once. Twice.

The pain I felt today was the deliberate cruelty of a man who I can honestly say I fell in love with of my own accord, who said he was in love with me in return.

The pain in my chest almost chokes me. Please, Alison, pick up, baby. Give me a chance to explain.

I hear a click as the phone is answered. "This is Jared."

That pain intensifies. There's no way to reach her.

The yelling by the Freemans starts. The only one not saying a word is Corinna.

Above the cacophony of sound, I yell, "She can't have left so quickly. I'm going to her house. There has to be some kind of clue as to where she is." My sister's eyes flash up to mine, filled with both pain and gratitude.

Caleb walks me outside of the conference room, where the family is still badgering his brother-in-law for information. "Call me if you need me." Clapping me on the back, he squeezes my shoulder tightly.

I didn't think I'd need to make the call when I got there.

I called within ten minutes.

Caleb arrived five minutes later.

We both stood in Alison's bathroom in shock, knowing there was no way to explain this to the family without explaining everything.

Something I was going to have to do before getting a chance to say it all to the woman I love.

~

A MARSHALL *man...a diamond...another woman. I should have known better than to think you were different, or that I was. YOU BROKE ME.*

I think those words written in bloodred lipstick on her mirror will haunt me for the rest of my life, all because of my damned ego. Because I never admitted I had a stalker. And now, Alison is gone because of my lack of explanations.

Alison is gone.

Alison can't be found.

Caleb immediately turned the full resources of Hudson into looking for her.

Her car was sitting in the garage of Watson, Rubenstein, and Dalton.

Jared had her phone.

Her credit cards hadn't been used.

Her clothes were missing.

The last cash withdrawal from her bank had been substantial, which included a transfer deposited to the company account of Watson, Rubenstein, and Dalton. She had also pulled out several thousand in cash.

There were no rental cars listed under her name under any agency our databases had access to.

Caleb had already tried to work Jared. Because of attorney-client privilege, and since she didn't commit any crimes and wasn't a witness, Jared was under no legal obligation to disclose her location.

I could practically hear Jared's sneer through the phone when he said, "She's not a missing person. She is in contact, with me. She chooses to not share that information with anyone else. Now, if you and Mr. Marshall have a need to bring my client back for any criminal proceedings, Caleb, please let me know. Otherwise, don't bother me with such a ridiculous request," right before he hung up on us.

I pick up my iPad and throw it across the room. It crashes into the wall and cracks with a sickening sound.

"We'll find her, Keene. I promise you, brother. We'll find her," Caleb swears.

"How? She's completely off the grid, Caleb! We can't find any record of her anywhere," I yell. Pressing my back against the wall of Caleb's office, I sink down. The heels of my hands press hard against my burning eyes.

"You know, you stupid boy, if you'd just told her it was a damned op, you wouldn't be in this fucked-up mess." I don't even lift my head as I hear Charlie's voice berate me.

I'm not surprised by the underlying fury I hear in his tone. Charlie Henderson is the original investigator who worked with the Freeman family so many years ago before Caleb and I ever purchased Hudson Investigations. His relationship with the family evolved into an avuncular one. He's watched over what he consider's his adopted family ever since.

"What do I do, Charlie?" I whisper.

"Something you completely suck at, Keene," Charlie replies. "You have to wait. It's not going to get fixed overnight. In the meantime, I suggest you start repairing the relationships you can. You're going to need them when you can find her."

Still crouched down by the wall, I try to stand. I glance up and see a beefy hand held out to me to help me up. I feel a burning hotness in the back of my eyes when I clasp his hand. "Thanks, Charlie."

"Don't thank me yet. You're in for the fight of your life, Keene. Even Cassidy may draw blood over this one." He transfers his look of concern from me to Caleb. "You're not immune from this either. And with her pregnant..."

"Yeah." Caleb lets out a long, drawn-out sigh. He's feeling more than his own measure of guilt, which isn't his to bear.

It's mine.

Charlie steps back. "Get to work, boys. Get my family back together, pronto." He lumbers his way out of the office.

Once the door closes behind him, Caleb asks me, "Do you ever wonder if he's really the one in charge around here?"

Feeling the first glimmer of hope since this morning, I respond. "Frequently. But then I remember you hired him and I feel better about life."

We exchange brief smiles before sitting down to start strategizing how to find my Alison.

When we're done, the pieces of my iPad are still on the floor, but I leave knowing I have to talk to the Freemans.

I'm not sure what I'd rather do—face Alison's family or be shot again.

Either. As long as Alison comes back to me.

39

MELODY

"You just couldn't leave him alone, could you, Melody?" I hear through the plastic phone attached to the wall. There's a face I haven't seen in close to five years.

Since the last time I got into a "situation." When he made me change my name for my own "protection."

"Father," I say respectfully. I dare not use any other tone right now.

He holds my fate in his hands once again.

And my ability to get out to get to Keene.

"You promised me that if I helped you start a new life, you would get help. You swore you did. You swore this to both your mother and me." He takes a deep breath.

I look at the difference five years has made on his face. He's aged. His hair, which had been more salt than pepper, is now fully gray. His eyes, dark like my own, are tired.

Disappointed and infuriated.

After all, when you're a judge, you have big issues weighing on your shoulders.

"How many others have there been, Melody? Other than the two you got caught for?" he demands.

I can't answer. I don't know.

It started so long ago. My high school biology teacher was the first. I smile with relish, remembering the way I improved my grade for the year. Blinking back into focus, I see nothing but disgust on his face.

"This time, you stand on your own, Melody. I won't help you. Not financially, not with counsel."

Not with Keene. It takes me half a second to realize that.

I jump up and bang at the glass in between us. "You bastard! You were never there for me! Never! You were always too busy for me!" I scream at him.

His expression never changes. "I was busy, Melody, yes. But I was never too busy for you."

"Liar!" I scream.

"There's nothing I can do to help you now." My father stands, the phone still in his hand. "Nothing your mother can do." My father shakes his head. "When they prosecute you, we won't be there to support you." He takes in a deep breath.

My hand not holding the phone runs through my hair agitatedly. I'm waiting for him to drop the bomb.

There's always one with Judge Arthur McDonald, United States Supreme Court Justice. The man who made his name in the judiciary world when he sentenced the man behind the South Carolina human trafficking ring to 144 years in prison.

His star has been on the rise ever since while mine exploded.

"We'll be there to support the prosecution." He removes the phone from his ear and hangs up.

I start screaming, "No!" at the top of my lungs. I'm banging on the glass. "Father! Get your fucking ass back to the phone and get me out of this mess! God damn you! No!"

The guards are on me before I can raise my hands against the glass again, wrestling my arms back into shackles. I struggle, earning me time in the box.

After I'm moved into solitary confinement, I'm left alone, contemplating on how I can get out of this mess to get to Keene.

He's mine. Always. They're all mine.

40

KEENE

"Tell me you're kidding right now, Keene. Tell me this is all some awful nightmare that I'm going to wake up from and you didn't cause my sister to leave because you're too much of a pansy-ass wimp to admit you had a problem." Cassidy lumbers to her feet and is leaning forward on her desk. Her petite body is so dwarfed by the children she's almost carried to term, I'm wondering silently if she's as round as she is tall.

"Tell me you didn't trust your woman enough the night you gave her Mama's diamond necklace, the night you finally told her you were in love with her, to tell her the truth of what had been going on the last two months," she continues brutally.

"Cassidy, love." Caleb steps in to save me, and she turns her anger on him.

"I have never been disappointed in two of the three men I love as much as I am right now. While a lot of what was building in Ali had to do with *this family*"—she stresses the last two words, putting me and Caleb on the outside—"the spy games you two played were the straw that broke her back. She fell in love with you, Keene!" she screams. "And you didn't prepare her for a scene like that? You didn't let her know it would all be fake? You didn't trust the woman you loved enough?"

Cassidy turns away from me and stares out the window. Her next question is worse than a slap. "Did you like it?"

"What are you talking about?" I ask.

"Having another woman...multiple women? Is that something my sister needs to worry about should she ever take you back?" Her voice is sad.

"No! Fuck no! Cassidy, how can you ask me that?" Fury propels me from the chair I'm sitting in.

"How can you not expect me to protect her the way she always tried to protect me?" she whispers. "Even from you."

I feel that punch straight through to my heart. Jesus.

"She knew you weren't happy about my having the twins, and she stood in front of you for me. Even when I didn't ask her to. She took a verbal beating from me in this very room. I made her apologize to you, and for what? For you to break her heart? To break this family apart? I have to ask myself why. Should I have protected her better? Should I have listened better?" My sister's voice is filled with tears.

I'm frozen. I never expected this kind of attack. When I lay awake last night, thinking of every possible scenario, this wasn't anywhere in my thoughts, earning my sister's doubt in the kind of man I am.

"Pixie, Keene's not like that. You know that." Caleb tries to touch her, but she shrugs him off. His shock is palpable.

"Right now, I can't have either of you near me. I love both of you, but I can't have you near me. Keene, this was yours, to share all the details." She turns fully away from the window, and I can see the tears flowing freely. Caleb sucks in a breath. "But Caleb, you could have told me something to have warned Ali. You watched what was happening. I could have called her. And now, she's gone." Cassidy's tears shift into sobs. Caleb steps forward, but again, she stops him. "No. I need to be alone. Please go, both of you. I have a lot of work to do since Ali's...please, just go." Her voice holds a note of finality.

I make my way over to the office door and fling it open. The sound of it hitting the wall is like a gunshot. I leave Caleb with the chance to make up with his very pregnant wife.

Taking the stairs two at a time, I make my way to the first floor when I hear a quiet voice behind me. "Charlie called me and Jared last night."

Quickly, I spin to see Corinna standing there, holding a kitchen knife in one hand and a mallet in the other. Not your average baking tools. "Corinna—" I start.

"We lost her—*I* lost her because of your damned ego. Do you think I can forget that so quickly?" Her aim is true. It was because of my ego that Alison is lost.

Gone.

"Do you think this is what I wanted?" I hiss out. "I was trying to spare her."

"Her or yourself, Keene? Because the Ali I know could've handled honesty. What she can't handle is believing she's a worthless game," Corinna hisses right back.

"From the first night you met her, that's what you treated her like —a game. She wanted to be so much more to you. She was so excited yesterday morning. Something wonderful happened the night before where she finally got the chance to tell you how she felt, and it wasn't a game anymore. She felt she had all of you, Keene." Corinna pauses. "But it was just another game, wasn't it?" Her arms drop to her sides. "It's time to grow up and stop playing games. The people you do it to don't deserve it."

Corinna begins to make her way back down the hall toward the kitchen. I find my voice. "She was never a game, Corinna. Not one minute with her was a game," I call down to her. "I was just figuring out how to let her in."

She doesn't turn around as she calls back, "Then maybe it's a good thing she's gone if that's what she got when she finally got in there."

I'm still standing there, gutted, when Caleb comes down the stairs. His face shows he didn't fare much better.

"Is Cassidy okay?" I ask.

"Okay, being subjective. Phil came in at the end. He'll watch out for her and bring her home later. I overheard some of that." His thumb points down the hallway toward Corinna's kitchen. "Are you okay?"

I shake my head. I'm bleeding, broken, but I don't have anyone to blame but myself. "Charlie tried to soften the blow."

"Did it help?" Caleb asks.

"Not with Corinna, but he also talked with Jared. We might want to talk to him again. Maybe this time in person?" I suggest.

"Good idea." With a last concerned look upstairs toward his wife's office, he says, "Let's go."

We leave Amaryllis Events and walk toward his Porsche to head back to New York City.

JARED'S FACE is impassive as Caleb explains the stalking I had been enduring the last few months. Caleb lays out everything, every interaction, every altercation we've documented. He shows Jared the restraining order we have in place and explains the fact the video was on yesterday in my office to show how completely Melody had gone off her rocker.

Pulling the files closer to him, he reviews them, flipping through pages of transcribed notes by our analysts. I refuse to give in to the embarrassment warring with my anger. I want to unleash the anger instead. Anger that Jared didn't know the kind of man I was after years of friendship, and that I would never break Alison's heart. That he didn't find a way to stop her from leaving. That he wouldn't tell us where she was yesterday so we could have told her all of this.

Finally, he sighs and pushes the files away. "I wish you had taken me into your confidence even yesterday morning. Then, perhaps, we'd have had a different outcome." He rubs his hand over his eyes. "She's my client, guys. I can't break that trust. I'm sorry." To me, he says, "I truly am sorry."

I feel the hope I'd been holding on to start to wane. "It's not your fault, Jared. It's mine."

He hesitates. "If you want to leave a message, I can be sure to get it to her. Whether it's verbal or written."

It's a huge concession, one I wasn't prepared for. When I stand, Jared and Caleb stand as well. "I need to think about what to say to her. I have to think..."

Jared nods, and Caleb says, "Come on, buddy. Let's get you home."

I look at him blankly. "It's not a home anymore. Alison's not there."

"I know, Keene. Trust me, I know."

I nod and start to follow him out of the partners' boardroom at Watson, Rubenstein, and Dalton. "Wait." Both men pause. "Jared, did she..." I swallow. "Was she sitting in here yesterday?"

He takes his time responding. "There." He points toward the chair nearest to my hand.

I take the single step toward it, brushing my hand over the leather. I imagine the warmth of her strong body cocooned in it as she held her emotions in tight, refusing to give in as she drafted her resignation notice. I imagine the pain she was in while she was writing her goodbye letter. As she called her sister, making her plans to run.

From me.

I can't help but break.

My hand on the back of the chair, I drop my head to it as the tears fall, the gut-wrenching sound pulled from the depths of my soul. I release the pain I felt from the minute I saw her standing in my office, and the pain I felt when I couldn't get past Caleb to get to her. The frustration of not being able to find her. The heartbreak of knowing she's gone. The knowledge that she blames me.

I broke her. I broke us. I can't fix it.

My grip on the chair tightens as the storm passes. This is the last tangible thing I can touch that Alison did. I don't want to let it go, but I have to.

I have to.

I drag my hand under my eyes and see Caleb next to me. Always there for me. Jared's standing behind him, his face racked with torment.

"Okay. Let's go. We have an evil she-bitch to prosecute." I plan on finding every piece of information I can on Melody Dempsey in order to have enough charges to make her plead for mercy. And when I have none, then, maybe then, I'll feel some measure of redemption for my Alison.

41

ALISON

Thank God the offices of Watson, Rubenstein, and Dalton have their own reserved parking, or I would abhor having to drive in downtown Charleston every day. Parking in the city is a complete nightmare. Even as the height of the tourist season wanes, people still flock to the beauty of this antebellum city. One of the reasons is the absolutely delicious food, which I've taken more than a little advantage of. I'm grateful I'm still able to handle my morning runs while pregnant, or I'd likely have gained more weight than my doctor told me to expect.

Though at my last OB/GYN appointment, I did have to have a talk with my doctor about mileage. I signed up for the Race 13.1, the Halloween-themed half marathon that's on a hard-packed dirt course. I love the idea of dressing a little wild for fun, helping out a children's charity and getting to run at the same time. My OB/GYN, also a runner, suggested I try the run/walk/run method to give myself a break. Despite my initial sneer, which she had a good laugh at, she explained that if I tried it, I would have more endurance. Despite my disbelief, I gave it a try. Damned if it didn't work. And now, we have more energy for the runs.

Right now, the only thing maintaining my sanity is running.

I organized the Charleston office in about a week. I think the daily challenges of working for Amaryllis Events overprepared me for this job. When I called Jared to let him know I was done, he laughed and said, "Set them up for when you're gone."

Good. Jared wasn't planning on having me permanently stay in Charleston. Despite everything, there are still a few too many ghosts in this town for my liking.

I knew leaving was the right thing for me to do. With my wildly raging pregnancy hormones, there was no way for me to have listened to anything that Keene said with any sort of calmness. I'd have gutted him with one of Corinna's knives that afternoon, and we'd have been planning a funeral instead of giving him an opportunity at life. There was no way I could have trusted him or anything that came out of his mouth. And at that point, there was no way I could have told him or anyone else about the baby. I'd have been in the same situation, but miserable every second. With the distance of almost two months, I know I did it in the wrong way.

I left myself no way home.

And then there's Keene.

One night last week, I called Jared to find out about how the family was doing, and Jared broached the subject of Keene. For the first time, I was ready to listen. After I heard the story, I was paralyzed in my chair at the office. I remember vaguely whispering, "I'm such a fool. He'll never forgive me, Jared," before disconnecting the call.

And then I wrapped my arms around our child and cried.

Jared hasn't brought up the topic since, and neither have I. Instead, I've only allowed myself time to think about Keene on my runs, the times when I have no distractions. I want all the happiness in the world for him. I want him to have a woman who's strong enough to stand up under the pressure and stick with him. I want the beauty of love and a lifetime of happiness for him.

I want him to have what I couldn't give him, but he still deserves to know about our child.

God, what a mess I've made.

In the early Charleston air, I'm coming up on mile eight of my run and look down at my pacing watch. Nine-and-a-half-minute-mile average? Not bad at all. In this humidity, and with my little apple growing into an avocado, I'm not trying to set a personal record. I just want to finish safely. Tomorrow is a rest day before my twelve-mile run over the weekend. With the race next weekend, I'm more than ready to relax and let the little one enjoy the cooler weather. Wherever Jared sends me next.

Reaching for my water during the cooldown portion of my run, I rub my hand along the little bump just beginning to show. "One more week until race day, my little angel. Let's head on home."

THE FIRST CALL rings my cell phone around 1:00 PM. I'm staring out my office window when the sound jerks me from my woolgathering. Since only one person has this number, I ask, "Jared? What's wrong?"

"Ali. I need you to take a deep breath and tell me you're sitting down."

Oh, God. Something happened to Cassidy and the babies. I don't realize I say it aloud until he responds. "No, it's nothing like that. I swear but..." He hesitates.

"Just say it." I snap. I'm hormonal about to cry at any second.

"There was an attack on a diplomatic escort a few days ago in London."

"I heard about it." I'm perplexed. Why is he so concerned to tell me?

"When we were talking at the family dinner last night, Caleb mentioned he knew some of the soldiers who were wounded." A strange knot forms in my chest. It's not the baby kicking. "Ali, I only met him the one time but..."

"Colby," I whisper. "They sent him back out into the field."

"Yes," Jared says grimly. "I don't have the details, but he's been transported back from overseas. He's been listed as serious; downgraded from critical."

My head rests back against the high back chair. "How are Corinna and Holly handling this?" My voice is husky even to my own ears.

"Not well. Holly was in tears. And Corinna? She stormed from the room saying the only person who had the right to kill him was her. She was noticeably upset as well."

"I just bet she was."

Jared hesitates. "Once he gets settled here stateside, we can arrange for a routed call through the office if you want to talk with him."

"Do that," I say firmly. Despite the walls between my family and I, I want him to know if there is a way for me to help, I'll do my best.

"Consider it done." Jared leaves a weighty pause between us before he adds, "I don't think it's going to be much longer before Cassidy has the babies. She was having contractions all night."

"Oh." I hope my voice holds the right amount of enthusiasm. This latest news just makes me feel more alone than ever.

Well, not entirely alone. I smooth my hand over my precious angel to comfort myself. "Keep me informed--about both Colby and Cass-- will you?"

"Of course. I'd do nothing else."

I look around my office. I find a dust bunny on a bookshelf demanding my immediate attention. "I've got to run."

With a sigh, Jared lets me go. For now. "Okay. We'll talk soon." Right before he hangs up.

∼

THE SECOND CALL comes in at 4:18 p.m.

"Jared, what's up?"

"Cassidy had the twins!" His voice is pure excitement. "A boy and a girl!"

I close my eyes and feel the wetness seep out. I remember how I thought I would be there, jumping into Keene's arms as his sister pushed our niece and nephew into the world. "I'm so happy for you, Uncle Jared," I say softly.

"I'm just as happy for you, Aunt Ali," he says back.

I shake my head. "No, Jared. I gave all that up, remember? I'm sure they don't consider me that anymore."

"Then you're a fool, Alison. They ask about you every time I see them. They haven't let you go any more than you've let them go." His voice is direct, and it pierces my heart.

I'm quiet for a minute. "Do you..." I hesitate. "Do you think Cassidy would be open to a gift?"

"I think Cassidy would be open to a gift if you walked it into that hospital room. So would Keene," Jared says bluntly.

"I'm sure Keene's given up on me. I mean, come on. The first challenge and I run like a cat getting sprayed with water?" I scoff, rubbing my hand over my stomach.

"Ali, you don't get it. That man would crawl over broken glass right now to find you. If I told him where you were, he would be down there in a matter of hours."

"Not if he knew everything," I whisper.

There's silence on the other end of the line. "Did you meet someone in Charleston?" Jared's footsteps are heard rapidly moving away. I begin to suspect he's at the hospital.

"Not exactly," I hedge. "I knew something before I left, and I didn't tell anyone."

"You're talking to your attorney, Alison. You know I can't tell him."

"You swear?" I need this additional promise.

"Alison, I swear. I won't tell Keene. I won't tell anyone."

Still rubbing my hand over the small knot in my lower stomach, I say quietly, "I had planned a special birthday gift for Keene, which is why I needed to get back into the house. I couldn't have him finding it."

There's an eerie stillness over the phone. "What was it?" Jared's voice is low.

I bite my lip.

"Ali? What was it?"

"My early pregnancy test and sonogram pictures of our child." It all comes out in a rush. "No one else knows, other than my OB/GYN."

"Oh. My. God. I have to sit down." I hear Jared's back slide against the wall. "How far..."

"Fifteen weeks," I answer quickly.

"Ali, now that you know what happened, don't you want him with you?" Jared asks, confused.

I start to cry. "More than anything, but how can he forgive me? How can he understand how hurt and scared I was?"

"Probably because he's feeling the same way now. He's petrified he's never going to see you again. Maybe if you tell him, it'll make it easier," Jared offers helpfully.

I sniffle. "Do you think so?"

"Want to test it out? I can have him down the hall in about a minute."

"He's there?" So close. If Jared had stayed where he was, I could have heard his voice. And your secret would have been out, my head yells back.

"Ali, do you want to talk with him? You don't have to tell him where you are or about the baby. Just that you're safe and thinking of coming home," he urges.

"Okay," I whisper without thinking.

Seconds later, I hear the slap of wingtips against a hospital floor as Jared races down the hall before I can change my mind. My heart feels like it's about to pound out of my chest. I hear quiet voices, and I start to panic. This can't be good for the baby. I'm just about to hang up when I hear his voice after months.

"Alison, is it you?" Keene's voice sounds like it's manic.

"Keene," I whisper. "I'm so sorry."

"What? No, baby. No. There's no need to apologize. Just tell me where you are," he pleads.

I'm sobbing into the phone. "There are things I didn't say before I left. Important things."

"Can you tell me now?" His voice is gruff.

"No."

"Are you coming back?" His voice is laced with pain.

"Soon." Hearing Keene's voice again has locked in the decision I've been waffling against.

He lets out a deep breath. "That's something, at least."

"Even if I have to leave again after telling you, I need to see you one more time." I don't realize I've spoken the words out loud until Keene's voice comes through the phone ominously.

"Alison, tell me where you are, damnit." His patience is gone. Back is the demanding, autocratic man I fell in love with.

"I can't. I have to go. I love you all—always. Goodbye, Keene." I move the phone away from my ear, even as he's shrieking my name.

"Alison!"

I disconnect the call. And before I can lose myself in the memory of Keene's voice, I feel it for the first time.

A tiny little flutter.

"Oh, angel. You need Daddy too, don't you?" I moan as I caress the tiny bump below my waistline. "We both do. I made such an enormous mistake by running. What do you think about going shopping for Cassidy and the babies tomorrow, hmm? We'll send them a gift?"

After a while, I'm finally calm enough to drive back to my empty, barren rental apartment.

THE NEXT DAY, I head to an antique store that's been in Charleston since long before I was born. I remember on rainy Saturdays, my mother used to bring me in to wander where we'd "look with our eyes" over the beautiful marvels imported from other countries. If it wasn't busy, Miss Julie would tell me stories about the pieces they collected.

It seems fitting to give Cassidy's babies a gift from my soul, as well as my heart.

Opening the door of the corner store, I inhale the musky scent and hear a faint "I'll be right with you."

And then she's right before me. Frailer than she used to be, her hair snowier than gray, but I recognize that welcoming smile anywhere.

"Miss Julie?" I whisper in disbelief.

Her head tilts to the side before her lips part in shock. "Little Louise? Oh my, child! Come give me a hug. Where did you go?"

Walking immediately into her arms, I feel centered for the first time since I left Connecticut. "You have no idea how good it is to see you," I mumble.

I feel a whack on my shoulder. "Where have you been all this time, young lady? Your mama would have had a switch to your hide for being gone so long and not letting anyone know where you were," she scolds me.

I pull back, and the ever-present tears prick the back of my eyes. "That's a story that'll take all day to tell you."

"I ain't got nowhere to be, girl." She gestures to a set of overstuffed chairs and a table with a pitcher of sweet tea. She arches an eyebrow. "Do you?"

"No, ma'am." Immediately chastised, I move over to the chair and drop down. After pouring us each a glass, I ask her, "Where do you want me to start?"

"Always the beginning, Louise." Patting my hand, she sits back. I tell her everything. What really happened with my father, to my new family, to Keene, and the baby. By the time I'm done talking, she hasn't said much, and I'm practically hoarse. All the sweet tea is gone, and I haven't got a lick of shopping in.

Miss Julie stands up and flips the sign on the front door to Closed before coming back to sit next to me. "Do you miss your man, Louise?"

I turn the empty glass around in my hands. "With every breath I take." Putting the glass down before I drop it, I ask her, "How can he ever forgive me for not telling him about the baby sooner?"

"The same way you forgive him for not telling you about something that broke your heart. You love each other through it. You think this is going to be the worst thing you're going to face in all your lives together?" Miss Julie lets out a laugh that echoes years of love, sorrow, and loss. "Young people these days don't take vows seriously enough, Louise. Just think about the first one for a minute. For better or for worse doesn't mean until your next fight. It means fighting with, for, and against each other until you make it through whatever battle you face. Together." She leans forward and captures my hand. "Don't you think being with Keene to fight this battle with will be better than being apart? It seems like apart is killing you both."

"I don't deserve him," I hiccup through my tears.

"Why? Because your father was a horse's ass? I want to show you something." She walks over to her laptop. After a few clicks, she gestures me over. Looking over her shoulder, I see a local article about my father's incarceration. What shocks me is the large portion of the article asking, "What happened to Louise Sibley?"

I'm floored.

Friends from middle school and early high school are quoted, taking a chance in showing me they still cared. "Seems there's a lot of people out there who think there was a lot of heart to love back then. Bet they'd love to know the brilliant, beautiful woman you are now."

"I never knew," I murmur, my fingers drifting over names I haven't seen since I was sixteen years old, leaving South Carolina in the rearview mirror.

"They're only one call away. Just like your man, Alison." My head snaps up. It's the first time Miss Julie has called me by my legal name since I entered the store. "Now, we've been gossiping like two biddies all day. Didn't you come in to buy some baby gifts?"

Nodding, I do something I haven't done in months. I smile. "Thank you, Miss Julie," I whisper, before reaching out to hug this woman who reminded me of something I forgot along the way. I was never completely alone in this city where hell first rained down on me. Nor was I alone in the last one I ran from.

Like running, love can happen anywhere. You just have to want to find your course.

AN HOUR LATER, I found two antique English silver-plated baby cups —one for a boy and one for a girl.

A cast brass and carved wood Art Nouveau magnifying glass that looks like it jumped out of the pages of Sherlock Holmes catches my eye. It immediately reminds me of Keene.

"Miss Julie?" My voice is breathless. "Can you wrap up the magnifying glass too?"

She looks down in the case. "Not going to haggle the price, Alison?" I can hear the shopkeeper in her tsking me for not trying for a better deal.

"I don't care. I know the exact message I need to send with it," I whisper. Keene's and my mutual love of Sherlock Holmes. He'll understand.

"Ah, sending it to your man." I can't respond—all my thoughts are centered on Keene. She prattles on. "In the interest of true love, I'll take fifteen percent off and wrap it for you too."

A few minutes later, I'm on my way to the Watson, Rubenstein, and Dalton office. I grab a FedEx box and a few notecards; then taking a deep breath, I pick up the phone.

One ring. Two. Finally, he answers. "Charlie Henderson."

"Charlie, it's Ali." I listen to him splutter into the line for a minute before I cut him off. "I need your help."

"Anything, little girl. Whatever you need," he says immediately.

"I'm sending you a package. And a video. Think you can get them to Cassidy and Keene?" I grin.

His voice is choked up when he replies. "It'll be my pleasure, little girl. My absolute pleasure."

I let out the breath I've been holding. "I've missed you."

"We've been waiting for you to say that, little girl. Now, come home."

I look out of my office window. "Soon, Charlie. Soon."

42

KEENE

I've been turning my conversation with Alison over and over in my head. She sounded scared and afraid. She wouldn't be if she was here. I bang my steering wheel in frustration.

The impatience I thought I had a handle on is back in full force. The only thing preventing me from tackling Jared and stealing his cell phone at this point is she said she'd be home soon.

Soon.

Then, even if I have to tie her to a chair to force her to listen to me, I'm going to tell her everything that happened. After, if she still wants to walk away... Fuck that. She isn't going anywhere.

I park my car in the lot at Greenwich Hospital and reach for the stuffed elephant and giraffe sitting in the seat next to me. Cassidy said the twins should be heading home tomorrow. Little Jonathan Ryan and Laura Faith are only a few days old and are already working miracles on everyone's hearts. Especially mine. Even without Alison here to share this joy, they're a tangible miracle every time I hold them.

If I'm this bad with my niece and nephew, I can only imagine what I'm going to do with my own child one day. I let out a sigh. Now I just need to get the future mother of my children home.

"Keene! Hold the door! Blasted box is marked fragile," Charlie grumbles.

I smirk. "You realize Cassidy is going to kill us both, right? The minute we walk through the door with more gifts, we're both targets." My sister swore the next person who walked in with a gift was going to get pelted.

"Maybe in your case, boy, but she'll want mine," Charlie brags.

"Whatever." I push the button for the maternity ward, where we ride the elevator in silence. Since both Charlie and I have already been cleared, we're already wearing the necessary wristbands to enter quickly. "What's in the box?" I'm curious.

"Don't know. Came to the house, special delivery. Had to race to get it here on time," Charlie admits.

I blink at him. "Seriously? Did you check it for a bomb first?" Is he insane, bringing a box like that here where my niece and nephew are?

Just as we're about to enter Cassidy's room, he says, "Don't be a jackass. I know who sent it, of course."

The hairs on the back of my neck stand straight up. "Who sent it?" I demand.

"Calm down, Keene. I have a message that goes with it too." Shoving me aside, he enters the room before stopping so hard, I run right into the back of him. "Holy God, I didn't need to see that, little mama!"

My sister is breastfeeding Laura, while Caleb is burping Jonathan. I can't help but laugh. "Should've let me go in first and maybe you might not have." I stroll over to the bed and place the stuffed animals next to my sister before kissing her on the cheek. "Doing okay?"

Cassidy's face has transformed in awe of new motherhood. "I can't even describe how I feel, Keene. It's like, suddenly, there's this remarkable cord of love that can't be cut, no matter the time or distance." Looking at Jonathan in Caleb's arms, she amends her statement. "Times two." Realizing Laura is asleep, she pops her nipple out and hands her to me to burp while she adjusts her gown. "I've been getting emotional all day thinking about Mama and how she must have felt when I was taken, not much older than they are now." She shakes her head and turns to Caleb. "Are you sure we can't LoJack them?"

He laughs out loud. "We will do everything possible, short of putting microchips in them, Pixie." He brushes his hand down her dark curls.

Turning back to me, she says, "I'm going to be harping on this for some time, you understand."

"Of course." Nuzzling my cheek against my niece, I misdirect her somewhat morose thoughts. "But Charlie has a mysterious package for you."

She picks up the giraffe I just placed by her bed and hurls it at him. I laugh.

"What was that for, little girl?" Charlie roars.

"I have to cart all this, plus two brand-new babies home tomorrow, Charlie. Gifts couldn't wait until then?" Cassidy wails.

Charlie shifts with the package in his hands. "Okay. If you don't want your message and gifts from Ali until then, I suppose I can take them home." He starts to make his way toward the door.

Still holding my niece, I block it. "Alison? That box is from Alison? You know where she is?"

"I think you need to see the video she sent me first," Charlie says. Pulling his iPad from under the box, he moves over to the bed where Cassidy is sitting.

Still holding Laura to my chest, I think of her namesake, my mother, and pray for a miracle. I move over to the bed to stand behind Cassidy as she holds the device. My eyes are trained on the screen. "Whenever you're ready, Cass."

My sister's trembling finger presses Play on the video. For a moment there's nothing, and I'm a heartbeat away from choking Charlie for taunting us. But then I see her.

"Hey, everyone," Alison says softly. She looks tired. She looks beautiful.

She looks like she's been crying.

"I am so happy for both you and Caleb, Cassidy. This is the most joyous time in your life. Be blessed by every second. Jared said you had a little boy and a little girl. I know they're going to grow up just as beautiful as their Mama and Daddy.

"I hope you don't mind my intruding on family time to tell you how incredibly proud I am of you for being so strong, for never giving up hope, and for knowing that Caleb was the one for you. Look at what precious miracles you got for those dreams, Cass. I'm so proud. So proud."

I watch as she blinks rapidly and clears her throat. At her next words, it's me who can't breathe.

"Keene must be over the moon with joy that you delivered safely. I know he was worried this whole time. Even though it was for reasons he and Caleb didn't share right away, you have to admit, you probably felt better having both of them so close during your pregnancy. All the little worries disappeared when they were around. It was hard for you to lose control so fast, but they helped you through it. That's what having an amazing husband and brother are for.

"You were right, you know? All those times you got on my case about your brother? Keene is...everything someone could wish for, and nothing they could ever dream of. I hate I held that dream in my hands and I lost it by being so careless. So foolish.

"Promise me you'll convince him it wasn't him or his actions, but it was me who was broken. Please, Cass. If there's just one more thing I can ask, it's that.

"There are things I'll be back to share soon. Things I should have shared before I left. I just couldn't leave my apology to you any longer. Not when your life is filled with so much joy.

"That's all I want for you, Cass, is for you to always smile. To always be happy. To always feel the same joy you did the moment your children were placed in your arms."

I watch as my Alison blows a kiss at the video with tears cascading down her cheeks.

"All my love, Cass and Caleb. And congratulations again."

The screen goes black.

The room is silent. I'm choking on emotional overload since I heard her voice for the first time thirty-six hours ago. I can't begin to speak.

"Cass? Here's her gift to you," Charlie says softly. He's holding out a plaid bag with white tissue paper. An odd choice for a baby gift.

Cassidy immediately drops the iPad in her lap and wipes her eyes. Reaching for the bag, she pulls out the tissue. Inside is a note-card with the letterhead of Watson, Rubenstein, and Dalton printed on it.

Mama and I used to walk around antique stores all the time. It wasn't until I was shopping for your bundles of joy I remembered that. Thank you for giving me that goodness of my past—XO, A

Inside are delicate silver baby cups. Obviously hand etched, one is for a boy and the other is for a girl. "They're so beautiful." Cassidy turns her face up to mine. "Keene, you can use these to find her, can't you?"

I damn sure can. I'm about to tell her so, when I hear Charlie say, "I don't think he'll have to."

My head snaps toward him. He's holding out a long flat box toward me.

"Give me my niece, Marshall, and I'll give you the box with your name on it," Charlie jokes.

Walking on unsteady legs, I move around the bed. Charlie puts the box at the foot so he can accept little Laura into his arms. "There's a baby girl," he coos. Nodding toward the package, he says, "Go ahead."

I pick up the elongated box wrapped in plaid wrapping paper. There's a card attached to the top.

Remember when we watched "The Reichenbach Fall"? When Holmes said alone protected him? I needed that for a while. Not anymore. Unlike Holmes, it's not how I want to live. I had a different gift planned for your birthday. Until I can give it to you, accept this one. —XO, A

Carefully opening the wrapping paper, I find a brass and carved wooden magnifying glass. Lifting it gently out of the box, I hold it, knowing Alison had her hands on it just a few days ago, thinking of me.

The box flutters to the floor with a thud.

"Keene, are you okay?" Caleb asks. He's been silent this whole time, letting Cassidy and I absorb Alison's gifts.

I shoot daggers at Charlie as I gather the box from the floor where it crashed. "If you don't tell me everything you know about how to track her, I will hurt you. Badly."

"All I know is the box arrived at my house today from New York," Charlie admits.

I glare at him. That piece of information is useless. Alison isn't in New York.

"But we haven't broken down the video yet. I wanted you both to see it untouched in the event there are any safeguards on it," Charlie says.

"Keene," Caleb interrupts.

"Hold on, Caleb." I order Charlie, "Break down the video. I want to know where it was shot by the end of the day."

"Keene," Caleb interrupts, more urgently.

"Hold on, Caleb," I say impatiently.

"Jesus, Keene. Look at the bottom of the box," Caleb snaps, exasperated.

My head drops to the floor. There's a sticker from the store on it. Charleston, South Carolina.

"She's in Charleston? The whole damned time?" I shout.

"Oh, holy hell," Charlie mutters.

Caleb shakes his head.

"Charleston? Why would she go back to Charleston?" Cassidy's confusion is obvious.

"Because nobody in the world would ever expect her to go back there, Cass, that's why. She's been living with her memories for the last two months on top of her emotional state when she left," I yell. Shifting slightly, my feet kick the remaining innards of the box on the floor.

"Keene, look!" Cassidy points down excitedly. Folded cardstock sticks out beneath the cotton cushioning that held my magnifying glass. The embossment indicates it's from Stafford Antiques, Charleston, South Carolina.

I pick it up and read aloud.

I've known Louise since her mama was alive. If you're half the man I expect you are, based on what she's told me, you'll be looking for her. Here's a hint, Keene. There's a race being run in our beautiful city this weekend to benefit a children's charity. My Louise and your Alison is running in it. I'll be cheering her on at the finish line. Will you? —JS

"What is it, Keene?" Caleb asks.

I drop my head. The search for her is over.

Walking over to Charlie, I lean over and kiss my new niece. Before I lift my lips, I whisper, "Thanks, Mom. I love you." I walk over to my new nephew and do the same to him as well. Then I hand Caleb the note.

"You found her," he breathes.

"What? Keene? We know where Ali is?" Cassidy's excitement is palpable. "When are you leaving to go get her?"

"Soon, Cass. I know where she'll be in a few days," I murmur.

"Screw that," Caleb says. "Go tonight."

I grin. "I was kind of hoping you'd say that."

"I'm officially throwing you out." Cassidy picks up the elephant and throws it at my head. "Bring my sister home."

"Yes, ma'am." I mock salute her, then look over at Charlie. "Charlie...there are no words."

"Bring her home. Then we'll celebrate."

Celebrate is right. Quickly snatching up the pieces of my gift, I hurry out of the maternity ward. I've got a bag to pack and a flight to catch. Not only do I know what city to look in, I know where to find my woman.

And now, I know just what she's going to get as her medal for finishing her race.

43

ALISON

I pop another cracker into my mouth as I make my way through the humid air to my starting corral. The Saltine cracker had settled my stomach acid slightly. I'm glad I thought to toss them in the car when I drove to the race start in Charleston at 4:30 this morning.

This isn't the first time race nerves have made my stomach jump. I've run a half marathon before, just not like this. I look down at my bib in disbelief. It has a bright white *C* stamped on it. I knew my qualifying 10k time was pretty fast, but I didn't know it would put me this far up. I'm going to enjoy all the extra time afforded to me. I want to cross the finish line, but not at the risk of injury to me or my little avocado.

I can't help but smile as I look around at some of the crazy costumes people are wearing. I think I saw someone in a full zebra outfit out of the corner of my eye. I just hope it was a one-person deal, or someone was going to have to deal with race farts while bent over, trapped in a costume built for two. I know it's for charity and all, but still, there are some limits.

My racing costume is pretty kick-ass while still being comfortable. I'm Sherlock Holmes, of course. I have on a plaid running skirt and a white, long-sleeved running shirt with a plaid vest over it. The plaid of my hat doesn't match, but I managed to score white knee-high running socks last night at the local running store. I even managed to fashion a magnifying glass out of a paper towel roll and tinfoil.

Not too shabby if I do say so myself. I mentally pat myself on the back, especially since I was up late packing boxes to be shipped back to Connecticut.

It's time to go home and face whatever it is I'll find upon my return.

I know my family will always love me, and maybe one day they'll forgive me. Maybe they'll find it in their hearts to open their arms to me again. God knows, every minute I spend away from them is tearing deeper wounds into my soul.

I've spent my days barely going through the motions, barely doing what needs to be done to function. The other parts of me are reliving every moment since Cassidy, Phil, and Em walked into my life. I've found myself outside of our old trailer park half a dozen times without knowing how I got there. I've been desperate to pick up the phone and call, needing to hear their voices.

When I'm not thinking of them, I'm replaying every hour I spent with Keene—the good and the bad. The desperate love I have for him. When I wake up in the middle of the night, I know I'll never be able to escape the memories of him or the pain of losing him. I walked away when I had it all in the palm of my hand.

I give my head a quick shake to clear it before the all-too-familiar tears can well in my eyes and my throat closes up. Probably not such a great idea before tackling a race. Blanking my mind, I ignore the other runners completing their pre-race prep around me. In the cool morning air, I do a final check of all the items in the pack around my waist. Water, music, backup earbuds, ID, and a large bag of mixed candy since my little avocado is now making Mama nauseous regardless of which running energy GU I try.

As I shake out my limbs one final time, I realize I've been wool-gathering longer than I thought. It's now 8:00 a.m., and the elite runners and corral A racers have already gone off. Walking with my corral, we ease closer to the start. Corral *B*s take off and my pulse begins to thrum faster. I regulate my breathing. Three in, two out. With the little avocado inside me, it's super important to keep my heart rate steady.

I quickly do a final check of my sneakers and earbuds, when I hear the announcer call out "Corral *C* runners, are you ready!"

I crouch down.

And within seconds of being told to go, I take off in a loping stride over the hard-packed earth of the wooded course. Within minutes, my mind wanders back over the last four months.

By the end of the first mile, I want this race to be over so I can go home and begin mending the relationships I ran from out of fear of love.

I'M on mile eight when my phone starts ringing. I answer it breathlessly.

"You know, I'm in the middle of a race, Jared. Probably not a good time to talk about the movers."

"Movers? Now I'm more than glad I lifted Jared's phone out of his pocket a few seconds ago. Caleb's holding him back because now I can tell you what I told you before every race. Do the best you can and don't hurt yourself."

Cassidy. Sweet Jesus.

"Cass. Oh God, Cass." The sob is ripped from me without a chance to stop it.

"What mile are you on?" she asks conversationally, as if this isn't the first time we've spoken in two months.

"Close to mile nine," I huff out.

"What, are you crawling the damn thing? Phil, Ali must be on crutches doing this half marathon. It's almost nine-fifteen in the morning and she's only on mile nine," Cassidy calls out to my brother.

I giggle through the tears. "The race didn't start until eight, Cass."

"Sadistic bastards down there, Ali. Must be the humidity messing with their brain. It's why you need to come home." Now, it's her voice breaking. "You hear me? It's time for you to come home."

Snot mingles with my tears, and I wipe both away on my running shirt. "I hear you. I'm mostly packed."

"Good. Now, tell Jared you don't hate him for us finally figuring out where you are, and you'll get a few more calls during your last few miles," Cassidy tells me.

"I don't—oomph!" I stumble.

"Ali! Are you okay?" Cassidy yells.

"Yeah. Just stumbled over a tree root." Probably because I can't see through my tears. "Put Jared on."

There's shuffling noise over the phone line, and finally, Jared says, "I swear, I didn't say a word."

I slow down to walk. "I know. You've been the best boss anyone could ask for, but as my attorney, you're officially fired." I pause. "Wait, am I on speaker?"

"No."

"I need to tell Keene about the baby before everyone else, Jared. I had planned to originally." I start running again, and my voice comes out breathless. "So, from that aspect, you're still under privilege."

He laughs. "Duly noted, counselor. What's your pace?"

"Nine-minute miles or so. I'm trying to keep cool. Running through trees is helping with keeping me shaded, and I'm drinking a lot," I tell him.

"I'd expect calls from these lunatics every nine minutes, then," Jared says wryly, before disconnecting the call.

Suddenly, I want this race time to be my worst ever. I want it to last forever so I can hear from all of my family.

And maybe, if I'm being blessed with a second chance, I'll hear from Keene too.

Putting one foot in front of the other, I head into the next shaded section of the course.

∾

"THE WAY I FIGURE IT, you owe me a new phone. You said you were going to call me, so since you didn't manage that, a new phone will do. Rose gold, please." Corinna's drawl comes through the line, along with a roomful of people laughing. Mile eleven was going to be the joke mile. "Besides, I've been getting calls from annoying rodents, so I need to change my number."

"Huh?" I'm confused but then again, so much information has been thrown at me at once I'm on sensory overload.

"Colby." Holly pipes in. Ah, I open my mouth to suggest she should give him a chance when Corinna continues.

"Like I said; the rats are calling. I need a new phone. You will provide it. Win, win for me."

At this point, each member of the family has called and put me on speakerphone to hear each other's antics. Phil called me at mile ten, daring me to stop along I-95 at one of the titty bars and see if they'd let me put my pole dancing classes to use. Everyone screamed at him for that. "Jesus Christ, Phil. We're trying to get her home, not get her picked up for solicitation!" Em yelled.

I begged Holly to tell me she was getting this on camera. She promised me she was.

Now, I hear the babies cry. I start sniffling when Caleb gets on the line and says, "Auntie Ali, I'd like for you to meet Jonathan. He's an impatient little guy who always wants to be sucking on Mommy's boob."

"Sounds just like his daddy," Phil yells in the background. Then, "Ow, Jason. That hurt, damnit."

I half giggle, half sob when I hear Cassidy say, "Laura is much politer. It must be the Marshall genes coming through."

"Please. Keene loves nipple play more than the average toddler," I say without thinking. The other end of the line goes silent. I hiss out, "Fuck."

I pick up my pace and my heart monitor starts beeping. Jared yells, "Slow the hell down, Alison!"

"Talk about sounding like Keene," Cassidy murmurs.

"He's been in my office enough the last two months. I may have picked up a few traits," Jared says.

"And there goes the firm," Ryan drawls.

Everyone starts laughing again, except me. I hear the clatter of the phone as it's taken off the speaker. "He loves you, Ali. Still. Always. Time, distance, it doesn't change that kind of love." Caleb's voice is soothing.

How will he react to me keeping his child from him? My heart monitor starts going off again.

"What's that noise?" Caleb asks.

"Nothing." I press Mute on my wrist.

"Jared! What's the beeping on Ali's side?" Caleb yells to his brother-in-law.

"It's her heart monitor. If she's setting it off, tell her to slow the hell down or stop stressing out. We need her back in one piece." Jared's voice can be heard in the distance.

Caleb's voice is amused as he says, "You heard your boss."

"Caleb, about that..." I hesitate. It's been months. What if they don't need me? "I have an idea for Cassidy's leave."

"Good. Get home and tell us." Caleb hangs up the phone.

I switch to walking. A princess and her prince run by, giggling as they chase each other through the forest. It's so cute, I almost want to throw up. Then again, maybe my little avocado is trying to tell me he or she is hungry.

"Sorry, angel. I've been talking to your crazy aunts and uncles. And they've made Mama so incredibly happy." Unbuttoning my vest pocket, I undo the Ziploc filled with jelly beans. Grabbing a small handful, I munch on them. Slugging back some water, I can see the twelve-mile marker a few hundred yards ahead.

Just another mile plus to go, then I can go home.

"Let's go, angel." I rub my hand over my stomach before slowly starting to run again.

Nine minutes later, the noise around me is intense. I just passed mile marker thirteen. I have one-tenth of a mile to finish. Hootie is blowing out of the speakers, telling me I'm going to rise above when my phone rings.

Blocked number.

I almost don't answer. The screaming cacophony of the after-party is underway, and you can barely hear above the celebration. I hit Answer anyway. Today's the day for good surprises.

"Alison Freeman," I pant. Just a few more steps, Ali. Then you're done.

"That's some costume you have on, baby. Personally, if it were up to me, I'd give you best dressed. But I think it's going to go to those assclowns who wore a zebra suit," Keene yells through the line.

"Keene?" My head swivels, looking through the swarms of spectators on the left and the right, trying to find him.

"Don't worry about trying to find me, love. Just keep running. For once, you're running in the right direction. Toward me." Keene's voice is all I can hear. The surrounding noise is washed away.

I cross under the finish line and start walking past the race monitors. "Where are you?"

"You'll see me soon enough. I've got my eye on you." He pauses. "It's like every fantasy I've ever had. Naughty schoolgirl meets Sherlock Holmes with those damn socks."

I start to cry as I search for him. "Keene, I need to get my medal. Where can I meet you?"

Suddenly, I'm jostled to the right, in front of one of the medal presenters. They hand me my medal, which is a child's drawing of a pumpkin. I look down at it and grin. It's fantastic.

Then I feel my earbud being removed from my ear. "Aren't the medals great?" Keene murmurs. My whole body trembles and I swallow convulsively. "I don't think they're quite as nice as the one you deserve."

And then I see the sunlight glint off the facets in the sun.

Keene's mother's diamond.

"Keene..." I choke out.

"I understand why you took this off, baby, but it's time to put it back on. Unless you tell me in the next thirty seconds you don't love me." Keene's eyes bore into my wet ones. "We can work anything out, as long as we're together, Alison. Together."

I nod my head slowly before whispering, "Together."

He sighs heavily. Slowly, he slides his mother's necklace over my head, his fingers trailing down my neck, shaking. "Can I kiss you, my love?" he whispers as he starts to lean in.

I'm trembling. It's now or never, Alison.

"No." He pulls back as if I slapped him. I take his hand and place it over my stomach, right where our little avocado has been growing. "But you can kiss your family." I bite my trembling lip, waiting for his reaction.

Ecstatic finishers push past us, bumping us closer to one another. One jostles me particularly hard in the back.

Keene snarls at him, "For fuck's sake, my woman's pregnant. Watch where the hell you're going, asshole!"

"Dude, sorry. You should probably move though," the runner says.

"Right after I do this," Keene breathes. Then, he crashes his mouth down on mine.

Heaven. I must have died on the race course. Otherwise, there's no other explanation for being locked in Keene's arms with his scent wrapped around me and our baby.

Ripping his mouth away, he says, "Alison, what in the hell is that beeping?"

Tossing my head back and laughing, I say, "That's my heart monitor going wild."

He smirks. "Bet your ass it is."

Sliding his hands under my rear, he picks me up and wraps my legs around his waist, then moves us through the crowd. "Now, let's get back to your place so we can figure out how soon we can get you home."

Sliding my fingers through his thick hair, I tell him, "Okay."

As Keene carries me through the masses of people, I catch a

glimpse of snowy-white hair standing at the rail. Seeing Miss Julie's face smiling, I blow her a kiss, knowing down to my soul that she's somehow responsible for Keene being at the finish line.

After catching it, she mouths to me, "For better or worse."

Dropping my head in Keene's neck, I guess we're about to find out.

44

KEENE

After we get past the crowd, I slide Alison down my body. I didn't want to let her go, but she told me she needed to relax her muscles after running.

We walk back to the parking lot, stopping briefly to grab her a banana and a bottle of Powerade. I watch her devour the banana. "I'll get you something else in just a few minutes, angel," she murmurs down to her stomach, patting it reverently. Her body goes stiff before her other hand reaches for the diamond, like it's a lifeline.

"Alison, we have to talk before we go back," I say quietly. Her body begins to shake, but she nods her head.

"Why don't you follow me back to my place? It's not far from here."

I pull out my phone. "What's the address?" She rattles it off. Just a couple of minutes in normal traffic, then I can see where my heart's been for the last few months.

"I'll walk you to your car," I say firmly.

The expression on her face softens. "Keene, I'm done running."

My chest heaves as if I was the one to have just completed 13.1 miles. The thoughts flying through my head are hitting me with a painful, enormous, brutal beauty.

She didn't run from me but walked up to me, ready to figure this out.

And holy shit, I'm going to be a father! A father.

We start walking toward her car before the impact of that fully hits me. My knees almost give way, even as I stride along next to her. I look to the left where she's close enough to touch. Her eyes are red-rimmed, but the beaming light beneath her nervousness is something I've missed seeing.

It isn't hard to remember when that was. Before she left me, her family, her life. When she lay in my arms after I placed the diamond around her neck. Before she walked into my office and her world was rocked on its foundation. Before my own arrogance came back to bite me in the ass.

The truth is, it isn't Alison who has explanations to make, dreams to reconfigure, and trust to regain. I have as many, if not more.

I've learned a lot about myself in the last few months. There wasn't a day in the beginning that I didn't blame Alison for leaving without listening to me. For not believing what the words "I love you" meant. And somewhere along the way, I understood something.

I love you is just a phrase...words. It's supposed to uphold the strongest of storms and fight the hardest of battles, but it's delicate, fragile, and unless it's built on a firm foundation, it can be shattered. It needs to be fed with trust and openness from both sides for it to thrive.

Caleb tried to warn me about this. His continuous prodding at telling Alison wasn't due to any blowback he expected. It's because he knows what it takes to nurture love.

Reaching her car, she lifts up her white shirt for a hidden zipper, which highlights the small bump the average person who hadn't memorized her body would have never noticed, but which I devour with my eyes.

Our baby.

Pulling out a single key, she unlocks the door and stands beside her car. "Do you want a ride to your car?" She leans over into the car, turns on the ignition, and rolls down the window.

Seeing the quizzical look on my face, she mutters, "I can't stand getting into a hot car with leather seats down here. I have to let the AC run for a few minutes."

A grin slashes across my face. "Afraid of scalding your ass?" I tease.

She responds instantly. "More like I'm afraid of melting the baby despite what the doctor says. I mean, if they're not supposed to be in hot cars alone after they're born..." Her voice trails off.

The grin on my face fades and transforms into a soft look. "I like this protective side of you, Alison."

"No one else ever has," she mutters to herself.

God, we have so much to talk about. I decide to ignore her and say, "I actually wouldn't mind a ride to my rental. I know parking was fairly liberal for the race, but I'm not certain if I can leave my car there long."

She laughs. "This is Charleston, Keene. Someone will tow you faster than you can breathe to take your parking spot—they're sacred down here."

I walk around to the far side of the car and slide into the compact vehicle, frowning when I realize it isn't terribly large. "This is pretty small, Alison."

She shrugs. "It gets me to and from work. That's about all I needed." Backing out of the space, she asks, "Where are you parked?"

I tell her and sit back as she efficiently drives over the bumpy grass that makes us both groan and grunt. "Are you shaking up the bean doing this?"

We slide off the grass and onto pavement. "Avocado, and no. He or she is well insulated." Driving for a few moments in silence, I absorb what she says. Our baby is the size of an avocado. "Keene, which car is yours?"

Dazed, I look at Alison, who is staring ahead with fixed concentration, trying to not hit runners and pedestrians alike. Her skin has lost its flushed appearance and has smoothed back to its normal glow. Her hair is slightly longer and lighter. I can't stop staring at her.

Her lip is pulled between her teeth as she shoots me a quick look. "Keene! Which car is yours?" she snaps.

"I honestly can't remember right now." I scramble for the key in my pocket with the make and model on them. "Right there." I point to a late-model SUV at the end of the row.

Letting out a puff of air, she pulls up alongside my car and puts on her flashers. I get out and walk around to the window she's rolled down, leaning in to talk to her.

She says, "I'm about a five-minute drive from here. Ten, maybe. Are you following me?"

"Anywhere you go, baby." Reaching out, I stroke a single finger down her cheek.

"I'll see you in a few minutes." Slowly, her window rolls up, and I'm forced to step back and walk to my car.

For now.

~

WE PULL up in front of an apartment complex a few minutes later. Alison hops out of her car and gestures for me to roll down my window. "Visitor spaces are along the back. I don't want you to get towed."

Nodding, I roll up the window and turn into one of the spots. In my rearview, I watch as she uses her key to pop open her trunk to grab her purse.

Following her, we climb a well-maintained set of outdoor stairs and walk down a short hallway. Opening her door, she says, "Come on in."

"Not bad, but not exactly as nice as home," I remark about the cramped space. I'm happy to note the cardboard boxes and tape guns on the coffee table.

She pauses on her way to what I assume is the bedroom. "I honestly don't think I knew what it looked like for the first few weeks I was here." Ducking her head in embarrassment, she turns. "Let me jump in the shower really quick?"

"Take your time." I'm antsy. "Can I make you anything in the meantime? Are you hungry? Is there anything you shouldn't have?" I have no idea what she needs for her pregnancy.

"Anything in the fridge is good for me, Keene. Have at it." The door closes quietly between us as I make my way over to the small kitchenette. Opening up the fridge, I smile. It looks remarkably like her refrigerator at home, filled with fresh fruit, vegetables, dairy, eggs, and—oh holy hell, there's an avocado in there. Almost blindly, I reach for it and hold it, shutting the refrigerator door absently.

This is the size of my baby. This isn't molecules or cells. This is a measurable weight in my hands. My chin drops to my chest as I stare down at the ripe green fruit.

Her state of mind when she left wasn't because I betrayed her by withholding information; it was because I betrayed them.

My family.

Just like my father betrayed his.

I'm suddenly unable to breathe as the impact of every mistake I've made comes crashing down on me like a tidal wave. I asked her to dive in with me and open up her heart to what we were building, but what did I give back? Just enough so I wouldn't be hurt.

I'm still holding the avocado in my hand, lost in thought when I hear my name. "Keene?"

Concerned, Alison stands there in a camisole top and running shorts, her hair wet from her shower. My eyes rake over her body, taking in each and every change. Her breasts are slightly larger, and her stomach is no longer concave. Other than that, you'd never know that she's... "How far along does the size of an avocado mean?" I blurt out.

Her lips part slightly. "Sixteen weeks." She clears her throat. "Or once I calculated it back..."

"The first time we slept together," I conclude, doing the mental math myself.

"Yes," she replies softly. "I swear I was on the pill, but the doctor said..."

I wave my hand, the one not cradling the avocado. I believe her.

Alison doesn't have it in her to lie about something so critical. "When did you find out?" My voice is low.

She sighs. "I'll answer all your questions, but can I grab some food? I'm starting to get shaky."

Shit. I got so lost in holding the avocado, I forgot to make her something to eat. I just can't bring myself to put it down. I look at her with this wildly panicked expression.

Alison bursts out laughing. "Move out of the way, Keene." Alison joins me in the cramped kitchenette. Pulling open the fridge, she yanks out a Tupperware of cubed cheese, some fruit, and grabs some bread off the counter. Leaning past where I'm still standing with my avocado, she grabs a knife, a couple of paper plates, and napkins. Popping everything on the bar top, she walks past me, calling over her shoulder, "Grab some bottles of water, would you?"

I jump into action and follow her to the living room, to find her muttering at the mess on the coffee table. "Want me to move anything?"

Bent over, showing me an outstanding view of her rear, she replies, "If you could twitch your nose and get all my stuff packed for me, that'd be great. Other than that, no. I've got it."

I'll be calling the movers after we're done talking.

Putting the bread, cheese, and fruit down on the table, she turns to me and holds out her hand. "Fork it over, Keene."

I give her a confused look.

"The avocado. I'm hungry. If you want to feel your baby, I'll let you touch the real one after we talk." She holds out her hand.

I practically throw it at her. "Thanks. I've had these cravings for avocado and cheese sandwiches for weeks. When I saw the doctor this week, I said it felt a little morbid. She said if that was the case, I wouldn't have eaten grapes or lemons, or anything else on the baby size chart." Alison masterfully begins peeling the outer skin of the avocado. Slicing the inside, she squeezes and lays the slices on her plate. Using her knife, she also slices off some cheddar and grabs a hunk of bread. Popping a bite of the unusual combination into her mouth, she moans. "So good. If only I could handle salsa."

I pick up the conversation gambit. "Can't handle spicy?"

She shakes her head. "Not right now. I don't want to take antacids unless I need to." She looks at her plate. "This is kind of like feeding that need without actually feeding it, if you know what I mean."

I nod, even though I have no idea. "Alison, when did you find out?"

She finishes chewing her second bite before looking at me directly. "The week before I left."

I'm stunned, and more than a little hurt. "And you didn't say anything?" I yell. I can't help it.

She quirks an eyebrow at me.

Shit. She's right. I have no leg to stand on. "Why didn't you say anything?" I try again.

Taking a drink of water, she swallows before answering. "I had it all planned. It was your birthday the following week. I had the original test, the first ultrasounds, and the frame filled with a collage of pictures Holly made for me. I slipped in some of the ultrasounds to give that to you as your gift." She lets out a deep sigh. "I was so certain you would've been as shocked, and then just as thrilled as I was. It was early for us, but I thought we were on the same page." Her breathing increases and her hands shakes. "Then I walked into Hudson, and my world fell apart." My heart hollows out hearing her tell the same story I lived through. "I felt I had no choice but to leave. What was I going to do? Be convinced it was a onetime thing?" Her laughter is hollow. "I knew I couldn't do that. I—we—deserved more than that."

"I got that point when I saw your message," I say quietly. She flinches before reaching down to wrap her fingers around the diamond around her neck.

"I never felt so attuned to your mother than I did at that moment. I thought I fell in love with a Marshall, only to be betrayed." Her voice is laced with sorrow, regret, and remembered pain. My eyes close with my own regret.

So many things could have been avoided if I'd just shared some of what was going on. So many moments lost.

"I need to tell you about that day. About Melody."

"Jared told me some of it," she whispers. "I'm so sorry I wasn't there for you, that I didn't stay and listen."

I scrub my hands up and down my face. "It would have made it easier, that's for sure."

She winces but doesn't respond.

What am I doing? I need to be explaining to her what happened, and all I keep doing is hiding behind my fear. She's brave enough to stand up and admit her mistakes, and she's been carrying our baby with a broken heart.

Alison stands, setting her plate on the coffee table. "I have something for you." I turn and watch her walk to her dining room, which is set up like an office. Picking up a book, she walks back over to the couch.

"Why don't you spend a little time getting to know your child? I'll be in my room packing," she suggests. Picking up her plate of food and bottle of water, she walks away.

In my hands is a journal in pale yellow stripes. I flip it open to the first page.

In Alison's beautiful handwriting, I see the date of the first sonogram and the words "Holy shit. I'm pregnant. What the hell is Keene going to say?" Below that is a copy of our baby's first sonogram.

Taking a deep breath, I turn the page and read about how she decided to tell me. Then I read about her drive to Charleston, pain in every word when it mentions me, and love when it comes to our child.

For the last two months, Alison has spent her time writing out her feelings and documenting her emotions about me, her family, and her pregnancy. Every moment, in preparation for today. Well, maybe not today, but the day she told me about our child.

It's late in the afternoon when I close the book and go in search of the other half of my heart. When I find her just a few steps away in her bedroom, I completely melt.

She's asleep on the bed, one hand holding our child, the other wrapped around the diamond I placed around her neck earlier. The clothes she had been packing are scattered around the room. Boxes are open and partially filled.

My heart turns over in my chest as I quickly reach for my phone. I take a picture of my world curled up on her bed and save it as my background before I crawl next to her. Pushing her hair away from her face, I start to wake her.

"Alison, baby," I whisper.

Her response is to roll closer into me and snuggle into my chest. I want nothing more than to wrap her in my arms and hold on forever. I need to know I have that right.

I stroke her hair for a few more minutes in wonder. How did she do it? How did she survive these weeks thinking I had betrayed her with part of me growing under her heart? I drop my nose into her hair and breathe deeply.

Her hair still smells the same. I don't know why I expected anything different. Maybe because if we had been in reverse positions, I'd have tried to eradicate everything from my life that reminded me of her. But not my Alison. She held on to the love she had for my child and has been beating herself up ever since Jared told her the truth. My arms tighten.

Her sleep-filled eyes blink. "Keene," she breathes.

"Hey," I say quietly.

"I fell asleep and thought it was a dream." She reaches up to touch my face before pulling her hand back. I capture it and pull it to my lips.

"It's not a dream. I'm right here."

Her body begins to shake as she tries to hold in the emotions racing through her. "I'm so sorry, Keene. I should have trusted you." A solitary tear escapes.

"Alison—" I begin, but I'm interrupted.

"When Jared explained what truly happened, I hit a low. I knew no one would ever want me to come back." Her face is turned away from mine. "I knew I'd have to come home and explain, but it would likely be the last time I saw you all."

"That's not true," I rasp. My fault. She's shouldering the blame for something I could have stopped.

"Then I kept getting calls today. Cass, Phil, Em, Corinna, Holly, Jared, Ryan, Charlie. Everyone called during my race. You. I thought maybe I'd have a second chance to make it right." She sighs. "I understand if all of this is too much for you." A wry expression crosses her face. "Fatherhood may not be what you were looking for."

I groan as I pull her closer. There's no way she can't feel the frantic beat of my heart. "Will you let me tell you what happened?" I have to stop her from thinking this is her fault.

Her body tenses next to me, but then I hear her quiet "Yes."

Throwing an arm over my eyes, I tell her from the beginning. About Melody. About the lonely drunken night at the bar. About the offensive advances at work, and how I thought I was putting an end to it before I came home from DC that final time.

The next hour is spent explaining how I argued almost persistently with Caleb that we needed to protect the family against my psychotic stalker. I walk her through my logic—Cassidy's pregnancy, my budding relationship with her, my overinflated ego. All of which seem so trite when I think of the things we lost. Time. Trust. Each other.

By the time I'm done, Alison hasn't asked more than a few questions, and I've laid it all out. The room is almost oppressive in the wake of what I've said. Now, I wait.

"You know what I've been crying the most about lately?" Her words cut through my heart like a knife.

"No, what?"

"Whether or not we would have failed solely because I didn't have enough confidence in myself. Would I have failed us?" she muses aloud. "I don't know. I'd like to think I'd have had these epiphanies without all the drama." Her eyes meet mine. "I'm not sure you would have though."

My heart starts to crumble in pain.

"I was ready to come home and beg, Keene. Kneel before your feet, knowing that what I did was wrong. I knew that within weeks of coming to Charleston before Jared told me the truth. Would you have ever told me about Melody and the threats if you didn't have to?" Her voice is quiet but strong.

And it's then that I understand what she's asking. Would I ever have trusted her without the catastrophe of the last few months? I open and close my mouth because I can't answer her the way she wants.

"There are some things I'll never be able to share, Alison," I hedge.

"Which I knew from the beginning, but something that's going to strike so deep at the core of us?" She takes my hand and places it on her stomach where our child is growing. "At the core of all of us, Keene, you have to figure out how to let us in.

"I think we fell apart so we could lose the blush of what we had to become what we need to be. We had to figure out who we are, not who we thought we were, to raise this life between us." Her voice is intense.

"What are you saying, Alison?"

"We were both damaged. We fell hard. We fell fast. I thought I was betrayed. I thought I was letting go of every dream of forever, Keene. I thought I was in this all alone for the rest of my life. We didn't have enough time for us to know what was real and what wasn't before all of this happened," she concludes, her hand rubbing circles around our child.

"So, where does that leave us?" I ask, feeling like the world might be slipping through my fingers.

Her hand stops over mine and squeezes. "It leaves me knowing I still love you. It leaves me coming home to have our child, and it leaves you with a decision on whether you want to be a part of that and how much you're willing to bend to be a part of that." She looks at me a moment before brushing her lips against mine. "I need you to be my rock, Keene, but not a rock if you see the difference."

Alison's words resonate deeply. Not since I was a little boy have I let someone in. The last time was when my mother told me Cassidy was missing. Over and over, I was let down by everyone I came in contact with, except Caleb. I shut down some part of me willing to trust on faith. Even when Cassidy was found, I still didn't open up to my little sister, let alone to the woman I love.

I never let her in. Is it any wonder she thought I'd be racing to get out?

"I can work on that." I croak out.

"Then let's go home, Keene," Alison whispers. Her eyes flood with tears. "I miss you. All of you."

I wipe her eyes gently with my free hand. She's still clutching my hand against her stomach when I feel it, and so does she. A tiny little flutter against her stomach. "Is that...?" I breathe.

"Yes," she hiccups. "Daddy."

Sweet Jesus. I bury my head in her neck and let my tears fall. "I'm so sorry, baby. I am so damned sorry. I love you so much."

"We'll figure it out. Somehow, we'll figure it out," she murmurs in my ear.

EPILOGUE - ALISON

TWO YEARS LATER

Aristotle said we depend on ourselves for happiness, and knowing our self is the key to opening up the wisdom within ourselves. I both agree and disagree with his statement. I feel it's imperative to know yourself—what you'll tolerate and where your boundaries lie. But wisdom is found all around us.

It was found in the heart of my family, who embraced me when I walked through the door after months of being away. It was found in long conversations, emotional outbursts, accusations, and tears. I was reminded once again why being a Freeman was so special. Ours was a family that wasn't born but built from strength and pride.

It's found in the brains of your boss who assigns you to work for your family, doing your old job during your sister's maternity leave, after which he promptly fired me with an open offer to come back and work for him anytime.

Wisdom is found in the eyes of the man who loves you. The man who decided the family we've developed is fine to split its time between Connecticut and New York until our daughter starts school. The man who's making plans for a satellite office in Connecticut. The man who didn't want to bind me to him because of the baby we were sharing, but because I felt so comforted by the blanket of trust he wrapped around me.

It took a long time. I still know I fell partially in love with him when he swept me into his arms off the fountain that night at the Plaza. The thing was, Keene never believed in love enough until he met me. And he had so much to learn about himself too.

When he dropped the masks he wore, it wasn't just my relationship with him that changed. One night, as my due date grew closer, Cassidy confided in me that she finally felt like she had a brother versus a friend.

Even as I smiled at her, I knew what she meant.

There are no more shadows behind Keene's eyes hiding his soul. He's become my best friend, my partner, and the man I intend to hold in my heart until the sun no longer lights the path I run down each morning.

HAVE you ever tried to pull off a surprise wedding with a fifteen-month-old, your family not having a clue, and hell, the groom doesn't even know about it yet?

One word—nightmare.

I can't turn to my family to share the angst of wedding day jitters. None of them are here to tell me if my dress looks good. I have to remember the old, new, borrowed, and blue crap myself.

What's worse? No one is here to help me keep my daughter out of the makeup she's trying to smear all over her adorable pink patent leather shoes.

"Katherine Laura Marshall! What did Mommy say about playing with her makeup?" I remind my daughter for the third time. Her lower lip wobbles and my heart flops in my chest. Our little girl has Keene's hair and my eyes. She looks a lot like Cassidy. Funny, she acts a lot like Corinna. Keene always rolls his eyes when I say that and mutters, "Or her mother."

She's a handful, and we both love her more than our next breath.

"Listen, beautiful girl, we have a super big surprise for Daddy when he gets off of work today."

"Dwaaddeeee!" Kalie shrieks. Losing interest in my makeup, she teeters over in her pink puffy dress. "Mama, up!" Kalie demands with a stomp of her little foot.

"In just a minute, sweetie. Mama's almost ready." I put my gloss in my bag and glance in despair at the bathroom vanity in our condo in the city. It's a disaster. Knowing we have no time to clean it up, I say, "Mama will just worry about this mess later," I sigh.

Kalie nods and points. "Mess!" She falls on her tush and giggles.

I look down at my short cream sheath with the long bell sleeves. I'm wearing Laura Marshall's diamond and a pair of her sapphire earrings Keene had given me when I pushed Kalie out. I reach for the blue sapphire bangle I borrowed from Corinna last week and "forgot" to return. Stepping into the silver Choos that started it all so long ago, I reach for my daughter's hand, knowing she'll want to walk as far as the elevator. "Ready, baby?"

"Go!" Kalie toddles off, and I'm not far behind.

It's going to be an interesting night.

FOR A LONG TIME when we got back from Charleston, Keene and I practically lived like roommates. Even though we slept wrapped in each other's arms every night, we were like two teenagers in the back of a car than two people who were about to have their first child.

It was sweet.

It was frustrating.

It was Keene's idea.

One night, about a month after I came back, when we were sitting in his condo and he was rubbing his hands over my protruding stomach, he told me our lack of sex wasn't due to lack of interest. He was trying to give me the courtship I should have had. Here we were, about to have a child, and we barely knew a thing about each other. He confessed that wasn't what he wanted to tell our daughter—that we rushed into everything, including our physical intimacy. He wanted to understand me and for me to understand him. He wanted me to know who was going to be by my side for the rest of my life.

My pregnancy hormones wanted to kill him. My heart wanted to jump him even more. I settled back, waited, had faith, and believed.

I was well rewarded.

The first time Keene and I came together after I came home was earth-shattering. I was sitting in bed, writing in my pregnancy journal when he came in, in all his naked glory, with a bandage around his thigh.

Tossing the journal aside, I swung my legs over the side of the bed and pushed myself up. "What happened? What happened to your wound?" Since I was well aware Keene had been shot in the leg protecting Caleb years earlier, I had every right to be concerned.

Sheepishly, he cleared his throat. "Nothing...exactly." Slowly, he peeled the bandage back, and I stumbled to the bed for purchase.

His tattoo.

Hooking off his sister's name, he entwined his mother's name, the name we chose for our daughter. And at the base of the maze of names, my name.

"Keene." My hand involuntarily reached out to trace around the reddened area.

He looked down at his leg and grinned. "Came out fantastic. All the women who own a piece of my heart, with you at the foundation." His fiery green eyes met my tearful blue ones. "It's always been you, Alison. It will always be you. I need you to carry me through the big things, the little things, the crazy things, the Phil things."

I let out a hiccup and a sob.

"We worked before. We work better now. I'll give you as much time as you need to be ready for forever, but you're it for me, Alison. There will be no other after you." Keene cupped my face and tipped my chin up before kissing me with such tenderness.

Slowly, carefully, he lowered me back to the bed before he made love to me, pouring every ounce of love he had into it.

I've never had a doubt about his love and absolute trust since then.

~

THE UPSTAIRS ROOM at Daniela Trattoria is empty, with the exception of Kalie and me. You would never know there's anything earth-shattering about to happen unless you happened to take notice of tables covered with white tablecloths that are scattered with amaryllises.

Jared and Ryan arrive first. "I can't believe you managed to pull this off." Jared shakes his head. He's the only one who knew what I was planning, as I needed to know if he could marry us legally in New York.

"We have to do it again in front of a clerk to make it legal tomorrow," I say ruefully. "Kalie, honey. Can you leave the flowers alone?"

"Pretty!" my daughter exclaims. Ryan saves the day as he scoops up his honorary niece and kisses her neck, causing her to squeal in delight.

"When is everyone else due to arrive? You look stunning, by the way," Ryan says. He's holding my daughter away so she doesn't kick me as he leans in to kiss me.

"Thanks. My nerves are all over the place." I press a hand to my stomach when I hear footsteps on the stairs. I'm petrified that Caleb won't be able to keep Keene at the office until the agreed-upon time. Caleb thinks I'm planning a special anniversary dinner, as it was two years ago today since I came home.

Oh, it's going to be special.

Georgio, who knows Keene, Kalie, and me from many a dinner at the trattoria, comes out from the kitchen with a tray of food. "Ali, where do you want these appetizers?"

Scanning the small upstairs space, I point against the brick wall. It will keep them away from Kalie and still allow us room to maneuver.

Providing Keene says yes when I propose.

Jesus, did I remember his ring? I run over to my purse and unzip it. Letting out a sigh, I find the rings. I need a drink, or I'm going to throw up. There's no in-between.

"What on earth is going on? I had to practically sneak out of the office to get here in time," Charlie announces as he reaches the top of the steps.

Kalie shrieks, "Unca Charwee!"

Taking a deep breath, I reach for my daughter's hand when she tries to race by me to get to Charlie. "Well, if he accepts, I'll be marrying Keene tonight. You wouldn't mind performing the ceremony like you did for Cass and Caleb, would you?" Before the words are out of my mouth, I'm engulfed in a hug by my surrogate father.

"It'd be my honor. My absolute honor," Charlie croaks. Leaning down, he hooks an arm around my daughter and brings her into our circle.

Now I wait for the family to arrive so I can ask the man I love the most important question of our lives.

⌇

EVERYONE KNOWS we're celebrating something. Phil asked one of the waiters for a notepad. He's walking around and taking odds on if I'm pregnant again since I'm not drinking anything. If he'd been paying any sort of attention, he'd also see I haven't eaten anything either, but let him have his happy little delusion until Keene arrives.

Speaking of that, I glance at the clock over the bar. He should be here any minute. And then I feel it—the charge in the room electrifies. Turning around slowly, I see Keene ascend the last of the steps.

He's stunning in a black suit and a blue tie, shot through with platinum threads. I left the suit and tie out for him. It bounces off the white shirt he's wearing, making his eyes gleam. He's been letting his beard grow, defining his jawline even more than normal.

He also has a smirk on his face.

God, it makes me want to jump him right now.

"Dwaaddeeee!" Kalie shrieks, teetering forward. Keene's face softens as he reaches for our daughter.

"Hi, precious. You're up past your bedtime, but don't you look pretty?" He searches the crowd and finds the entire family is present. "Are we celebrating something?" he asks mildly. A hush falls over the crowd, and I fidget a bit. Okay...a lot.

"Why don't you give her to me, Keene? Ali's been busting at the seams for the last hour," Phil drawls.

Thanks, brother. Remind me to adjust your running workout to take you uphill both ways. Jackass.

I step away from the crowd and move toward the man I love, looking much more confident than I feel. I suddenly have so much more empathy for the men of this world. I know there's a 99.9 percent chance Keene's going to say yes, and still, I feel like I'm going to be ill.

Keene checks out my outfit, looking appreciative. "You look beautiful, my love." His eyes rake over me from head to toe, and his lips twitch back into a smirk. "Nice shoes." His eyes heat as they meet mine. "Brings back some memories."

I'm suddenly calm because he remembers the shoes. This is going to work out perfectly. "Honey, can you sit down for a second?" Colby comes up behind Keene with a chair.

"Thanks, Colby," I say gratefully.

He winks before melting back into the semicircle.

"Oh! I need my purse. Can someone get it for me?" I call out.

Corinna steps forward. "Here it is, Ali."

I do a quick list in my head when suddenly, I feel it.

Keene's thumb rubbing back and forth across my wrist. "I'm going to love it, whatever it is, Alison," he promises.

Where do I start? I can't kneel. That will give everything away. I drop down into his lap, and he catches me so I don't fall.

I expect nothing less.

That's who we are now.

"It started with these shoes and Phil's wedding. I took a dare and it changed my life, Keene." Suddenly, the room fades away as I talk. I'm bombarded by memories large and small. "You were so irresistible and intolerable all at once." Everyone laughs. "I never knew which end was up with you. We were so afraid of what we could be that in our own ways, we both ran. Then we stopped running and found ourselves right back where we started, with each other, where we're always supposed to be."

"Alison." Keene's voice holds a warning, and his hands shift to my hips. I lift my finger to his lips.

"Please, let me finish?"

His eyes blaze, but he nods.

"When you're a runner, you always look for sure footing because there are so many things that can trip you up along the route. Because of you, my life is the race I'll always win. You've made sure I have the right gear, know where each footfall is going to land, and that I'm safe. And every moment, every day there's the thrill I'm out for the run of my life. On the course, there's the love and joy I feel when I wake up and see you in the bed next to me. The thrill I feel when I see our daughter. There's nothing like it." I take a deep breath and continue. "I want to ask you in front of everyone we love if..."

He's already shaking his head. "No."

There are gasps in the crowd.

"No?" I challenge him. I know my man. This has absolutely nothing to do with love and everything to do with ego. My eyes narrow.

"You are not going to be the one to propose, damnit! I had it all planned." Keene is pissed. He stands up and plops me into the chair he was in. "Now, sit and listen to me."

"Stay, roll over." I sigh dramatically. Our whole family bursts out laughing. Phil howls like a dog, and Corinna and Holly screech in laughter.

"Oh, are you in trouble when we get home." Keene's breath is mingled with mine, his lips are so close.

"Look at me shaking in my boots," I say sarcastically, crossing my legs.

"You're not wearing boots, and don't pout. I have a few things to say too, and then you can finish, okay?" Without waiting for a response, he starts talking.

"I didn't have a label for it because I didn't know what love was.

After everything I went through, I never thought I deserved it. Certainly, I never expected to find it. But if I'm honest with myself, I've been falling in love with you every minute since that first night at the Plaza." I hear sniffles from my other siblings around the room, Cassidy's the most prominent. "I felt like part of my soul had been ripped away when I walked out." A lone tear trickles down my face, and Keene brushes it away.

"I don't think I'd be the man I am right now if it wasn't for the battles we fought against each other, for our families, for our daughter, for each other. I had to know how to be that safe place for you to come to when you need to run, and not be the person you ran away from." Our eyes clash as so many memories pass in a second. He raises my hand to his lips.

"You slay me with the amount you love, Alison, with your warrior heart and your loyalty. With your beauty, inside and out. You taught me that, no one else. You want to share that life with me every day, and that's a blessing I'll never understand." His head drops. I run my hand through his thick dark hair that matches our daughter's perfectly.

God, I love this man.

"You beat me to it, baby." He smiles as his head raises, and he's holding a ring—a sapphire flanked by two diamonds set in platinum —in his hand. There's a collective gasp around the room. "This represents the love we have now, this represents the love we'll have tomorrow, and this one, the love we'll have for eternity," Keene says, explaining the setting. "I was all set to meet you here in this place, where you said all of your best beginnings happened, and ask if you were ready to take that final step with me." Keene holds the ring over the third finger of my left hand, a tender smile on his face.

Tears are pouring down my cheeks, but I still manage to say, "Actually, I was going to skip over the whole engagement." I reach inside my purse and pull out two platinum bands. A war whoop goes up around the room, and Keene's eyes go round. "Yes to your engagement, Keene. It will last all of"—I look at the clock over the bar again —"four minutes."

"Plenty of time to figure out vows." His voice drips with sarcasm as he slides the ring on my finger. Pulling me to my feet and standing, he kisses my finger just above the ring. "Four minutes, huh?"

I step into his body. "Yep. Think you can handle it?"

"What kind of bachelor party do I get?"

I roll my eyes. "The kind where you take your daughter to go potty before she ruins her dress."

Keene tosses his head back, bellowing out a laugh. "Deal. Right after I kiss her mother."

And before our family and friends, Keene kisses me as if we've already spoken our vows, with our souls colliding on the promise of forever.

I just hope our mothers can see how it all turned out. Maybe through the eyes of their granddaughter, they already are.

THE END

WHERE TO GET HELP

Every day, agents work to uncover, dismantle, and disrupt human trafficking.

Human trafficking victims have been found in communities nationwide in the agriculture, hospitality, restaurant, domestic work and other industries, as well as in prostitution that is facilitated online, on the street, or in businesses fronting for prostitution such as massage parlors. These victims are not only children, but men and women of all ages – many of whom come into the countries they are found in because of promises of legitimate jobs, a better life, only to find their dreams destroyed.

I was compelled to add this addition to the Freeman family dynamic when I was traveling through Hartsfield-Jackson Atlanta International Airport over a year ago. As I was walking one of their terminals, every other "advertisement" was urging people to report suspected or known human trafficking. I contacted a friend who lives in the area, shocked, because I was unaware of the critical state of affairs. And so, the backstory behind Ali, Corinna, and Holly began.

In fiscal year 2016, Homeland Security Investigations (a critical investigative arm of the US Department of Homeland Security) initiated 1,029 investigations with a nexus to human trafficking and recorded 1,952 arrests, 1,176 indictments, and 631 convictions; 435 victims were identified and assisted.

It's not enough.

In the United States, if you notice suspicious activity in your community, call the ICE Tip Line at 1-866-DHS-2-ICE

COMING SOON

I've played a lot of roles in my life. I can make you laugh, make you cry, make you want to dance in the aisles or fall to the ground weeping. But one day shattered all of that.

I don't know who I am anymore, but I'm determined to find out by whatever means necessary.

My name is Evangeline Katherine Brogan.

And it all starts in New York City...

Close Match by Tracey Jerald
October 3, 2019
Amazon/Kindle Unlimited
Add to your Goodreads TBR
Sign up for Go Live Notice

Want a Sneak Peak of Close Match? Sign up for my newsletter. After subscribing for the newsletter, you will be emailed a special link to read an excerpt of **Close Match.**

ALSO BY TRACEY JERALD

Free to Dream

Free to Run

Free to Rejoice

Free to Breathe

Free to Believe

Coming Soon:

Close Match

ACKNOWLEDGMENTS

To my husband. I know I say this every day, but I love you. You are my heart, my soul, and my beloved. There is no way I could be sitting here typing this without your constant love and support. Thank you for sacrificing so much for me to live this dream. And since this is coming out so close to the day we promised each other forever - happy anniversary, my love.

To my son. Every day you are growing right before my eyes. You're taller, your smarter and your heart's bigger. It's the last one that's the most important, baby. And remember, the word of the year is "try".

To my mother, there is no support and love greater than yours. Knowing my book sits on your shelf is as incredulous to me as it is to you.

To my father – for teaching me every day. I just wish I had a chance to say thank you before it was too late.

Jen, if we were still being charged by the minute for phone calls, your mother would have grounded me (again) for the phone bill during the creation of this book. There is no one else who quite understands me the way you do. I love you to the moon and back. Thank you for being the sister of my heart and the sister of my soul.

To my Meows; Jen, Tara, Alissa, Greg, and Kristina. Every day you inspire me just by being who you are – the best friends a woman can have. My framily – I love you all so much.

My Betas, Spoon and Toasty. Those random sections of the book I would send you and you both would say "and...?" waiting for the next page – when I hadn't written it yet. I'm so sorry – not sorry! I love you both for putting up with my whacky thought process!

To Jennifer Wolfel. I think I owe you at least a winning lottery ticket in addition to genuflecting. Thank you for diving head first into this crazy because of a simple question.

Ash, I think I might be a little co-dependent on you and your mad skills, your sassy mouth, and your brilliant brain. I should have just brought you home after Denver. Love you, babe.

Alessandra Torre, for continuing to be that person I can turn to with all the crazy questions. You have my eternal thanks.

Jenna Jacob, I love you so much, woman! Thank you for your love, your support, and being so damn kick ass I just can't stand it!

To my editing team, Trifecta Editing Services. Amy, Lyndsey, and Dana – trying to find the right words to express how overwhelmed with love and gratitude I am when I think of the three of you is impossible. And I'll just say it – I can't write Phil without thinking of how to make y'all laugh harder.

To Sandra Depukat from One Love Editing. From the moment we met, I knew I'd love you (and it's not just because of your accent that I could listen to all night!). Thank you for adding your special touch to this story.

My cover and brand designer, Amy Queue of QDesigns, I'm still laughing over my Meows contacting you. If my mother does, we know we're all in trouble! Thank you for living in my head. Thank you for getting it just right. Thank you for being you, being inspired, and having no problems with crazy requests because you are so amazing.

To the team at Foreward PR. Linda Russell – If home is where your heart is, then I've been home for a while now. I can't say I love you enough. I know this journey may have happened, but there's no way it would have been close to being as remarkable as it has been with you all at my side. To Alissa Marino - I don't know what I would do without you having my back, my front and everything in between. You are an amazing woman and friend. All my love and hugs.

To all of the bloggers who first took a chance on Free to Dream and now Free to Run, thank you from the bottom of my heart. I'm still so honored you chose to read my book is an honor – one I don't take for granted.

To my readers, I love each and every one of you. Thank you for being people with enormous hearts and souls. Thank you for continuing to follow me on this journey. I am choosing to read my words.

And to Sir Arthur Conan Doyle. I still can't believe you didn't love your character of Sherlock Holmes.

ABOUT THE AUTHOR

Tracey Jerald knew she was meant to be a writer when she would re-write the ending of books in her head when she was a young girl growing up in southern Connecticut. It wasn't long before she was typing alternate endings and extended epilogues "just for fun".

After college in Florida, where she obtained a degree in Criminal Justice, Tracey traded the world of law and order for IT. Her work for a world-wide internet startup transferred her to Northern Virginia where she met her husband in what many call their own happily ever after. They have one son.

When she's not busy with her family or writing, Tracey can be found in her home in north Florida drinking coffee, reading, training for a runDisney event, or feeding her addiction to HGTV.

To follow Tracey, go to her website at http://www.traceyjerald.com. While you're there, be sure to sign up for her news-letter for up to date release information!

44761633R00204

Made in the USA
San Bernardino, CA
21 July 2019